THE SMOKE-SCENTED GIRL

MELISSA MCSHANE

Night Harbor Publishing

Copyright © 2015 Melissa McShane

ISBN-13 978-0692368497

Published by Night Harbor Publishing

This book is a work of fiction. Names, characters, businesses, organizations, places, events, and incidents either are the product of the author's imagination or are used fictitiously. Any resemblance to actual persons living or dead, events, or locales is entirely coincidental.

Cover design by Clarissa Yeo

❀ Created with Vellum

For Jacob,
who laughed in all the right places

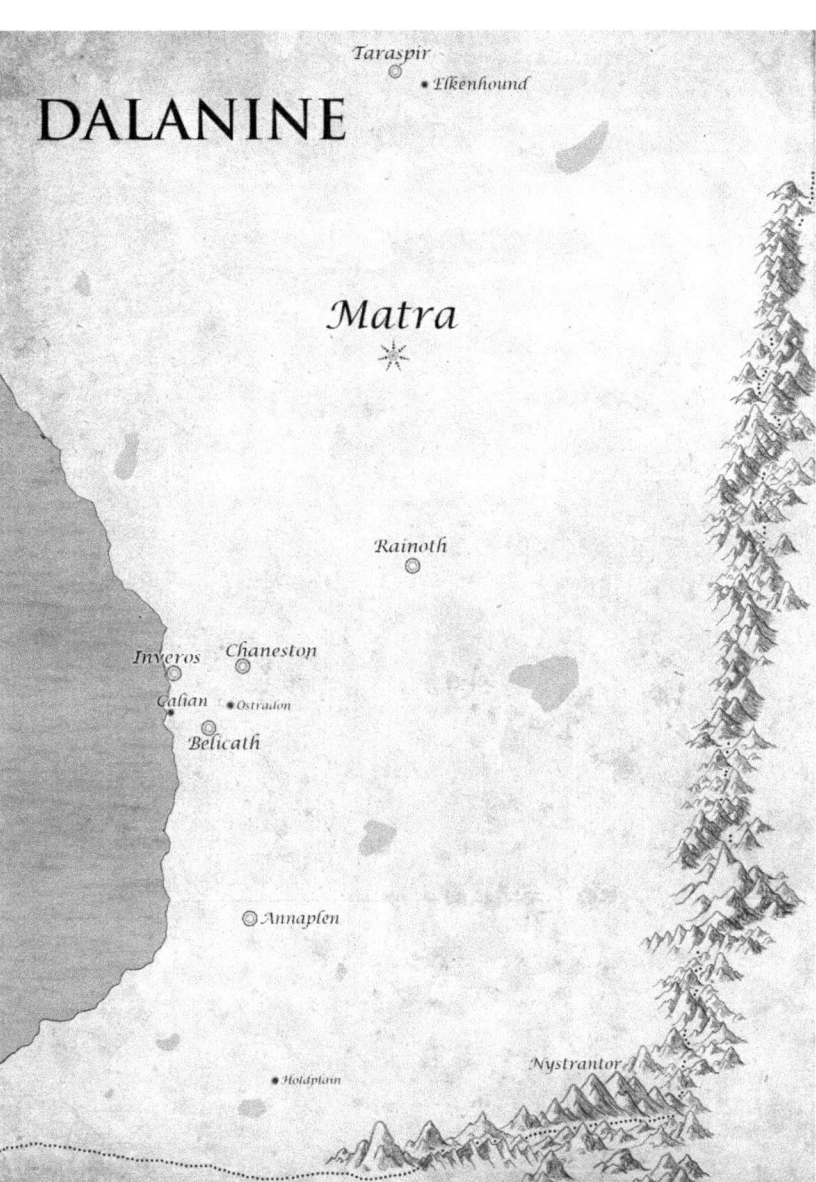

DALANINE

Taraspir

• Elkenhound

Matra

Rainoth

Inveros Chaneston

Calian • Ostradon

Belicath

◎ Annaplen

• Holdplain

Nystrantor

Gray areas are places of power

PROLOGUE

*B*eing reborn hurt more than dying did. She felt as if she were being sculpted by giant hands, molded like clay and forced back into human form. Skin grated on bone, bone crushed her lungs and stomach and the heart that never stopped beating, even when it was disintegrated into a burning mist. She cried out in agony, but heard nothing, and wondered if she had ears yet.

Then, as always, the fire left her, and she was Kerensa again. She fell to the ground, her hands and knees cracking the brittle, glassy crust that was all that was left of the bare earth beneath her. The air felt like knives in her chest as she sucked in a breath, then another, and sobbed great tears that steamed as they struck the ground. She crouched naked and alone in the center of the firestorm's aftermath. Smoke wreathed her, blinded her, filled her nostrils with the smell of wood and bubbling tar. She pushed herself to her feet, wobbled, took an involuntary step back to steady herself on the rapidly cooling surface and felt her foot come down on something hard but brittle. She kicked it away in terror and revulsion, felt ash stick to her bare foot, and choked back bitter bile. There weren't many bone fragments this time. Only one victim, thank the Twins—not that They were interested in her thanks.

She'd tried to lead the man away from the houses, but he'd shoved her into the narrow, dark space between them, and now both were blazing, the fire spreading too rapidly, as if it were a living thing crawling up walls and across roofs after its prey. The roaring in her ears, the sound she could never identify, was replaced by more normal sounds, screams and shouting and the distant nasal honking of the fire brigade's horns. The thick smoke flowed into the street like drifting fog. Everyone who could still see was looking at the burning buildings; no one was looking at her. That wouldn't last long. A naked woman drew even more attention than a burning one. She staggered through the narrow space and went around a corner to duck into the alley. She'd stowed her bag here when she felt the fire begin to take her. Her fingers shook as she dug through it—plain rough linsey-woolsey dress, her precious shoes, a kerchief to wrap around her long blonde hair. Someday some urchin would find her bag before she returned to it, and that didn't bear thinking on.

She came back out of the alley, bag over her shoulder, and looked up at the burning buildings. The fire had nearly consumed the house on the right; the other burned less fiercely but was still doomed. The fire brigade was taking far too long; the fire would spread to both houses' neighbors before they arrived. She closed her fist hard on the leather strap and turned away. Nothing she could do.

Hoarse, desperate screams cut across the clamor of the bystanders. Kerensa glanced over her shoulder and saw a man tearing at the hands restraining him, trying to reach the front door which was limned with orange fire. The man's screams were unintelligible, but she had no trouble interpreting them. Fire tore at her heart. *My fault*, she thought, *my fault*, and she tossed the bag back down the alley, kicked her shoes after it, and darted through the crowd, shoving hard until she reached the front line of onlookers who stood well back from the blaze. They watched the fire silently, with the expressions of people who were grateful it wasn't their lives being devoured. No one heeded her, just another woman in the crowd, so no one stopped her as she pushed through the line and ran for the door. Another shout, but it was too late; she had the door open and shut behind her in two seconds.

That brief gust of air made the fire roar. She ignored it. However much air she fed it, it could not consume her. The claustrophobic hall of the cheap lodging house had narrow doors opening off it on both sides, single rooms that would house two or even three families each, and she moved down the hall quickly, glancing inside each room. Empty. Steep stairs that would have been unstable even if they weren't wreathed in fire waited at the end of the hall; she took a deep breath, choked on the heat and smoke, and began to crawl up them. One snapped in half as she put her weight on it. She lurched, and clawed at the next step to keep from falling through. Eyes watering from the smoke, she kept crawling.

The hall at the head of the steps was identical to the one below. Grateful that there were only two floors, she crouched low to stay below the smoke and then had to scramble backward as a burning beam sagged and fell almost on her head. She yanked on the hem of her dress, caught beneath the fiery wood, and slapped at the glowing, shriveling fibers to put them out. The fire was spreading more quickly. She climbed over the end of the beam that wasn't on fire and began checking the rooms, trying to hear human sounds above the laughter of the fire.

She mistook the woman for a bundle of old rags and would have moved on if the woman hadn't seen her and cried out. She huddled in a corner, cradling a toddler who wasn't moving, and shied away from Kerensa in mindless terror as she approached. Fire rolled along the ceiling and crept down the walls toward them both. Kerensa cursed and snatched the child out of the woman's arms. She couldn't tell if it was even still alive, but the mother wailed and lurched forward, and Kerensa grabbed her upper arm and pulled her into the hallway, over the beam and down the stairs, heedless of the flames, driven by the crackling and howling of the fire devouring the house. Near the foot of the steps she tripped and tumbled to the bottom, dragging the woman and the child with her. She half-landed on the child, who stirred and began to cry. Not dead, then.

The woman heard her child's voice and clawed desperately at Kerensa, who pushed the toddler into its mother's arms and then shoved the woman to the ground when she would have risen to her feet. "Stay low!" she shouted, though she knew the woman was too terrified to understand her, and crouched in demonstration. She took the woman's upper arm again and urged her forward, creeping on hands and knees to match the woman's halting pace. Her kerchief hung loose and her hair fell forward over her face, curling up from the heat. It was going to be too hot to breathe in a moment, even low to the ground as they were, and they still had to get through the front door. Flames scurried up the walls and across the ceiling, gold and yellow and red like autumn leaves. The fire was beautiful and she loathed it.

The door was entirely aflame now, and Kerensa imagined she could see the heat radiating from the latch and from the iron hinges. The woman reached out for the latch, but Kerensa pushed her aside and took hold of it herself. It was so hot her brain told her it was cold, bone-searing cold, and she gripped it tightly and pulled it open. Fire erupted around her as air blew through the opening and the flames went wild. Part of her sleeve caught fire, but she didn't have time to think about that, she needed to get those two out, two lives for one — surely that would make up the balance.

She turned, and couldn't see the woman for the smoke rushing past, so she dropped to the ground and felt around. She found a piece of cloth, an ankle, groped her way up the woman's body and found her arm, now so familiar to the touch. The woman didn't move. Kerensa found her face, which felt blistered from the heat, and thought she could feel breath sighing in and out of her nostrils. Kerensa's muscles burned with fatigue and heat, and she wanted to collapse, but she got under the woman and heaved her over her shoulders, then picked up the child, unconscious again, and half-crawled, half-staggered toward the door.

She was barely aware of passing across the threshold, there was so much smoke, but then someone lifted her burden from her back and she took that as a sign that she could lie down. She curled gently around the child and hoped it wasn't a corpse she was cradling. A fit of coughing struck her, and someone lifted her head, another person took the child from her, and then she was choking on cold water that tasted of soot. Or maybe it was her mouth that tasted of soot.

"Damn fool woman, like to get yourself killed," said the man holding the flask.

"She saved two lives," said a woman.

"Still a damn fool thing to do," the man muttered. The flask was withdrawn. "Can you stand?"

Kerensa shook her head. The damn fool thing wasn't running into the fire, it was letting everyone see her come out. *Shouldn't have done it. Couldn't have done anything else.*

A great moaning creak sounded over the dull roar of the fire, and a cry went up. Her two ministering angels left her side, and Kerensa rolled to her feet and ran. Behind her, the house collapsed on itself with a crash, and the fire's clamorous roar redoubled. It sounded victorious. She didn't look back.

Her bag was still where she'd thrown it. She put on her shoes, wrapped her hair around her head and tied the kerchief over it, dunked her still-smoldering sleeve in the downspout of a rain gutter to douse it, washed her face with what water was left. In the distance, thunder growled. The rain would come too late to make a difference. She wiped her face with a clean kerchief from her bag, then walked away down the street. Two lives. Two lives, against who knew how many dead. She'd stopped counting months ago. She walked faster, though she knew it didn't matter how fast she moved or what direction she took. The leather strap of her bag felt slick in her left hand; she closed her right hand, unmarked by the red-hot latch, into a fist. Thunder, again, like the laughter of the gods mocking her. She walked until the fire was far behind her and then kept on walking out of town, trailing behind her the acrid scent of smoke.

1

Failure was a puddle of liquid wax, seeping through the cracks in the blackened oak table and dripping noiselessly to the tile floor beneath. Evon dropped heavily onto the low stool that put his eyes even with the table top. From that perspective, the molten ivory beeswax made a thin meniscus in which the lonely wick, defying gravity, still stood erect, white and uncharred. The wax had no odor to it, but if it did, it would probably reek of his growing despair. Evon closed his eyes, which felt dry and gritty as if he hadn't slept in...how long had he been working on this spell? A day? Two? He could feel his diminishing magical reserves as a knot of tension at the base of his spine that radiated cold down his legs and up his arms. He rubbed his eyes, blinked, and stood to find a cloth to wipe the table with, quickly, before the wax solidified and he had to waste time chipping it off. The hanging lamps, glowing dimly with spells that he ought to renew soon, cast strange, fuzzy shadows over the table and whitewashed walls. He swept the cooling wax off the table and into his hand, squeezed it, then pinched it into a roughly human shape. Man of wax, subject to his whim. He really had been working on this spell for too long.

Being able to create a defensive shield independent of his body had turned out to be the easy part. Making it flame resistant, heat resistant, was proving more difficult. He refused to think it might be impossible; Miss Elltis was not paying him for impossible. And if he didn't find a solution soon, she wouldn't be paying him at all. He threw the wax-smeared cloth toward the dustbin and picked up the palm-sized ceramic tile from the center of the table. Wax had puddled in the grooves of the runes he'd carved on it, and he lit one of the dozens of candles in the room and heated the tile in the flame until the wax ran like oil off its surface, then took it over to one of the tall windows that let in the cold blue winter daylight and held it up to examine it. Perhaps the rune was wrong. He'd tried everything else. Silica glass bell, so the shield would manifest at a distance. Ceramic tile for fire resistance, and he couldn't think of anything more symbolic than that. And *presadi* was the standard command word to shape magic into any shield. It had to be the rune.

He threw the tile after the wax-coated cloth and heard it clatter across the floor instead. Nothing he'd thrown at the dustbin in the last four hours had come anywhere near it. He must be tiring. He eyed the cot in the corner of the room. No. He wasn't yet so tired as to sleep before he discovered the secret, and he was running out of time. It had to be the rune. Maybe he was overthinking it. Maybe the rune needed to be simpler, not more complicated.

A knock sounded at the door, and Evon, startled, reached up to straighten the neckcloth he wasn't wearing. Miss Elltis had strong opinions about the behavior and attire of the magicians belonging to her cooperative, and finding Evon in his shirtsleeves with, he suddenly realized, a thin film of ash and copper chalk dust coating said shirtsleeves would prompt her to make one of those subtly cutting remarks that reminded the recipient that she was first among equals, even if Evon was more equal than most.

"I must say, Lore, I didn't expect to find you quite so disheveled," Piercy Faranter said, pushing the door open with his hawk-headed walking stick. He'd started carrying the thing when he was twenty-one, probably in an effort to look more mature than his youthful face suggested, and in the last three years Evon had come to think of it as an extension of his body. "I had the impression that professional magicianing—is that a word? Well, it is now—was rather cleaner than being a chimney sweep." He sniffed dramatically and held a linen handkerchief to his nose. "And it's rather more...fragrant...than I would have imagined. When did you last bathe?"

Evon sat down on the stool again, realized he was looking up his friend's nostrils, and stood back up. "Piercy. What in the Twins' names are you doing here?"

"I'm crushed, dear fellow, crushed indeed. Can a man not visit an old friend at his place of employment without being greeted with such dismay?" He tucked his handkerchief back into the pocket of his elegant maroon waistcoat, straightened the front of his equally elegant black frock coat, and gave Evon a look of sorrow that on his long face looked more comical than injured.

"I'm working on confidential government research—visitors aren't allowed. I wonder that you were able to pass the doorkeeper. Tell me you didn't bribe him."

"Merely a trifle. Besides, I told him I was on official government business. I have the most brilliant secretive gaze, you know. Gets me into so many places." He winked, his brown eyes merry as always.

Evon picked at the wax that, despite his best efforts, had coated the table with a thin veneer. After hundreds of tests, that was to be expected. "If I don't solve this problem soon, we'll lose our contract. I'm very busy."

"Yes," Piercy drawled, and poked Evon in the sternum with the head of his stick. "I inquired at your home. Your mother informed me that you've been 'very busy' for several days now. Haven't slept in your own bed for a week, I believe was her precise wording. I heard in her unspoken plaint a clear message to me. It was a message that said, 'Piercy, your old friend Evon Lorantis has once again chained himself to his desk, possibly not metaphorically, and it is your duty, nay, your Gods-given responsibility to free him from his shackles, possibly not metaphorically, and ensure that he cleans himself up and eats something more nourishing than the hunk of cheese he has stowed in a bag hanging out of his window.'"

Evon glanced at the window. "There's bread too," he said defensively.

"You have the most distressing tendency to become wrapped up in your work these days," Piercy said. "What are you doing that is so important you forgot to keep your appointment to dine with me?"

Evan's stomach sank. "That wasn't today, was it?"

"It was two days ago, and I was deeply wounded. Well. In truth I was merely put out a bit, since I have known you since we were both ten years old and I'm accustomed to your little quirks." Piercy looked around for a chair, dusted its seat with the same dove-white handkerchief, and sat. "In all seriousness, Evon, I'm concerned for you. You can't possibly do your best work if you push yourself past breaking, and based on what I see before me, you are very close to breaking."

"I'm very close to *succeeding*, Piercy, I've almost figured this out! A fireproof, heatproof shield! Think how much it will mean to the war effort!"

"And I'm sure the Despot of Balviros trembles in his sweaty boots to know it, but a day's rest isn't going to change the course of the war. You need food, you need sleep, and you need something else to think about to give your prodigious brain time to recover." Piercy removed a sheaf of papers from inside the greatcoat draped over his arm and slapped them against Evon's chest. Evon reached out to take them automatically, turned them over and nearly dropped them.

"These are restricted-access government documents! Piercy—"

"You can thank me later, Lore."

"From inside my prison cell? Or will I be sharing one with you?"

"I have my superior's tacit permission to show this to you. He may be under the impression that you're somewhat older than you are and have a quarter-century's experience in all things magical, but I couldn't exactly tell him that my 'specialist' has barely a quarter-century's experience in *life* and is a junior member of a magicians' cooperative."

Evon squared the pages without looking at them, as if they carried some contagion transmitted through the eyes. "Why *didn't* you take them to an experienced magician?"

"Because we have many experienced magicians in Home Defense, and all of them are stymied by what's in those papers. You have a flexibility of mind that they lack, something I know from personal experience of all the times your cleverness has gotten me into trouble. And you clearly need a new challenge."

Evon scowled at him, but turned over the pages and began scanning. Almost immediately, he said, "You can't be serious."

"I am very serious."

"There's no mystery here. Fires start all the time. Particularly in parts of cities built with a great deal of wood and very little space between buildings. There doesn't have to be some supernatural explanation for it. And I see here that some of this information has come from the *Weekly Gazette*. They claimed last week that the King of Dalanine is really a woman with a hairy chest. I think their reliability is questionable."

"A great many men and women in Dalanine's government, sober people with very little sense of humor, are taking it very seriously indeed," Piercy said, and there was nothing teasing about him now. "These fires are hot enough to melt stone and vaporize flesh—and have done, at every site we've investigated. Whatever this phenomenon is, if we can harness it, it could tip the balance of the war in our favor. And I don't mind telling you that the Despot is pushing forward faster than anyone thought possible a year ago."

"Yes, I know; did I mention I have a deadline?"

Piercy waved that away. "We need this, Evon, we need to know who or what is causing it, and I think you're the man to figure it out."

"I—that's praise indeed, Piercy, but I don't know what you want me to do."

Piercy tapped the sheaf of papers. "This is all the information we have to date. Places, times, deaths, anything our agents could learn. Find a pattern. See if you can identify the magician behind it."

"Are you certain that there is an intelligence behind it? It could be some naturally occurring phenomenon."

"Find that out, too. Whatever it is, the government wants to know." Piercy grinned, once again the carefree man about town. "With you working on fire-resistance spells, who knows? It might turn out to be related to your work after all. Now, put your clothes on. I refuse to be seen in public with you in this state. Besides, you'd freeze in just your shirtsleeves. It's snowing again, did you realize?"

"I can't leave now. If I don't solve this problem in the next two days—"

"If you do not *rest*, dear fellow, you won't be solving it at all. You know I'm right. Home, bath, food, bed, possibly not in that order, and a fresh start in the morning."

Evon sighed, but buttoned up his waistcoat and tied his neck-cloth, then submitted to Piercy retying it for him properly. Now that he thought about it, he was very hungry and a little cold now that he wasn't lighting fires every ten minutes. Perhaps he needed food, and some rest. He glanced down at the papers. Mysterious fires. Melted stone. If Piercy was right, and this wasn't simply sensationalism, it would be a fine challenge indeed.

It was, in fact, snowing rather heavily outside, and Evon turned the collar of his overcoat up against the fat flakes and filled his lungs with cold air that cleared away the last funk of hot wax and fire that clung to him. In the wintry light, the businesses lining both sides of the wide, well-traveled street looked gray and tired, upper stories jutting out above lower ones, threatening to overbalance entire buildings. He glanced at the neatly-painted letters on the leaded window above him, lit from within despite the morning sun. ELLTIS & CO., FINEST MAGICS. Someday he intended it to read ELLTIS, LORANTIS & CO. or, if he really dared to dream, LORANTIS & CO. He buttoned his overcoat and said, "Where are we going?"

"I told your mother I'd bring you home like the little lost lamb you appear to have become," Piercy said. They proceeded up the street, stepping aside when a carriage rattled past on the rough cobbles, throwing up a fine spray. By evening the carriages would be sending up waves of filthy water to douse unsuspecting pedestrians. Evon nodded and tipped his hat at a pair of young women whose full skirts were already a little dirty from the road. They glanced at him and giggled as they passed, and he felt his face grow warm. How disheveled must he be, to inspire such a response? He knew himself to be reasonably attractive, even handsome according to more than one young lady, but at the moment he felt like a hideous creature out of myth, something the legendary hero Alvor might have slain with his equally legendary mace. He self-consciously pushed his hair back behind his ears. He needed a haircut. He needed a bath.

"How have I come to this?" he muttered under his breath.

Piercy had very good ears. "Do you mean your current physical condition, or the extremely prestigious employment that caused it? I am certain that Elltis woman is grateful for your tendency to become absorbed in solving a problem to the exclusion of all else, but when you're not obsessed with your work, you can be quite charming. Those young ladies certainly thought so."

Evon reddened again. "I think they were more amused by whatever odor I'm emitting."

"You have never been good at interpreting the intentions of the fairer sex, Lore. You are, in fact, almost as bad at it as you are at recognizing when your own heart is engaged. As I recall, I had to tell you that your interest in Velena Torenter was non-platonic because watching you moon about in unhappy ignorance was more painful than I could endure."

"I'm at least capable of knowing when my condition is less than appealing to anyone, let alone women. I swear, Piercy, I won't let myself go this seedy again."

"You almost certainly will. Come now, Lore, why so despondent?"

"Piercy, I've been working at this problem for days and I feel I'm no closer to the solution than I was at the start. Yes, I know, I need to think about something else, give my thoughts time to come together, but I've...I realize it's arrogance, but I've never encountered a magical problem I couldn't solve before."

"You mean you haven't faced a challenge that hasn't bowed down and kissed your boots in ten seconds before. I have tremendous faith in your abilities, old friend, or I wouldn't have brought you my little problem." He tapped Evon's breast with his walking stick, making the papers tucked inside rustle.

"You're trying to distract me."

"No, I'm selfishly trying to get you to work on something that could mean a promotion for me if I can bring in a solution. I know you can read and walk at the same time. It gives you an undeserved air of studiousness that as I recall usually concealed your planning some kind of mischief."

"You never complained at our exploits, though you probably should have done." Evon sighed. "I can't read and walk in this weather. Why don't you just tell me the essentials?"

"I was rather hoping not to do quite so much work, but if it will halt your slide down the slope of despair, then I will make the sacrifice. What do you know about these fires?"

"Nothing, since until twenty minutes ago I believed they were naturally occurring events strung together by superstitious thinking."

"Harsh, Lore, very harsh. As I said, they burn so hot as to melt stone—our agents, who are as unimaginative as men can be and still walk upright, have visited the sites and confirmed this. That alone should tell you that we are not dealing with a mundane phenomenon."

"I believe you."

"More significant is that with a single exception, all the fires have had exactly the same dimensions—a rough circle ten feet in diameter. The anomalous event was more than one hundred fifty feet in diameter and destroyed fifteen buildings."

"Was it the first event?"

Piercy looked at him narrowly. "You're thinking whoever is behind this might have had trouble controlling the spell initially."

"I was. Though I think it is a mistake to assume there's a person behind it. Go ahead."

"Molten stone, identical dimensions...there's no regularity to the timing of the events, and they are always within cities."

"Unless there are fires your people don't identify as part of the phenomenon because they happen where there are few witnesses."

"You're already thinking further than we have, Lore." Piercy wiped a clump of snowflakes from his eye. "Most disturbingly, there's always at least one body—or the charred bones and ash of a body—within the circle of devastation."

"That suggests the possibility that these people are spontaneously combusting."

"That occurred to us, too. And then there are the eyewitnesses, who are as reliable as eyewitnesses ever are. Some claim they saw a person fleeing from the fire, despite its being so hot that nothing could survive within it. Others say a dark-robed figure walked up to the victim and struck him or her with a ball of liquid fire. Don't ask me how they knew it was liquid. And of course there's the inevitable Alvorian conspiracists."

"I don't believe 'conspiracists' is a word."

"Well, it is now. *They* believe Dania caused the fires as a harbinger of Alvor's return."

"Dania, as in Alvor's magia? How can anyone believe that?"

"It's been almost a thousand years since Alvor and his companions are supposed to have destroyed the warlord Murakot and then disappeared. Some people believe he's destined to return to save the country from the Despot."

"Dalanine can save itself, I think. With the help of hard-working magicians like myself."

"I agree, but these conspiracists see Alvor's hand in everything. And one of the rumors is that a bald woman stands near the fires and watches the victim scream. You might recall that one of the legends has Dania shaving her head to use her hair to capture Murakot's chief lieutenant and force him to give up Murakot's weakness."

"I admit I don't know much about Alvorian myth, but I don't recall Dania being so coldblooded as to simply watch a person burn to death."

"I don't recall Dania being a real person."

"There's always a kernel of truth in these legends. After all, Murakot was a real warlord, though probably not a creature of magic. And I imagine there's a kernel of truth in these stories as well."

"So what do you think it is, if I may take the liberty of assuming you've already made some conclusions, clever fellow?"

Evon side-stepped a rivulet of water running toward a nearby drain. "I believe there *is* a person behind all of this," he said. "Unless there is something in these papers you haven't told me, not one of the witnesses declared that the victim had simply gone up in flames.

That's the sort of thing people would remember. We are dealing with some individual who is capable of creating fires far hotter than any spell we know can manage."

"That's unsettling. I might even say, frightening."

"It is indeed."

They crossed the street into a neighborhood of narrow, tall houses that stood four and even five stories above the quiet street. All were built of black stone and in the light of the wintry day looked foreboding, what with the beds of frozen, snow-covered flowers and the bare trees that lined both sides of the street. The only cheerful note was the brightly colored doors, reached by short flights of stairs, red and purple and green set off by the golden brass of door latches. Evon and Piercy had the street to themselves, shrouded in the strange hush that was the sound of millions of soft flakes drifting to the ground. Their boots left prints on the sidewalk that immediately began to fill with snow.

Evon turned to ascend the stairs of the fifth house on the right. "Will you come in? Mother will undoubtedly want to thank you for escorting me home. She believes I'm flighty and easily distracted, which I find amusing since you've told me I'm the opposite."

"I have a dinner engagement, so please give your mother my apologies." Piercy tipped his hat at Evon, causing a small avalanche to fall from the brim. "Good luck, and my thanks for tackling that somewhat knotty problem. And, Evon?" This as Evon had put his hand to the latch. "You're not obsessive. You're simply very focused. Try to keep that in mind?"

Evon smiled and shrugged. "If I must be very focused, I promise to turn that focus on your problem rather than my own. At least for the day."

He shook the snow from his hat and brushed off the shoulders of his coat before entering his home. The blue door creaked a bit, as it had for the last seven years; his parents always said they'd have to do something about it, but it remained unoiled and continued to make a sound somewhere between a squeak and a moan. It was better than a doorbell for announcing one's presence. Even so, no one appeared to greet him as he entered and shucked his overcoat. Well, Father would be at work at this hour, and Aunt Mayda and Uncle Findlay would be at the tea shop, and his odious cousin Jessalie would be at school, thank the Twins, and Mother might be at the church supervising preparations for the upcoming winter fete. He had the house to himself. The idea made him feel lonely.

The entry, unfurnished except for the coatrack, was painted a plain white and bore only portraits of long-dead Lorantises; the doors to his father's study and the dining room were both closed. It felt empty and as silent as the snowy street. Evon shivered a little and ascended the stairs to the fourth floor and his bedroom. The fire was unlit, the logs cold on the andirons, and that combined with the pale blue wallpaper and the winter sunlight filtering through the falling snow made his room feel frozen. *"Forva,"* he said, snapping his fingers at the fireplace, and fire sprang up golden and cheery from the thick logs. The word left a taste of hot metal in his mouth and made the knot of tension in his spine twinge as it tapped his nearly depleted reserves further.

Now that he was home, exhaustion sank into his bones and his eyeballs, and he could almost hear the bed calling to him. No. He was too filthy. Bath first. He removed his frock coat and unwound his neckcloth, which suddenly felt stifling, tossed both on a chair, and went down the hall to the bathroom and turned on the tap. It had been his first magical gift to his family, years ago, when he'd first learned to enspell the water tank to produce hot water and installed the filter that purified the waste water before it reached the street. He'd won the gold medal at Houndston School for it. He was fourteen. And now here he was, ten years later, trying and failing to *keep* things from getting too hot. He stripped off the rest of his clothing and sank into the hot water. Two days, or he would—no, he wouldn't lose his position, he was too valuable to Elltis and Company, but— He sank further under the water until only his nose and mouth were above it. He wasn't going to think about it. He'd promised Piercy.

So. Someone capable of producing fire on a scale no one had ever seen. No, that was wrong. If there was a kernel of truth in legend, it was fire on a scale no one had seen for centuries. He didn't know very much about the stories of Alvor and his companions, except that they'd gone on a quest to find a way to defeat the warlord Murakot, who'd supposedly had great magics at his command. Including powerful fire spells. *That can't be the answer, though,* he thought, sitting up and making the water splash over the edge of the tub, then lathering up to keep from falling asleep in the wonderful, warm, soothing embrace of the bathwater. *I might be convinced that some creature from a thousand years ago exists and is present in this time, but there's never been any evidence that magic was somehow different in the past. Someone's discovered a new spell.*

He scrubbed at his hair. It took two rinses before he felt truly clean. His cheeks burned to think of how he'd let himself go. *Focused, Piercy? I really think 'obsessed' is the better word.* An unexpected pang of loneliness struck him; he was suddenly conscious of how isolated he'd become, how alone he'd managed to make himself even in the midst of his large family. And yet he couldn't remember how he'd gotten this way. At school, he'd been a top student, but he'd always had time for sport and courting young women and, of course, getting Piercy into trouble. He'd been popular, damn it, and now he hardly ever saw his friends from those days, except Piercy, always had his head down over some work project or other. It couldn't be healthy. *And it's not making me happy,* he thought with some surprise. Satisfied, maybe, content, possibly, but there was definitely something missing in his life.

He dried himself and ran back down the short hall, naked and clutching his clothes in front of him because he'd forgotten his dressing gown. Safely in his room, he put on a clean shirt and trousers and collapsed onto his bed. He was starving now, but he was more tired than he was hungry. His bed was the best bed that ever was made by human hands. He began to drift off. No more fires of any intensity. Just his sleepy brain putting up a soft barrier between himself and—

His eyes snapped open. It couldn't be that simple, could it? Not rigid; flexible. He leaped out of bed and began rummaging in his desk. So many odds and ends, broken pieces, discarded spell components—there was a cowrie shell, no idea how it had gotten there but it would have to do. Nothing fireproof, nothing fireproof. He finally found an old silver snuffbox, which was puzzling because he didn't use the stuff, and scrabbled at his coat pockets until he found the piece of coppery chalk no magician was ever without. Carefully he drew a single straight line and a wavy one on the surface of the snuffbox. The chalk filled the grooves of the snuffbox's engraved top as if it were liquid rather than powder. Evon shoved the papers and other detritus of work to one side of his desk and set the snuffbox down in the center of the clear spot. He laid the cowrie shell beside it, then took his penknife and cut a chunk of candle off the ancient taper on the windowsill and put that next to the other objects.

Now he needed oil. He used magic to light his room, a globe hanging from the ceiling in a translucent glass basket, but there had to be oil somewhere in the house. He thundered down the stairs all the way to the ground floor and into the kitchen, where he startled a shriek out of the cook. "May I have some cooking oil?" he demanded.

"Mr. Evon, sir, whatever d'ye need cooking oil for?" she said, her eyes wide.

"A spell. Quickly! I don't need much. In a cruet, if you can."

The cook, still stunned, found a glass cruet of oil and handed it to him, her hands shaking a little at his intensity. Evon nodded his thanks and dashed back upstairs. His own hands trembling, he dribbled oil in an awkward circle around candle, snuffbox, and shell, then set the cruet far away on the other side of the room and clenched his fists to steady himself. This had to work. It was so simple. He closed his eyes briefly and said, "*Presadi*," feeling the all-too-familiar numbness pass briefly over his tongue.

A silvery dome that looked like a soap bubble, its surface slick with rainbows that sparkled rather than gleamed, sprang up around the three objects. Evon held his breath. It looked the same as any other shield. He exhaled, slowly, then snapped his fingers and said, "*Forva*."

A ring of white fire sprang up along the line of oil, over a foot tall. Evon was several feet away, but the heat parched his face and hands and crisped his hair. It felt as if all the air in the room were being sucked into it. Evon shielded his face and shouted, "*Desini!*"

19

The fire went out. So did the shield. He'd need to be more careful about directing that command word. Evon went forward, his lips still tingling from *desini*. Shell. Snuffbox.

Candle. Completely intact.

Evon sucked in a breath, then shouted a wordless cry of triumph. It worked. By the Twins, it actually worked! He picked up the candle stub. Not only wasn't it melted, it was cool to the touch. So were the other two objects. He clasped them to his chest and did a joyful little dance around the room. Piercy had been right; all he'd needed was to think about something else for a while. He stopped dancing and drew in several slow breaths to calm his racing heart, set the spell components on the desk, and sat down on the bed. Sleep was out of the question now. He might as well turn his attention toward Piercy's little problem. It couldn't possibly be as difficult as the one he'd just solved.

2

_____

*E*von shivered and once again wondered why Miss Elltis was so opposed to installing some form of heating in her magicians' offices. A series of metal grills with a radiant heat spell cast on them, for example, would fit neatly under the long row of windows and not interfere with the rest of the wall space. He rubbed his hands together, then pressed the tips of his index and pinky fingers together and whispered, *"Presadi,"* and the iridescent shield rose up around him, two inches from his nose. He immediately felt warmer, felt his breath coming up against the shield and rebounding to brush his face. His breath was damp and warm and smelled slightly of hazelnuts, for no reason Evon could imagine. After demonstrating the fireproof shield to Miss Elltis and a handful of government officials from Home Defense, he'd worked long hours coming up with the gestures that would replace the runes and material components of his initial experiments. The shield had turned out to be airtight as well, which made it dangerous for long-term use. Eventually he'd have to work out a solution for that, too, but at the moment he felt he'd earned his bonus, as well as Miss Elltis's grudging approval. They both knew Evon was Elltis & Company's brightest rising star, though Miss

Elltis behaved as if Evon were just another junior member of the cooperative and Evon behaved as if he actually thought of her as his superior.

He dismissed the shield with a word and a flick of his left hand and felt the chill descend upon him again, oppressive and distracting. Time to take another look at Piercy's project. The map tacked to the wall was the biggest map of Dalanine and environs that he could find. He'd marked the sites of the...fires? Events? Explosions? that Home Defense had identified. Why they didn't just come out and call it the War Department, given that Dalanine was actually at war, he had no idea. Then, with some pride, he'd marked in a different color the sites *he'd* identified. True, he'd had to resort to the dubious help of the *Weekly Gazette*, but when he'd stripped away all the Alvorian nonsense and talk about people being struck by acts of Gods, he'd actually found truth hiding away at the core. Three more sites, all of them matching the specifics of the other explosions. Three more sites proving that this...this epidemic had been going on much longer than Home Defense believed.

Someone rapped at his door and opened it without waiting for an invitation. "Lore, I half expect to find you frozen to your chair one of these days," Piercy said. He wore padded kid gloves and an overcoat with a fur collar turned up to shroud his ears and hairline and had his walking stick tucked under his arm. "Doesn't your Miss Elltis believe in the basic human right not to freeze to death in one's place of employ?"

"Miss Elltis believes in the basic human right not to spend unnecessary money, and she defines what is unnecessary," Evon said, rubbing his hands together and blowing on his fingers. "And I forgot my gloves. Did you bribe the guard again?"

"The guard is under the impression that I am Home Defense's liaison with this cooperative, which is true except for all the ways in which it is false. For the Twins' sake put on your coat, at least. You make me cold just looking at you."

Evon crossed the room to where he'd left his frock coat and overcoat and put both on. Piercy went over to the map and stood with his hands behind his back, gazing at the marks. "You've been a busy boy these last three weeks, dear fellow," he mused. "I hope this represents actual progress."

"You have such little faith in me. It represents the progress of the Fearsome Firemage through Dalanine."

"The 'Fearsome Firemage'? How very alliterative of you."

"A term coined by the *Weekly Gazette*. I may have to take out a subscription, it's been so useful. Care to know the latest act of Gods? Strange creatures emerging from the magical places where nature's law no longer applies? Or perhaps some Wystylth sightings? It's a full moon, always good—"

"Thank you, no, I encounter enough insanity at my place of employment every day." Piercy riffled through one of the stacks of the pages tacked to the wall beside the map. "I recognize this name. Lendan Hansaltis. One of the victims."

"I think not. It's his wife those clippings are about. Charra Hansaltis was accused of viciously abusing her husband and children over a course of several years."

"Abusing her husband? That seems unlikely."

"You'd be surprised at what some women are capable of, and what some men are incapable of resisting. Don't you want to know why it matters?"

"Since you clearly want to tell me, yes."

Evon tapped another stack of papers. "Only six victims in four events were ever identified. But four of the six have criminal histories. Harkel Stantis, who turned out to have six bodies buried beneath the foundation of his home. The most recent one, Frandon Toltis, who was accused of poisoning both his wives. Charra Hansaltis. And Storna Cathelter, whom Joral Donalter says—"

"Gimpy? How is the old fellow, anyway? Haven't seen him in a dog's age."

"He's fine. He's employed in the constabulary in Carshan, where Storna Cathelter lived. He says they had complaints all the time about her from her neighbors, serious criminal allegations even, but no one ever brought her up on a charge." Gimpy had been surprisingly happy to hear from him, and Evon felt a renewed pang of guilt at having let that old friendship slip by, a pang intensified by his feeling that he had only looked Gimpy up because he needed something from him. One more friendship he'd let fade.

"I'll wager he still has the fastest legs in Dalanine. I would hate to be a criminal run down by him. Lore, is there a point to this?"

"Isn't it obvious? All four had what I think Gimpy would call a criminal nature and none of them were brought to justice for their crimes. I would wager, as long as we're placing bets, that if we could identify the rest of the victims, we'd find similar evidence. In fact, in Alsenth, where the first event occurred, there was a series of unsolved murders that stopped after the explosion. I was thinking of contacting Chess Blaketer, see if he's heard anything more."

Piercy shook his head. "Not a good idea. He joined Speculatus after two years at university. He and Odelia were both recruited pretty heavily. I'm surprised you didn't at least know about Odelia. I was under the impression that you kept a careful eye on her so you would never again have to share the same breathing space."

Evon scowled. "I really have no interest in what she does with her life. And I don't see how Chesley being employed by Speculatus means I shouldn't reach out to him for information. In fact, that might make him more likely to know something."

"Their unsavory reputation, according to my inside sources, is more than a little deserved," Piercy said. "I realize none of their members has ever been convicted of shady dealings, but there are people employed by my department who watch them like a starving man watches someone else's meal, waiting for them to misstep."

"I can't imagine Chess being involved in anything like that."

Piercy shrugged. "Maybe not, but it's still better not to bring him in on this. For all we know, Speculatus might have an interest in finding our mystery magician themselves."

"That's an excellent point. Well, I would like to have more evidence about Alsenth, because I realize it's a stretch, but it fits the evidence. I think the Fearsome Firemage is targeting evildoers whom the law has no hold over."

"But Storna Cathelter—"

"Was killed with her child, yes. It's likely some of these victims were innocent bystanders. The spell isn't exactly discriminatory."

"Then you know how it works."

Evon shook his head and shoved his hands into his overcoat pockets. "I wish I did. I've been able to duplicate the ten-foot diameter, but nothing I've tried has come close to being hot enough. Either the Fearsome Firemage—"

"You really do enjoy saying that, don't you, dear fellow?"

"It has a certain appeal. She's either using a combination of runes and gestures I've never heard of, or she's found some material component that is far more potent than anything we have access to."

"Then you believe your Fearsome Firemage is a woman." Piercy riffled through the clippings again, as if looking for her identity among them.

"It can't be coincidence that witnesses at every location have reported seeing a woman either fleeing the place, or watching the fire, or standing out in some other way. There's too much consistency —a woman with long blonde hair, of average height, young or at least not yet middle-aged. That's discounting the witnesses who saw a *naked* woman leaving the site, which simply proves that some people have very low minds." Evon grinned. "I think we're looking for a woman."

"That's—what do you mean, *we're* looking for a woman?"

Evon grinned more broadly. This was how he used to feel all the time, everything knife-edged and clear in his mind, all the steps laid out before him and all he had to do was leap from one to the next, towing Piercy with him, or occasionally pushing him out ahead. Piercy needed danger in his life, and Evon needed a challenge; their friendship was based on that symbiosis. "You and I," he said, savoring the words, "are going to make a journey. South."

Piercy shook his head, slowly but emphatically, and held up his stick as if to ward Evon off. "No. No. You have that look in your eye, Evon, and besides, I can't exactly leave my work and go haring off with you on whatever mad quest you have in mind."

"You won't have to leave your work, Piercy. Your employers are going to pack you a box lunch and kiss you farewell, metaphorically speaking, because you are going to tell them that you know how to track down the Fearsome Firemage. Though you might not want to call her that in front of them. They'll think you read the *Weekly Gazette* and the Twins only know what kind of mental instability that might mean."

"I, track down the Fearsome Firemage? Evon, if anyone is displaying mental instability right now, it's you."

Evon rapped on the map with his knuckles, then blew on them to warm them. "Would I lead you astray?"

Piercy covered his face with one gloved hand. "I am experiencing a vivid memory. Would you like me to tell you what it is?"

"I already know it's a memory of our fifth year at Houndston, winter term, when we rearranged Mistress Goulter's personal spell components so she mistook her hair growth tonic for her skin cleanser and grew what I recall to be a very fine beard."

"Yes, and because you made me handle the jars, I spilled some of the tonic and grew hair on my palms. As if my in-house suspension wasn't enough of a trial."

"To be fair, I confessed my part in the adventure and stood suspension by your side, as a true friend would."

Piercy raised his head. "My *point*, Evon, is that our mutual history could be construed to be a long, long line of events in which you led me astray."

"Well, I promise I'm not leading you astray now." Evon pointed at the map again, then covered his nose with his cupped hands and breathed heavily to warm his face. "There's a pattern there," he said, his voice muffled, "or rather a trend, since there's no consistency in the timing of the events or the distance between them. The trend is southward. The Fearsome Firemage is seeking out criminals who can't be or haven't been apprehended by the law. We just have to find those criminals first."

"Evon, did I mention that you are out of your mind?"

"I've already received a leave of absence from Miss Elltis. You tell your superiors that you are accompanying your, whatever you called me, civilian expert as the government's representative because said expert needs to examine the evidence personally. Tell them I'm close to discovering the secret. It's true, I am. I'll wager they won't have any problem letting you go."

Piercy took a deep breath and let it out, slowly. He smiled, brown eyes twinkling. "I have to say, it *is* good to see your old self is still in there somewhere, dear fellow."

"I feel the same." Evon looked around the dismal workroom and wondered if he even wanted to come back to it. Lorantis & Company. Right. He could endure a little dullness for the sake of his dream, be satisfied with mere contentment, but Piercy was right: his old self had been locked away too long. Time to see what that self could accomplish.

It was the most tedious and most anxious two weeks of Evon's life. He and Piercy took the coach from Matra to Chaneston, site of the most recent event, and searched outward from there, looking through newspapers for reports of unsolved violent crimes in the larger cities, asking after female strangers in the smaller ones. They took coaches down narrow roads that were more like game trails, bare tree limbs and spiny brambles almost scraping along the sides of the vehicle. They spent nights in villages so tiny they weren't even marked on Evon's map, sometimes bedding down on the floor of a willing cottager's home because there was neither inn nor tavern with rooms to let. After the first week, Evon began to fear that his plan wasn't as brilliant as he'd thought. He found it hard to meet Piercy's eye, though his friend never complained or criticized. It was that lack of complaint that worried Evon; if Piercy's flow of pointed witticisms dried up, it meant Piercy was as frustrated as Evon, and that made Evon feel guilty at having dragged Piercy into this.

Ten days and sixteen villages after Chaneston they rode through the streets of Rainoth, which was a fairly large city only three days' journey south from the capital. New construction on every corner proclaimed its prosperity, though Evon observed that the builders hadn't taken advantage of the opportunity to upgrade the existing properties. The mix of styles gave the city a lopsided look, older wooden houses with upper stories jutting out over lower ones pressed cheek to cheek with the flat brick façades of the newcomers.

It had snowed the previous night, and the streets were already churned into a dirty slush the horses kicked up with every step. Evon stepped down from the coach at the way station and stretched to get the kinks out of his back. They'd slept cold on some farmer's hearth the night before, and Evon had wakened several times imagining the unknown magician had passed and was far ahead of them preparing to strike down some new victim. His eyes felt dry and itchy and his shoulders ached. The Fearsome Firemage would have had to backtrack to strike in Rainoth, but it was the last large city between Chaneston and Matra and he was running out of ideas.

"Did you want to begin searching immediately, or find a bed? Or send your Miss Elltis an update?" Piercy asked. He, damn him, looked as fresh and impeccably turned out as ever.

"An inn," Evon said, "to drop our gear. I'd rather not haul it all over town." *And*, he thought, *I want to delay the moment where I have to tell Miss Elltis I've still had no success as long as possible.* At first he'd communicated with her by mirror every evening, then every other day, and now his contacts with her were sporadic as he convinced himself he shouldn't waste her time by telling her he had no news. He dreaded seeing her severe visage in his mirror, hearing her precise voice, tinny with distance, dressing up her message in formal words but always saying the same thing: come home successful or don't come home at all. He thought the last part might be a little extreme; Miss Elltis couldn't afford to lose him. Even so, every time he felt the palm-sized round mirror in his inner pocket press against his chest, he cringed.

"That one looks promising," Piercy said, gesturing across the road to a three-story stone building with a wooden sign over the door that said THE FIREBRAND. It did look prosperous and the sign depicting a burning torch was new, the paint fresh. Evon's eye returned to that picture. "Interesting," he said.

"Well, it looks no more or less promising than any of the other inns I've seen on the way here, but it has the virtue of being in our immediate vicinity," Piercy said.

"Fire," Evon said. "I wonder."

Piercy glanced at him. "You aren't suggesting that after ten days of searching, we step off a coach and just happen to stumble upon our quarry's trail?"

"This is the coaching stop for Rainoth," Evon pointed out, "and there are three inns within sight of it. If she did stop in Rainoth, chances are she put up in one of these places. She had to decide between them somehow. Maybe she's drawn to fire. It's worth inquiring, anyway."

"I suppose so," Piercy said. "And I have a plan. Follow me."

The idea of Piercy having a plan filled Evon with dread, but he obediently shouldered his bag and followed Piercy across the road, dodging carriages and skidding a little on the wet cobblestones, and ducked through the door of the inn.

They entered the taproom, which was well-lit and clean and smelled of stew. Round tables with surfaces unmarred by time dotted the room like flat-topped mushrooms, circled by narrow chairs that were surely too skinny to support an average person. Piercy crossed the taproom to the bar. "Excuse me," he called out, rapping on the bar with the head of his walking stick. "My friend and I are thirsty."

After a moment, a tall, skinny woman came through a door at the far end of the taproom, wiping her hands on a none-too-clean rag. "You want beer?" she said. She sounded a little surprised that anyone might want beer at nine o'clock in the morning.

"If you please, madam," Piercy said. He'd adopted a grand manner that told Evon he was about to tell a grand, unnecessary lie. "Piercy—" he began, but Piercy shushed him with a wave of his hand. Piercy took a seat on one of the glossy new bar stools, and after a moment, Evon joined him. As the woman's back was turned, Piercy gave Evon an intense, wide-eyed look that said *Just agree with whatever I say.* Evon sighed. It was true he'd gotten Piercy into a lot of trouble when they were younger, but Piercy had gotten himself into trouble enough on his own with his habit of making up wild, implausible stories to get himself out of whatever trouble Evon had gotten him into. Evon leaned his elbow on the counter and rested his chin on his hand. Fortunately Rainoth had no shortage of inns, because it was possible Piercy was about to get them kicked out of this one.

The woman set two foaming glass mugs on the counter before

them. Evon's stomach revolted at the idea of beer before breakfast. Piercy raised his and took several large swallows, making appreciative noises. He set the now half-full mug on the counter, wiped his mouth, and gave the woman his most brilliant smile. "That is the most delicious brew I've had in weeks," he said. "Do you make it yourself?"

"It's ordered in," the woman said. She looked at Piercy with suspicion, as if she thought he might be making fun of her. Evon couldn't blame her. Piercy sounded so enthusiastic that it came across as insincerity. He took a sip of his own beer and nodded and smiled at the woman. It *was* good, even if it made his stomach demand eggs and fried ham.

"Well, you've found an excellent supplier," Piercy rallied. He took another long drink. "I was wondering if perhaps you could help us. We're looking for a woman we believe passed through Rainoth some...?" He looked at Evon, eyes pleading. Yes, Piercy hadn't thought this through. Evon did a little quick calculating in his head, aided by his instincts.

"Five weeks ago," he said.

"Why are you asking?" the woman said, drawing back from them a little in suspicion. Evon mentally kicked himself, then Piercy. Of course it would look suspicious, them asking about a woman without being able to say why. Telling this barkeep that they were after the magician who'd caused all those fires would either make them sound crazy or start a panic.

"She's run away from her family," Piercy improvised. "They're very worried about her. She was...she was going to be married, and she ran off two days before the wedding. They're afraid something's happened to her." Evon wished he could kick Piercy for real. Too much detail, when the Fearsome Firemage might have told any story. Suppose she wasn't as young as the reports made out?

The woman shrugged and scowled. "Plenty a woman changes her mind before she reaches the altar," she said. "Maybe the young man wasn't her choice." But the scowl didn't reach her eyes, and Evon noted that she'd said "young man." Maybe Piercy had unwittingly hit on the truth. Evon's heart beat a little faster.

"They were childhood sweethearts," Evon picked up the tale, afraid of the look in Piercy's eye that said he was about to come up with something outrageous. Evon had always been the better liar. "Her relatives think she might have been in the family way and was ashamed. They don't care about that. They just want her to come home."

Something in his words shifted the woman's attitude. The look in her eyes went from suspicious to warily sympathetic. "What did she look like?"

Piercy turned another pleading look on Evon. He tried to remember the details of the reports on the mysterious woman's appearance. "Not very tall," he said. "Long hair...maybe a little darker blonde than mine. In her early twenties," he added, making an instinctive leap as he watched the woman's face.

The woman folded her arms across her chest and stared them down. "She said her name was Kerensa," she said. "Came here looking for work maybe five weeks ago. I gave her a job in the kitchens, cleaning up, then set her to waiting tables when she proved willing. Popular with the men, if you take my meaning, though she never led them on. Brushed off the ones got too friendly without being mean. Never said where she was from or who she'd been and I didn't ask. Didn't much care so long as she did her work. Didn't like that she had a tobacco-smoking habit. Never saw her doing it, but she always smelled of smoke."

Evon made a mental note of that odd piece of information. "When did she leave?" he asked.

"Two weeks ago. Just vanished one night. Didn't even ask for her pay, and stole my daughter's spare dress on top of that." The woman scratched her nose with one thin finger. "Can't say as we were surprised. She always had this air said she had one foot out the door all the time. But she might've asked about the dress. You gents from her family?"

"Old friends," Evon said, stepping hard on Piercy's foot when he opened his mouth, probably to claim they were this Kerensa's loving brothers. "We were headed this way and they asked us to inquire after her."

"Hope you find her," the woman said. "Figured she was higher class than she put on, seeing as you gents talk so fancy. Come from good family, does she?"

"The best," Piercy interjected, prodding Evon's shin with his booted toe. He sounded annoyed that Evon was doing all the talking.

"Strange, a girl from good family being so capable in the kitchen." The woman started to look suspicious again.

"She felt she should understand what it took to run a household," Evon improvised. "She is rather progressive."

"Her fiancé is still working his way up in the world," Piercy said. "Good prospects, but still, ah, working his way up in the world." Piercy's voice was pitched a little too high, sign that he was about to panic and ruin everything. Evon said, "The family approves the match, but they're realistic. And progressive."

The woman's eyes narrowed. Piercy opened his mouth. Evon said, "You've been so helpful, miss...?"

"*Mrs.* Kelnter," the woman said, but she softened a little, pleased at being thought young enough to still warrant a "miss."

"Mrs. Kelnter, we've been so worried about Livian—that's her real name, I'm not sure where she came up with 'Kerensa'—and I'm sure you can imagine, having a daughter yourself, what it must feel like not to know where she is or if she's safe. Livian's parents will be so relieved to hear that their daughter found shelter here for a time. I don't suppose you know if she made any friends, spoke to anyone who might know where she intended to go next?"

Mistress Kelnter pursed her lips. "Never spoke much to anyone," she said. "I know she was on foot, I can tell you that. Couldn't have afforded a horse or coach fare." She shook her head. "Wish I'd known her story, or I would've made sure she had her wages."

"Thank you, Mistress Kelnter. And thank you for the beer." Evon put some coins down on the countertop and took a long swallow from his mug. His stomach had gone from hungry to excited. So close. "We should be going," he added, directing a pointed look at Piercy, who looked mulish but followed him outside.

"You nearly ruined everything," Piercy said in a low voice when they were safely on the street.

"*I* nearly—Piercy, you were going to babble!"

"I was not. I had her believing everything I said."

Evon snorted. "I have two words for you. Master. Harntis."

Piercy flushed. "That would have worked if you hadn't sneezed."

"Master Harntis was never going to believe you were there for extra tutoring. Particularly after you panicked and told him his daughter was extremely attractive. Except you were looking at a rotogravure of his son."

"I maintain that the boy had a very feminine face."

"It doesn't matter. We know the Fearsome Firemage was here up until two weeks ago. That was when she went to Chaneston. Didn't you think it was odd, what Mistress Kelnter said about the young woman always smelling of smoke?"

"If she has a tobacco-smoking habit, no, I do not find it odd."

"But Mistress Kelnter said she never saw her doing it. I think we've found another characteristic of our mystery magician."

"I wonder that you are so fond of alliteration, dear fellow. Besides, why does that matter?"

"I don't know yet. We need food, and then—no, I still should send Miss Elltis a message—but *then* we can be on our way. We need to go back to Chaneston, now that we have more information."

"I suppose you will now ask after young blonde women of average height who smell of smoke?"

"Not exactly. But I think I can do something with that fact."

3

―――――――――

The road to Coreth was little more than a dirt track. Evon grasped the edge of his seat and held on as the carriage bumped over the frozen ruts. He'd given up his fur rug to Piercy about an hour ago, and now rode with his teeth clenched together against the cold and the jostling ride. He'd forgotten what a poor traveler Piercy could be. His friend lay slumped in the opposite corner, one fur rug bundled up beneath him as protection against the thinly padded bench, the other covering him so only his nose and eyes were visible.

"Do you want to change seats?" Evon said quietly. If the past was any indication, Piercy would have an agonizing headache on top of his other maladies.

"We should have ridden. We should have *walked*," Piercy moaned.

Evon eyed Piercy's stack-heeled boots with the sharply pointed toes, all shiny black leather and hand-stitching. "We're almost there," he said. "There ought to be an inn or something." *I hope.* They'd been well on the road to Chaneston when they'd heard about the Fearsome Firemage striking in Coreth, only half a day's journey out of their way. Evon thought Coreth would be better suited to his plan, as fresh a site as it was, but Piercy had wanted to press on to Chaneston and Evon had had to override him. Now, looking at Piercy's sallow face, he felt a little guilty at his insistence.

Piercy groaned again and pulled the rug over his face, and muttered something of which Evon only caught the words "eat" and "bedbugs." He pressed his face against the glass and tried to see into the distance ahead of them.

A few stone houses, their thatched roofs a dull brownish yellow, lined both sides of the track. Their gray, weathered doors didn't quite fit their frames. Smoke trailed from a few chimneys, but no one came out to watch the coach or peered out the window at the strangers, though Evon thought he saw movement behind some of the drab white curtains. Cottages gave way to more solid-looking buildings, roofed with slate rather than thatch, some of them two-storied with actual glass windowpanes. They passed a general store and a smithy, and then the coach pulled up in front of a long, low building with a peaked roof and a tiny second story that looked like it had been stuck on as an afterthought. The coachman leaped down and opened the door. "Coreth," he said. "You stoppin' here for the night, gents?"

Evon gave the building another look. "I suppose we are," he said. "May my friend wait here while I make arrangements? He's quite ill."

The coachman peered at the pile of furs. "Just so's he's off the coach afore I leave," he said. Evon left him removing their baggage from the roof and went into the building. He had to duck under the low door frame, but once inside he found the rafters were much higher than he'd anticipated and he could stand upright with ease. The planed wood floor, warped with age, creaked as he crossed the taproom, its boards many different shades of brown as if they'd been replaced, one by one, with whatever lumber was handy. The chairs were as mismatched as the floorboards and some of the tables canted a little, though Evon couldn't tell if it was the floor or the table legs that were uneven.

A portly man with wisps of white hair flying from his round head looked up as Evon entered. "Can I help you with summat, gent?"

"My friend and I would like rooms for the night," Evon said.

The old man frowned. "Ain't got but the one room, though it's got two beds. That do for you?"

So it was a tavern, not an inn. Evon was just grateful he wouldn't have to share a bed with Piercy, who he knew from their nights in the school dormitory was a restless sleeper. "That would be excellent, thank you," he said.

"Upstairs," the man said, and led the way through a dark doorway and up a narrow, unlit flight of stairs to a room that seemed to comprise the entire second floor. It did have two beds, and was remarkably warm and smelled of soup and mutton and fresh bread. "Hope you don't mind it's over the kitchen," the man said.

"Not at all. It smells wonderful. When do you serve supper?"

"Half past six, in winter. Nothing fancy, just good plain fare." He turned and left the room without another word, leaving Evon gaping in the middle of another question. He closed his mouth and looked at the two beds. The blankets were thin, but there were several of them, and the mattresses didn't seem infested. He set a light to bobbing over his shoulder to illuminate the stairs and went to fetch Piercy, who had recovered enough to support most of his own weight as they ascended the stairs. Piercy collapsed onto one of the beds and flung his arm over his eyes, letting his walking stick fall from his other hand to clatter and roll under the bed. "If I die here, don't let them bury me in the pig pasture," he moaned.

Evon knelt to reach under the bed after the walking stick and nearly dropped it from its unexpected weight. So Piercy wasn't carrying it just for show. "I don't think they have a pig pasture."

"Of course they do. Anywhere this far away from civilization must be awash in pig pastures. What is that smell?"

"Supper, I think."

Piercy moaned again, but more quietly. "I must be feeling better, because it actually smells quite delicious. Not to be rude, dear fellow, but would you mind terribly taking yourself elsewhere? The sound of your breathing makes my head throb."

Evon descended the stairs and almost ran over a young woman with large, pretty brown eyes and a thin face. She wore a coarse brown wraparound apron and a white kerchief that completely covered her hair. "Oh! Beg your pardon, gent, but I didn't see you comin' down there."

"No, it was entirely my fault. Please excuse me."

The girl blushed. "Don't you talk fancy, there! Mam sent me to see if the young gents wanted to order aught special for supper. Only there's mutton, and soup, or mam could kill a chicken."

"Mutton's fine. Thank you." The girl blushed and made a half-bow, half-curtsey. "Wait," Evon said as she turned to go. "Can you direct me to the home of Corlis Fullanter?"

The girl's expressive eyes went cold and she crossed her arms over her chest. "Ain't no home left. Burned to cinders, it was."

"I know. I wanted to see what was left."

"Ain't naught left but smoke. You one o' them city gents comin' here to make mock of us?"

It was the first he'd heard of anyone coming to gawk at the site of an event. "No," he said in an indifferent tone, "I'm investigating the...fire...to determine what caused it."

"Ain't a mystery," she said. Her eyes were still cold and angry, but she let her arms drop to her sides. "The Gods struck Mr. Fullanter down, him and his evil ways."

"What ways are those? If you don't mind my asking. I promise I'm not here to mock you."

The girl pressed her lips together into a thin white line. "We all knew what he did," she said in a tight voice. "All the mams knew to keep their littles away from his door. Was evil, he was, and the Twins took note and burned him where he stood."

"Did you see it?"

She hesitated, then shook her head. "But we all heard the sound, and Mr. Lenter's house near took fire though it's nigh fifty feet away."

"Did anyone see it? Or see anything strange afterward?"

She shook her head. She looked as if she were gearing up to ask some questions of her own, so Evon said, "Thank you so much for your help. Would you mind pointing me toward Mr. Fullanter's...well, where his house used to be? I'll need something to tell my superiors back home," he added with a smile and a wink, and the girl blushed redder than before. Maybe Piercy was right, and he did have a little charm at his disposal. He couldn't remember the last time he'd accompanied a young woman to a play, or a lecture, or even down the street. The way he'd been going, it was unlikely any woman would have consented to go anywhere with him. He shrugged away the self-pitying thought. Perhaps, when this was over, he would ask Piercy to make some introductions for him. Piercy never seemed to have a shortage of young women fluttering around him. He could probably be induced to part with a few.

The girl ducked her head and gave him a shy look through her eyelashes, but said, "Out the taproom door and to the right. Follow the road and you can't miss it," then bobbed another half-curtsey, half-bow and retreated toward the kitchens. Evon followed her instructions, nodding at the few patrons seated in the taproom. They watched him openly, their faces blank as if he were a new specimen of bird and they weren't sure which way he might flap. At least they weren't hostile.

Evon's top boots were only slightly better for walking across muddy roads than Piercy's custom-made footwear. He watched his footing carefully, avoiding the deep ruts filled with icy slush and the occasional pile of half-frozen animal waste. Villagers stopped to stare at him as he passed, and he nodded at them, though he wasn't sure how friendly he looked, what with how hard he was concentrating on not falling. They did look as if they were accustomed to strange gents from the city wandering around their village. Evon sidestepped a particularly large turd and glanced around. He had walked nearly half the length of the village and passed half a dozen depressed houses. He felt a little depressed himself, looking at them. He hadn't realized how much a creature of the city he was until that moment.

He nodded again, this time at an elderly couple who were walking toward the tavern, hand in hand, and felt unexpectedly jealous. When this was all over, he was going to take a leave of absence —he was certainly owed one—and go to the theater, and the menagerie, and the Royal Gardens, with...his imagination stuttered to a halt. It had been six years since graduation; all the young women he'd known at school had returned home, or gotten married, or any number of things that put them beyond his reach. He drew in a deep breath of frozen air that tasted of snow and mutton, and moved on. It could wait until later. Right now, he had a mystery magician to find. About a hundred feet ahead he saw winter-dead yellow grass give way to blackened turf, and shortly he stood before what was left of Fullanter's house.

It hadn't burned entirely. The outer walls, made of large river stones, still stood, though the roof was gone and the wall over the doorframe had collapsed, leaving a fall of stones for Evon to step over. Inside, the packed dirt floor was black with char that stirred as Evon walked through, sending up a bitter smell of old fire and dead earth. If Fullanter had owned any furnishings, they hadn't survived the fire. Snow drifted shallowly against the inner corners of the cottage, clean and white against the burned stones.

The cottage had originally been bisected by another stone wall. Now that wall lay in a heap in the center of the cottage, not a heap of stones but a pile of what looked like fossilized mud. Evon touched it with his finger. It felt like cold stone, exactly as it should, except stone wasn't supposed to flow like water. He crouched so his eyes were level with its top and examined it. It looked a little glossy, as if it had been polished, and the grain seemed finer than that of the stones in the wall. He laid his palm against it, not sure what he expected, but nothing happened. It might as well have been sculpted into this bizarre shape.

Evon stood and brushed his hands off on his coat, then reached into his inner pocket and pulled out a quizzing glass with a smooth brass handle. He'd scratched runes along the frame of the lens, which gave it a seedy look, but Evon didn't carry it to show off. He polished the lens with the lining of his waistcoat, then passed his open palm across the glittering crystal and said, *"Epiria,"* and held it to his eye.

He was nearly blinded by the glow of residual magic the glass revealed. Blinking hard to keep from tearing up, he turned away and looked at the stone pile from the corner of his eye until his vision adjusted and he could see clearly. Even then, it was almost too bright to bear. The revelation spell showed the remnants of the fire spell as flying, twisting ribbons of blue-white light that left afterimages printed on Evon's eyes. Runes scrawled up and down the ribbons, as blindingly dark as the ribbons were light. He leaned in to examine one more closely and it drifted away, as if, impossibly, it was aware of his interest. No matter how he approached, the memory of the spell stayed just far enough away that he couldn't make out the runes. After a few failed attempts, Evon stepped back to look at the spell as a whole, and realized it had a larger pattern.

The twining ribbons outlined two human figures, one much taller than the other. The taller one reached out toward the shorter one with both arms, the shorter one raised its hand above its head, then both dissolved into fluttering ribbons of light only to come back together and repeat the strange dance. Evon watched the little scene play out a few times, then lowered the quizzing glass and said, "*Desini*." Two people, present at the center of the extraordinary spell. They had to be Fullanter and the Fearsome Firemage. Standing in the wreckage of Fullanter's cottage, surrounded by the remnants of the most powerful fire Evon had ever heard of, the whimsical name didn't seem so funny. He tucked the quizzing glass back into his pocket and dusted his hands again, though they weren't dirty, and licked his lips against the dry taste *epiria* had left in his mouth.

He breathed shallowly, inhaling the scent of char and snow and, distantly, someone's dinner. He had no idea if this next part would work. He'd worked it out by candlelight the last two nights while Piercy muttered in his sleep, scribbling notes and crossing them out and sketching the shape of a spell he wasn't sure was even possible. Tracking someone when you had a piece of them, a hair or a drop of blood, that was a commonplace. His quarry hadn't left anything like that behind. But she had left something else, if Evon could manage to find it. If it even remained here. If the spell worked.

He chalked a rune on the back of his left hand, then closed his eyes and let his mind wander. The bitter brown scent of burned earth. The clear crystal smell of snow melting. Mutton boiling over a fire, cold damp stone like ancient caverns. He pinched his nostrils shut with his left hand, pressed down on his eyelids with his right, and whispered, "*Olficio*."

Even with his fingers clamped over his nose, the raucous clamoring of a thousand odors made him stagger. There was a river—he remembered their coach passing over it—a quarter of a mile away, and he could smell the water rushing past its banks, throwing up the rougher scent of the rocks it wore away at. The nearer smell of mutton drilled into his lips and tongue, warring with the bitter coffee flavor of *olficio* and making him want to vomit. He swallowed hard and kept his eyes shut. Trees with green sap flowing through their veins waiting patiently for spring. The sharp musk of a fox in its den. And somewhere, in all of this olfactory noise, a scent that didn't belong.

He became gradually aware of a more human smell, the noxious odor of a body infrequently bathed and the warm, slippery scent of greasy hair. It permeated the stones, but faintly, as if the air was tugging it free and blending it with the wind that blew through the wrecked cottage. Fullanter. Then, even more faintly, the scent of smoke. Not the smoke of a campfire or even of a burning building, but a darker, thicker smell, slightly sour, as if someone had smeared grease on a hunk of ancient cheese and then set it alight. Evon let it seep into his closed nostrils and into his lungs. It wasn't exactly an unpleasant smell, but it made him uneasy, as though he'd invited something to take residence in his body that might not be the most gracious of guests. But nothing happened. He let the scent fill him to the core, then said, *"Desini,"* and the smells vanished so completely that even after he lowered both his hands, he felt as if his sense of smell had been surgically excised. Only the thick, sour smell of smoke remained, trailing away out of the cottage and down the road south toward Chaneston.

Staring down at the melted lump of stone, Evon ran through his careful deductions in his head and realized just how much guessing he'd done. Suppose he was right that the...he couldn't call her that name anymore, he'd have to say "the unknown magician." Suppose the unknown magician really *was* turning her devastating magic on people she believed deserved punishment. That didn't mean she was incapable of turning it on innocent people. Or that she was incapable of turning it on *him*, even though he only wanted...well, what did he want? He wanted to know how to wield that fire. He didn't want to hurt her, or stop her vigilante quest, he just wanted the fire. The realization shocked him. Even if she was killing evil men and women (and that was another guess he could be wrong about) innocent people were being killed along with the guilty. Shouldn't that matter too? Evon shook his head to clear it. First, they had to find her. Everything else could wait until then.

4

"*I* have already explained that we are moving as fast as we can, Miss Elltis," Evon said. It became harder for him to control his frustration with his employer every time he spoke with her, which was increasingly rarely. "This tracking spell—"

"I am not interested in the tracking spell, Mr. Lorantis," Miss Elltis said. Today she wore her flaxen hair parted in the middle, coiled in ringlets on both sides of her face and braided into a bun at the back of her head. Her small blue eyes peered at him myopically; he'd never understood why she refused to wear her spectacles when communicating with someone. She pursed her lips, causing a host of wrinkles to erupt around them and deepening the ones at the corners of her eyes. "I am interested in the fire spell. How soon will you have it?"

Evon ground his teeth against a host of angry words he wanted to fling at her. "We are very close now."

"Which is the same as saying you do not have it and can make no guarantees as to when you will." Miss Elltis leaned forward, narrowing his view of her until she was nothing more than a pair of bulging eyes and a twitching nose. "I am beginning to think this excursion of yours is a waste of my time and money."

"I fail to see how you can say that, when I have already achieved more than anyone else the government has set to this project," Evon said, and was afraid his words sounded like a snarl. "Have patience."

"Do not tell me what to do, Mr. Lorantis," Miss Elltis said, and she *did* snarl. "The government expects results from us, and they are not accustomed to patience. Find the magician, Mr. Lorantis. You have five days. After that—"

Evon cut the connection. He didn't need to hear any more. She wasn't serious; she could not afford to fire him. But it was a measure of how much she had promised the government that she could even imply that threat. He tucked the mirror away inside his coat and went outside to mount his horse, an indifferent gray gelding that always seemed to be laughing at him.

"Inveros, then?" Piercy said, his voice a little muffled by the collar of his coat, turned up against the chill wind. He prodded his own horse, a much nicer animal, and led the way out of the coaching inn's busy yard.

"It's the next place south of Chaneston," Evon said, "and although I think she came through here twice, I'm fairly confident she went south instead of west the second time."

"I am confident in *your* confidence, dear fellow, but I wish we had acquired horses sooner. It feels as if we are traveling faster, though I realize that is likely an illusion."

Evon only nodded. He felt an urgency now even greater than the one that had propelled him to discover the fireproof shield, a fear that they would reach Inveros only to learn that a giant explosion had leveled three buildings the day before. Knowing that he could now track the woman, having her scent in his nostrils day and night, couldn't dispel his fears. The smell had become so familiar he no longer perceived it as an odor, but as a compulsion, drawing him onward like a fish caught by a silver hook for the last two days.

Piercy had fallen silent when Evon did. Evon had no idea what thoughts preoccupied his friend. Regrets for the life he was missing in the capital, possibly, or something more mundane, like what hovel they might sleep in that night. So it surprised him when, a few hours later, Piercy said out of nowhere, "It appears our Fearsome Firemage is a young woman, then. Named Kerensa."

"It seems so," Evon said. "Though I wonder if that's her real name."

"True," Piercy said. They rode a few minutes in silence, then Piercy said, "Evon, would *you* be capable of such destruction?"

"I? Do you mean, could I so callously kill so many people, or could I cast the spell?"

"The latter, of course. You've too much compassion for the former."

He said it in such an offhanded way that Evon felt the tips of his ears redden with embarrassment rather than cold. "I—no, I can't imagine casting such a powerful spell. I can't imagine *anyone* capable of such power."

"And you are the most powerful magician of your generation. Don't protest, we both know it's true. No one else in our class was recruited to a highly prestigious cooperative directly out of school, bypassing university entirely. No one in the history of Houndston took the gold medal six years running. And if this woman is of an age with you, or younger...." His voice trailed off.

"You're wondering what else she might be capable of."

"I'm wondering what might happen to us if we face her directly. You know I have the utmost faith in your abilities, dear fellow, but I also have a deep and abiding love for keeping my integument intact. Perhaps this isn't the best idea we've ever had."

Evon blew out an explosive breath. "She's been targeting men and women who've done great evil to those around them. I was hoping I could convince her to turn that desire for justice on the Despot of Balviros's armies. You know better than I how his forces are advancing. You know the kind of destruction he leaves behind him."

"I know that his atrocities have multiplied in the last year," Piercy said. "It seems as if he no longer cares whether the countries he conquers remain a viable part of his empire. But...Evon, I'm beginning to agree with you that the Fearsome Firemage, whatever her name is, might not be sane. Convincing her of *anything* might be impossible."

"Do you think we should go home, then? Report...what? I don't know what we could even tell our superiors that wouldn't see us out on the street, unemployed and unemployable due to no references." He chose not to think about Miss Elltis's probable reaction.

"I don't know. I simply wish we had a better plan of attack."

"So do I." Evon wiped his nose, which had begun to drip from the cold. Another two hours and it would be too dark to go on. "Let's just focus on finding her. We can decide what to do from there. If we're right, and she's taken a job somewhere, we might be able to confront her in public so she's less likely to simply attack us."

"There is still a great deal of 'if' and 'might' attached to that plan, but I agree it's better than nothing." Piercy sniffled and wiped his own nose. "Not to complain, dear fellow, but I am so weary of sleeping on floors that I become less interested in the fate of our mysterious quarry with every mile that passes."

"Let's push on a little farther," Evon said, flicking his reins, "and with luck we'll find a bed rather than a floor."

They rode into Inveros around eleven o'clock in the morning the following day, following a wagon caravan laden with raw lumber headed for the port. Evon felt as if the city grew up around them, new construction giving way to established buildings of brick and limestone and then to granite quarried and hauled from over fifty miles away, tangible evidence that the more prosperous residents of Inveros could afford the same amenities as their wealthier neighbors in Matra. Inveros was smaller than the capital, but it felt bigger because of the wide streets, wide enough for two carts to pass without inconveniencing pedestrians on either side. There were few riders on horseback, and Evon and Piercy had trouble navigating between coaches and carts that regarded the streets as their property. By the time they found a satisfactory inn—satisfactory to Piercy, who dismissed Evon's first three choices as lacking in amenities, by which he meant an en-suite bath—Evon was more tired and irritable than he'd been the past three days living rough on the road. They turned their horses over to the care of a perky stable girl, paid far too much for a room with two beds and the essential bath, and collapsed onto their respective beds. "Is she here?" Piercy asked.

"She's here. Somewhere. We should start looking," Evon replied, but he put his arm over his eyes and let the tension drain out of his shoulders. He needed to get up if he didn't want to fall asleep. He wanted to fall asleep. He groaned and rolled over, then stood, his whole body aching more than if he hadn't taken that moment to rest.

"Piercy," he said, prodding his friend on the shin with his boot. "Piercy. We can't sleep now."

"I believe you are entirely mistaken in that statement. I feel that I am quite capable of sleeping." He had his arm flung over his eyes much as Evon had done moments before.

"Piercy, we need to track this woman down. Let's at least find out where she is. Then we can rest and decide what to do next."

"*You* do it. I await your findings with great anticipation."

"Do you want me to face this woman alone? She might kill me. Then you'd feel horrible and never be able to sleep comfortably again."

Piercy removed his arm and stared at the ceiling. "Why is it that you take such pleasure in having guilt as a major weapon in your rhetorical arsenal?"

"Because it's worked on you for nearly fifteen years. Come on. Get up. Her scent is very strong—I don't anticipate this taking very long."

Inveros was beautiful in the bright winter sun, everything sharp-edged and crisp like the smell of snow that still hung in the air and blended with the tangy salt of the sea. They left the horses behind at the inn and set out on foot. Everyone they passed had a smile or a greeting for them; even the sweepers at the street crossings had bright, eager faces. Brick and glass storefronts displayed wares from all parts of the world, and Evon had to remind Piercy why they were there when his friend kept falling behind to examine an exquisite pair of shoes or the perfect top hat. The scent led them through that major shopping district toward the heart of the city, where red and brown brick and greenish-white limestone gave way to quarried granite and wrought-iron gates and fences. There were fewer pedestrians now, and they had to walk more carefully to avoid the gray slush cast up by the passing carriages.

They turned a corner and found themselves facing a long, low gray brick wall, beyond which leafless trees and bare brambly shrubs spread out past the limits of their vision. The entrance to the park was some hundred steps to their left, and despite the season men and women still passed its gates. Evon sniffed again. "The route's directly through there," he said.

"Then let us by all means be tourists, albeit tourists who were woefully misled as to the season Inveros shows itself best to distinction," Piercy said.

But they hadn't taken more than ten of those hundred steps before someone behind them said, "Evon Lorantis, by the Gods! And his shadow. I certainly didn't expect to see you here. And don't you both look so...well, your sartorial decisions have always been unique, Evon, but you might at least make an effort not to look as though you'd been tramping the long and muddy roads for a week."

Evon stiffened. He hadn't expected to hear that voice here. Or wanted to hear it, ever again. "Odelia," he said as he turned around, trying for a cheery greeting. "How unexpected to see you here, too." He didn't dare look at Piercy, whose expression, whatever it was, would make him lose his composure in the face of this woman.

Odelia Cattertis stood in her familiar pose, legs slightly akimbo, fists on hips, her lips quirked to one side and one eyebrow raised. It was a pose that said she was ready to fight anyone who cared to come at her, though Evon knew her preferred weapons were words rather than fists. She wore her stiff black bonnet dangling down her back, hanging by its tied strings, and her dark brown hair was pulled sharply back from her face and knotted at the base of her neck. A black cloak lined with sable nearly concealed her full-skirted, multi-tiered black gown of finely woven wool, and she wore jet earrings that dangled almost to her shoulders. It was mourning garb, but Evon had known her long enough to know that black was simply her preferred color. That it put people at a disadvantage, wondering how to speak to a grieving woman, was a side benefit.

"I mean, we're all aware of your work ethic," Odelia continued, "so it really is surprising to see you on a...really, Evon, you *do* realize most people take their holidays when the weather isn't so nippy?"

"I might say the same for you, Odelia," Evon retorted, "but since you seem happiest when other people are miserable, I suppose it's no surprise that you're taking your holiday now."

Odelia pretended to be hurt, but her wounded expression was marred by her trilling, beautiful laugh. "You know me so well, don't you?" She glanced at Piercy. "Nothing to say in greeting, Evon's shadow?"

"Good morning, Miss Cattertis," Piercy said in a monotone. His hand was gripping the head of his walking stick so tightly Evon could see the tendons standing out. Piercy had never liked Odelia, even before he began hating her on Evon's behalf. He was also the only one who didn't believe that the scholastic rivalry she and Evon had shared had ever become a romantic relationship. Looking at her with an impartial eye, Evon could see why someone might have believed it. Odelia had a lovely heart-shaped face, pink lips that seemed permanently on the verge of a kiss, and enormous blue eyes fringed with the longest, blackest lashes Evon had ever seen. She also had the heart of a snake and a mind to match, all steel edges and indifference as to whom she cut.

"Good morning, Mr. Faranter," Odelia said, imitating his deep voice with a mocking bow. "Evon, it really is *so* good to see you again! Still slogging away at At-last and Company?"

"I understand you're working for Speculatus now," Evon said. There was no point in engaging her ridiculous taunts. "Congratulations. Are they treating you well?"

"Indescribably well," Odelia said, smiling coyly. "It's a pity they didn't approach you. We *did* work so well together, didn't we?"

Evon nodded, unable to speak as a hundred infuriating memories surged up. It didn't matter that he'd ultimately taken the top prize in their graduating class, he could only remember how innocently he'd accepted her first friendly overtures, how pleased he'd been at the thought of finding someone who matched him intellectually, how furious and humiliated he'd been when he realized she'd only collaborated with him to make him look like a fool.

Their relationship hadn't been so much a rivalry as a hotly contested war.

"I don't suppose you really *are* here on holiday?" he said politely, casting his eye over the oncoming conversation for a way to leave it gracefully and get back to their task.

"Business," she said. "*Secret* business." Her blue eyes twinkled at him. This was the signal for him to try to drag the secret out of her. He was about to decline taking the bait when he noticed that Piercy had tensed up, meaning that something wasn't right. Piercy might be a terrible liar, but his instincts about people were excellent. So Evon said, "*Secret*, is it? Can't you give an old friend a little hint?"

"I really shouldn't."

"That's a shame." Evon paused, then let a sly smile touch his lips. "Oh, Odelia, you nearly fooled me. There's no secret. Really, is your work so pedestrian that you have to pretend otherwise?"

"My work is far more interesting than whatever you've been doing, holed up in that poky old building for the last six years," Odelia said hotly.

"You know where I work? Really, I'm touched that you cared enough to drop by. Not that they'd let you in, of course, trade secrets and all that. Oh, that's true, you wouldn't know anything about that."

"I'm privy to more secrets than you can possibly imagine, Lorantis," Odelia said.

"Oh, I believe you," Evon said as insincerely as he could manage without giving the game away.

"Really? Watch the newspapers. Speculatus is on the verge of something big, and I'm the one who's going to find it. Magic like no one's seen before. We'll see how important your secrets are then, won't we?"

"I'll be watching the papers for your name with great interest," Evon assured her. "We should let you get back to your...*secret* business."

Odelia sneered at both of them and walked away, kicking up her skirts to keep them out of the slush. Evon and Piercy watched her go without speaking. When she was out of sight, Evon said, "Good instincts."

"Speculatus *is* going after the Fearsome Firemage," Piercy said. "I'd bet on it."

"She seemed pretty confident. Whatever other flaws Odelia has, she never acts on impulse. They must have a way to track the magician. We have to move quickly."

"I ought to let my superiors know about this," Piercy said.

"Now?"

"This could mean bringing Speculatus to justice. I think some of my superiors would call that more important than locating the Fearsome Firemage."

"That's true." Evon chewed his lower lip. "I can continue on my own."

"Is that safe?"

"I have no idea. But we can't afford to halt the search while you send a message. I won't approach her unless I think Odelia's about to attack. Do you have a mirror?"

Piercy patted his front pocket. "I may not be much of a magician, but I can manage a communication spell."

"I'll contact you when I find her. Go back to the inn when you're finished."

"I think this is a terrible idea."

"So do I. But we've run out of good ones." He nodded at Piercy and walked rapidly to the park gates.

The park would be beautiful in the summer, leaves in every shade of green, close-trimmed grass, gravel crunching underfoot as you strolled the paths, possibly with an attractive companion. It was still beautiful in the heart of winter, though in a different way, the bare branches making runes against the cloudless blue sky, thin drifts of snow over the winter-yellowed grass. Evon walked as quickly as he dared without drawing attention to himself. It wasn't impossible that Odelia had companions, and that they were watching him; Odelia's mind was that suspicious. But it was hard not to break into a run, especially since the scent was growing stronger. His heart rate picked up, not from exertion but from excitement. He wanted to see this woman. He wanted to ask her a million questions. And he was so close he could, literally, smell victory.

He emerged from the park into a paved pedestrian zone, a place he guessed in summer would be thronged with holiday-goers and the kind of street artists who painted poor reproductions of the scenery for far too much money. The scent still led directly forward, across the pavement and...stopped. He'd expected it to cross the street that terminated in the pedestrian zone, but it ended somewhere in the middle of the vast brick-paved promenade. She was here. One of these women walking past.... He went forward slowly, using his eyes as much as his nose. Long blonde hair, an oval face, not too tall, young. All the women had their hair bundled up under bonnets or kerchiefs. It was impossible to tell the shape of their faces. And from this distance, they all seemed to be the same height and age. He continued moving forward, narrowing his search. She was in that group of about ten women, but which one? All looked identical in dark cloaks and bundled hair, though one of them wore a kerchief while the rest had dark bonnets. The woman in the kerchief carried a bag over her shoulder and was moving faster than the others. She was in such a hurry that she pushed the others aside and proceeded at a near run across the street, not waiting for the sweeper.

It was her.

Evon broke into a faster pace himself, no longer afraid of Odelia's unseen, possibly non-existent watchers. The woman was moving so quickly that he feared losing her in the crowd. Though she was frequently obscured by other, taller pedestrians, her dingy white kerchief stood out and gave him something to follow. He had to do a little shoving himself to keep her in sight, but soon he found a pace that matched hers and was able to stay about fifteen feet behind her, a comfortable distance. His heart was pounding. Where was she going in such a hurry? Suppose she'd found a new victim? Would he be able to stop her? Would he *want* to stop her?

The woman didn't notice him following her, didn't seem concerned that anyone might be following her, just kept walking rapidly without looking to left or right, out of the central district. They passed stores with barred windows, tall houses narrower than

Evon's own, mansions that made Evon nervous, aware of his scruffiness and afraid the local constabulary might roust him for a vagrant. He continued to follow her through the wealthier parts of Inveros and into less prosperous but still attractive neighborhoods, all the while heading toward the outskirts of town. The farther they went, the thinner the crowds became, until Evon was certain she would notice him simply because they were the only two people on the street. He slowed his pace, but she still didn't seem aware of his presence. They passed through neighborhoods that became plainer and more worn until they reached a place where wooden houses blasted gray by the airborne sand and salt leaned against one another, some so visibly canted that Evon expected to see them tip over at the next gust of wind. They were close enough to hear the ocean but not see it, and the air tasted briny and smelled of seagull. The street, which terminated in scrub grass and sand dunes, was empty except for the two of them.

The woman dropped her bag in the street and began to run toward one of the houses near the end of the row. Without thinking, Evon ran after her. She was almost certainly going to kill whoever was in that house, and now that the moment had come, Evon realized that he couldn't allow someone, even someone evil, to die in that inferno. "Wait!" he shouted, again without thinking, and the woman slowed her steps and turned to face him. Her face was unexpectedly lovely, even twisted with rage as it was now.

"Go back!" she shouted. "You're not the one I'm here for!" She had the slightly broad vowels of a northerner and sounded as if she were pleading with him rather than commanding him.

"I can't let you do this," Evon said, stopping some ten feet away. Maybe there was still hope. She'd stopped to talk; maybe she was willing to listen.

Her face contorted with a choking, mirthless laugh. "You can't stop me," she said, mocking. "Get out now. Stay away. You don't deserve to die." She threw her cloak on the ground and kicked off her shoes, then whipped the kerchief from her head and dropped it on the pile. Her blonde hair came loose from where she'd wrapped it around her head and fell heavily around her shoulders. She stood facing him in a thin country dress with a straight skirt, her shoulders heaving as she drew in great, sobbing breaths.

"Whoever that person is doesn't deserve to die either," Evon said, pointing at the house, wondering if it was true.

She laughed again. "You think I don't know that?" She turned and sprinted toward the house. She moved so quickly that Evon was caught off guard. "*Desini cucurri!*" he shouted, flicking both his hands up and out like a conductor raising his baton, wincing against the jaw-numbing chill of the spell, like biting a chunk of ice, but she was inside the house before the spell could affect her. Evon cursed and ran full-out, yanked the door open so hard it nearly tore free from its leather hinges, and pulled up short.

The door led directly into a single small room with a stone fireplace that seemed more sturdy than the house it warmed. The magician stood in the middle of the room, her whole body clenched as if she were fighting some strong impulse. "You can get away if you run now," she said through clenched teeth, and Evon realized she wasn't speaking to him. A short, fat woman rose from a rocking chair near the fireplace, staring at both of the intruders as if she couldn't believe their presence.

"Who are you? Get out of my house! *Jontis!*"

"Just *go*," the magician said. Her skin looked rosy in the firelight. "Don't call him. Get out."

"*Jontis!*" the woman screamed. She limped over to the magician and raised both her hands as if to strike her. The magician's skin went from rosy to bright red. Fiery yellow lines, irregular and jagged, roiled beneath her skin. "It's too late," she said through her clenched teeth. "I'm sorry, I'm sorry, I'm—"

Pure instinct threw Evon to the floor. He pressed the tips of his index and pinky fingers together and shouted "*Presadi!*" just as the world went white around him.

Heat battered at him, dried his nostrils and his eyes and lips and pulled his skin tight across his cheekbones. Sweat sprang up and instantly evaporated. He squeezed his eyes shut and covered them with his arms, terrified that he'd already gone blind in that first exposure to the magician's fire. His ears rang with a high, keening sound that was probably the blood singing through them, propelled by his too-rapidly beating heart. He panted like a dog in the heat, then tried to calm himself. He only had so much air in this bubble and he was using it up too fast. He could already feel himself becoming dizzy — or was that the heat?

He risked a peek at his surroundings and found the air had gone from blinding white to a flickering yellow-orange. It was still brutally hot inside his shield, and he could feel himself becoming increasingly light-headed. Either he was going to die of suffocation in here, or he could die by fire out there. He decided to take his chances with the fire. As he dismissed the shield, he sucked in one last breath, just in case; it burned all the way down.

Thick smoke that smelled of salt-dried wood filled the air, rendering everything in the room dim and wavery. He was just outside the edge of a black-burned, glassy circle of earth, the foundation that lay beneath the floorboards. The fireplace stones had melted and flowed like mud over the hearth. Half the roof had collapsed and all of it, the entire house, was on fire. Evon stood and staggered a little at the heat, which was nothing close to what he'd experienced inside the shield, but was still hot enough to remind him that he needed to get out, fast.

He looked down and saw the grotesque outline of a human skeleton at his feet, and behind it, the magician. She was on her knees, shaking hard, her hair obscuring her face and her arms around her chest. She was also naked. Without thinking, Evon removed his coat and put it around her shoulders, then half-lifted her to her feet. She turned to look at him, her eyes dull and confused, and said, "You didn't burn."

"I will if we don't get out of here," he said, and urged her toward the door. It was entirely aflame, and Evon had to cast another spell to open it without setting himself on fire, all the time listening to the creaks and moans of the house under siege by the flames and thinking *hurry hurry hurry* until they were both safely outside and in the street, well away from the burning building. A few people had gathered to watch the house burn, but made no effort to rescue anyone who might be inside and paid no attention to Evon and the magician. She didn't try to get away from him, only leaned heavily on his arm as if she were exhausted. Evon stopped to pick up her belongings and overheard a man say, "Probably just as well, her going like that."

"Never did find out what happened to her son," his neighbor said.

Evon half-dragged the magician down the street past the last houses and out of sight behind a dune, then released her. She made no effort to keep his coat closed over her body, and Evon, embarrassed for both of them, turned his back on her and held out her cloak and satchel. "Thank you," she said. Her voice was husky, almost raw-sounding. He heard her rummage in her bag, and after a few minutes she said, "You can turn around now," with what almost might have been humor.

Evon turned and found her fastening the last few buttons on her dress. She bent and picked up his coat and handed it to him, gingerly, as if she expected him to take hold of her again. "You're not dead," she said. "You should have burned."

"Did you want me to?" he asked.

She reacted as though he'd slapped her. "Of course not," she said. "But everyone burns. There's never been a single survivor. So I want to know, why you."

Her directness, and the calmness with which she spoke, unnerved Evon more than if she'd screamed at him or threatened him. "It's a new kind of shield," he said. "It almost didn't work. I think your spell is a good deal more potent than any fire I expected it to defend against."

She wrapped her cloak more securely around herself and shivered, then lifted her bag to her shoulder. "What do you want from me?" she asked.

Evon was again unnerved. "I want to understand that spell," he said. "It's what I've been researching, fire spells and protecting against fire. I think we can use it in the war. Will you—I can teach you the shield spell in return, if you like. I don't mean you any harm," he insisted.

"I'm not a magician," she said. "And you don't want this spell."

She turned and began to walk away. Evon grabbed her wrist, realizing how stupid that was only after he'd already taken hold of her. She stopped and looked down at his hand. "Let go of me."

"Look," Evon said, feeling desperate, "I've been trying to find you for weeks. I just want to talk to you. Come with me. Just an hour. Maybe two. Then...I don't know. But—" She looked up at him, and her face was so empty of emotion, her eyes so dead, that he was seized with a wrenching sympathy for her. "I think you need help. My name is Evon Lorantis. I want to help you. What's your name?"

Confusion, and some other emotion he had no name for, flickered across her face. "Kerensa," she said. "Kerensa Haylter."

5

$\mathcal{J}$t was Evon's turn to lead the way, retracing their steps toward the heart of the city and the inn where he and Piercy were staying. He had to resist the urge to take Miss Haylter by the hand and tow her along after him. Every time they turned a corner he expected her to take off running in the opposite direction. But she stayed close by his side, not speaking, not even looking at him in the brief moments when he glanced over to reassure himself that she was, indeed, still with him. The scent of smoke that drifted from her wasn't as pungent as he'd imagined it might be, this close to her, more of a memory of a smell than the smell itself. He wondered what she was thinking. She hadn't sounded insane, but that haunted look in her eyes suggested that whatever grasp she had on reality was tenuous. And nothing she'd said, from the moment he'd confronted her, fit the picture he and Piercy had drawn from the evidence. How could she not be a magician, with magic like that at her disposal? And yet she'd seemed reluctant—no, that was far too tame a word for the way her whole body had gone rigid as she'd screamed at the victim to get out. It was as if the spell was under someone else's control, and that was simply impossible. He glanced at her once again, and this time met her eyes as she did the same. Her skin appeared too creamy, as if she had no pores, and he wanted to touch it to see if that were true. Her face was expressionless, and after a moment she looked away. Evon flexed his fingers, once again resisting the urge to tether her like a kite to keep her from drifting away.

He kept an eye out, as they walked, for Odelia or anyone who looked like a member of Speculatus, casting their net wide in the hopes of catching Miss Haylter in it. It was a pointless impulse; Odelia and anyone she had with her would be dressed just like anyone else. But meeting Odelia had roused some of the old paranoia he felt whenever he dealt with her. Suppose she had approached him because she knew why he was in Inveros, and had used him to find the rogue magician? Evon felt his shoulders beginning to hunch defensively. It was not beyond possibility that Odelia would attack them in the middle of the street, despite the throng of innocent bystanders.

"Is something wrong?" Miss Haylter said. Her husky voice had no emotion to it.

"Nothing," Evon said, straightening and trying to walk normally. All he needed was for her to panic and run away, forcing him either to chase her through the crowded streets or start the whole process of finding her again. He scanned the crowd again. Surely Odelia would stand out, dressed like the harbinger of death she was?

His heart pounded once, hard, as he realized Miss Haylter was no longer beside him. He turned to see her standing three feet away, looking up at the sky, not moving. Pedestrians brushed past her, but she seemed unaware of their presence. Evon went to her side and took her arm, not caring that it was a stupid idea. "Is something wrong?" he asked, echoing her earlier words.

"This is a bad idea," she said. "I can't help you. You can't help me."

"Just...give me one hour. Please." Her arm lay unresisting in his grasp. "You can't know what's possible if you won't even talk to me. Please." How far would he get if he picked her up and carried her away? About ten feet, that's how far, and then she'd start screaming and he'd either be tackled by concerned citizens or arrested by a stern constabulary, and either way he'd lose her again.

She lowered her head to look at him. "You don't understand anything."

"Then explain it to me. But do it at the inn, not on the street." Evon tugged gently on her arm, and after a moment she began walking. He kept hold of her until they reached the inn, then indicated she should precede him through the door. An older woman at the desk glanced up briefly, then gave them both a longer, disapproving look. "No guests," she said.

"My sister," Evon said, "and she won't be staying long. You don't mind, do you?" He gave her what he hoped was his most winning smile, when inside he was screaming at yet another delay. Miss Haylter stared at the wall above the woman's head, focused on something only she could see. The woman looked at Miss Haylter, then at Evon, and began tapping her fingers in a one-two-three rhythm on the desk. Evon slid a coin across the desk toward her. She slid it out of sight. "Good day to you both," she said, "but your...*sister*...better be gone in an hour."

"Thank you," Evon said, and bowed Miss Haylter toward the stairs, carefully ensuring that she went first so she wouldn't have anywhere to flee to, if it came to that.

"She thought I was a whore," Miss Haylter said as they passed the second floor landing.

"I'm sorry," Evon said.

"It doesn't matter." They left the stairs at the third floor and Evon led the way to the fourth door on the left.

"Oh. I'm traveling with a friend. He's no danger to you, but I wanted to warn you."

She turned that blank gaze on him. "You're no danger to me either," she said, and Evon wasn't sure if she was talking about his motives or his abilities. He opened the door and indicated she should enter; she did so without hesitation.

From the en-suite bath came the sound of gurgling water and a voice loudly humming a popular music-hall tune. "Evon? Did you find her? I was just drawing a bath—my superiors were most assuredly pleased to hear about Speculatus, though 'pleased' is probably too subtle a word for their reaction." Piercy, naked at least from the waist up, poked his head out of the bathroom and said, "I —*Evon!*" He slammed the door and added, "Was it so impossible for you to declare in a loud and carrying voice that we have company of a very feminine nature?"

Evon put his hand over his mouth so Piercy couldn't hear him laugh. He looked at Miss Haylter and was surprised and comforted to see her eyes lose that dead look for a moment. "Piercy, put your trousers on and come out here to greet Miss Haylter. *Kerensa* Haylter," he said.

After some banging and the sound of water draining, Piercy emerged, fully dressed though not as sprucely garbed as he usually was. "Miss Haylter, did you say? A pleasure," he said, taking her hand and bowing over it. "You have been a difficult woman to find, and I say that with great feeling. Too few cities are equipped with adequate laundry facilities, and some of my clothes will never be the same again. So your name is actually Kerensa? We wondered, Lore and I—"

"Will you sit, Miss Haylter? Piercy, stop babbling and get Miss Haylter a drink of water. One for me too, if you don't mind. It's been rather hot for both of us."

Piercy stopped halfway to the jug, his face ashen. "Are you all right?" he said in a low voice. "Evon, did she...were you actually *there?*"

"I think Miss Elltis owes me a promotion for that shield spell," Evon said. He held the only chair in the room for their guest, then took a seat on the edge of his bed and waited for her to take a long drink before tossing back most of a glass himself. He felt dry and itchy and wished he could have taken the bath Piercy had drawn and then drained. "I don't think we were followed, though I'm not sure how I would have known if we were. I didn't see Odelia, at least. But she implied she had some way to find Miss Haylter, so I think we should assume she will eventually find her here."

"That's not good, Lore. My superiors were quite specific on the topic of Speculatus. They demanded that we stay out of their way, and I am more than happy to abide by their wishes on this point, if all their members are as virulently antisocial as Odelia Cattertis. Pity you can't—" He clamped his lips tight on the end of that sentence, addressed to Miss Haylter, and Evon glared at him. Miss Haylter seemed not to notice. "That is to say, I sincerely hope we do not have to deal with Odelia and her postulated companions," Piercy finished lamely.

"She wants to find me," Miss Haylter said.

"Her organization wants your secret and they won't be gentle in extracting it," Evon said.

She turned her empty eyes on him. "And I suppose you will be."

Evon was stung. "I don't mean to *extract* anything from you. I simply want to talk." He knelt on the floor in front of her and put his hand on her forearm. "Miss Haylter," he said, "this spell isn't under your control, is it. It's something that's been done to you."

She nodded, turning her face away. "Something," she agreed, "though I don't know what."

"You find certain people, and when you're close enough, the spell activates," Evon guessed, spinning out what they'd already learned with what he'd observed just an hour ago. "You don't choose the...targets. You burn them. And it starts over again."

She nodded again. "It drives me," she said. "It goes away for a while. Six days, or five weeks—I never know how long. Three months, once. Then the urge falls on me, and I have to go where it drives me. I don't have any choice."

"Could you not, perhaps, ignore it?" Piercy asked.

She looked up at him, her too-smooth skin glowing in the light from the window. Her eyes were as dead as ever. "I tried, once," she said. "The second time, I knew what it meant and I wouldn't follow. It ached inside me for weeks, months even, and then I was standing in the marketplace and it was like—" She turned away again. "Do you know what it's like to burn from the inside out?" she said, as calm as if she'd just asked them if they preferred coffee to tea. "After the first few seconds, it hurts so much you can't feel the pain. That sounds wrong, doesn't it? But it's how it is. I burned, and I died, and then I was myself again and there was nothing alive but me for hundreds of feet, all around. So many people dead, and more dying, and I walked away unmarked. Other people paid for my fear. I don't ignore the urging anymore."

"How did it start?" Piercy asked.

She ignored him, fixing her gaze on Evon. Her eyes were hazel, more green than brown, and dark-circled as if she hadn't slept in days. "How did you find me?" she asked.

The image of himself sniffing the wind made his face grow warm. "I...cast a spell. A scenting spell. Following the, um, your unique...." Her unwavering eyes unnerved him yet again. Even when she spoke, she seemed to live at the center of a stillness so profound he felt as if he were losing himself in it. "It was quite difficult," he added, though he didn't know why.

She smiled a faint, amused smile. "Such a polite way of telling me that I haven't bathed in weeks," she said. The smile was so at odds with her demeanor that it threw Evon off balance even more.

"It was the scent of the spell we tracked," Piercy said. "Lore is right, it was difficult."

"I thought I'd be easy to trace, with the trail of destruction I was leaving," Miss Haylter said. "I was going to turn myself in, several times, but I couldn't risk being locked away when the urge struck."

"You think you should be punished for something you had no control over?" Evon asked. "It's not as if you're doing this intentionally."

"Does it matter to the people I kill?" Miss Haylter looked at her lap. "You can't help me," she said. "I've done too much evil to be forgiven. I'd like to die, finally. It hurts, coming back together, more than the dying. Every time, I think, maybe this is the time the Gods let me stay burned. And every time I come to myself and it starts again. I only want to be allowed to die."

Evon and Piercy looked at each other. Evon wondered if the look of shock on Piercy's face mirrored his. "Powerful or not, this is just a spell," Evon said. "A spell that has somehow gotten tangled up inside you." He didn't say that he had never heard of such a thing before, that it should be an impossibility. No sense driving her further into despair, if that was even possible. He had never heard anyone speak with such hopelessness as she just had. "If I can remove it, you can return to your old life. You don't have to die."

"I saw them all burn," she said, unexpectedly angry. "How am I supposed to live with that?"

"Every person who died from your spell was a monster," Piercy interjected. "Someone who had caused pain and torment to anyone they encountered. I cannot imagine what you must have gone through, but you should not blame yourself for innocent deaths. They were all far from innocent. One man had raped and killed six young women and buried them in his cellar. Whoever put this geas on you was using you, true, but it seems to have been as the unwitting hand of justice. This is a guilt you do not deserve to carry."

"Not all of them," she said. "That little boy—"

"Was a horrible accident," Piercy continued. "And one whose blame no doubt lies at the feet of the malefactor. I assure you, Miss Haylter, you may have been the instrument, but you bear no guilt."

She looked at Piercy, then back at Evon. She seemed to be struggling with some emotion, something she feared to embrace. "Why do you care?" she exclaimed. "I'm nothing to you. Why are you telling me these things? What do you want from me?"

Evon and Piercy exchanged glances again. Piercy shook his head, minutely. Evon took refuge in the truth. "When we thought you were a magician with a powerful new spell, all I wanted was that knowledge," he said. "But now...." He trailed off, not knowing himself what he wanted. Her despair overwhelmed him. "I want to help," he said. "If I could remove the spell...could you learn to...to live again?"

"You can't remove it," she said, but she didn't sound certain.

"Believe me, Miss Haylter, if anyone can do it, Lore can," Piercy said.

Her impassivity faded away, replaced by the faintest expression of hope. "If you can," she began, then her eyes rolled up in her head and she fell off the chair, still in a seated position, stiff and unmoving. Evon jerked back and looked at Piercy. "What—" Piercy began. Evon tore his quizzing glass from his waistcoat, fumbling a little, passed his hand across it and said *"Epiria"* with his eye squinted shut against the expected blinding glow. Instead, faint blue light played across his eyelids, and he opened his eyes to see the familiar ribbons of blue light, scribed with runes he still couldn't make out. Rough red cords tangled with the blue, binding Miss Haylter's arms and legs and neck. *Desini cucurri.* "They've found her," he said, ending the revelation spell and putting away the glass.

"Found her, but not us, you think?" Piercy said.

"If they knew we were with her, they'd have tried to immobilize us as well. Probably succeeded. Any spell that can affect someone the magician can't see has Odelia's grubby fingerprints all over it. No, I think they believe she's alone. Get your things. You'll have to carry her. We're leaving."

He slung his bag over his shoulder and cracked the door open, listening, while Piercy hefted his own bag and stick and awkwardly tried to find a way to carry the frozen young woman. He was somewhat taller than Evon and ultimately put his burden over his shoulder, her bent knees catching at his shoulder and helping him balance her. "I won't be able to support her like this indefinitely," he warned.

"Just to the stable yard. Now shush." Evon listened. The stairway was a bottleneck they couldn't afford to be caught unawares on. "Quietly. Let's see if we can surprise them." He pushed the door open and they silently proceeded down the short hall to the landing and down the stairs. Evon's rapid breathing echoed in his ears so much he was afraid he might not hear them, but as they passed the second floor landing the sound of footsteps, rapid and loud, came to him from the floor below. He gestured to Piercy to stop and flexed his fingers. Despite the danger of their position, Evon grinned. Speculatus was in for a surprise.

The footsteps approached. Evon looked down over the bannister and saw three men and the flash of a black, tiered skirt. Even better. He flicked his hands up and out and whispered, *"Desini cucurri."* The three men dropped, frozen in place as Miss Haylter had been. The black skirt hesitated, and Evon took a few steps down and around the landing to face Odelia. Shock gave way to anger, and she clenched her fist and opened her mouth to speak —

"*Presadi!*" Evon shouted, and the iridescent, airtight bubble sprang up close around her, silencing whatever she'd been about to say. Something fatal, judging by her expression. She raised her hand and clawed at her nose and mouth, then at her throat, then closed her eyes and fell hard on the bottom steps. "Let's go," Evon said, and he and Piercy with his awkward bundle made their way around the fallen bodies and out of the stairwell. Evon looked down at Odelia for a long moment, then dismissed the shield spell and took a minute to cast a stronger, longer-lasting paralysis. He couldn't bring himself to kill her, though he wondered if he'd made a mistake exposing the new spell to her. She was smart enough to possibly work out the details for herself. It didn't matter. It was time to leave.

The woman at the desk leaned against it, frozen in the act of speaking, her hand raised and her index finger pointed past them at the stairs. Piercy led them the back way through the kitchens and into the yard, where they began rapidly saddling their horses, shooing away the stable hand. Piercy had to set Miss Haylter down in a pile of hay, solicitous of her comfort though they both knew she couldn't feel anything in that condition. Pulling yet another buckle secure, Piercy said, "Where to now, dear fellow?"

"Somewhere far away. I wish I knew how they were tracking her, because I might be able to do something about it. But we need to find a place where I can examine that spell."

"What if she's correct, that there isn't any way to remove it?"

"And here I thought you had such faith in my abilities."

"Faith in your abilities doesn't extend to, for example, a belief that you can make the sun rise in the west. Some things are simply impossible."

"Well, I'm going to behave as if it's possible, for the moment, and we'll deal with impossible if we come to it."

"Can you wake her up?"

"Unfortunately, no. There's no spell that breaks *desini cucurri*. Let's get a few miles down the road. And hope none of the local constabulary sees us and wonders why we seem to be abducting a young woman."

They mounted up, the paralyzed Miss Haylter perched in front of

Evon's saddle, and rode out at the fastest gait they dared in the middle of the city, once again dodging carriages and carts and throngs of pedestrians. People did look at them strangely as they passed, and some even eyed their unconscious burden with concern, but no one tried to stop them. They took the eastern road out of Inveros, which was less well traveled than the coast road but turned north, opposite to the trend Miss Haylter's journeys had taken her. Evon reasoned that if Speculatus was working out Miss Haylter's position based on the path she'd taken, this might throw them off, if only for a short while. It was a wild hope, but he couldn't think of anything else to do. The northern road passed through broad fields, bare-limbed trees growing here and there, with the road sunken some five feet below ground level. It felt like riding through a tunnel, sheltered from watchful eyes.

Two miles past the city limits, Miss Haylter twitched, then began to stretch her legs. Evon stopped and put his hands under her arms to keep her from falling off. "You were struck with a paralysis spell," he told her in what he hoped was a calming voice. The last thing he needed was for her to panic, start struggling, and fall off the horse to the frozen ground below. "It's fading. There aren't any lasting effects. Just relax and let it wear off. It feels a little strange, I know. I had to go through it as part of my training. The part I hated most was how my face stayed numb long after I could walk around again."

"I thought that part was very amusing," Piercy said. "Evon Lorantis struck speechless."

"Well, *you* couldn't turn your head for two days," Evon retorted. "It was the longest any paralysis had lasted in the history of Houndston and we made a game of how often we could make you turn around just to look someone in the eye." He dismounted and helped Miss Haylter off the horse, then steadied her as she gradually regained control of her body. "If you rub your arms and legs, the stimulation will make the paralysis wear off faster," he said, and almost began to help her with that before he caught himself and had to turn his face away to hide his embarrassment. Who knew how she would react to him manhandling her? As soon as she could stand erect, he removed his hands from her waist and took a few steps away. "I'm afraid Speculatus found you," he said. "Odelia knew enough about your location to be able to strike at you from a distance, which is something of a specialty with her. She didn't know you weren't alone. We're free for the moment, but I don't know how long that will last."

"You should've let her take me. I don't want your deaths on my conscience." Her words were indistinct but comprehensible, her face still a little stiff.

"Odelia wouldn't kill us," Evon said, though he remembered his last look at her face and wasn't sure that was true. "And we're not going to abandon you. Did you have a destination in mind, after this last...event?"

"Why didn't you leave me?" she said, ignoring his question.

"Leave you in the hands of Odelia Cattertis? Miss Haylter, we wouldn't leave a diseased rat in her hands," Piercy said. "She'd enjoy it too much. Besides, she and Lore have fought one another for years, and he is physically and emotionally incapable of allowing her to win even the smallest advantage."

"Am I a prize, then? An advantage?"

Piercy's mouth fell open. "Ah...I didn't mean it that way...."

"Ignore Piercy, he lives with his foot in his mouth," Evon said. He took Miss Haylter by the shoulders and made her look at him. Her hazel eyes were almost angry now, and it relieved his mind to know that she was still capable of feeling. "You want me to tell you you're not worth saving," he said. "You have lived with this guilt for so long that you have forgotten that you are as much a victim as the people this spell kills. Well, Miss Haylter, it's true I came after you for selfish reasons. That spell could make my career. But can you think that I—that either Piercy or I—are such monsters as to not see another person suffering and not want to help?"

"At the cost of your lives?" she exclaimed.

"It won't come to that. Remember, I survived your attack once already, and Piercy has the best sense of self-preservation I have ever seen."

To his amazement and dismay, Evon saw tears come to her eyes.

"I—I can't," she began, dashing them away with the back of her hand. "I just want this to be over."

Evon released her and stepped away, disturbed that his next impulse had been to embrace her, which would have made things worse rather than better. "Let's find a safe place," he said, "and I'll see what I can do about making that happen."

6

———————

The road eventually rose to ground level, and they rode along it between acres of fallow ground, weeds bent and snow-blasted into dead tangles. These were not farmlands, but unclaimed territory between the ocean and the forests that lay to the north and east, tenanted only by a few desperate folk scrabbling out what living they could on the land. Evon kept his attention southward, watching for riders, and wished he'd brought a pair of spectacles to cast a distance-viewing spell on. He could try enhancing his own eyes, but given the extraordinary success of *olficio*, it was likely he'd just blind himself. So he merely watched behind them and left the guiding of the party to Piercy, who'd taken Miss Haylter up behind him. Nothing moved except sea birds wheeling in the sky, occasionally descending on the weed-choked fields to snap up whatever insects had survived the first freeze. Their white bodies stood out against the gathering gray clouds. Snow was coming.

"Evon," Piercy said, and Evon turned around to see Piercy pointing into the distance. "A farmhouse. Is that what you had in mind?"

"Yes. No." Evon chewed on his lower lip in thought. Did he really want a farmer's family as audience for this attempt? It wasn't that he minded failure, or that he was afraid of looking ridiculous, it was that he wasn't sure what might happen when he tried to remove the spell. He'd been almost dismissively certain when he told Miss Haylter he could remove it; now all the concerns he should have had before clamored for his attention. Suppose he managed to trigger the spell? No, all things considered it was better not to have bystanders.

"We should ask to use their barn," he said finally. "I think it's better to have some privacy for this."

Miss Haylter turned to look back at him. He wondered if she could read his fears in his face and tried to look as unconcerned as if he were proposing a winter outing. "I assume I am your sister again," she said.

Piercy laughed. "Is that what you told the old dragon guarding the gate? You do have similar coloring, though I must say, Miss Haylter, you are a good deal prettier than Lore."

"You have a flattering tongue, Mr. Faranter," she said, in a voice that said she didn't much care for his flattering tongue. The smile dropped from Piercy's face. Evon felt sorry for him. Piercy flirted with women the way he breathed: unconsciously, but with sincerity, and courtship came as naturally to him as magic did to Evon. He did it so well that women never seemed to mind that his flirtations never led anywhere serious. Miss Haylter, for her part, didn't seem to realize she'd hurt his feelings. She turned away from Evon and looked out across the fields toward the farmhouse. "There's no smoke coming from that house," she said.

"Are you sure?" Evon said.

"I'm familiar with fire," she said, once again emotionless. "I think there's no one home."

"Let us by all means find out," Piercy said, rallying, and they went forward until they found a narrow track that led across the fields toward the small house. Miss Haylter's assessment was correct; no smoke rose from the small chimney, and no one moved between the house and its outbuildings. As they neared the farmhouse, they saw missing shingles, a broken step, and windows missing their glass. "I don't think this has been inhabited for many years," Piercy said, dismounting at the foot of the three steps leading to the narrow porch. He pushed open the door with the head of his walking stick and stuck his head inside. "Definitely uninhabited," he said, crossing the threshold and letting the weathered door, with its trace of yellow paint, swing shut behind him.

Miss Haylter made as if to follow him, but Evon restrained her. "Piercy will make sure it's safe," he told her. "An abandoned house like this, there might be anything residing here now. Animals, probably, but also drifters. Piercy will take care of whatever he finds."

"You're good friends."

"The best."

She regarded him for a moment. "You're lucky," she said.

Piercy put his head out through one of the empty windows and said, "Come inside. I think this may meet your needs admirably, Lore."

Evon held the door politely for Miss Haylter, then shut it behind himself. With the light fading behind the clouds outside, the interior was almost black. Evon sent a light bobbing to the ceiling to cast a soft glow over the three of them and the small room they stood in. The farmhouse's front room was bare of furnishings, though there were dark marks on the wall where pictures had hung. The unvarnished floorboards, pale and uneven, were blackened from soot and sparks from the brick fireplace against the far wall. Evon looked through the inner door to the next room, which was a small kitchen containing only an old cast-iron stove that sagged into the floor, its chimney dangling loose. Light came in from the hole in the ceiling where the chimney had once exited. Another door at the far side of the kitchen hung by its lower hinge, swinging gently.

"That's merely an empty room," Piercy said. "Probably someone's bedroom once."

"We really only need this front room, though I wish we had a chair or something." Evon looked at Miss Haylter, who gave him a guarded look. He wished he knew what she was thinking. It looked bad, objectively: she'd gone off with two strange men, who now had her alone in a place where no one would hear her if she screamed, with no way to defend herself against anything they had in mind. Either she was a total innocent, or she genuinely didn't care what happened to her. "Do you mind sitting on the floor, Miss Haylter?" he asked. She looked even more skeptical, but lowered herself to sit near the front door with her legs crossed. Evon couldn't tell if she was positioning herself to flee, but guessed that her skirts, while not as full as Odelia's, would still hamper her getting to her feet quickly. She folded her hands in her lap and looked up at him, waiting.

"Stand over there, would you?" Evon said to Piercy, then squatted in front of Miss Haylter. "The spell on you is complex," he told her, "and I'm just going to look at it at first, to see what I can learn. It won't hurt."

Her eyes had regained that dead look she'd worn before, but Evon noticed that the knuckles of her clasped hands were white, the tendons straining against the skin, and he felt relieved, again, that she wasn't entirely indifferent to her fate. The idea that someone so young and beautiful—and she *was* beautiful, he now had time to realize, despite the shadows under her eyes and the strange, poreless appearance of her skin—that someone like her could have given up hope so completely seemed sickeningly wrong to him and left him with a renewed determination to free her from this spell.

He removed his gloves, took out his quizzing glass and cast the revelation spell. Once again the flowing, fluttering blue ribbons of magic appeared, their color and intensity as muted as they'd been when he'd looked at them back in their inn room. When he'd seen them in Coreth, at the site of Fullanter's death, they'd been so brilliant he could barely endure looking at them. He already knew, from what Miss Haylter said, that the spell had a dormant phase, but this suggested that the spell actually exhausted itself when it was triggered. Why its reactivation was variable, he didn't know, but that question could wait.

His calves burned from crouching so long, so he sat cross-legged in front of Miss Haylter, holding his quizzing glass about seven inches from her heart. As he turned the glass, she inhaled sharply and said, "Is that...does it really look like that?" He looked up to see her craning her neck to see through the lens. With his free hand, he took one of hers and brought it up to grasp the glass.

"It does, and it doesn't," he said, as she ran the glass across her legs and up her arm. "Magic isn't something we can comprehend in its...I suppose you could say its natural state. The runes and command words we use are a sort of compromise between our limited perception and the vast incomprehensibility that is magic. *Epiria* reveals the structure of spells, but in a form that we can make sense of."

"Does it look different from other spells?"

"Very. May I?" He accepted the glass from her and held it in a position about midway between their bodies. "It keeps moving, for one thing, and it's also covered in runes. A rune is supposed to be a focal point that gives shape to a spell, not part of the magic itself. I've never heard of anything like it. Would you mind being quiet for a moment? I need to concentrate on this. But I'd be happy to answer any questions you have, later. You have a perfect right to know what this thing is about."

She nodded, and Evon went back to studying the spell. The movement wasn't random, he realized, but he was damned if he could identify the pattern. He felt as if he ought to recognize it, but the longer he stared at the fluid magic, the blurrier his vision got. What he needed was to see it all at once, not just through the two-inch-diameter lens.

He stood and dug in his pocket for his chalk. "No, don't get up, I'm going to try something else," he said absently. He glanced at Piercy, whose face was so expressionless it had to be on purpose. "What?" he said.

"You have that look again," Piercy said.

"What look?"

"The mad genius look. Should Miss Haylter and I seek shelter?"

"Don't be ridiculous. Just because I'm trying something I've only ever read about in books." He drew a large, lopsided circle around Miss Haylter and began chalking runes inside it. "This will extend the range of *epiria* to cover your entire body at once," he told her. "It should be a better perspective. Just stay still."

Out of the corner of his eye, he saw her clasp her hands together in her lap again, once more clenching them tight. He stopped mid-rune and went to kneel in front of her, careful not to smudge the circle. "I apologize," he said. "Piercy will tell you I have a regrettable habit of getting too caught up in my work. I forgot that this is personal for you."

Hazel eyes met his with that disconcerting gaze. "I have nothing to lose," she said. "Why shouldn't I trust you? After all, I couldn't kill you; that should count for something." To his astonishment, a smile touched her lips, just briefly, but long enough that it transformed her face and made him wonder what he could do to make it return. *Get her free from this spell, of course.*

"I hope to be worthy of your trust," he said, and finished chalking runes on the uneven floorboards. He once again seated himself cross-legged in front of her, put the chalk away and dusted his hands on his trouser legs. He held his quizzing glass in front of him, tilted it so the runes scratched on its rim lined up with the ones chalked on the floor, and pictured it enormous, a lens five feet in diameter, rim the thickness of his upper arm. With that image firmly in mind, he said, *"Epiria."*

The writhing blue ribbons of the spell blossomed into full view. They twisted and rolled around Miss Haylter's body, making her look like a statue wreathed in tendrils of blue smoke. Miss Haylter sat unmoving except for her eyes, which darted in every direction as if she couldn't decide which spell-ribbon to follow.

"Do you see a pattern?" Evon asked Piercy, who left his position by the wall to stand next to where Evon sat on the ground.

"I don't. But it feels as if I should. It seems very familiar."

"That was my sense as well." Evon stood, focused on a single twisting ribbon and watched it flow slowly down Miss Haylter's left arm and back up again, around her chest and back to her arm again. It wasn't a continuous circle, but there was a clear sense that it was following a path dictated by the shape of the spell. Up, down, around and back. "It's a circulatory system," he said, absently watching the ribbon flow through its path. "It mirrors Miss Haylter's own body, not perfectly, but close enough."

"By the Twins, you're right," Piercy exclaimed. "What does that mean?"

"I don't know. I think it's how it stays bound to her. You. Excuse me. This spell is damned—excuse me, Miss Haylter—very complex, if it can have an entire aspect devoted to staying connected to you."

"So you can't free me."

"I didn't say that." He leaned in to examine one of the spell-ribbons more closely and once again it moved just far enough away that the black runes thronging it remained indistinct. The spell was definitely reacting to his presence, which spoke to a level of awareness that worried him. He tried, absurdly, to take hold of one of the strands, but it was as incorporeal as any other spell and didn't even bother moving out of the way of his hand. Evon felt he was being taunted. Irritably, he clenched one fist, slapped his open palm over it, and growled, "*Desini cucurri.*"

The entire spell froze, all movement ceasing in an instant. Evon's mouth dropped open. "Good Gods," Piercy said weakly, "did you break it?"

"Should it not do that?" Miss Haylter asked.

"Ah...." Evon looked down at Miss Haylter, half-expecting to see her go blue and begin choking due to lack of blood circulation. She seemed only curious and a little uncertain. "Do you feel any pain? Any discomfort or unusual sensations?"

"I feel just the same," she said, flexing her fingers. "A little cold, though I don't think it's a good idea to light a fire in here. That chimney is probably full of smuts and birds' nests."

"What did you do, Evon?" Piercy asked. He came forward and leaned in so his nose was inches away from one of the unmoving spell-ribbons.

"Lost my temper, just a little," Evon said. "I think this spell is sentient." He mirrored Piercy's gesture until he was close enough to make out the tiny black runes. They quivered with energy, their edges blurred, but Evon could still make them out. His heart sank. "They don't mean anything," he said. "I recognize some of the runes, but they don't trace out any spell I'm familiar with. They're more like fragments of spells, but...I'm thinking about this the wrong way." He closed his eyes and tried to think about something else, give his subconscious time to work out the solution. "How long since the first time you felt the pull, Miss Haylter?" he asked.

"Almost a year ago," she said, her voice once again expression-less. It was the sound, he was beginning to realize, her voice took on every time she spoke about the spell. "And I've felt compelled to...eleven times now."

"We established that there's no pattern to the...incidents, they aren't evenly spaced geographically or temporally."

"That's right."

"Does this have a point, Evon?" Piercy said.

"I'm just lining up everything we've learned. I beg your pardon if this is painful, Miss Haylter."

"No more painful than being pulled apart and put back together again."

Evon's eyes flew open. "Are you speaking literally?"

She shrugged. "It's how it feels to me. The fire destroys me the way it does my victim. And then I come back together." Her tone was flatter than ever.

Evon leaned over and traced the curve of one of the spell-ribbons. "They aren't fragments," he said, "they're links in a chain. No, a chain mesh. Each link is broken and it makes a spell when it comes together with another link, or several links. They break and reform dozens of times a minute. This is *extraordinary*. Miss Haylter, the—" He saw her face. "I beg your pardon," he said more quietly, "I'm being insensitive again."

"I'm starting to think you might be able to remove this thing from me," she said with that tiny, fleeting smile. "Be as insensitive as you like."

Evon felt his cheeks redden. "Well, um, it's just that the ribbons, Miss Haylter, they are how the spell...remembers you. It's how it's able to...reassemble you after...it destroys you. And the runes are...I'm not exactly sure yet, they seem to do so many things, but I imagine they decide where you should go and who you should find, and how to know when you've reached your desti-nation to trigger the event. If I could read the runes more completely, I could be more specific. Whoever invented this spell created hundreds of new runes to do it, which is simply unheard of. Are you certain you can't remember this being done to you? A loss of time, perhaps, or an unexpectedly long sleep, or an encounter with a stranger?"

She shook her head. The smoky blue ribbons turned with her, their edges starting to quiver like the runes. "Nothing like that. I was just a barmaid in a small northern town, no one who would stand out at all."

Evon regarded that beautiful face, her graceful limbs, and thought her assessment was highly unlikely, but he said, "I think the chances of you simply waking up one morning with this spell fizzing through your veins are remote. And yet I can't come up with any other explanation. You didn't have any remarkable ancestors?"

She shook her head again. "Perfectly ordinary."

"As far as you know," Piercy pointed out. "How many of us can trace our ancestors back more than a handful of generations?"

"*You* can," Evon said.

Piercy waved his hand dismissively. "My family is hardly representative. And some of our proudest connections may be spurious, which simply proves my point. You, Miss Haylter, may well be descended from some great magician of yore, but we have no way of proving it. Which makes it irrelevant, Evon."

"True." Evon examined the quivering runes again. "How odd. They're—" The spell jerked into motion, and Evon flinched, bracing himself for the furious spell to lash out at him, wrap its tendrils around his neck and choke the air from his body in retaliation. Instead, the spell-ribbons resumed their slow orbits as if they'd never stopped. Evon blinked in astonishment. "I've never seen anything break *desini cucurri* before. It's as if the spell was straining against it until it gave. That speaks to a remarkable amount of power...well, of course, if it's capable of burning someone to ash, it would have to have a lot of power." He cast *desini cucurri* again, and stood staring at the unmoving spell. "I'm starting to wonder about the creator of the spell. This is quite intricate and yet quite specific. I know of no one who could have created it, and certainly no one who'd have created it and not taken credit."

"It *does* murder people, even if they happen to be deserving, Lore.

That might put a damper on the fellow's desire for the accolades of his peers."

"True. But I think you should suggest that your people start looking for the magician, now that we know it's not Miss Haylter here." He smiled at her, he hoped reassuringly, and she gazed back at him. Her eyes were once again emotionless, and his smile faded as his last exchange with Piercy replayed itself in his head. *Do you need a dictionary so you'll understand the concept of insensitivity when you see it next, Lorantis?* "I'm sorry," he began, then cleared his throat. "All right. I think I can try to remove it."

"With that cursory examination? Evon —" Piercy began.

"It's in two clear pieces. If I can...I think the best way to describe it is that I'll remove its memory of you, Miss Haylter. The spell will still exist, but it won't have any connection to you. And then I can figure out what to do with it once you're free."

Her hazel eyes met his. "Do it," she said.

Evon sat cross-legged before her and held out his hands. She put her hands in his without further prompting. "This could hurt," he warned her. "And at the risk of unnerving you, I'm not as certain about this as I sound."

"You have no idea what pain is," she said. "Go ahead."

With another jerk, the spell-ribbons snapped back into motion. Evon withdrew his hands from Miss Haylter's, thinking to cast *desini cucurri* again, but the writhing, looping movements made him hesitate. Leaving it free — and he was unnerved all over again at how easy it was to think of the spell as a living creature — might make it more difficult to focus his magic on the spell, but instinct told him that it needed to be in motion if this plan of his was to have any chance of working. He grasped Miss Haylter's hands and gave her what he hoped was a reassuring smile.

The spell-ribbons continued to flow over Miss Haylter's hands, looping through Evon's rather than passing around them. He felt nothing, not cold or pain or even the brush of the flexible matter they appeared to be made of. Well, they were linked to Miss Haylter's body; perhaps they would respond to a variant on a healing spell. He focused on one no thinner than a strand of yarn that darted up and down her index finger and blinked twice, slowly. *"Vertiri."*

Every ribbon stopped moving at once, but where *desini cucurri* had frozen them all in place, they now seemed alert, as if they were listening for what he might say next. Evon held his breath. He'd meant only to prepare that one piece of the spell to be altered, but somehow he'd hit on something far more powerful. *Might as well try it,* he thought, and encompassed the entire spell in his gaze. Miss Haylter's eyes were closed, her fingers gripping his loosely; she was far more composed than he. Evon took in a deep breath, let it out slowly, and said, *"Frigo."*

A faint taste of lemon passed over his tongue. The ribbons of blue light expanded, stretching width-wise like dough as they pulled away from their orbits. The blue light went from dull to sunlight-bright in an instant. And Miss Haylter crushed Evon's hands in hers, her nails cutting into his palms, and screamed as if he'd knifed her through the heart.

7

"*Desini! Desini desini!*" Evon screamed, his voice cutting across Miss Haylter's. Miss Haylter ripped her hands from his and scrambled backward until she hit the wall, kicking her feet as if trying to force her way through it, scrabbling at it with her nails. She'd stopped screaming and her voice now came in short, whimpering grunts. Her eyes were wide, the irises completely encircled by white, and Evon didn't think she could see either him or Piercy. Evon hesitated, torn by the need to provide comfort and reassurance to someone in distress and the awareness that he'd been the one to cause that distress. "Piercy," he whispered.

"Don't," Piercy said, and crossed the room to crouch at the woman's side. "Miss Haylter," he said quietly, "can you hear me? Just try to breathe. This will pass. Just breathe."

To Evon's surprise, Miss Haylter nodded. Her eyes were still fixed wide open, but her fingers stopped scratching at the wall and her breathing began to steady. Piercy continued to murmur to her as she began to relax, and Evon, cursing himself, turned and went into the kitchen. He'd been so stupidly confident, so eager to prove himself to this injured young woman, and he'd just made things worse. She would never trust him again—not that it mattered, since the spell was clearly beyond his abilities. He looked at his palms. They were marked with sore red crescents, blood seeping from one of them. Compared to what she'd felt, it was nothing. He rubbed his thumb across one row of them. A reminder that Evon Lorantis wasn't nearly the magician he claimed to be.

"Evon," Piercy said from the other room, and Evon steeled himself for whatever look might be in Miss Haylter's eyes now. Anger? Fear? Contempt? He went through the door and saw the two of them standing together in the center of the room next to the scuffed coppery circle.

"I'm so sorry, Miss Haylter, I can't tell you how sorry I am," he began.

"You didn't hurt me, Mr. Lorantis," she said. "I was terrified. I didn't think I had it in me to feel anything, after all these months. I wish I could tell you what I was afraid of. Maybe...if it's true that this spell is aware of us, maybe it was its fear I felt. I just want you to know I don't blame you for anything. It was...kind of you to try." She was more animated than he'd seen her before, which still meant her words came from a core of stillness so profound she made everyone around her look manic. She held out her hand to him, and, stunned, he extended his own, but she jerked away before he could clasp her hand. "Did I do that to you?" she asked.

Evon turned his right hand palm-up to display the bloody crescents. In his surprise, he'd forgotten about them. "It's nothing."

"I'm sorry." They both stared at his hand for a moment, then Miss Haylter gathered her cloak around her and said, "I do appreciate your efforts," and turned to leave the house. Evon and Piercy both jumped. "I don't think that's a good idea, Miss Haylter," Piercy said, putting his hand over hers where she grasped the door latch.

"You can't help me," she said, a statement of fact rather than an accusation.

"But Speculatus is still after you," Evon said.

"They can't hurt me."

"I wish that were true," Piercy said. "They will do whatever they can to learn the secrets of that spell, and they will certainly not care how you suffer in the process."

"And, forgive me for being callous, but Piercy and I are determined to understand the spell ourselves, and keeping it out of Speculatus's grasp is just as important," Evon said.

"You think of me as a tool," she said, regarding Evon with an expression verging on anger.

"No, I think of you as a woman caught up in unfortunate circumstances. I admit there's a great deal I don't understand about that spell that has you tangled up inside it, but I'm positive it's self-aware, which means that if anyone thinks of you as a tool, it's the spell. Miss Haylter, I failed just now because I was too arrogant to give that spell the analysis needed. I won't make that mistake again. The spell *is* separate from you and it *can* be removed. I just don't know how yet."

"Why should I trust you?"

"You couldn't kill me, remember? And what other options do you have? You could go on as you have been, dragged all over the Gods' creation and forced to kill according to the spell's whim. You could wait for Speculatus to grab you. Or you could give me another opportunity to figure this out." Evon closed his aching fists. "I wish I could swear to you that I can free you. But all I can promise is that I'll do my utmost, and this last failure aside, my utmost has always been excellent before."

Miss Haylter's anger had been replaced by that same unreadable impassivity. "And what will you do if the urge comes on me before you've unraveled the spell?"

"Follow you. Cast a better shield." Evon smiled. "Bring you a spare dress?"

The tiny smile touched her lips and was gone, but even that brief glimpse eased Evon's heart. "If I say no, you'll just follow me anyway," she said.

"How observant of you, Miss Haylter," Piercy said. "Lore is the most stubborn and obsessive man I've ever known, and those are some of his best qualities."

"You told me I was merely very focused," Evon objected.

"I only said that to keep you from falling into despair."

"I don't know whether to thank you or punch you."

"You will give Miss Haylter an entirely wrong impression of yourself if you strike me." Piercy straightened his overcoat and brushed his hair back from his head. "Why don't we all go back to the capital and bring in a few more magicians on this problem? You might be the preeminent magician of your generation, Evon, but more minds ought to make light work, yes?"

Evon exchanged glances with Miss Haylter. "If I'm trapped there when the urge strikes, the explosion will be worse. I'd just be a danger to all those people," she said.

"True. I'd forgotten," Piercy said. "I wish we knew how Odelia found Miss Haylter back at the inn. I'm not certain whether we are safer finding secure lodgings or staying on the move. I take it you don't feel the...urge...now, Miss Haylter? No?" He scuffed at the floorboards with the toe of his boot, now badly in need of a polish. "All things considered, I think we are better off in a city, at least for the moment. I can find us defensible lodgings and provide some security while you do whatever it is you do, Lore. Will Calian do? I believe it's the next large city south of Inveros."

"Does south matter?" Miss Haylter asked.

They both stared at her. "You've been moving steadily south this whole time. We assumed you had a reason," Evon said.

She shrugged. "There were other things on my mind." Her voice had gone flat again, and Evon's heart sank. He'd hoped having companions, having the possibility of being free from this life, might give her some hope. It was stupid of him to think that a year of guilt and agony could be so easily erased.

"Well," Piercy said, sounding as uncomfortable as Evon felt, "if we get on the road now, we can reach Calian just an hour after sunset. Is that acceptable to you, Miss Haylter?"

Miss Haylter shrugged again. "Not to sound ungrateful, but as you pointed out, Mr. Lorantis, I don't have any other options." But she smiled as she said it.

Snow was falling when they left the farmhouse, sleety wet drops that only barely qualified as snow by being too thick for rain. They mounted up, Miss Haylter riding behind Evon this time, and retraced their steps past Inveros and on down the coast road. Miss

Haylter rode with her arms clasped lightly around Evon's waist, which made him self-conscious. He hadn't been this close to a woman, even platonically, in years. He really had become isolated. Someday, when this was all over, he would ask Piercy to introduce him to one of his many young women. Lancie Bierter, possibly, or Shelena Gerantis—no, he'd heard she was engaged to Biffy Valatertis. How old Biffy had gotten someone that attractive to even look in his direction was a mystery. The horse jogged left to avoid a pothole, and Miss Haylter clutched at his waist more tightly for a moment, but said nothing. She was well-spoken for someone who'd been only a barmaid. He wondered if she'd left anyone behind, wherever it was she came from. Family, friends, a beau—given her appearance, that was probably beaux plural. How *had* she come under this spell, anyway? One more thing to investigate, though he thought it likely that unravelling the *how* would point directly at the *who*. And then he would track down the spell's creator and shake that magician into teeth-rattling submission. The whole thing spoke to such incomprehensible arrogance that thinking about it infuriated him.

It was full dark when they reached the city, worn out and soaked through, and even Piercy was happy to stop at the first inn they passed. Evon took one look at Miss Haylter's face when he helped her down from the horse and all thoughts of research fled. "A room with a bath for my sister," he told the man at the desk, "and another room for my friend and me." He removed his hat and a thin trickle of water poured over the brim and onto the black and white diamonds tiling the entry hall, mingling with the brown sludgy water he'd tracked in from the yard. The desk clerk's expression was clearly visible in the light from hundreds of walnut-sized orbs decorating the wrought-iron lamp that hung from the ceiling, two stories tall. Evon stiffened his spine and glared coldly back. As if the kind of patrons this man was accustomed to never were caught in the snow or had to trudge through the yard muck...all right, they probably had minions to do their trudging for them, but they were as human as anyone else, and Evon's money was just as good. Well. Miss Elltis's money was just as good.

Finally, the man extended a hand holding two keys, Evon

brushed aside the offer of help with their bags—that probably did look strange, two canvas sacks and a small bag between the three of them—and they trudged up two flights of stairs to what turned out to be a suite of two bedrooms and a conjoined bath. It took Evon only a little persuading to get Miss Haylter to make use of the facilities; her lips were outlined in purple and the circles under her eyes were darker than before. While she bathed, Evon and Piercy changed into drier clothes and consulted. "I'll need to tell my superiors all about this, dear fellow," Piercy said.

"Why do you sound so apologetic?"

"Because—" Piercy dropped his voice to a whisper, though their door to the bathroom was closed—"this changes everything. My people were operating on the assumption that we were looking for a magician casting a spell. Now the magician is nowhere to be seen and the spell itself may be aware, which I don't mind telling you is going to be hard for the old boys at the home office to believe. They are certainly not going to be happy with the idea that Miss Haylter is not at all to blame."

"She isn't."

"That's a subtlety that may be lost on them."

"Then you'll have to convince them otherwise."

"I'll do my best, dear fellow, but you should be prepared for them to arrive here and attempt to take over your investigative efforts."

"They can't take her back to Matra. It's far too dangerous."

"Another subtlety that may etc., etc. I intend to present my findings in the most salubrious fashion I can muster, and I intend to do it tomorrow. Do you suppose she's used all the hot water? I did rather fancy a soak myself."

"I don't know. I'm going to go cast a few forbiddances on her windows and the door, just in case Odelia is an exceptional tracker. I'm not looking forward to tackling Miss Elltis tomorrow, either."

He knocked loudly at Miss Haylter's hall door, then slipped inside and shut it behind him. The bathroom door on this side was half-open. "Miss Haylter?" he said, keeping his eyes averted. "I'm just putting some protective spells on the windows and door." There were two windows, neither of them tall enough to admit anyone larger than a child, but he took out his chalk, slightly damp from the journey, and began tracing copper runes on the sill and the glass panes. The dim light from a single lamp near the bed cast up his reflection in the dark window.

Water sloshed. "Are they to keep intruders out," Miss Haylter asked, "or me in?"

"You're not a prisoner, Miss Haylter," Evon said. He breathed out a command word, and the runes turned black and then vanished. He went to the next window and began to repeat the process.

"I was joking," she said. "I realize it's hard to tell."

"If I were in your position, I'm not sure I'd have much of a sense of humor left." One rune failed to blacken, and Evon scrubbed everything out and started over again.

"It surprised me, too." More water sloshed, the sound of someone stepping out of the tub. He fumbled the chalk and rubbed at the flawed rune irritably. "I really do appreciate what you're doing, Mr. Lorantis."

"I haven't exactly done anything warranting your appreciation, Miss Haylter."

Water began gurgling down the drain. "You didn't burn," she said. "You didn't see me as a monster. Who are you, that you weren't even a little afraid of me?"

"I didn't think to be afraid." The runes blackened and vanished, and Evon crossed to the door. Miss Haylter emerged from the bathroom and closed its door behind her. She was fully dressed in her spare gown, a dark striped woolen thing that was too loose in the bosom and too long at the hem, and her dark gold hair hung nearly to her waist. Her poreless skin made her look unreal, like a woman wearing her own skin as a mask, but in the dim light the effect was lessened, and Evon thought she might be the most beautiful woman he'd ever seen. He closed his fingers tight on the chalk, its damp grittiness anchoring him to the here and now.

"I realize it's informal," he said, "but if you're meant to be my sister, we should really call one another by our given names. If you don't mind."

She tilted her head just a little. "It makes sense," she said. "I mean, it's not as though you haven't seen me naked."

Evon blushed so hard he thought his head might pop open, and she smiled, her eyes merry at how she'd discomfited him. "I didn't look," he stammered, and felt like more of a fool for saying anything.

"I wouldn't have mentioned it if you had. Thanks for being a gentleman...brother Evon."

"Thank you for still having a sense of humor, sister Kerensa. Even if it *is* at my expense. I'm going to seal this door now. If you need to exit, you'll have to come through our room."

He took his time scrawling runes across the door, the frame, and the threshold. No one would pass through this door without his knowing about it. *Especially Odelia*, he thought, putting a few extra flourishes around the knob. Probably Odelia was still scrambling to catch up, but if she came anywhere near Kerensa, she'd have more than a simple paralysis to deal with. He muttered a handful of command words, then pulled out his quizzing glass and used *epiria* to check his work. Tight and tightly bound, and he felt no small measure of pride at his accomplishment.

They ate supper together in the inn's large dining room, speaking rarely, even the normally talkative Piercy worn out from the day's travels, then retired to their beds. Evon watched the bathroom door close on Kerensa and, around a jaw-cracking yawn, said, "I really wonder what she makes of all this."

"She's certainly not what I expected to find at the end of our chase," Piercy said, unbuttoning his waistcoat. "Astonishingly attractive, for one, though I don't think she appreciates being told as much."

"Maybe you've finally found the one woman immune to the Faranter charm," Evon said. The idea made him cheerful. It would do Piercy good not to have *every* woman in the world fall at his feet.

"Unlikely. I simply haven't found the way to this one's heart yet."

"Don't toy with her, Piercy."

Piercy looked surprised. "I never toy with women, Evon, you know that. And this one...she's pretty enough, but there's something about her I don't dare touch. I'll leave her to you."

Evon turned away to remove his shirt so his friend wouldn't see how his face had reddened. "I'm afraid there's a conflict of interest there, what with me more or less using her as a research subject. Unfortunate for both you and me, then." He had a sudden image of Kerensa standing inside the bathroom, her ear pressed to the door, and wondered if he could cast a spell to make the floor open up beneath him. Dropping him into someone else's bed. What a solution.

"When we get home, you should ask Vansie Aldenter to attend the theater with you," Piercy said, flopping down onto his pillow. "She's been asking after you for weeks."

"I should do that," Evon agreed, pulling the covers over his chest, but as he tried to remember which of Piercy's many lady friends Miss Aldenter was, the only image that came to mind was the too-smooth oval of Kerensa Haylter's face.

8

———————

"Y"ou'll want to make yourself scarce while I talk to the authorities back home, dear fellow," Piercy said over breakfast the next morning. "I don't dare use the public communication network for a thing like this."

"I thought Miss— I might take *my sister* shopping for a new dress," Evon said. He laid his napkin down and squared his knife and fork across his plate. "What with our luggage mishap and all."

"Oh," Piercy said. "Of course. Miss...Lorantis shouldn't have to wear that old thing forever."

"You shouldn't worry about my clothes, *brother*," Kerensa said, glaring at Evon. "I don't want to be a burden on your pocketbook. This dress is just fine."

"No one will believe I let my *sister* go out in public in a dress that clearly wasn't made for her."

"I didn't think I'd be going out in public much, since I'll be assisting you with your studies."

"That won't last forever, will it?" He stood and offered her his hand. "Shall we go?"

"I may not be here when you return," Piercy said, pushing his chair back from the table. "I intend to make a tour of this fair city and ascertain that our dear friends won't come upon us unawares. Good luck in your studies, Evon. Miss...Lorantis." He bowed to Kerensa and left the dining room.

"I was serious about you not spending money on me," Kerensa said under her breath as she wrapped her cloak around herself. "I don't want a new dress."

"And I was serious about you not looking much like my sister in that thing," Evon retorted in the same tone. "I would think you'd be happy to be rid of it. It doesn't look comfortable, what with it dragging at the hem like that."

They exited the inn, Kerensa holding her skirts high to keep them clear of the mud of the inn yard. The air was clear and cold and smelled of new snow and salt brine and, to Evon, of Kerensa's smoky scent. Across the street from the inn, half-timbered shops did a busy trade in housewares, tobacco, books, and spices, and the jingling three-toned sound of an apothecary's bell rang out constantly. The inn stood at the top of a gentle slope, and to the west Evon could just barely see the ocean, gray-green in the winter sunlight. He offered Kerensa his arm, and after a moment's fumbling with her heavy skirts, she accepted it and they crossed the street, dodging carriages and a horsewoman who sneered down at them.

They walked down the street in silence for a while, Evon looking at the shops, Kerensa looking at the ground, until Kerensa said, "I'd rather not spend money on something that'll probably just be destroyed."

Evon glanced at her. The curve of her cheek was all that was visible of her face. She had left her kerchief behind, saying that it made her look too much the country girl to be seen walking around with Evon in his frock coat and top hat, and her dark blonde hair was pinned neatly at the base of her neck. She'd need a bonnet, too, he reflected, though it seemed a shame to cover up that hair. Her voice was back to being toneless and dull. Without thinking, he said, "You could always take it off before you go."

Her head snapped up. "What?"

"It would save on having to buy new clothing all the time. And it's not as if you'd have to worry about what the person thinks of you." His mouth was operating independently of his brain, which was screaming at him to *shut up, what are you thinking, you're insulting her and you need her to trust you.* Kerensa's eyes were wide and her mouth hung slightly open. Evon smiled at her; he was sure his smile looked insane.

Then she laughed. It was such an unexpected sound, warm and rich and deeply amused, that Evon stopped in the middle of the street and gaped at her, releasing her arm. "Take it off," she said. "I can't believe you just said that to me."

"I apologize—I don't know what I was thinking—"

"I'm not used to this, having someone else share this secret. You don't see it the way I do."

"I assure you, I didn't mean—"

"That wasn't a criticism. You genuinely believe this...curse isn't a part of me. That it's something I can be rid of. All I've known since this started is despair and self-loathing because I thought it was something I was doing. I'm tired of that feeling. I wish I could see things through your eyes."

"Even if I suggest that you engage in public nudity?" A passerby gave them both an astonished, embarrassed glare.

"You made me laugh. I can't remember the last time I laughed at something funny." She took his arm again and squeezed it in a companionable way. "All right. But I'm paying for my own dress."

"No, Miss Elltis's expense account is paying for your dress." They proceeded arm in arm up the street, Kerensa's hem dragging in the mud once again.

"Who is Miss Elltis? You talk about her as if she's something between a dread maiden aunt and a dragon."

"That is fairly accurate, though I do have a dread maiden aunt who is not nearly so terrifying as Miss Elltis. She is my employer, though technically she's just the senior member of my cooperative. I had to have her approval to take on this quest to find you."

"You make it sound like you're Alvor looking for the Dirn-Hound. I'm not sure that's very flattering to me."

"I don't know that story."

"It's not a popular one. Alvor's dearest friend Carall was killed fighting the legions of Murakot, overwhelmed and overpowered, his body lost and his soul a prisoner of the Underworld. Alvor couldn't defeat Murakot without him, but no one knew where the gates of the Underworld were except the Dirn-Hound, which had never been captured. So Alvor went to the King of Westorn to ask his permission to hunt the Dirn-Hound on his lands, and the king of Westorn granted his request, but warned him that his heart's desire would keep him from finding what he looked for. And Alvor found the Dirn-Hound, but every time he came near it, it was suddenly half a mile distant. He chased it across the lands of the Princess of Cambrian and the Lord Regent of Esternis, and both rulers gave him permission to cross and both told him what the king of Westorn had. Finally Alvor was tired and angry, and he sat on the grass at the top of a hill and decided it was a waste of his time. And then the Dirn-Hound stood next to him, and allowed Alvor to harness him."

"That sounds like metaphor to me."

"Me too. It's not popular because people don't like to think of Alvor as someone who had to ask permission for anything. Some versions of the story have him ordering those lords to let him pass, but I don't think that makes much sense—if he had to order them, it means they had the power to say no, which still makes him their inferior. And my version fits better with the rest of the historical evidence, that Alvor was just a man who became great because the times demanded a hero."

"You know a great deal about Alvorian myth. Forgive me, but you don't speak like a barmaid."

Kerensa shrugged. "I went to school in Taraspir for a few years, and I listened to every story of Alvor every passing storyteller could give me. All those different versions, from Alvor's call to glory to his disappearance after killing Murakot, and the truth was somewhere in the middle—it fascinated me. I wanted to go to university in Matra to study more, which is why I was working in the tavern, to earn enough money, but that was before...." She ducked her head again, but she didn't sound quite as despondent as she had before.

Evon cast about for something to distract her. "You come from Taraspir, then?" It was a city near Dalanine's northern border.

She shook her head. "From Elkenhound, east of Taraspir. You won't have heard of it. It's not very big."

"You're far from home, then," Evon said, then cursed himself. *Of course she's far from home, she's been driven across Dalanine by a murderous spell that burns her to death every few weeks.* "I've never been out of Matra myself, not more than half a day's journey away, anyway," he said. "This is the farthest I've ever been away from home."

She was silent for a moment, and Evon ran through all of the possible ways his words might have sent her back into despair, but she said, "Do you have family in Matra, then?" and her voice sounded curious rather than despondent.

He laughed. "I sometimes think I have more family than any man deserves to have. My parents. My mother's parents. My father's married sister, her husband, and my odious cousin Jessalie. My father's unmarried sister, my dread maiden aunt. My younger brother Goderon. And we all live together in the family home except my older sister, who had the good sense to marry and flee."

"You still live at home?" Kerensa said, and now the twinkle was back in her eye. Evon felt a weight lift from his chest.

"I do, and you can forgo the rest of the comments I see gathering in your mind. It's a family tradition. Everyone works to provide for the household and we all benefit from the support of the family. And truthfully, except for my Aunt Etta and the odious Jessalie, I like having my family around. I just didn't realize how stifling they can be, without meaning it, until I made this journey. So I suppose I should thank you for opening my eyes."

"You're welcome. Now I want to know more about Miss Elltis."

"There's not much to know. She's a talented magician, but her real skill is in administration. Elltis and Company is one of the most experienced and prestigious cooperatives in Dalanine thanks to her efforts. But she's brusque and severe and demands a great deal from her 'partners,' including me."

"Will she be angry that you didn't find a magician at the end of your quest?"

"She wants the spell. She'll be annoyed at the delay, but she can't afford to fire me—I'm her top researcher and I bring the cooperative substantial sums of money from my creations. Let's try this shop."

The shop assistant who came to meet them concealed her distaste for Kerensa's dress imperfectly. Evon spun out a tale of broken-down carriages and lost luggage so well that even Kerensa behaved as if it were true. It had been a long time since he'd needed that skill, and he was pleased to see he hadn't lost it since leaving school. While Kerensa tried on dresses, he fell into a reverie involving Piercy and himself raiding the headmaster's liquor cabinet to bribe the gatekeeper to open the gates for them after curfew. He was so distracted that he didn't notice Kerensa had returned until she waved a hand in front of his face and said, "Gathering wool again, brother?"

He blinked and focused on her. She'd chosen a full-skirted gown in deep blue, fitted closely in the waist and bust to flatter her excellent figure. The color brought out the gold in her hair and made her too-creamy complexion seem less unnatural. She smoothed the bodice and shook out the skirts, and said, "I think this is much nicer, don't you?"

He nodded. He was having trouble speaking. He caught the shop assistant watching him suspiciously, realized he was not looking at Kerensa in the way a brother would, and said, "It looks very nice. Miss, would you mind wrapping the old gown for us to take away? We really should return it to the kind woman who loaned it to my sister. Not her fault they're very different shapes, yes?"

He paid for the dress and a charcoal gray bonnet, and with parcel in hand he escorted Kerensa back to the inn and their suite. "Would you mind waiting in your room for a moment?" he asked. "I have to update Miss Elltis on my progress." His instinct was to prevent Miss Elltis from seeing Kerensa, who would look with suspicion on Evon's motives if she knew the spell was attached to the body of an attractive young woman. Evon didn't know why she held such a dislike for attractive young women; he only knew that Miss Elltis employed no one of that description and had rejected at least one applicant on those grounds alone.

Kerensa took the parcel from him. "I'll see if I can't get this mud off," she said, "and it can be my alternative to running around naked."

Her hazel eyes twinkled at him, and once again he found himself without a ready response. He stared after her for a long moment after she'd closed the bathroom door behind her, then cleared his throat and drew up a chair in front of the small mirror over the shining parquet surface of the dressing table. He huffed on the mirror and quickly drew a pair of runes in the resulting fog. "Tifana Elltis *eloqua*," he said, and the surface of the mirror fogged over completely. *Eloqua* tasted pleasantly of mint, strong enough that he imagined he could smell the illusory taste. He sat back in his chair and waited. He was fairly certain that Miss Elltis always delayed responding to his communication spell to remind him that she was in charge, at least nominally. He leaned back further and tilted the chair so it balanced on two legs. In school, he'd been able to keep that position up indefinitely. He took out his pocket watch.

Seventeen minutes later, the fog cleared and Miss Elltis's face loomed out at him from the mirror. Her smooth, round cheeks were rosy, as if she'd been running, and the creases at the corners of her eyes and mouth were deeper than usual. Something had occurred to upset her. "Mr. Lorantis," she said. Her voice, by contrast to her face, was expressionless.

Evon set his chair down on all four legs and said, "Good morning, Miss Elltis."

"I hope you have news for me."

"I do. I've located the carrier of the spell."

"The 'carrier' of the spell? Are you being deliberately opaque, Mr. Lorantis?"

"No, I'm being deliberately precise, Miss Elltis." Evon summarized the last twenty-four hours' events, emphasizing what he'd learned about the spell and omitting the part where he'd spent her money on Kerensa's clothing. When he was finished, Miss Elltis's eyebrow was twitching, a tic Evon recognized as a sign that she was thinking furiously. He resisted the urge to fill her silence with more words.

"If I understand you," she said finally, "this girl has no control over the spell."

"Correct."

"Which indicates that she is of no use to us in using the spell to our advantage."

"Not in the sense that she's a magician who can teach me the spell, true, but I can't separate it from her, so in a different sense, she's crucial to my understanding of it."

Miss Elltis pursed her lips again. "You've made this report to Home Defense as well."

"Mr. Faranter has, yes."

The eyebrow twitched. "I'm inclined to tell you to leave it to them and return home."

Evon's jaw dropped. "Miss Elltis, we are so very close to understanding this spell —"

"Mr. Lorantis, by your own account you haven't even begun to investigate this spell."

"Which is why it would be foolish to give up before we've started."

"Are you calling me a fool, Mr. Lorantis?"

"Of course not, Miss Elltis, I'm saying that Elltis and Company hasn't prospered all these years by stepping aside from a challenge before fully engaging with it. I'm prepared to do whatever it takes to discover the workings of this spell. I think you know what I'm capable of. I merely want your support."

Twitch, twitch. "I don't like the idea of this cooperative's resources being squandered, Mr. Lorantis. You had better be able to produce results."

"I assure you, Miss Elltis, I am quite careful of our resources. I anticipate success very soon."

"For your sake, Mr. Lorantis, I sincerely hope you are correct." She cut the connection without another word.

Evon gently knocked his forehead against the dressing table. Someday, he'd be in a position to give Miss Elltis orders, and what a sweet day that would be. What could have upset her so? Well, it wasn't his concern, and frankly, he wasn't all that sorry to see Miss Elltis discomfited.

"I've caused you trouble," Kerensa said from behind him. He

turned to see her standing in the bathroom doorway, her hand on the knob.

"No, Miss Elltis delights in finding ways to cause me trouble," he said, "and she is using that spell as a pretext. Were you listening?"

"Not on purpose. No, that's a lie. I wanted to hear what your dragon maiden aunt sounded like. She *is* nasty, isn't she?"

Evon thought he should probably take her to task for eavesdropping, but found he didn't really mind. It wasn't as if he'd said anything he wouldn't have told Kerensa later. "She can be, yes. She was in a foul mood just now. Normally she's more polite."

"I think it's too bad you have to put up with her. Why don't you form your own, what did you call it, cooperative?"

"It's hard to make a name for yourself, and I'd have to give up too much of my research to run such a thing. My hope is to gain equity in Elltis and Company and thereby gain more control. Miss Elltis has to retire someday, after all."

"I didn't think dragon maiden aunts ever retired. Sit in a corner and make rude noises at people, possibly."

Evon raised his eyebrows at her. "You're...pardon my saying, but you're in a remarkably cheerful mood."

She twirled in place, making the skirt flare out. "I didn't realize what a difference clothing that fits makes. I haven't had a comfortable dress for...is it seven months, or eight? I feel light all over."

"If I were really your brother, I would point out that I was right and you should listen to my wisdom in future."

"If I were really your sister, I would roll my eyes in your direction."

"Do you suppose we could begin investigating that spell? I know I sounded dismissive, but I don't want to disregard Miss Elltis's instructions entirely."

The smile left her face. "I forgot," she said. "For a moment I forgot about it entirely."

She looked so lost that Evon's heart went out to her. "Let's see if we can let you forget about it permanently," he said, and offered her the chair he'd been sitting in.

When Piercy returned half an hour later, Kerensa was once again wreathed in blue spell-ribbons, still dark and dormant and frozen in the grip of *desini cucurri*. Evon was so caught up in his work that Piercy's entrance startled him, and he dropped his pencil.

"I beg your pardon," Piercy said, retrieving it and handing it over. "Miss—should I call you Miss Haylter when we're alone?"

"I'd like for you to call me Kerensa, Mr. Faranter, since Evon is doing the same. It makes me feel less awkward, like I'm really among friends."

Piercy looked a little startled, but said, "Then if we are friends you should call me Piercy. And now that we are entirely friendly, dear fellow, I think I should tell you about my day, if you're in a position to be interrupted."

"I lost my place when I dropped my pencil, so you might as well." The spell-ribbons jerked and resumed their motion. "It seems the spell is ready for a rest too."

Piercy sat on his bed and laced his fingers together in front of him. "My superiors are sending someone to take charge of Miss— Kerensa, that is."

Evon stared. "Piercy. You promised—"

"I said I'd be at my most persuasive. It seems my most persuasive wasn't good enough to overcome the fact that the spell is under no one's control. You must realize how they'd feel about that."

"What do you mean, take charge of me?" Kerensa asked. She'd clasped her hands in her lap and her knuckles were showing white.

Piercy sighed. "They weren't forthcoming with the details. I'm afraid they don't understand the danger of your being forced to miss your rendezvous, so to speak. Evon, you'll have to convince them. They know I know almost nothing about magic; they think this is a simple matter of national security."

"Should we run?" Evon asked.

Piercy blanched. "Dear fellow, aside from that being ultimately pointless because the government has virtually unlimited resources to bring to bear on finding us, it would be treason. I had the feeling, in talking to them, that the war is not going well at all and certain factions within the government have built up this spell as our salvation. How they intend to use it is anyone's guess, but as I said, they don't seem to understand how the spell works at all. I've been instructed to stay here and wait for whomever they send to...I hope not relieve me, but it might come to that."

"Piercy, this is disastrous."

"I know, dear fellow, but you have four days to unravel that spell before they arrive."

"And suppose Kerensa is forced to move on before then?"

"Then I will have to remain behind." Piercy looked grim. "I cannot seem to be disregarding orders, even for such a justification as that. I just hope it doesn't come to that, because I doubt they'll accept any excuse for Kerensa not being here when they arrive."

"I can't wait on them," Kerensa said.

"No one's telling you to," Evon said. "If the urge does come upon you, we'll move ahead and I'll keep Piercy apprised of our progress and location. But it's not going to happen."

"How do you know?"

"I don't. I'm being unreasonably optimistic because I'm filled with dread. If your next words are to tell me that Odelia will be here in the next fifteen minutes, I may begin screaming."

"No, I've seen no sign of Odelia or her companions," Piercy said. "No suspicious lurkers, no one asking after us. But it might not be a bad idea to blanket this inn in whatever protective magic you have at your command."

"It's a large inn, Piercy, I'm not sure how far my reserves will extend. But I'll try."

Piercy jabbed a finger at one of the spell-ribbons. "They quite match your dress, Kerensa, which is lovely. You must have excellent taste, because Lore is practically color-blind."

"I am not. Just because I don't think an afternoon spent choosing a neckcloth to match a new waistcoat is enjoyable."

"I didn't think of the color when I chose it," Kerensa said, eyeing a spell-ribbon that hung in front of her left eye. "I wonder if they influenced me at all?"

"More likely it was that shop assistant," Evon said absently, going back to his notes. "I've been building a lexicon of the new runes. It's really astonishing. Whoever built the spell didn't use runes the way we do at all. He, or she, treated the runes as pictograms, representing words instead of symbols. It's a narrow distinction, but an important one. I think these—" he traced the line of a ribbon with the tip of his pencil—"are sentences. If I can work out what the other words are, I can read the spell as easily as if it were a book."

"That's unusual, is it?" Kerensa said. "And please don't poke me in the eye."

"Sorry. Yes, extremely unusual. Everything would take forever if we cast spells this way. *Desini cucurri* is so much faster than saying 'Blue porcelain vase next to the brown table, stop falling now,' for example. But our spells are also far less complex than this one. The whole concept is groundbreaking. It opens up a whole new paradigm for spell-casting. This alone could keep me busy for the next ten years."

"Your enthusiasm is, as always, terrifying to behold," Piercy said, "and it's dinnertime. Kerensa, if your stomach could produce a lady-like growl at this point, it would do wonders toward helping me convince Lore that he needs to eat just like the rest of us."

"I can't growl on command," Kerensa said, "but I can say 'dear brother, I'm starving, could we please eat now?'"

Evon scowled. "I've made the biggest breakthrough in magical theory this century, and you two mock me. You'll be sorry when you read my memoirs."

"I would tremble at that threat, dear fellow, but I know you'll be too distracted to remember to write them."

9

*E*von scribbled through a word, pressing hard enough that the tip of his pencil snapped and flew off to *plink* against the window. He swore. Behind him, Kerensa said, "I had no idea gentlemen used that kind of language. Should I pretend I didn't understand?"

"Gentlemen can be just as vulgar as anyone else, given the right provocation, and right now I am extremely provoked. I don't have enough information to interpret this rune, and without it I can't interpret this entire branch. I haven't made any progress in the last half hour. I think we should take a rest."

Kerensa put her book down. "I'd like to stretch," she admitted. "And this book is interesting, but I wish it had more original material."

Evon dismissed *epiria* and sat down on his bed, flexing his stiff fingers. He'd been working for three and a half hours and had discovered the meaning of fifteen runes, not his most productive session, but at least he was making progress, or had been. He had the nagging feeling that he was going about this the longest possible way, that if he could just find the right perspective it would all fall into place. But he couldn't find that perspective, so he kept slogging away while Kerensa read or stared into the distance or, on one occasion, took a nap. Four days, and Piercy expected his superiors to appear at any moment. Evon had copied out five hundred unique runes and he understood barely a hundred of them. Fragments of runic sentences swam before his eyes when he lay down to sleep: *and make it the*, or *can find*, or other useless phrases. Nothing that would unlock the secrets of the spell; nothing that might free Kerensa from its grasp.

"I'll have Piercy get you another," he said. "This must be so boring for you."

"You keep saying that," Kerensa said, looking out the window. "My life's been exciting enough, these last months. Boring is nice. Boring with a book to read is nicer."

Evon flopped back to lie on the bed and put his hands behind his head. "So it's at least a good book."

"The author believes that Alvor will return soon to free us from tyranny, though she doesn't say whose tyranny we need to be freed from. Aside from that, she tells some good stories."

"So you're not, in Piercy's phrase, an Alvorian conspiracist."

"That's a good phrase. No, I think Alvor and his friends were real people, but not immortal or anything like that. I'm interested in working out what's true and what isn't in all these legends. Like this one, about how Dania gained her powers. It says she challenged a magician called the Wooden Man for his secrets, though I'm not sure why she would need to."

"A thousand years ago magicians were secretive about their spells. They would surround the command words with gibberish to prevent rivals from learning their spells, or cast them from a distance so the words couldn't be overheard. Magicians would sometimes challenge each other to contests in which they each might put up a spell as a stake."

"Oh. Well, in this story, Dania had no magical powers and she challenged the Wooden Man for all of his spells. He was supposed to be actually made of wood and so never got tired or needed to eat or piss or anything like that. But I think it's more reasonable to assume that a magician of that power probably had spells that would give him those abilities. Am I right?"

Evon considered. "I don't know of any spells that exist now that would, for example, remove the need to sleep. But I could probably create one."

"Yes. So what I think is that Dania challenged a powerful magician who was capable of altering his body—"

"Wait just a second." Evon bounced up and went to the dressing table, covered with sheets of his notes. "I know I—that's it. This rune means 'alter.' The spell altered your body so you couldn't be damaged by normal fire. It must be why you look so...." He waved his hand, holding the sheet of paper, in a circle in her direction.

"Why I look so what?"

"Um. So...smooth?"

"I don't know what you're talking about."

He had the feeling he'd walked into a trap. "You must know," he said, "the way your skin looks like it doesn't have pores...?"

She stared at him as if he'd lost his mind. Evon reached out and took her hand, used his other hand to push her sleeve up to her elbow, then rolled back his own. "Obviously your skin would be smoother than mine in any case, but—"

She snatched her hand out of his and held her forearm up to her eyes. Then she dashed to the mirror above the dressing table and leaned in close, scattering some of Evon's notes. "I look *awful*," she moaned. "I look like I'm wearing a flesh mask. I can't believe I've been walking around, thinking at least I look like a normal person, when all this time—"

"It really isn't that bad," Evon said. "No one's commented on it before, have they? Not even when you were able to settle down for a while? You're really very pretty, you know."

"Am I?" she said absently, prodding at her cheeks as if she thought the mask might come off.

The words *You are the most beautiful woman I've ever seen* froze behind Evon's lips. He just nodded. "Piercy thinks so too. And when the spell is gone, you'll look like yourself again."

"I feel so shallow, but now that I've seen this, removing that spell seems more urgent," Kerensa said, stepping away from the mirror and grinning ruefully at Evon. She went back to the window and leaned on the sill. "Not really, but you know what I mean."

"I do. And I don't think it's shallow to want your life back, even if just in that small way."

"I want it back in every way, but I'm afraid to hope. I—" She stiffened. "Evon," she said, her voice sounding strained, "Piercy's coming. And he's not alone."

Evon came to join her at the window. He was just in time to see Piercy pass out of sight below, headed toward the inn door. Behind him were five or six people, all wearing the plain black cloaks and wide-brimmed hats Evon associated with Home Defense. Their heads were constantly moving, as if assessing possible threats from any direction. One looked up and seemed to gaze directly at them; Evon resisted the urge to duck out of sight.

"Sit down," he told Kerensa, and cast *epiria* but not *desini cucurri*, so when moments later Piercy tapped at the door and then opened it, Kerensa sat demurely in the center of the room, wreathed in flying blue spell-ribbons that glowed with a light that burned the eyes of anyone who looked at it too long.

Evon looked up from a page of notes, pencil in hand. "Piercy," he said. "And these must be your colleagues." His hand holding the pencil was shaking a little; he gripped the pencil tightly and willed the tremor to vanish.

"Evon, may I make known to you Mr. Garaid Terantis," Piercy said, inclining his head in the stranger's direction. "Mr. Terantis, Evon Lorantis."

Mr. Terantis nodded at Evon, more curtly. "You're too young," he said. He was a broad, bulky man with a thick mustache that covered most of his mouth and neat black hair parted in the center and swept back over his ears. Under his cloak, he wore a black frock coat with a white shirtfront and black waistcoat from which hung a silver watch chain. His feet were enormous and seemed to take up most of the space between himself and Evon, vast black shoes whose shine was somewhat diminished by the filthy slush that covered the toes. He looked like a prosperous undertaker, and Evon was suddenly reminded of Odelia and her funereal garb. Behind him stood a man and a woman, both wearing black cloaks, the woman dressed in trousers like the man.

"I have more than enough experience to handle this situation," Evon replied, biting back a harsher response.

Mr. Terantis glanced over the room, saw Kerensa, and in an instant his self-possession deserted him. "What the *hell* is that?" he shouted.

"That, Mr. Terantis, is the spell Mr. Faranter and I were searching for," Evon said calmly, though his stomach was in knots and his heart pounded as if trying to break free of his ribcage. "You can see it's not like other spells. It—"

"What the hell do I know about other spells? Mr. Faranter, this is not what we were led to expect. We'll have to take her into custody immediately. Who knows what damage she might do?"

Kerensa's knuckles went white. Evon said, "She's no danger to you, sir. The spell is dormant now and Miss Haylter has no conscious control over it, so she could not harm anyone even if she were minded to do so. Which I assure you she is not."

"That's exactly what I'm afraid of," Mr. Terantis said. He stepped closer to Kerensa, though not within arm's reach of the spell-ribbons, and walked around her, examining her like a mare he thought he might buy. "She's got no control over it, so who knows what it might do?"

"Mr. Terantis, please stop talking about me as if I wasn't here," Kerensa said in a quiet but firm voice. "My name is Kerensa Haylter."

"Miss Haylter, I ought to arrest you for murder," Mr. Terantis said, coming to a stop in front of her. "Ten incidents—eleven, now, I've just learned—and nearly forty dead. I've seen the remains of some of your victims. You expect me to believe that you're not dangerous?"

"Miss Haylter is a victim of the spell you see surrounding her," Evon said. The dead look had returned to Kerensa's eyes and he felt like beating the huge man senseless. "It is attached to her, but it acts of its own volition. She is in no way to blame for those deaths."

"So you say," Mr. Terantis growled, turning on Evon. "I've never heard of a spell like that before. Far more likely she's a magician who got some idea in her head about prosecuting her own justice and found a way to do it." He spun back to face Kerensa. "Tell us how to work the spell, and you'll go free, much as it pains me to let a murderess go unpunished."

"I didn't do it," Kerensa said, her voice dull. "I don't know how it works. I can't help you."

"You'd better change your mind before we have to change it for you."

"Don't threaten her," Evon began, and Piercy cut in with, "Mr. Terantis, I assure you Mr. Lorantis knows his business. If he says the spell is independent of Miss Haylter, he is speaking the truth."

Mr. Terantis waved his hand in the direction of the spell. "You expect me to believe something as damned unsettling as this isn't dangerous? That she doesn't have control over it? We need this spell, Faranter, and I didn't come all this way to be told that's not possible."

"If you would *listen* instead of tossing off threats," Evon said, "I will explain everything I've learned about the spell. It's certainly a weapon—"

"Under no one's hand!"

"—as I said, it is a weapon, and I think if it is safely detached from Miss Haylter—"

"Forget about that," Mr. Terantis said. "We'll take her back to Matra where our magicians can examine her."

"You are not taking her *anywhere*," Evon shouted, "because if you interfere with the spell's function, the results will be disastrous. Remember the second event? That's what happens when Miss Haylter is prevented from following the spell's direction. Do you really want that to happen in the center of Matra? Of your head-quarters? You can't be that foolish."

"Evon," Piercy said, "I think—"

"Don't call me a fool, boy," Mr. Terantis shouted back. "You think to threaten me? You've already said the spell is under no one's control and now you pretend you know when it will strike? Abretis. Wylter. Find a way to get rid of these...things...and prepare to transport the girl."

"No," Kerensa said, her voice firmer now. "I won't go with you."

"Stay away from her," Evon said, stepping in front of Kerensa and flexing his fingers. Frantically, he ran through spells in his mind, looking for something that might stop them without escalating this nightmare. Were they magicians? Surely not, or they'd have slapped him with *desini cucurri* or something more potent the second he moved. Abretis and Wylter both took a step and then halted, hands on the clearly not decorative blades at their hips. They eyed his hands as if assessing their chances at reaching him before he loosed a spell. Evon tried to look fiercely determined instead of filled with despair. Mr. Terantis had come with no intent to listen to him. In a moment he would realize that Evon couldn't attack his people without committing treason, and he would take Kerensa back to Matra, and the Gods only knew what disaster would come of that.

Footsteps sounded in the hall. "Garaid, the area is secure," said a woman, and the next moment she came into view. She was in her mid-forties, a few years younger than Mr. Terantis, with graying brown hair and a square face with a prominent chin. Her blue eyes took in the situation in one glance, pausing briefly on Kerensa wreathed in blue, catching Evon's eye and then moving on to rest on Mr. Terantis. "Stand down," she said to Wylter and Abretis, who quickly stepped back all the way into the hall. "Garaid, is that the girl?"

"You can see she's dangerous," Mr. Terantis said.

"It's not true," Kerensa said, her voice trembling, but to Evon's surprise with anger, not fear. "I don't want to hurt anyone."

Mr. Terantis ignored her. "Get out of the way or I'll charge you with treason," he snarled at Evon.

"The only danger she poses to you is if you try to take her back to the capital," Evon said, not moving.

"May I see?" the woman asked, and walked around Evon without waiting for his permission. He fell back, startled, and Mr. Terantis grabbed his arm and twisted it painfully behind his back and put a pistol to his side. Piercy said, "Don't!" and moved toward Mr. Terantis, but hesitated when the man pressed the gun more firmly into Evon's side.

"Stop!" Kerensa leaped to her feet, a look of horror on her face. The spell-ribbons flew wildly about her body. The woman glanced at Mr. Terantis and Evon with no sign of agitation. "Let him go, Garaid, don't turn this into something we can't come back from," she said. "*Let him go,*" she repeated when Mr. Terantis showed no sign of moving. Mr. Terantis stared her down for a moment, breathing heavily, then released Evon and shoved him away. Evon stumbled to his knees, caught his balance, and looked up at Kerensa. "It's all right," he said, though he wasn't sure that was true. She reached out and helped him stand, gripping his hand tightly before releasing it to clasp her hands in front of her.

"Mr. Faranter wasn't clear on the details," the woman said, "but I can see now that this spell defies easy description." She turned to face Evon. "I'm Brenla Petelter," she said, "deputy minister in the department of Home Defense. I take it you are Mr. Lorantis?"

Evon nodded. "Miss Petelter—"

"Mrs.," Mrs. Petelter said with no rancor. "Tell me about the spell."

"Ah," said Evon, caught off guard by her directness. "Well. It's made up of hundreds of runes—do you know anything about magic, Mrs. Petelter?"

"I have some magical training, yes."

"Then you know how unusual that is. The runes make sentences that describe and execute the function of the spell. I've already been able to decipher about a hundred of them, enough to make out a few details. It's definitely a weapon—that is to say, the spell's creator built it specifically to target and...and attack based on certain criteria."

"So there's a pattern to whom you choose to kill?" Mrs. Petelter said, addressing Kerensa, whose face went expressionless. Evon could almost see her withdrawing into herself.

"*She's not doing it,*" he said, so frustrated he wanted to scream it at the woman. "The spell is using her as the means to fulfil its instructions. Miss Haylter *dies,* Mrs. Petelter, every time the spell is released, and it puts her back together again to repeat the process. Does that sound like something *anyone* would willingly undergo?"

"I beg your pardon," Mrs. Petelter said, eyeing Evon with a calculating expression. "You can see how that would be hard to believe."

"I know. It's also the truth. Mrs. Petelter, I have been studying this spell for days. I admit there's still a great deal I don't understand. But I am convinced that the spell is separate from Miss Haylter and I am trying my best to detach it. Then we might be able to use it as a weapon in this war."

"You see how dangerous it is?" Mr. Terantis said. "It's not under anyone's control, Brenla. We can't take the chance that it might injure innocent people. We have to take it back to Matra with us."

"That would be a huge mistake," Evon said. "If Miss Haylter is prevented from reaching her target, the power builds until it can't be contained, and the resulting explosion is devastating. As I explained to Mr. Terantis."

"You claimed to have some control over the spell," Mr. Terantis growled. "You dare to threaten us?"

"I did *not* make such a claim, and if you weren't such a self-involved—"

"*Enough*," Mrs. Petelter said, with enough force that Evon fell silent. "Garaid, I want you to check my assessment of the security of this building. Take Abretis and Wylter with you."

Mr. Terantis blinked at her, his broad face going red, but he left the room without another word. "Mr. Faranter, if you would shut the door, please," Mrs. Petelter continued, and Piercy did as she asked. When they were alone, she said, "I would say that Garaid means well, but none of us would believe it." She removed her cloak and draped it over her arm.

"Mrs. Petelter, I apologize for my outburst—"

"No apology needed, Mr. Lorantis. Garaid is enough to try anyone's patience. Now, let me see if I understand you. The spell has an ongoing existence that is independent of—Miss Haylter, was it? —and is not under her control. It chooses targets based on some unknown criterion. And it was made specifically to do this."

"That's correct, though I've seen Miss Haylter resist the spell's activation for a short time, and I think that period might be extended. And I'm beginning to understand why it chooses the people it does." Evon went to the dressing table and shuffled through his notes. "The phrase 'no soul' repeats itself throughout, and while it's perhaps overly poetical, it probably means people who have no regard for human life. People who see other people as things. It fits with what we know of the victims who have been identified."

"You speak of it as if it were alive."

"It seems to have some limited self-awareness, based on its reactions to my spells."

"Self-awareness...and self-preservation?"

"I...actually, I hadn't thought of that. It certainly resists being separated from Miss Haylter. But it's never objected to *desini cucurri,* other than to break its hold after a time." He cast the spell as he said the words, and it froze. Mrs. Petelter jerked backward, then leaned in to inspect the motionless spell-ribbons. Kerensa raised her arm and the spell moved with her.

"Astonishing," Mrs. Petelter said. She poked one of the ribbons and her finger passed through it. "Why does it respond to you and not me?"

"Evon—Mr. Lorantis—tells me it's altered my body to see it as part of myself," she said. "It's made me unable to be burned by normal fire, and to be able to...communicate with it, or something, so I know where to go to find the next..." She took a deep, shuddering breath. "Mrs. Petelter, I swear I don't mean to hurt those people. I don't care if they're evil or not, I don't want to be forced to kill anyone. I don't think I'm a murderer."

"Kerensa—" Evon began, afraid of the look in her eyes.

"Based on the evidence, I don't think you are either, Miss Haylter." Mrs. Petelter looked in Piercy's direction. "Nothing to say, Mr. Faranter?"

"Evon's the expert. I am merely the government's eyes and ears," Piercy said. "I'm sorry to learn that this department has such little faith in my abilities as to ignore my report."

"Careful, Mr. Faranter. I took your report very seriously. It's fortunate you *weren't* more specific; what I've heard here today would have truly set the cat amongst the pigeons, and you three would have had far worse than Garaid to deal with. I don't suppose you have any ideas as to the identity of the magician who cast this spell, Mr. Lorantis?"

Evon hesitated. There had been hints, all along, nothing substantial, but he could make an informed guess and something about this woman encouraged him to be honest. "I think the magician is long dead," he said. "This isn't a new spell. It's old. Centuries old. How it came to survive all those years, how it came to attach itself to Miss Haylter, I have no idea. But I'm afraid finding the magician, and compelling him to give up his secret, is impossible."

Piercy and Kerensa just stared at him. Mrs. Petelter pursed her lips. "That's...unfortunate," she said, though her tone of voice said "unfortunate" was far too mild a world for what she was thinking. "How certain are you of this?"

"As certain as I can be, given what little I've learned. The phrasing of the spell...text, I suppose you could call it...is archaic, as if it's written in an ancient version of our language, and there's nothing modern about how it's assembled. And there are places where a piece is, well, put together awkwardly, as if the creator didn't know how to do it the simple way any modern magician would. It's just possible that someone today put it together using old-fashioned techniques, but instinct tells me that's not the case." He didn't tell her what else he knew, that there was a depth to the spell that almost frightened him at times, that sometimes as he studied it he had the feeling that something ancient was looking back at him. He'd become the most skilled magician of his generation not only because of his knowledge but because of the instincts that led him to make intuitive leaps beyond what his rational mind understood, and all those instincts told him he was dealing with something older than anything he knew.

"And you're certain Miss Haylter cannot be taken to Matra?" Mrs. Petelter said.

"You saw the destruction at the second event site," Piercy said. "That's what happens if Miss Haylter refuses to follow the spell's urging when it comes on her."

Mrs. Petelter turned away from Kerensa and wandered over to

the window. "What I am about to tell you does not leave this room," she said, putting her hands on the sill. "The war is not going well. Despite the snow, the Despot moves farther north every day, driving refugees ahead of him and leaving utter destruction in his wake. If nothing changes, he will cross Dalanine's southern border by spring. Our generals are confounded at the Despot's ability to see our greatest weaknesses and exploit them ruthlessly. We need an advantage. We need this weapon."

"I understand the urgency—"

"I'm not certain that you do, Mr. Lorantis, but I take your word that you are fully committed to providing Dalanine with something that will change the outcome of this war." She turned to look at him. "I do wish we had understood the nature of Miss Haylter's involvement. We have been gathering magicians in Matra to study the spell, but as it seems taking her back to the capital is impossible, we will have to continue to depend on you for now. I'll send word for our magicians to join us here as quickly as possible."

"I've had a great deal of success on my own," Evon said, concealing his irritation.

"Your desires don't enter into it. We cannot afford you the luxury of working at your own pace. More magicians mean more expertise —or do you deny that you lack the experience of maturity?"

"Mrs. Petelter, Evon is the finest magician of his generation and far more skilled than many magicians with more, as you put it, experience of maturity," Piercy said. "I brought this task to him for that reason."

"The department is grateful to you, Mr. Faranter, but now I will be supervising this affair, and my assessment is that Mr. Lorantis's efforts will be more productive with the assistance of his fellows." She settled her cloak over her shoulders. "Home Defense has already declared this spell war materiel, and under our jurisdiction. You will all three of you serve your country as I dictate or face charges. I am sorry it must come to this, but the Despot has left us with no choice but to appropriate whatever we believe will win us this war."

"I'm not a thing, Mrs. Petelter," Kerensa exclaimed.

"It is unfortunate for you that you are, for the moment, inseparable from the spell, but that changes nothing. I suggest you accelerate your efforts if you wish her out of this, Mr. Lorantis."

"What of Speculatus?" Piercy said. "They pose a not inconsiderable threat to us."

"We are aware of the danger and our people are prepared to defend the spell if Speculatus comes against us. If we are fortunate, Speculatus will overextend themselves and commit to an action that will expose them for what they are, and leave them vulnerable to the law. The best circumstance would be for Speculatus to succeed at abducting Miss Haylter and then be captured by us."

Kerensa's expression was even more wooden than before. She seemed not to hear what Mrs. Petelter was saying. "And suppose you didn't capture them? You would dare put her in danger like that? Speculatus wouldn't shrink from torturing her to gain secrets she doesn't have," Evon said hotly.

"Control yourself, Mr. Lorantis. Miss Haylter is far too valuable to risk. If I decide such action is necessary, she will have every protection we can muster."

"Stop treating her like she isn't human!"

"Careful, Mr. Lorantis. I am your advocate in this situation. Would you prefer I leave things to Garaid? Miss Haylter, I apologize, but I'm sure you understand better than anyone what it means that this spell is part of you. Mr. Lorantis, I expect a report on your findings at the end of each day. Mr. Faranter, walk with me. I have further instructions for you."

Piercy's lips were set in a thin, hard line, but he held the door for Mrs. Petelter and followed her into the hall. When the door was again shut, Kerensa sat in her chair and stared blindly at the wall. Evon said, "I'll figure it out. I swear."

"I know," she replied in the dull, emotionless voice Evon had hoped he'd heard the last of. Damn Mrs. Petelter, and damn Mr. Terantis, for doing this to her. He dismissed *epiria*, then knelt at her side, scuffing the chalk circle, and took her hand in his. "Mrs. Petelter's going to leave us alone. This changes nothing, do you hear me? I'll work harder and soon they'll have their damned spell and it will be nothing to do with us anymore. Kerensa. Look at me."

She turned to face him, her poreless skin pale, her eyes haunted. "Will you start work again now?" she said. "I want this to be over."

He squeezed her hand, gently. Her skin was warm and soft and felt just like ordinary skin. "I will," he said, "if you remove that expression that says I just killed your favorite puppy."

Her eyes widened, then she smiled. "I like cats," she said. "And I think you come up with outrageous things to say to me so I'll laugh."

"That's true," Evon said, and released her hand. "I lie awake at night inventing insults and absurdities to keep your spirits up. It keeps me sane when Piercy snores."

"Well, it works. Thank you. And, Evon? Thanks for defending me."

Her hazel eyes were fixed on his, and he found himself tongue-tied. All he could do was smile, and nod, and turn away as gracefully as possible.

10

---

ow Evon fell into a pattern: breakfast, study, dinner,
study, supper, study, sleep. Piercy had to force him to
take rests and ultimately resorted to pointing out that Kerensa had
begun to look haggard from inactivity, which made Evon feel
horribly guilty. After that, Piercy and Kerensa went for walks in
the mid-morning and after dinner, accompanied by one of the
Home Defense agents, and Evon organized his notes and made
more of them and analyzed his findings until his eyes ached. Occasionally he joined Piercy and Kerensa, but he was always so preoccupied with his thoughts that he was a poor companion and
sometimes had to be steered out of the way of other pedestrians
and lampposts.

His lexicon grew slowly, which infuriated him. It felt like the
spell was taunting him, becoming more obscure the more he learned.
More phrases: *fire to destroy, tell it to return, bind the call*. Too many long
sequences of indecipherable runes. Some of the five hundred runes
seemed to be variants on others, and he didn't know what to make of
that; were they the same words, written differently, or did the variants alter the meanings, change present to past tense or turn a noun
into a gerund? He used up his paper and sent Piercy to the station-

er's for more, set Kerensa to sharpening pencils, and drew runes until he felt he would overflow with them.

At the end of the third day, Evon sat at the dressing table, staring at his notes, wondering why anyone had ever thought he was a brilliant magician. He'd deciphered another fifty runes since Mrs. Petelter had descended on them, trailing agents in her wake, and they hadn't made any difference. The problem, he knew now—and discovering this had been important, so maybe he shouldn't be so hard on himself—was that it was actually a host of smaller spells working together for one purpose. He'd worked out many of the small spells already. He knew how it made Kerensa impervious to normal fire—he'd used that one to improve his own shield spell. He knew how it was able to resurrect her after the explosion. He understood the tangle of spells that caused the spell's activation, though he still wasn't sure how it chose its specific targets beyond the unhelpful "no soul" cluster of runes. And he knew how it directed Kerensa to find its next target. He just didn't understand the great central spell that all the rest connected to, the spell that contained the secret of the magical fire. And he didn't know how to break Kerensa free of it.

A hand removed the pencil from his. "Stop," Kerensa said. "Rest. It's not so urgent that you have to kill yourself figuring it out."

He looked up at her. Motionless blue spell-ribbons made a halo around her head. "I want you to be free," he said.

"So do I, but not at the cost of your sanity."

"Those other magicians will start arriving in a day or two, Kerensa. My work will effectively end then, because even if they let me continue working, I'm going to spend days explaining what I've already learned to magicians who won't respect me enough to listen."

"Let's just start again tomorrow, all right? You need sleep, and honestly, so do I. I'm exhausted and I'm going blind because of this blue light. Can you turn it off, please?"

Evon gestured and the spell vanished. "I can't sleep. I see runes every time I close my eyes."

"You need something else to think about," Piercy said, entering in time to hear Evon's last words. "But I'm afraid I am all out of new projects for you, dear fellow."

"How is our dear friend and patroness Mrs. Petalter?"

"Friendly and patronizing as ever, Lore. She greeted my suggestion that in remaining here we are a more obvious target for Speculatus with polite dismissal and the unspoken suggestion that I should take myself off so the adults could make decisions. I didn't bother speaking to Terantis, of course." He sat heavily on his bed. "I need a drink."

"So do I." Evon lay back on his bed.

"You need hot milk and a bedtime story, dear fellow."

"Hot milk sounds disgusting, but...Kerensa, wait." Kerensa paused with her hand on the bathroom doorknob. "Why don't you tell us a story about Alvor?"

"Aren't you a little old for bedtime stories?" she asked, raising an eyebrow.

"It will give me something to think about besides runes. Please?"

Kerensa shrugged and took her seat again. "What do you want to hear?"

"I barely know any of them," Evon said. "Pick one of your favorites."

She tapped her lips with her index finger, thinking. "All right. Do you remember the story of the Dirn-Hound?"

"No," said Piercy.

"It helped Alvor find the gates of the Underworld," Evon told him.

"Is this a true story?" Piercy asked.

"Depends on who you ask. Do you want to hear it or not?" Kerensa said. "Then stop talking. All right. Alvor's best friend Carall was trapped in the Underworld, and Alvor needed his help to defeat Murakot. So he went on several quests to get him back. They all have their own stories, like the Dirn-Hound, but the short version—"

"Why can't we hear the long version?"

"Because you might want another bedtime story tomorrow, Evon, and I want to save something for then. Now shush. Alvor collected all sorts of things: a vial of magic oil, a stick from the oldest oak in Telwyth Forest, a hazelnut the size of his fist, and of course the Dirn-Hound and the leash he used to capture it. And the Dirn-Hound led him, with all his magic things, to the gates of the Underworld.

"None of the legends say what the gates looked like, just that they opened in the Dirn-Hound's presence and let Alvor walk through. The halls of the Underworld teemed with the spirits of the dead, none of them able to speak and all of them able to lead a mortal visitor down the wrong path. Alvor was prepared. He blindfolded himself and with the stick from the oldest oak in Telwyth Forest found the path that took him past the spirits and to the antechamber to the five Death-Lands, where he discovered five identical doors.

"Now, in the Twins' domains, there are doors you can only pass once, and these were the doors the dead go through to their final home. Alvor had to choose the one Carall had passed through, and if he chose wrong, he'd never be able to come back to choose again. So Alvor put the magic oil on his eyelids, and saw that one of the doors was blacker than a crow's heart. He chose that door and came through to a black hall filled with spirits, and every one of them was Carall.

"Now one of the people whose help Alvor had asked for was the Witch of Marhalindor, who was insane but saw things sane people don't. She told Alvor to take what Carall hated and give it to him. So Alvor took a giant hazelnut—stop laughing, Piercy! It's how the story goes."

"I simply think it lacks sufficient gravitas. Hazelnut, indeed. Much better a stinging nettle, if you must have some type of flora. Or some kind of vicious animal, like a cat."

"I like cats. And I'm telling the story. It was a hazelnut because Carall couldn't eat them, they made him sick. And Alvor took the giant hazelnut and tossed it into the middle of the throng. All ghosts love food, even though they can't eat it, and they dived on the nut— all except one. And Alvor took the Dirn-Hound's leash and tied Carall's hands, and led him out of the Underworld to the lands above."

"How did Alvor get out if he'd gone through the door you only pass through once?" Evon asked. Kerensa's low, musical voice had relaxed him nearly to sleep.

"He took the God Cath's route, the one the Twin takes when he leaves his realm. He had to fight his way free, that's how he lost his finger."

"And Carall was alive again?"

"No, he was dead, but he walked the living world like a breathing man. And he fought with Alvor against Murakot and defeated him."

Evon rolled on his side to face her. "So, where's the kernel of truth in that story?"

Kerensa stretched. "You want to know what I think? I think the whole thing's true."

"Dead men walking the earth?"

"Aren't there places people don't go because they're so saturated with magic the laws of nature break down? If I were going to hide the entrance to the Underworld, I'd put it someplace like that. But if you want a more realistic interpretation, Carall wandered into one of those places, Alvor went after him and had some kind of hallucination, and the place changed Carall into something not quite human."

"I prefer the second interpretation, but I am a pragmatist," Piercy said.

"I'm surprised you believe the more unbelievable version this time," Evon said. "You're usually so quick to dismiss the less likely elements."

"I just think the idea of Alvor going into death after the person he cared most for in all the world rings true," Kerensa said. "And now I'm going to bed. Good night."

"Good night," Evon said. "I'm starting to understand the appeal of these Alvor stories," he said to Piercy.

"Really? I prefer a good straightforward adventure novel in which the men are heroes and the women are grateful," Piercy said. He sat on his bed and began taking off his boots. "No concerns about whether or not it's true."

"You don't think Alvor really existed?"

"Oh, I think he did. *Somebody* killed Murakot, after all. But no one man, or even three men and a woman, or two men, a woman and a whatever Wystylth was, could possibly have done everything they're meant to have done."

Evon rolled off the bed and began to undress. "Don't you ever feel as if we've wandered into one of these old stories? Ancient spells, a wandering quest...though I have trouble picturing you as Alvor."

"I'm Wystylth, the sneaky one, and since you're a magician that makes you Dania. I'm just as happy not to be living in those times. No indoor plumbing anywhere, for one thing."

"Put out the light, would you? I'm saying, suppose one of those old stories found us. That spell is pretty old."

"As old as Alvor?"

"Maybe." Exhaustion overwhelmed him. If the spell were as old as Alvor...the thought reminded him of something, but he was too tired to dig it out of memory. He sank into sleep and dreamed of a faceless man fighting his way out of the underworld, towing Kerensa behind him.

EVON FLATTENED HIMSELF ON THE FLOOR AND PEERED UNDER THE bed, then summoned a light and looked again. Nothing but hardened dust clinkers and a deserted spider web. No pen knife. He searched under Piercy's bed, then dragged the dressing table away from the wall and looked there. The movement sent drifts of pages sliding to the floor. Evon put the table back with more force than necessary, knocking over the rest of the pages and jostling the wall mirror. He hadn't spoken to Miss Elltis in five days; between the arrival of Mrs. Petelter and her people, and the increased urgency to decipher the spell, there hadn't been time. He was lying to himself, of course. He didn't *want* to talk to Miss Elltis. What he wanted was to find the damned pen knife. Someone must have taken it.

"Evon—you look awful. Let me help." Kerensa came through from the bathroom and bent to help him pick up papers.

"I'm trying to find my pen knife," he muttered. "No, I need those in order. Thank you."

"You loaned it to me yesterday, to cut the pages of that new book," she said.

"Why didn't you say so? I need it!"

"I didn't know that. Here, I have it right here."

He snatched it out of her hand. "Finally. Couldn't you have returned it immediately? Sometimes I think no one cares about this undertaking but me."

Kerensa went very still. "You're probably right," she said. "The Gods forbid it could possibly matter to anyone else."

Evon's heart sank. "Kerensa, I'm sorry," he said. "That was thoughtless and insensitive and untrue and I should never have said it. I've become caught up in my work again...but that's no excuse. Please forgive me."

She surveyed his face, her eyes expressionless. "I'm going down to breakfast," she said. "You should probably clean yourself up before you do the same. You wouldn't want to get so caught up in research that you forget to eat. Again." She turned and left, slamming the door behind her.

Evon threw the pen knife at the dressing table and heard it slide and clatter to the floor. He sat on his bed and covered his face with his hands. He needed to stop thinking about this. He couldn't afford to stop thinking about it. That look on her face...she wasn't going to forgive him for that for a long time. The thought made his chest ache. *When am I going to learn to think before I speak?* He found he'd lost his appetite, or maybe it was just that he couldn't bear to meet her empty eyes again.

He stood and retrieved the pen knife, which was now chipped from its encounter with the table. It could be a reminder to him to stop being so caught up in his work that he forgot to be a decent human being. He moved most of the pages to the bed and spread fresh paper on the table, then drew up the chair. There was a tangle of runes he thought might be the key to the spell, if only he could work out which of their many configurations meant something instead of being gibberish. Knowing this was how ancient magicians had worked was different from seeing the technique in action. Evon picked up his pencil and began writing the runes on the blank pages, large and bold and separate from one another. Then he cut the paper so he had dozens of smaller, square-ish bits of paper, each with a single rune on it. He shuffled the papers and dealt them out as if he were playing a particularly fiendish game of patience. There was a combination that made sense, and he would find it.

He spread the papers, rearranged them, gathered them up and spread them again. He took notes on the configurations that didn't work. It was going to take forever. Shuffle and spread. Fragments of sentences took shape and dissolved again. More notes on his failures. His fingers became gray and dry with pencil lead.

And then, almost without him realizing it, the sentence took shape in front of him. He held his breath, afraid to disturb the light slips of paper, afraid that it was another dead end that simply took longer to reveal itself. But there it was. He read down the line of runes, consulted his notes and read on. A growing dread filled him the further he went, until he reached the end and found that his hands were numb from his having clenched them so tightly. He read through it again.

No.

But there's no mistake.

I can't tell her this. Not now.

"One day, I won't bring you food, and they will find you starved to death in some garret, a pencil clutched in your bony fingers," Piercy said, pushing open the door. He held the only food he was capable of making, a fried egg sandwich with two slices of bacon that was more a matter of assembly than actual cooking. He held it out to Evon, then said, "What's wrong?"

Evon accepted the sandwich wordlessly. He took a bite and nearly spat it out. "Where did you get this?"

"I admit the eggs are a little hard, but I thought the pepper might liven it up," Piercy said. "Evon, something's happened, I can see it. Did you learn something?"

"Shut the door, Piercy." Evon took another bite of too-peppery egg and choked it down, though his stomach churned with anxiety and he wasn't sure how long it would stay down. "And stand in front of it. I don't want Kerensa coming in."

"You did learn something, and it's bad news. Tell me."

Evon set the sandwich down on the last clear spot on the table. "There is a part of the spell I've been trying to decipher. I knew it had something to do with the people the spell targets and I hoped it would be the key to breaking that cycle. It's not, Piercy, it's so much worse." He gathered up the small pieces of paper and tapped them together into an irregular stack. "The spell is looking for someone in particular. One person. All these other deaths, they're *mistakes*. Similar to the real target in some way, but mistakes. It has this— there's this element of the spell that does a sort of, of assessment of the world—I don't know how it manages it—right after it explodes. If it finds evidence that the person still exists, it resets itself. Rebuilds Kerensa so it can try again. If it doesn't..." He couldn't finish the sentence.

Piercy didn't need him to. His face was white. "Who is it looking for?"

"I have no idea. It could be anyone. The next time she feels drawn to...by the Gods, Piercy, we can't tell her this. She's only just gotten used to the idea that she might have a future."

"I agree, dear fellow. Isn't there anything you can do?"

"I could remove that element right now if I wanted. But the magician who created the spell, may he be damned to burn eternally, set it up to destroy itself, and its host, if any piece of it was taken out. Apparently he didn't want anyone using his spells for themselves." He laughed, and it sounded hollow in his ears. "It never occurred to him that someone could just copy the spells and make new ones."

"You have to find a way to stop it."

"Elegant statement of the obvious, Piercy." He absently took another bite of the sandwich and winced. "You didn't think to bring anything to drink?"

"I'm not your serving girl, Evon." Piercy leaned heavily against the door. "We can't tell Mrs. Petelter either. She might decide it's worth the risk taking Kerensa back to Matra, if the alternative is losing the spell entirely."

"And it won't disturb her that it would mean losing Kerensa too," Evon said bitterly.

The door thumped. "Evon, other people need to use this door," Kerensa said.

Piercy and Evon looked at each other. "You look terrible. She's going to know something's wrong," Piercy said.

"You don't look much better. Try to think of something cheerful." Kerensa banged on the door again. "And open the door." Evon picked up his now-cold sandwich and took another bite. Maybe she would mistake the anguish he felt for disgust at Piercy's offering.

"*Thank you,*" Kerensa said, pushing past Piercy into the room. "Evon, I told you—what's the matter?" Her irritation was replaced by a look of concern that made his heart break. That *she* might be worried about *him*—the Gods were certainly playing with him.

"He doesn't appreciate the breakfast I brought him," Piercy said, sounding exactly as if nothing were wrong.

"Because it's disgusting," Evon said. He couldn't meet Kerensa's eyes, so he turned toward Piercy and added, "Not that I don't appreciate the gesture."

"If you keep bringing him food, he'll never leave this room," Kerensa said to Piercy. "You shouldn't encourage him. Especially since being alone makes him say stupid things." She smiled at Evon, her hazel eyes clear and untroubled, and he managed a weak smile in return. "I'm ready to begin when you are."

"I...actually want to go over my existing notes," Evon said. "You should enjoy your morning. Go to the shops, perhaps. Buy something nice."

"You're behaving awfully strange. Are you sure nothing's wrong?"

"Upset stomach," Piercy volunteered. "We should leave him to it. Would you care to take a turn with me? It's good for the digestion."

"I suppose," Kerensa said, but she was still looking at Evon with concern. "Do you want to work more this afternoon?"

"Yes, I should be ready by then." Evon realized he was still holding the stack of little papers and crushed it in his hand. "Enjoy your walk, both of you."

When they were gone, he dropped the crumpled papers onto his unmade bed and stared at them. He could try again, see if there was another meaning...but no. No, he was certain he had the right interpretation. The spell would eventually find its true target, and it would kill Kerensa permanently. He picked up a handful of pages of notes from the table, but instead of reading through them, he paced the room, seeing not the pale blue walls but the too-smooth oval of her face, the hazel eyes that hardly ever looked dead or despairing anymore. Telling her would do nothing but make her miserable. The secret had certainly made him miserable enough.

Paper brushed his thigh. He'd forgotten he was carrying the pages of notes. He sat at the table and sorted through them. Somewhere in all this morass of paper was the secret of freeing Kerensa from the spell. Failing that, there might be a way to keep it from activating without the devastating side effects of a delay. It was also possible that his notes contained the secret of creating the intense fire, though Evon wasn't surprised to learn he no longer cared very much about that. Miss Elltis would be furious if she knew, but since he didn't intend to tell her, her potential anger was irrelevant.

The mirror clouded over, startling him. *"Evon Lorantis eloqua,"* said Miss Elltis's voice. She sounded as angry as he'd just imagined, making him wonder if she'd been spying on him. No, if she had, she would have made an appearance much sooner. He tidied the dressing table, took a deep breath, and said, *"Eloqua."*

The fog cleared, revealing Miss Elltis's face, ruddy with anger. "Mr. Lorantis, why have you not reported for five days?"

"I had nothing to report, Miss Elltis. I didn't want to waste your time."

"I decide what is a waste of my time, Mr. Lorantis. How can you have nothing to report? You told me you were making great progress, last we spoke. I begin to think you have deliberately misled me."

"Miss Elltis," Evon said, making a great effort not to stand and shout at her image, "this is a complex and ancient spell that even I can't unravel in a day. It's true I haven't learned the secret of the fire yet, but—"

"Improving that shield spell of yours is merely a side benefit. The fire is what matters." Miss Elltis's perfectly coiffed flaxen hair seemed straggling a little today. "Mr. Lorantis, I have received an unpleasant communication from Home Defense today. They say they were misled as to your qualifications for investigating this spell. I assured them I had every faith in your ability. Do you realize how it pained me to have to lie to the government?"

"Are you saying you *don't* have faith in my abilities? After all these years?"

"You have been unable to make progress—"

Evon snapped. "I, make no progress? Miss Elltis, I defy you to do better! I have done nothing but try to take this spell apart for days and I can assure you that no living magician knows more about it than I do! I don't know what notions you've taken into your narrow-minded brain about the spell's capabilities, but I am making progress as quickly as *anyone* could."

Miss Elltis's face grew redder, the creases at the corners of her mouth deeper. "Mr. Lorantis, do not dare to speak to me in that tone!"

"Then do not insult us both by making allegations for which you have no foundation."

"No foundation?" She leaned closer to her mirror. "Home Defense has informed me that they are sending a host of experienced magicians to take over the investigation. When they arrive, you are to desist work on the spell immediately and return to Matra. Then you and I will have a conversation about your future here."

Evon gaped at her. "That would set progress back by days. Weeks, possibly. How are we—"

"Mr. Lorantis, I think you fail to grasp my meaning. Elltis and Company no longer has the right to investigate the fire spell. We are no longer in a position to develop it for the government, let alone for commercial uses. We have been what is euphemistically known as 'let go.' You should be aware that I lay the blame for this entirely on your head. Be grateful that I do not simply let you go as well."

"You wouldn't dare."

"Wouldn't I? You are fortunate in having been such a productive member of this cooperative for many years. I'm told the government's magicians will arrive in a day or two. I expect to see you back in the capital in one week." She broke the connection, leaving Evon with his mouth open and a shout dying on his tongue.

It was over. He'd failed Kerensa and he'd failed himself. All those promises he'd made to her—how could he ever face her again? Oh. Of course. He wouldn't face her again because he'd be gone. He raised his hand to fling all the papers to the floor, but stopped himself in time; it was stupid to have to reorganize everything again, after having just tidied up. Losing his temper wasn't going to help anyone.

Miss Elltis wouldn't even let him stay to instruct the new magicians on the research he'd already done. How humiliated she must have been to have some Home Defense official upbraid her on the failures of her subordinate— Mr. Terantis had to be behind this, he was stupid enough not to realize that in getting rid of Evon he was sabotaging the research he desperately wanted completed. Perhaps he could appeal to Mrs. Petelter...no, she wouldn't go against her superiors' wishes even if she did respect Evon's work, and even she believed the research would proceed more quickly with more minds applying themselves to it, whether or not Evon was one of those minds.

The door flew open and slammed into the wall. "Evon," Piercy said, and Evon turned to see both Piercy and Kerensa breathing heavily, Piercy with his hand on Kerensa's shoulders as if supporting her, Kerensa twisting her hands together so hard her knuckles were white.

"It's started," she said. "It's pulling me again."

Evon met Piercy's eyes. "How long?" Evon asked.

Kerensa shook her head. "I can't tell. It feels close." Her mouth trembled. "I can't do this again," she said. "I thought—"

Evon stood and embraced her, pulling her tight to him and feeling her arms clutch at him in desperation. "There's still time," he said. "But we have to move quickly. If those magicians—they'll just want you to stop while they waste time repeating all the work I've done. We're going to tell Mrs. Petelter that we have to leave immediately. Kerensa, Piercy and I aren't going to let you go through this alone, you understand? I'll be with you right up until it happens, and I will walk out of there with you." He stepped away and lifted her chin so he could meet her eyes. "I promised I'd bring you a dress, remember?"

She laughed, weakly, but it was still a laugh. "I'm counting on it."

11

They left Calian at noon and pushed as far as Belicath before night overtook them. Now the clear winter sky shone with thousands of stars made dim by the ever-burning lights of the city of the Gods. They'd passed the Twin Temples on their way into the city, Cath's a dark, sleek assemblage of narrow spires and clustering towers, Belia's squat and warm with glowing yellow stone. They faced one another across a wide open space that in summer was a garden lush with flowers and trees; now it was dormant, though the temples' auras kept it snow-free. Evon thought it would have been less depressing had it been covered in snow.

The inn Mrs. Petelter chose was smaller and less expensive than the one they'd stayed in in Calian, but she had compensated for this by evicting the current tenants and hiring the entire inn. She called it security; Evon thought it might be paranoia, but he knew nothing about the subject and had to defer to Mrs. Petelter in any case. If it kept Kerensa safe from Speculatus, then he was in favor of paranoia, though he was beginning to suspect that Odelia had lost them completely. The Home Defense agents hadn't seen anything suspicious at all, certainly nothing they could attribute to Speculatus, but they maintained a readiness that would have been more comforting had it not been so restrictive. He looked out of the window in Mrs. Petelter's suite of rooms, which were on the second floor and gave an excellent view of the wall of the pub next door. Security again, probably.

"I'm sorry, Mrs. Petelter, but there's no time to wait for the magicians," he said once again. He felt as if their conversation were going around in circles, him making this same basic point, Mrs. Petelter countering with some variation on —

"I do not see," Mrs. Petelter said, "how a day's delay will make any difference."

"We don't understand enough about the spell to know how much the damage is increased by *any* delay," Evon said. "Up until this point, Miss Haylter has simply walked away from whatever she was doing the instant she felt this urge. I think we should allow her to proceed as she always has."

"I don't like the idea of allowing our actions to be dictated by a murderous spell," she replied. "It cannot be right that we're proceeding in a course of action that will end with at least one person dead, possibly more. Standing by and doing nothing runs counter to everything I believe."

"I feel the same way," Evon lied, "but I see no alternative. I continue to make progress in understanding the spell, and Miss Haylter doesn't know how long it will take to reach her destination; it's possible we will unravel it before it comes to a death."

Mrs. Petelter eyed him narrowly, as if she could read the difference between his words and his thoughts in his face, but he maintained an innocently concerned expression, and finally she said, "I'll send word to our people to hasten their journey. You should have all the assistance you will need very soon now."

So she didn't know about Miss Elltis's ultimatum. "I hope it will be useful assistance, Mrs. Petelter," he said. He might be able to bluff a little while longer, pretend not to have received Miss Elltis's instructions, but if Mr. Terantis knew the truth, he'd be on his way back to the city the second those magicians appeared on the horizon.

He left Mrs. Petelter's room and went upstairs. Piercy and Evon once again shared a room, though the inn was large enough (and, thanks to Mrs. Petelter, empty enough) that they might have each had their own; they opted for the security of being able to make their own plans without being observed. Piercy sat up from where he was lounging on his bed when Evon entered, and said, "Well?"

"She doesn't like it, but she's agreed," Evon said. "I don't know how long we'll be able to stay ahead of the magicians, though."

"How bad could that be, really? Even if they aren't helpful, they can't possibly interfere with your work that much, dear fellow."

Evon drew in a breath. "Miss Elltis has commanded me to return to Matra when the magicians arrive. I won't have anything more to do with the investigation."

"No," breathed Piercy. "She can't do that."

"Apparently she can. So you see why it's essential to stay ahead of those magicians, so I'm not forced to disobey her."

"You'd stay anyway."

"If I could. If Mrs. Petelter and Terantis don't learn about her ultimatum. I have no doubt that the government doesn't want me working on this either."

"If you left, it would be disastrous," Piercy said. "It will take them days to understand the work you've already done, if they don't simply discard it and start over on the grounds that you're a mere stripling who could not possibly understand the forces of magic you've been fumbling with. And Kerensa will feel so betrayed. You know they'll treat her like an experimental animal."

"Are you *trying* to send me into despair?"

"I apologize, dear fellow. What can I do?"

"Find a way to keep your superiors occupied so they don't care that I'm still here. I can ignore Miss Elltis; the worst she can do is let me go without a reference, and I'd get past that. But Home Defense has the manpower to escort me back to Matra. In chains, if necessary. And I assure you it would be necessary." The idea of leaving Kerensa behind filled him with a terrible anxiety. Piercy was right; she would feel betrayed, and he couldn't bear to do that to her.

"I'll do my best, Evon, but you've noticed that Mrs. Petelter doesn't exactly respect my opinions or contributions."

"I have faith in your ability to confuse and bewilder everyone around you. Though Terantis shouldn't be hard to confuse or bewilder or both."

"I am fairly certain that both those words mean the same thing, but I take your meaning. How early do you think we can be out of here?"

"Not until a few hours after sunrise, unfortunately."

"Doesn't traveling all day interfere with your examination of our favorite research subject?"

"Don't call her that, Piercy."

"I was hoping to lighten the mood. My apologies. Well, doesn't it?"

"I can read and ride just as well as I can read and walk at the same time. I've copied out every rune I could see, so it really is a matter of figuring out where the secret is hiding." Evon blew on his fingers. "I'm for bed, though I'm too keyed up to sleep, I think."

"You could ask Kerensa to tell you another story."

"I can hardly bear to meet her eyes, I'm keeping so many secrets from her."

"She needs to know there's a possibility you might be dragged away," Piercy said. "Imagine the shock that would be."

Evon grimaced. "You're right. I'll go talk to her. Are you going to bed?"

"I'm going to have a drink in the taproom first. I'll be up shortly."

Kerensa's room was down the hall from theirs, and Evon missed the convenience of their all being in close quarters. Mrs. Petelter had posted a guard outside Kerensa's room and two more on a rotation below her window. Evon would have been more grateful for this if he hadn't suspected that Mrs. Petelter had made the arrangements the way she might have planned security for a valuable museum exhibit. He passed the guard, who didn't so much as look at him, and rapped on the door. "It's me," he said in response to her query, and let himself in.

Kerensa was standing next to the window, looking down. "They aren't very subtle," she said, and Evon went to her side to see two men in Home Defense cloaks and hats moving in a regular pattern from one end of the inn to the other. She wasn't yet dressed for bed, though her hair was loose and she held a brush in one hand. Her hair gleamed warm gold in the lamplight and Evon was seized with a brief, irrational urge to touch it, to see if it felt like hair or flowing metal. He closed his fist on the impulse.

"I was about to come find you," Kerensa said, turning away from the window, "because I thought you should maybe look at the spell, see if it's different now that I'm...being pulled by it."

"I should have thought of that," Evon said. "Go ahead and sit down."

Kerensa sat on the edge of her bed—there was no chair in the room—and Evon brought the spell into view and froze it. It was glowing more brightly, though not as brightly as the memory of it had in Coreth, and Evon suspected its brightness would increase as they drew closer to the target. She sat very still as he examined it. "There *is* something different," he murmured, "but I can't tell— would you mind standing and turning around?"

"I feel like a life-sized doll," she said with a smile, and did as he asked.

Evon bent to look more closely at the spell-ribbon hovering just above the small of her back. "It's a new set of runes," he said, "but it looks familiar, too. I know I've seen this kind of configuration before." He stepped back and rubbed his forehead. There were five or six others that were written this way, all of them impenetrable to decipherment, and now a new one.... "I need to take some notes," he said, and took her hand and drew her out of the room and down the passage, ignoring the startled noise the guard made when Kerensa, wreathed in blue, went past. In his own room, he rooted through his things for paper and pencil and made a copy of the new runes. He showed it to Kerensa, who'd been craning her neck watching him, then impatiently dismissed *epiria* so he could see her clearly.

"What's the thing around them?" she asked, pointing at a squared-off arc that cradled the runes.

"Something that binds them so they won't be used by the other spells. This is—here," he said, showing her another page. "There are more of these, but I don't know what they do."

"If you turn this one upside down, it looks like a bare tree with two branches, or a T," she said, rotating the page.

"And from this angle, this one looks like the old form for the letter F." Evon snatched the page from Kerensa, then quickly apologized. He rotated the page to several different angles. "They're not runes, they're letters," he exclaimed. "Where did I put—thank you. If they're all oriented the same way, like this—" he rewrote the symbols in a row—"it says...damn. Gibberish."

"No, if you rearrange the symbols, you get the word *fathlon*," Kerensa said, snatching the pencil out of Evon's hand. "I know that word. It means 'enemy.'"

"Among other things, yes—"

"No, you don't understand. It's Murakot's title. In all the oldest stories, he's Murakot Fathlon."

They stared at each other. Evon absently retrieved his pencil. "So what," he said, "is a name out of Alvorian myth doing in this spell?"

"You said it was old. Could it be *that* old? A thousand years?"

"I don't see why not, given all the other impossibilities it contains. Including this one. The spell becomes active, and an ancient name for Murakot suddenly appears? It makes no sense."

"What if the other ones are names too? Alvor and the rest, maybe?"

Evon scrabbled through his papers. "You do these. I'll tackle these ones."

Piercy found them that way, seated side by side on Evon's bed, scribbling and rotating pages. "This is as cozy a scene of domestic intellectuality as I have ever seen. I take it there has been a breakthrough?"

"Yes, though not quite what I hoped for," Evon said. "We found names embedded in the spell, and one of them is an old title for Murakot."

"So is the spell an Alvorian conspiracist, too?"

"Unfortunately, no. We were hoping to find Alvor's name, or his companions' names, or *any* names related to the myth, but there's nothing."

"Except we did find names," Kerensa said, laying down her

pencil. "Just nothing we recognize. Leandrie and Minta, Danior and Wadley."

"And Haderon," Evon said. "They at least confirm that the spell is about a thousand years old. People in those days didn't use surnames, just words indicating where they were from. Like O Dell or Der Lake."

"I'm so disappointed. I was really hoping Alvor might've had something to do with the spell," Kerensa said. Then, indignantly, she added, "But I would be so *furious* if he had!"

"Some progress is better than nothing, given what little time you may have left, Evon," Piercy said. "There must be some way to determine to whom those names belong."

"What do you mean, what little time?" Kerensa asked.

Piercy looked at Evon. "You didn't tell her."

"This distracted me."

"Tell me what?"

Evon said, "Miss Elltis has recalled me to the city. I'm to return as soon as the Home Defense magicians arrive here."

"What? You can't go!" Kerensa stood, knocking papers and pencil to the floor.

"I'll try not to, but if Home Defense tries to press the issue, I may not have much choice."

"I'll refuse to cooperate," Kerensa said. "I'll run away. You already said I was hard to find. I can be even harder to find if I try."

"Kerensa—"

"I'm serious. I absolutely won't have anything to do with a bunch of magicians who don't care anything about me except that I've got this spell bound up around me. If Mrs. Petelter wants this spell so badly, she'll have to do as I say."

"Kerensa, Mrs. Petelter has no interest in what you want or anything you might have to say," Piercy said. "She has a task to accomplish and you are nothing more than an obstacle to her getting what she wants. If she has even the slightest notion that you might possibly be considering flight, she will lock you in your room with a guard to watch you at every moment. If you fight her, she will tie you to a chair in that locked room and risk the devastation that will result."

"But—" Kerensa's jaw clenched. "I am not a *thing*," she said. Evon couldn't tell if she was close to tears or shouting, but her voice was hoarse and her eyes in their too-smooth mask furious.

"I'm not gone yet," he said, "and we're looking for a way for me to stay. Let's not worry about it until the time comes."

"Won't Miss Elltis notice if you don't show up soon? Those magicians can't be more than a day away."

"I think I quit her employ yesterday." Saying it was like a load off his chest he didn't know he was carrying.

"You didn't! Evon...."

"Not officially. But I do not intend to obey her instructions, which is essentially the same thing."

"But—I can't let you do that!"

"I know I've told you that Evon is the most stubborn man I know," Piercy drawled. "When he sets his mind to a thing, there is very little short of an act of Gods that can change it. And he has gotten the bit between his teeth with this one."

"And I don't desert my friends," Evon added, not happy at how Piercy had made him sound. He wouldn't have left Elltis and Company merely for the sake of an intellectual problem; he was doing it for Kerensa's sake.

"Oh, you most certainly desert your friends," Piercy objected hotly. "You deserted this friend one sweltering summer night ten years ago, when he was unfortunately detained by the housekeeper during a daring raid on the Houndston pantry. She was three inches shorter than I and gave me a hiding that had me standing up for a week."

"You certainly whined about it enough. I don't desert my friends except for Piercy," Evon said with a smile, but Kerensa didn't respond in kind. She walked to the window and looked down.

"It's like they know where I am," she said. "They march under these windows too." She looked back at Evon, her lips trembling. "What next? Piercy loses his position because Mrs. Petelter thinks he isn't detached enough? At what point do they decide the simplest thing is to cut me apart and see what part of my body this damned spell is tethered to?"

"Kerensa," Evon began.

She cut him off. "None of us has any power over this thing, do we? I'm going to bed now, and I'm going to pray to the Twins that those magicians get permanently lost. Maybe the Gods will listen to me now that I'm in their city. It's not as if they ever have before." She pushed past Evon and Piercy to the door. "And I'm not promising I won't run away. If I do, don't follow me." The door slammed behind her.

Evon walked to the window and leaned on the sill. Below, the Home Defense agents stopped in their paths to speak to one another. By the gestures, one needed to relieve himself. "I've already let her down," he said.

"You've done more for her than anyone else," Piercy said. "I've never seen you come so close to tearing yourself apart over anything like this before."

"And it's not enough."

"It's not over yet, dear fellow."

"It *is* over, Piercy, it was over the minute Miss Elltis told me to return." Evon went to sit on his bed and covered his eyes with one hand. Then he sighed and stood to gather the papers Kerensa had scattered. "I'm not tired. Do you want me to go to the taproom so you can sleep?"

"You'll never be able to concentrate down there. All the Home Defense agents are in there having an argument I'm not sure even they know the purpose of. I can sleep with the light on." Piercy yawned and began removing his clothes. "Try not to exhaust yourself. We'll need to make an early start."

Evon turned the lamp as low as he could bear it and sat on his bed, spreading out his notes. Knowing that those grouped symbols were names changed his perspective. If these five were names, then the surrounding runes...the names were like signatures, binding the larger parts of the spell. He found a piece of clean paper—he was so tired of looking for paper—and scrawled out the five names. They had to be the magicians who'd created the spell, and he was a fool for not realizing before that a spell of this complexity could never have been devised by only one magician, however powerful the magician. Haderon, creator of the resurrection spell. Minta, creator of Kerensa's immunity to fire, and Leandrie, responsible for Kerensa's being drawn to the next victim. And Wadley, whose tangle of runes caused the spell to activate when it reached its victim. What Danior's work did, Evon wasn't certain, but it had to be the fire—there was nothing left.

Now, the word *fathlon*. Enemy. It had other meanings, but none so accurate. Evon held his notes close to his eyes. He was going to go blind from eyestrain one of these days. There was a marker each name had in common that he was fairly sure indicated a proper noun. If Kerensa was right—and no one knew more about Alvorian myth than she did, he was certain—the word's appearance in the spell was meant to indicate *the* Enemy, Murakot. Evon chewed his pencil and made a face at its bitter taste. Murakot. The spell was old enough that it could have been contemporary with him. But even Evon, with his limited knowledge of history, knew that no one had ever attempted to kill Murakot with a spell of this magnitude.

He needed an expert.

"Where are you going?" Piercy muttered.

"I just need to discover something. Go to sleep." He slipped out of the room and went down the hall to where the guard drowsed in front of Kerensa's door. The guard came to attention and glowered at him.

"She's asleep," he said.

"She's not asleep yet. I need to talk to her." He reached past the guard to rap on the door.

"Mrs. Petelter doesn't approve of hanky-panky," the guard said.

"Just talking. No hanky and no panky." Evon remembered that fall of golden hair and wondered if thinking about running his hands through it met Mrs. Petelter's definition. He blinked hard to rid himself of the vision. *Never mind how attractive she is. You're supposed to be helping her.*

The door opened a crack. "I need to talk to you," Evon said to the sliver of Kerensa's face that was visible. "About Alvor."

Kerensa opened the door wider. "Tell me you're not looking for another bedtime story," she said.

"This is important."

"All right." She held the door open for him, then shut it, leaving both of them in darkness. "Don't move, I'll get the light," she said, and after a moment in which she bumped into something and swore softly, light kindled and grew in the lamp beside her bed. Kerensa was in her nightdress and had her hair braided up. She sat on the bed. "Did you learn something?"

"I hope to. Are there any stories of someone making a spell to kill Murakot?"

"Is *that* what you think this spell is?"

"It's old and I think you're right that 'Fathlon' in the spell means Murakot. And it's definitely targeting Fathlon, whoever that is."

Kerensa swung her legs up onto the bed and sat with her back against the headboard, her knees pulled up to her chest. "There are no stories like that," she said. "Nothing like that is even hinted at. Maybe that's because it's *Alvorian* myth, and that would be — I mean, even Dania never made a spell this complicated. So if it's really meant to kill Murakot, it would have been made by — "

" — Some magician, or magicians, no one ever heard of," Evon finished. "But Murakot's dead, isn't he? There aren't any legends about him returning the way there are about Alvor?"

"Definitely dead," Kerensa said. "There's one really gruesome story about what they did to his body that I wish I didn't know. It was what the Four Talismans were for, to defeat Murakot because he couldn't be killed by normal means."

"If that's what this spell was for, it would explain why the fire is so potent. I can't imagine anyone coming back from it. Except — "

"I know," Kerensa said tonelessly. "Don't apologize, Evon, this is just the way things are."

Evon sat at the far end of the bed. "I'm sorry," he said. "For everything."

"I'm sorry, too," she said. "You're as trapped by this as I am, though in your case at least you chose to be here."

"I'm not leaving," he insisted.

"Even if I tell you to?"

"Even then."

She smiled. "Piercy's right. You're too stubborn for your own good."

"I hope I'm stubborn enough for *your* good." He leaned back against the bedpost. "So why is this spell trying to kill someone who's a thousand years dead?" he mused. "Tell me about Murakot. What was he like?"

"Oh...he's the model for every villain of every melodrama written in the last thousand years. Pure evil. Liked to watch people suffer. Destroyed things just because he could, sometimes even when the destruction went against his own interests. I think he's the least believable part of the stories. Nobody's *that* evil."

"Except the Despot," Evon said, and stopped. They looked at each other. "No, the spell is clearly targeting Murakot, not the Despot. And you said there was no way Murakot could be back from the dead."

"Could his soul have been resurrected? No, that was what Wystylth's Claw was for, to pin Murakot to the Underworld, never to return."

"Maybe it means Murakot's spiritual successor? If he...what did you just think of?"

Kerensa wore a strange, distant expression. "There *is* one story," she said, "but it's not really part of the lore. The woman who told it to me said it was a late addition to the canon and most people wouldn't call it Alvorian myth. It was about Murakot and his shadow, or rather his other shadow, because according to this story he had two. One of them was a normal shadow and it did what all shadows do, show the way toward the Gods, because if you can see your shadow then you know which way to turn to face the light. But the other shadow pointed where Murakot was already inclined to go, into dark places, and it taught him strange magics and protected him against his enemies. The story says, when Alvor came to kill Murakot, he had two shadows, but when Murakot was dead, only one remained. It's sort of a horror story, I think. You know—is Murakot's shadow still out there, looking for someone new to whisper evil to. I thought it sounded made-up, myself." She didn't sound very certain now.

"It fits, though," Evon said. He was thinking so furiously that his voice sounded to him like it was coming from very far away. "If the 'Enemy' isn't Murakot, but something that was riding him—"

"Evon, that's ridiculous. You can't build a theory on one story that isn't even part of the lore."

"Can't I? Kerensa, the target word is clear and we're both certain Murakot isn't alive now. You're being drawn gradually south, in the direction the Despot's armies are camped. And you tell me there's a possibility that Murakot had some...entity...guiding him." He leaped to his feet and began pacing. "Oh, by the Twins, Kerensa—this all started a year ago, and that's when the Despot began to make headway in his conquest. It's when he stopped caring about doing anything but razing the lands he captured. He *changed* just about a year ago."

"You're serious."

"Deadly serious. And I think I can prove it. It's going to take a complicated spell—damn it, it's going to take *forever* now that we have to be on the road, never mind if the magicians get here and interrupt me—no, if you let them get caught up in examining you, they'll leave me alone—"

"Evon," Kerensa said, "stop pacing and take a deep breath." She went to where he stood restlessly in the center of the room. "Can you start now?"

Evon looked at her, surprised. She seemed more animated than she'd been all evening. "Aren't you sleepy? I've kept you up far too late."

"When you're so close to another breakthrough? I wouldn't be able to sleep now if I tried. What can I do to help?"

Evon thought. *More notes, and material components....* "Think of something physical that might represent Murakot, and the Despot," he said. "We don't have anything of theirs that might stand in for them in the spell, so it has to be something with...emotional resonance. I have to get things from my room, but I'll be right back." He grabbed her by the shoulders and kissed her forehead. "This could work," he said with a grin, and dashed out of her room, bumping the guard and ignoring the epithet the man spat in his direction.

Piercy was soundly asleep, so Evon moved as quietly as he could, gathering paper and pencils and snatching up a handful of material components: his pen knife, a coin from the detritus littering Piercy's bedside table, a piece of coal from the hod, his quizzing glass. He dropped to his knees and reached far back under the dressing table with a pencil to gather up cobwebs in a soft ball. It would—

Suddenly, it was daylight. Evon blinked. It took effort, as if something were pressing down on his eyelids. He blinked again. His arm was stretched out straight under the dressing table, and he couldn't turn his head. He could feel his knees pressing into the rough wooden floor, but his hands and his face felt numb, and the things he'd held were scattered on the floor around him. Paralysis. His thoughts were as numb as his face. He couldn't remember what he'd been doing or why he'd had to do it on the floor. He tried to move and discovered that his left leg and arm were both free from the paralysis. He pushed off from the floor and managed to roll onto his back. The ceiling was painted the same light blue as the walls, the exposed rafters stained almost black, and a crack like the silhouette of a mountain ridge ran between two of the beams. With a little rocking, he managed to roll onto his side facing Piercy, who was also awake and seemed to be in the same condition Evon was in. He said something Evon couldn't understand because his mouth barely moved. Evon flexed his jaw. "See if your legs or arms work," he said, more intelligibly than Piercy. Piercy blinked once and began to stretch his legs.

Evon stretched his left arm and managed to reach his right leg, and began massaging it. Something about this disturbed him, but he couldn't remember why. Obviously someone had attacked him and Piercy, but why? He would feel like a fool when he finally remembered. His right leg began to twitch on its own, and he concentrated his efforts on his right arm. At some point, his neck loosened, and he rotated it gingerly. Paralysis didn't leave you stiff once it had passed, the way you would be if you'd fallen asleep in such an awkward position, but it did take time to recover from.

Kerensa had recovered quickly from *desini cucurri*, back in Inveros—

Oh no.

"No, no, no, no," he chanted. Memory came back in a rush. He rolled onto his hands and knees and pushed himself up with the aid of Piercy's bed. Piercy sat up and flexed both his legs. "What's wrong?" he asked, still mumbling.

"It's morning, that's what's wrong," Evon said, and hobbled out of the room. From his doorway, the guard at the end of the hall appeared to be asleep. As Evon drew nearer he saw that the man was actually very dead, his throat slit and blood drenching the front of his coat and speckling the wall with rust-brown spatters. The door to Kerensa's room was ajar, but he pushed it open anyway. The bedclothes were rumpled. The lamp on the side table still burned. Kerensa was gone.

Speculatus.

1 2

$\mathcal{E}$von stumbled back down the hall, taking a wide path around the dead guard. "They've taken her," he said.

Piercy stopped rubbing the back of his neck. "How long ago?"

"I—let me think. Around ten o'clock last night." He swung his still slightly numb right arm up until his hand caught hold of his watch. "It's eight-thirty. Over ten hours. Piercy, they could be anywhere in ten hours."

"Evon, calm down. You can track her, remember? They can't have gotten that far away."

"Right." He took a deep breath through his nostrils. Kerensa's smoky scent tickled at his nose, faint but still distinct. "The guard is dead. We should see if Mrs. Petelter is all right."

"I notice you're not worried about Terantis," Piercy said as they left the room.

"I'm not so callous as to wish him dead, but I wouldn't cry many tears over him."

Once in the hallway, Evon could hear the noise of several people arguing, and doors slamming, and occasionally the sound of boots running. On their way down the narrow back stairs, they met one of the agents, who was limping and whose face seemed to sag a little from being paralyzed on one side. "Get back to your room," she said, though it came out as "Et ack to or oom."

"The guard is dead. Kerensa is gone. Where is Mrs. Petelter?" Evon said.

One of the agent's eyes widened, and she shoved past them without saying another word. Evon and Piercy continued their descent and found the hall below full of people. Some of them leaned against the wall, massaging their necks or arms, while some sat on the floor being helped by their fellows. Evon and Piercy went to Mrs. Petelter's door, which was open.

"See if anyone else is missing," Mrs. Petelter was saying to an agent as they entered. One arm hung limp from her shoulder, and she leaned heavily on her dressing table with the other, her leg folded beneath her. Her usual expression of placidity had been replaced by one of frustration and anger. She saw them, and her frown deepened. "Where's the girl?"

"*Kerensa* has been taken by Speculatus," Evon said. He bit back *And what a fine job you did guarding her*. His position was still precarious; no sense antagonizing Mrs. Petelter further.

Mrs. Petelter cursed. "They came upon us unawares," she said. "The guards outside were lax and they paid for that laxity with their lives. I had no idea Speculatus had magicians capable of casting a spell to blanket an entire building. Everyone in this place last night was paralyzed. *Everyone.* Who can defend against something like that?" She sounded as if she were preparing to report on this to her superiors and was looking for some way to excuse her complete failure. If Kerensa hadn't been in danger thanks to her, Evon might have felt sorry for Mrs. Petelter.

"Was anyone else killed?" Piercy asked, and Evon knew him well enough to guess that he was trying very hard not to say *I told you so*.

Mrs. Petelter shook her head. "We don't know yet. Her guard?"

"Dead," Piercy said, "though I'm not sure why, since he would have been paralyzed with the rest of us. Possibly they intended to make sure of him."

Mrs. Petelter rubbed the inside of her right elbow fiercely. "Our priority now is getting everyone accounted for and mobile again.

Then we will wait for the magicians to arrive in a few hours. I have no intention of confronting Speculatus until we have magic enough to counter theirs."

"We need to leave *now*," Evon insisted. Anxiety clenched his stomach. "Every hour we wait is an hour in which they will be trying to extract her secrets. They killed at least three men last night, including one who was no danger to them; do you think they'll be any gentler with her?"

"Mr. Lorantis, I have no idea of your magical capabilities aside from what Mr. Faranter keeps telling me, but I note that you were paralyzed along with the rest of us. I have no other magicians of professional level. How much success do you think you alone will have against whoever cast that spell last night?"

"It wouldn't have been one person, it would have been several, working together...." Evon's voice trailed off as he realized he was proving Mrs. Petelter's point for her.

"If you wish to be of assistance, help some of these people recover," Mrs. Petelter said. "Have patience. You are far too agitated to think clearly. I've already spoken to the magicians and they will arrive shortly. Then we can decide what to do."

THE MAGICIANS ARRIVED FOUR EXCRUCIATING HOURS LATER, while Evon was in his room failing to work out the spell he'd conceived the night before. Every footstep below jerked him out of his concentration. He didn't have the right components for this. He didn't know what he was looking for. Proving the existence of some...creature...he knew nothing about, could barely imagine—he must be out of his mind. But he needed something to keep his imagination from circling back around to Odelia, psychotic Odelia, trying to break Kerensa with every vicious tool she had in her arsenal. Kerensa was strong. He shouldn't be this worried about her. Odelia couldn't beat her. But Odelia could try, and Evon knew her too well to believe that she'd confine her torture to mere words. And Odelia must have a superior.... He went back to shuffling things on his bed, coal, coin, webbing, pen knife. He needed something to represent the Despot, something that could be easily divided...where could he find clay in this town?

"They're here," Piercy said, sticking his head in the door. "You're not going to like this. Caris Quendester is with them."

"Mistress Quendester," Evon said, frozen in the act of rising from the bed. He sank back down onto it. "Piercy, have I offended the Gods in some way?"

"No more than usual." Piercy looked grim. "It's always possible she's forgiven you."

"I humiliated her in front of the advanced spellbuilding class. Mistress Quendester doesn't forgive easily."

"True, but she's also rational. She has to see that your skills are essential to this endeavor."

They looked at each other for a long moment. "She'll send me back to Matra," Evon said. "Piercy, I can't go back."

"I know." Piercy pursed his lips. "No, wait." He grinned. "You're an idiot."

"I am? Thank you so much for the boost to my confidence."

"They can't send you home," Piercy said slowly, as if Evon were a very slow child, "because they need you to find Kerensa."

Evon suddenly felt ten pounds lighter. "You're right," he said. "There's no way Speculatus didn't cast an obscuration on their path. But no one knows about the scenting spell."

"Come downstairs, and for the Gods' sake be polite to Mistress Q.," Piercy said. "She can still make your life a misery, and you know how easily she gets under your skin, dear fellow."

Evon shrugged. "She's proud and arrogant and not as good as she claims to be. I can't help but want to show her up."

"Well, you'll do that with the scenting spell alone. Try to pretend that you are a mature adult for once."

"That's fine advice coming from you, a grown man still playing pranks on his co-workers. One of those guards told me what you did to the back door at your headquarters. She seemed concerned that I know exactly what kind of reprobate I put my trust in."

"You didn't tell her that was a jape I learned from you?"

"Of course not. *I* look like a mature adult."

Evon said this as they came out of the stairs and almost ran into a tall, thin woman with red hair piled high on her head. She wore a dark green gown with a full skirt and carried a white baton about a foot in length. She looked at Evon with a sneer and said, "Lorantis. I was told you were in the middle of this debacle. I'm not surprised."

"Mistress Quendester, good morning," Evon said with a small bow, barely more than a nod of the head. "I didn't realize you worked for Home Defense."

"I don't," Mistress Quendester said. "Home Defense put out a call for the best magicians to assist in this little endeavor."

Then why did you come? Evon thought. "I'm grateful for the assistance," he lied. "How many magicians are there?"

"Ten," Mistress Quendester said. "Not all of the same caliber, but all competent enough."

A man came down the stairs behind Evon and Piercy, holding a bundle of dark cloth. "Mistress Quendester, I believe we can begin," he said. "This belonged to the girl."

Evon realized it was Kerensa's dress, *she's only in her nightgown, she must be freezing,* and was filled with unaccountable rage that anyone would handle her things so carelessly. "You...are trying a finding spell," he said.

"Yes, Lorantis, when someone is lost that is indeed what we do," Mistress Quendester said. "You can observe if you want, but I don't think your assistance will be needed." She accepted the dress from the man and swept off down the hall. Evon hurried behind her.

"Mistress Quendester, that won't be necessary, I can already track Miss Haylter," he said, but Mistress Quendester didn't pause. "I'd be happy to show you the spell—it's really quite effective—"

"Lorantis, I'm not in the mood for your experimental spellcraft," she said without turning her head. "I'm sure our poor finding spell isn't up to your high standards, but I hope you'll do us all the courtesy of not criticizing our work. As if you could help yourself."

Oh, she has most definitely not forgiven me. And when the finding spell failed, and he demonstrated the scenting spell, she would look even more like a fool. Well, the Underworld take her. He'd tried. He followed her into the taproom, where nearly a dozen other men and women waited, some seated at the tables, others standing. He didn't recognize any of them, but he estimated that his and Piercy's entrance into the room halved the average age of the group. None of them paid him any attention. He went to a corner of the room and leaned against the wall. Piercy joined him, carefully studying his fingernails in a way that told Evon he was actually looking forward to the upcoming spectacle. Evon's anxiety returned. This was a waste of time. He thought, not for the first time, of simply taking his horse and riding off to find Kerensa, but Mrs. Petelter had a good point; his abilities and his determination alone would not be enough to rescue her. He was being irrational. So he stood, and stewed, and tried to run over possibilities for the new spell in his head. It would have to isolate the entity—wait, he could use part of Kerensa's spell for that, *if she were here, if she weren't in enemy hands. Stop thinking about it.* The spell would have to locate it—ironic, that he was thinking of a new location spell while Mistress Quendester and her cronies were about to fail at theirs. He definitely needed clay, and possibly ash—

"Join hands," Mistress Quendester said in that pompous tone that still irritated Evon to the point of wanting to prove her wrong even when she was right. She never failed to make him wish he'd gone to university and earned the title of Master, if only to force her to stop sneering at him. The group formed a circle around Kerensa's dress, lying on one of the small tables like a shed skin. Mistress Quendester stood just inside the circle, her baton raised. "All focus," she added, and the room went silent except for the sound of Evon's pulse racing, so loud he was surprised no one else could hear it.

Mistress Quendester took in a deep breath and let it out. "*Reperto Kerensa Haylter,*" she intoned, waving her baton in an intricate and unnecessarily detailed rune that meant "uncover," and a speck of light began to glow in the air just above the dress. It grew until it was nearly the size of an apple, spinning slowly on its horizontal axis like a roast on a spit. Then it drifted in the direction of the eastern wall. Evon saw one of the magicians smile. The smile faded when the glowing ball halted just past the circle and dissolved into specks of light. There was a moment of silence, then the magicians began arguing loudly with each other, unclasping hands to punctuate their sentences with broad, vehement gestures.

"*Silence,*" Mistress Quendester said, though she had to repeat herself twice more to command everyone's attention. "We'll try again. Better focus this time, everyone, and I think we should all cast at the same time."

Piercy poked Evon in the side. Evon said, "Mistress Quendester, may I—"

"No one is interested in your opinion, Lorantis," Mistress Quendester said, not bothering to look at him.

"Lorantis?" said one of the magicians, a portly man with strands of hair combed over his balding head. "Not Evon Lorantis? Aren't you Tifana Elltis's boy wonder?"

"I am Evon Lorantis, yes," Evon said, fuming over the "boy wonder," "and I think Speculatus has cast an obscuration on their path. However, when I found Miss Haylter before, I used a different method they don't know to protect against."

"I think I told you we're not interested in your experiments," Mistress Quendester said.

"I'd like to hear about it, Caris," the balding man said. "He did find the girl, after all, and I don't like the idea of the weapon being in Speculatus's hands any longer than it has to be. Speak, Mr. Lorantis."

Evon was suddenly the center of ten magicians' intense interest. "I—the spell has altered Miss Haylter's body in a way that gives off a particular...olfactory residue. I isolated the scent and used it to track her."

"Like a dog," Mistress Quendester scoffed.

"Yes, Mistress Quendester, if you want to put it that way," Evon said, feeling his irritation threatening to spill over, "but it works. I can find Miss Haylter and I can lead you all to her."

"Why not simply teach us the spell?" asked another magician, an elderly woman with a sharp-nosed face and short white hair.

"We don't have time for that," Evon lied. It probably wouldn't take more than an hour to teach them all the spell—longer, in Mistress Quendester's case—but he wasn't going to give them any excuse to send him away. "If you're willing to follow me, we can leave immediately."

"I think you should be able to prove that your spell works," Mistress Quendester said. "Your lack of experience doesn't fill me with confidence."

Evon had to pause for a moment; it was either that or scream obscenities at the woman. "I can't prove it except by finding Miss Haylter," he said finally. "But we can either sit here and watch your further attempts at a finding spell fail, or we can start the search we should have started the instant she was discovered missing."

Mistress Quendester's face went white with fury, but before she could speak, the elderly woman said, "Don't be testy about this, young man. We got here as quickly as we could. And now we're going to leave as quickly as possible."

"Thank you," Evon said. "Ma'am, if you would tell Mrs. Petelter your decision, and we should all meet in the stable yard as soon as we've made whatever preparations you think necessary."

The woman's mouth quirked into a sideways smile. "You're very decisive, Mr. Lorantis," she said. "A desirable trait in a magician, though not always a comfortable one for those around you." She glanced around the room. "Gather your things and find your mounts. We leave in half an hour—if that's sufficiently speedy for you, Mr. Lorantis?"

Evon blushed. "Thank you, Mistress—?"

"Belitha Gavranter," the woman said. "And I am interested in learning your scenting spell...when we have time." Her tone of voice suggested that she knew what Evon was doing, and approved. It comforted him to think that not all of these magicians were hostile. Mistress Quendester had enough hostility seething within her for all ten of them.

He and Piercy gathered their things, then Evon went and packed Kerensa's bag with what little she possessed. On his way out, he retrieved her discarded dress from the taproom and did his best to roll it up neatly. How women managed to pack their clothes was a mystery to him. He loaded his bag and Kerensa's on his horse, then mounted and wheeled the animal in a slow circle, trying to contain his impatience. The magicians seemed not to feel the urgency. Only a few of them had arrived in the stable yard, and they were standing near their horses but not mounting them. He sniffed the air, taking in a great deep breath, and released it, both trying to calm himself and seeking out Kerensa's scent. There it was, a thin line leading out of the stable yard and to the east. Fifteen hours now, but it was still strong. He once again controlled his impulse to simply ride off after it, Piercy no doubt following his lead even though he would be taking them both into disaster.

"Evon, you're making the horse dizzy. Be still," Piercy said.

Evon looked over at his best friend and a wave of misery hit him, bringing with it a simple realization. "I love her," he said.

"I know," Piercy said, and put a compassionate hand over Evon's. "I've been wondering when you would realize that."

"I—what?"

"I love you like a brother, Evon, but you can be remarkably dense at times," Piercy said, "particularly in matters of the heart. You began falling in love with Kerensa the moment we left Inveros."

Evon stared at his friend, dumbfounded. "I think I would have noticed," he began, and memories of every interaction he'd had with Kerensa played out, all the times he'd been mesmerized by her beauty and quick wit, how often he'd sought her out, and he felt like an idiot. "You're right," he said. "Piercy, we have to find her."

"We will, Evon."

"She's out there, having the Gods know what done to her—"

"You can't help her by stewing about it, dear fellow. She knows you'll follow her. Be patient."

"I've barely known her two weeks and already I can't imagine being without her."

"It happens that way sometimes."

"I can't tell her. What would I say? She's already depending on me to break her free of this spell; learning that I love her would just burden her further, since I know she sees me only as a friend."

"Are you certain of that?"

Evon finally met Piercy's eyes. "How many hours have we spent together in the last several days? I may be dense, but I'm certain she's never once looked at me that way. And suppose I declared my love for her, and she felt she owed me something, and...oh, Piercy, I really must have angered the Gods, that They're tormenting me like this."

The white-haired Mistress Gavranter approached, riding a horse nearly as white as her own hair. "I believe we're all ready, if you'd care to lead out, Mr. Lorantis."

Evon looked around the yard. Ten magicians, twelve Home Defense agents, and Mrs. Petelter and Terantis, the latter looking as if he'd rather stab Evon through the heart than follow him anywhere. He checked the air again, not caring that he looked like a dog casting for scent. "This way," he called out, and led the procession out of the stable yard and into the streets of Belicath.

13

The scent led Evon eastward, through the merchant district where every kind of religious artifact was for sale, icons for the home, medallions and amulets for people, even tiny charms for pets. Evon had never seen the point of outward religious observances, reasoning that the Gods knew how devoted you were without you rattling around weighed down by ugly necklaces, but now he wondered if there wasn't something to the practice. Perhaps he needed an ugly necklace so Belia or Cath, or possibly both, would turn Their attention elsewhere. He certainly felt like Their fool.

He barely heard the clamor of horses' hooves, of people behind him talking as if nothing were wrong. If he'd stayed just minutes longer, he'd have been with her when Speculatus struck. Yes, and he'd still have been helpless, and they'd have cut his throat like they had the guard's. There was nothing he could have done to stop them. All he could do now was reach her as fast as he could, and be prepared to kill as many Speculatus members as got in his way, if that became necessary. If he was capable of killing. He let his nose find the way and set to reviewing spells in his head, practicing gestures for spells he'd learned the theory of in school and never cast.

Defensive spells—Odelia was almost as good as he was, good enough that the difference wouldn't matter if it came to a fight, and he would need to shrug off whatever she cast without slowing down his own casting. He had a feeling he would be facing her; it would fit the way his life was going if he had to fight his nemesis in defense of the woman he loved. He was certain now that the Gods were using him as entertainment, watching from wherever They lived and possibly placing wagers on how it would all turn out.

Kerensa's face emerged from memory, looking the way it had when he'd seen her last, excited and hopeful that he might have found part of the solution. Excited, hopeful, but nothing more, no deeper feeling that might have matched his own. Evon closed his eyes and cursed himself. If the spell didn't exist, would he have been able to court her properly? *If the spell didn't exist, you'd never have met her.*

He let his nose lead him and made himself focus on the new spell, the one that would prove the existence of the entity, and was so engrossed in it that he didn't realize people were calling his name until Piercy said, "Dear fellow, are you certain of the path? Because you seem to have left it behind a quarter of a mile ago."

Evon looked around. The last he'd been aware, they'd passed the eastern gate of Belicath and proceeded along that road. Now, though, he was standing in a treeless, snowblown expanse somewhere well to the north of the road. He sniffed, then turned his horse in a circle, and felt the beginnings of dread.

"I knew it was a mistake to trust him," Mistress Quendester was saying to Mistress Gavranter as both approached him.

"We have a problem," he said. "They've turned northeast. Kerensa—Miss Haylter was being drawn south by the spell. If she ignores the urging, the power builds until it activates on its own. The results are devastating. The first time it happened, Miss Haylter simply stayed in one place, only knowing that following the urge resulted in a death. If she's taken in a direction opposite to the one the spell wants her to take—"

"The process will be accelerated," Mistress Gavranter said, cutting across whatever insult Mistress Quendester was about to fling at him. "Are you certain this northeastern heading is their true route?"

"Yes. Positive."

"Then proceed," the white-haired magician said. "And hurry."

They rode across snowy fields now, Evon taking the most direct route rather than trying to follow the roads. He learned to triangulate the course Speculatus took, cutting across corners, only once having to backtrack to pick up the scent again. Twice they caught sight of the heat shimmer of a magical trap, no doubt Odelia's work, both times before it could go off; Evon guessed they were avoiding dozens more with the route they were taking. Finally they reached the broad highway that led northeast from Belicath to Ostradon and from there all the way to Matra. The scent followed it precisely, and so did they, able to keep up a faster gait on the smoothly paved road. Carriages that would normally have expected the right of way pulled aside for the contingent of horses riding all-out along the highway. Evon leaned forward along his horse's neck and urged it on, chafing at the delays when they had to slow to keep from exhausting the horses. The scent was stronger now, but it was growing dark, and Evon despaired as twilight fell and the trail showed no sign of coming to an end.

"Mr. Lorantis," Mistress Gavranter said, coming up beside him, "we will have to stop for the night. I believe we can make Ostradon in half an hour." She reached out and took his arm, awkwardly because of the motion of both their horses. "I am sorry for the delay, but we *will* find her. Speculatus can't afford to kill her, not and obtain the secret of the fire spell."

Evon looked at her. In the fading light, he thought he saw compassion in her eyes. *Can everyone see how I feel?* "I understand," he said. "I'll see if they went through Ostradon. It makes no sense to continue on tonight."

Mistress Gavranter patted his arm again. "That spell of yours really is remarkable."

"It was hard-won. You're not going to like learning it," he warned her.

She laughed, a delicate bell-like trill much higher pitched than her speaking voice. "I haven't gotten to be this age without learning many things I didn't enjoy. Good luck, Mr. Lorantis." She dropped back into the gloom.

Evon sagged. He'd been so certain they could find her today. Unwanted images tried to rear up in front of his eyes again; he ruthlessly brushed them aside and refused to think of Kerensa alone among her captors. He concentrated so hard on blocking those images that he almost didn't notice that the scent had changed. He stopped and looked around. They were riding through a small forest of pines, heavily laden with snow that the moonlight reflected off, and by that light he saw a smaller road, unpaved, that left the highway going east, toward the mountains. The scent turned to follow that road.

"Wait!" he shouted, and guided his horse a few steps along the road. It was certain. Kerensa had gone this way. He returned to the group and sought out Mistress Gavranter. "It's definitely this way," he told her. "I wish I knew how long ago."

"We're all tired," a thin magician with plump cheeks said. "We should rest in Ostradon and return in the morning. I don't think it's a good idea to face their magicians when we're in this state."

"Mistress Gavranter, we have no idea what's at the end of this road," Evon said, "and by morning they may have moved on again. We have to pursue this."

Mistress Gavranter considered him, his desperation, and said, "Mr. Lorantis, I suggest that you and your friend follow the road until you have a sense of what we face, then join us in Ostradon. Do *not* engage Speculatus if you find them." She gave him a look that said she *did* know exactly why Evon was on this journey and warned him: if you want your woman back, don't be a fool.

"I understand, Mistress Gavranter." They arranged a rendezvous point in Ostradon, and then Piercy and Evon rode off along the side road while the magicians and agents proceeded north. It was even more overgrown than the main road, and dark under the branches where no snow had been able to fall. Evon ducked to avoid a low branch and said, "I'm sorry I dragged you into this."

"Which this? The part where we are riding along in the ebon-black heart of winter's night toward what may be our certain doom, or the part where *I* came to *you* asking for help to find the Fearsome Firemage?"

"All right," Evon said, amused despite himself, "so we did some mutual dragging. But right now I'm beginning to think Mistress Gavranter was right, and we should have waited until morning."

"You needed something to do, and she took pity on you, lovesick fool that you are. And *I* am along to ensure that you do not go racing off to the rescue and get yourself killed by a hundred Speculatus agents."

"Do you really think there are a hundred of them?"

"No. But there might be fifty."

"There couldn't have been that many that took Kerensa, or someone would have noticed—"

They came out of the woods into a wide plain covered in snow that gleamed pale blue in the moonlight. Far ahead, at the end of the road, lay an enormous manor house blazing with light, with a pillared entrance capped with snow and two pointed towers flanking it like a pair of giants protecting a fifty-foot-tall treasure chest. Dark shadows passed in front of its lower windows, sentries making their rounds in well-trodden paths in the snow. The house rose four stories high and was made of red or brown brick; the towers were made of what looked like white stone, though it was hard to tell their true color in the white-yellow light of the magic-lit lamps that burned in every window. Evon looked closer at the sentries. Smaller shadows paced beside them—dogs on leashes. Evon and Piercy looked at one another, then slowly moved their horses back into the comforting concealment of the forest.

"I am not going in there alone," Piercy said, "though I love Kerensa like the sister I wish I had in place of my own."

"I agree," Evon said. "Much as it kills me to." He dug in his inner pocket for his mirror. "I'll tell Mistress Gavranter what we've found. Then we'll make a plan."

∼

"WE AREN'T AT OUR BEST, AFTER RIDING ALL AFTERNOON," Mistress Gavranter said. They were once again gathered at the intersection where the smaller road left the main road. Evon saw disgruntlement and open annoyance on several faces. He had to find a way to convince them.

"It's dark," he said, "which gives us an advantage we won't have come the morning. And the longer we delay, the more time they'll have to improve their defenses. They know we'll come after them, but they won't expect us here so quickly—they have to believe their traps and obscurations slowed us down."

"I, for one, am not keen on the idea of that weapon remaining in Speculatus hands one second longer than it has to," the balding magician said. "Belitha, I know we're all tired, but we're none of us *that* exhausted that we can't perform."

"I disagree," Mistress Quendester said. "We ought not to attempt to retrieve the weapon until we're physically and mentally at our peak."

"They won't have more than five or six magicians," Evon said. "And they won't be expecting us."

"Mistress Gavranter, I think we should attempt an assault," Mrs. Petelter said, surprising Evon, who'd become accustomed to the idea that Home Defense had become irrelevant now that the magicians were here. "We've heard rumors of a Speculatus stronghold in this area, and it sounds as though this is it. We'd be wasting our advantage if we didn't strike now."

Mistress Gavranter looked from one person to another and ended with her gaze on Evon. "How certain are you about the number of magicians?" she asked.

"Ah...well, it would take five magicians working together to blanket a building the size of the inn with *desini cucurri* that creates a paralysis lasting ten hours," he said. He'd done the calculations in his head on the road, desperately trying to keep his mind off Kerensa. "And Piercy tells me—you can confirm this, Mrs. Petelter—that Speculatus doesn't have many magicians as a whole. He said it was why they recruited our old classmates so intensely. So it's unlikely they would have more magicians than they needed for that *desini cucurri.* And there are no magical defenses on that manor, no shields or anything like that, so they don't have enough magicians to spare maintaining them. So I estimate no more than seven magicians, and more likely only six."

"I agree with your reasoning," Mistress Gavranter said, "but I'm concerned about your report about the non-magical defenses and the location. It will be difficult to get close without being seen and losing our advantage."

"Piercy is working on that. He's a sneaky bast— sorry, a sneaky fellow when he wants to be. He's examining the patrol pattern and looking for a hole we can exploit. And, forgive me, but shouldn't a group of magicians this powerful be able to create a few camouflaging shields?"

"Camouflage, yes, but it's hard to move a group this size quietly."

"My agents have training for situations exactly like this," Mrs. Petelter said. In the moonlight, her face had the look of someone determined to prove herself competent.

"Then—"

"*Evon Lorantis* eloqua," a tiny voice in Evon's pocket said. Evon pulled it out and repeated, *"Eloqua,"* and the mirror cleared to show most of Piercy's face.

"They're sloppy," he whispered. "The guards' paths don't overlap, and there's one fellow who takes long breaks in a corner out of the wind. We can approach from that side, but there's still the problem of crossing the field."

"We have a plan for that," Evon said, catching Mistress Gavranter's eye and receiving a nod from her. "Wait there and we'll join you shortly."

"Your attention, please," Mistress Gavranter said. "We'll be moving forward on horseback, then proceeding to the manor on foot. When we reach the edge of the forest, we—the magicians—will cast *spexa* to determine the interior layout of the manor, then fall back to allow Mrs. Petelter's people an unimpeded view of the building. Please have patience; this is a complicated...operation, I believe you call it, Mrs. Petelter?"

"Are you sure this is wise, Belitha?" said someone near the back.

"I am sure it is the wisest option of a host of suboptimal ones," she replied. "Any other questions? Then let us proceed. Mr. Lorantis, to me."

Evon brought his horse alongside Mistress Gavranter's. "I assume you know the young woman well," she said drily, and Evon flushed. "Can you cast *spexa* on the move, so to speak?"

"I've never used it except on spectacles and the odd wall and door," Evon said.

"Then I'll have to teach you. It will help us to have a sense for where she is in the manor, if it's as large as you say, and it's likely Speculatus's magicians will have cast abjurations on the manor itself to prevent our using it on the physical building." Mistress Gavranter dropped her voice to a near-whisper, and she added, "I suspect those magicians are of better than average capability, if they are able to work so well together as to cast *desini cucurri* over an entire building. Some of our magicians are not ones who do well under pressure, so I hope they will stand firm when it comes to a fight."

"They seemed to work well together casting the finding spell. It was not their fault that it failed."

"Working well together when someone is trying to break both your arms at once is very different." Mistress Gavranter grimaced. "Now, *spexa*. When you draw the runes on a door, you think of *spexa* as creating a hole through which you may see. To cast *spexa* on air, you must believe the opposite: that *spexa* reveals a hole that is already there, that has always existed...."

It was a strange way of casting the spell, and the first time Evon succeeded he nearly fell off his horse because *spexa* was not so much a hole as it was a tunnel that led into emptiness. They were nearly to the edge of the woods before Evon cast the spell properly and had a good look at his bathroom back home. The image was so clear he thought he might be able to reach out and pull the chain on the cistern. He dismissed *spexa* and sat back heavily in the saddle, swallowing hard to rid himself of the cloying taste of strawberries it left in his mouth. Learning a new spell was exhausting, but it was also interesting and had the side benefit of keeping him distracted.

"You *are* good," Mistress Gavranter said. "Eight minutes. I thought perhaps your reputation was exaggerated."

"Thank you," Evon said. "I didn't know I had a reputation."

"If you tire of working for Tifana Elltis, see me first. I'm certain I can find employment for you."

"Again, thank you. I may need to take you up on that offer soon."

"Tifana isn't treating you fairly?"

"She wants me back in Matra. I'm not going."

"I see." Mistress Gavranter glanced over at her magicians, who were dismounting and making various preparations for spellcasting. "Let us see if we can find your young lady."

"Her name is Kerensa, and she's my friend," Evon said curtly.

Mistress Gavranter raised her eyebrows at him, but said nothing more. "To find a person, you should know the person well enough to picture her in your mind. Think of that image, keep it close at hand, and cast the spell."

All day and all evening Evon had tried *not* to think of Kerensa, but now he allowed himself to remember her as he'd seen her last, in her white nightdress, her hair braided and her eyes shining with the excitement of finally learning what had driven her all the long way from her home. He traced runes in the air and said, "*Spexa,*" and the air parted like an oculus and he saw her, close enough to touch. She lay on the bare wooden floor of an empty room, her back to him, her hair still braided but untidy. Someone's feet were in the circle of his vision, booted feet that paced near Kerensa's head. Evon made an involuntary noise of protest. "I can't see her face," he said.

"Take *spexa* by the sides as if it were a mirror, and turn it," Mistress Gavranter instructed, and Evon did so. The image wobbled along with his concentration as he felt a cool, soapy *something* in his hands, though he knew *spexa* was merely a construct of his mind. He turned it and imagined walking it around Kerensa until he could see her face. It was unmarked, but her hands were bound and as he watched he saw her body and face contort with a scream. The *spexa* fell apart; he sat on the horse, hands clenched, shaking with fury.

"Again," Mistress Gavranter told him. "Time enough for anger when we face our enemy. This will go much faster if you can locate her. Observe." She pointed at the balding magician and an ordinary-looking woman with intense eyebrows who were gesturing in tandem. *Spexa* sprang up in front of them, positioned where they could look through it at the house. The lens gave the house the appearance of an architect's drawing, the walls invisible, all the rooms laid out in stark black lines as if a child had gone over its bones with a black crayon. No furnishings were visible, and the image was empty of people. "That's the best we can do against their abjurations," Mistress Gavranter continued. "We can find a path to any room in the house, but unless we enter it and lay *spexa* on every door in the manor, we will not know where to look for the young woman. For Kerensa. Try again."

Evon calmed his breathing and cast the spell again. This time, when the image formed, he was looking at her as if standing near her feet. "Take the *spexa* and aim it upward. Find a window," Mistress Gavranter instructed him. Evon grasped the nonexistent handles and swiveled it, and found himself looking at Odelia Cattertis. She was talking to someone out of his sight. She looked bored. The image shook as Evon once again had to gain control of himself. Out of curiosity, he turned the *spexa* to see the person Odelia was talking to.

He saw a tall, broad-shouldered man with a heavy red beard and curly hair that hung past his shoulders. He was dressed in waistcoat and old-fashioned knee breeches, but he looked more like a pirate than a gentleman. He replied to whatever Odelia had said, then scratched his beard and stepped away.

"Can you show him to me?" Mrs. Petelter asked, startling Evon and causing him to briefly lose focus. He nodded and brought the *spexa* around. The man had taken a seat on an old sofa with the stuffing coming out of the cushion. He picked at the stuffing with his thumb and forefinger and with his other hand drew out a gold watch and consulted it. He said something, then leaned back and crossed his legs.

"Rayner Valantis," Mrs. Petelter said. Her voice had an unchar-acteristic eagerness to it. "We've suspected him of any number of illegal activities, but never been able to catch him in the act. This is an unlooked-for boon. We try to capture him, understand?" This last was directed at her people, who nodded their assent.

"We understand, but I can't make any promises, Mrs. Petelter," Mistress Gavranter said. "Magic in combat situations is imprecise at best. Retrieving Miss Haylter—" she glanced at Evon—"is our first priority."

"Yes, I know, Mistress Gavranter," Mrs. Petelter said, but Evon suspected she wasn't listening. She turned away to consult with one of her agents. Evon remembered what he was supposed to be doing and turned the *spexa* toward the walls, looking for a window. The room was on a corner, windows lining two adjacent walls. Evon looked out and saw nothing but fields and then forest, then thought to look down and saw a guard pass by, far below. There were three banks of windows below him, and about fifty feet away from the foundation there was a white boulder next to a lone pine tree.

"Excellent," Mistress Gavranter said. "Upper left corner...that one." The two magicians holding the lens turned it as she directed. Evon dismissed *spexa* and saw, off to the left side of the building, a white boulder with a darkish smudge next to it that might have been a pine tree.

"Plot a route, please," Mistress Gavranter told the two, then indicated that Evon should dismount. She joined him on the ground and beckoned to the rest of the magicians to gather near. "Those of you with combat experience know what to do," she said. "*Frigo* and *forva* only if absolutely necessary. If the weapon is close to triggering, we'll have more fire than we know what to do with. Those without combat training will hold *presadi* as we advance, then guard the rear. Mrs. Petelter?"

"My agents will follow as far as the front doors, then spread out to take on purely mundane attacks so you can save your spells for the other magicians," Mrs. Petelter said.

"Leaving her free to hunt for that Valantis fellow," Piercy said in Evon's ear.

Evon jumped. "Don't be so sneaky," he said irritably.

"If I weren't so sneaky, I'd have been caught seven times over by now."

Evon retrieved Kerensa's bag from his horse and tied it securely to his back. "I'm tired of waiting."

"How fortunate for you," said Mistress Gavranter, "because it is time to go."

14

$\mathcal{C}$ lear, bright moonlight lit the snowy fields with a bluish glow that made everyone look half-dead, eyes shadowed and cheeks hollow and dark. Near the head of their small force, Evon divided his attention between his footing and the half-sphere three feet in front of him, a transparent film that rippled with the movement of the magician who held it, the balding man whose name Evon still didn't know. It was about ten feet tall and thirty feet wide, an awkward burden, and Evon half expected it to be torn from the magician's hands like a kite in a strong wind. But the magician wielded it with dexterous ease, and the fifteen people who walked behind it had no trouble staying within its shelter. Beside them, the woman with the aggressive eyebrows held an identical shield protecting Mistress Gavranter's group.

"This makes me extremely uncomfortable," Piercy whispered. His boots, like Evon's, made no noise on the crusted snow; unlike the rest of the party, wrapped in a bubble of *desini cleperi*, only their boots and Mistress Gavranter's shoes were so muffled. No spells could be cast from within the area of silence, and while it was possible to extract yourself from it, that took time. So Evon and Mistress Gavranter remained unaffected, to cancel the spell when they reached the manor. Evon had excluded Piercy from *desini cleperi* as well, since he already moved like a cat and would need to be able to alert Evon to hidden dangers. "We ought not to be able to simply walk up to the manor shielded only by a filmy bit of nothing. It's hard to believe they can't see us."

"The most they can see is a ripple in the air, and in this light, even that won't be visible unless someone is very, very lucky. And they'll only hear our movements when we're too close for them to do anything about it."

"I still say it's unnatural."

"If it were natural, it wouldn't be magic."

They were near enough now to see the passing guard as a figure rather than a moving blob against the brightly-lit manor. He and the dog he led crossed in front of the manor's front door, moving toward the left. The dog lifted its head, and Evon cursed mentally, gestured and whispered, *"Olficio retexo."*

The guard said something Evon couldn't make out at this distance, looking down at the dog, whose head moved from side to side, up and down, and it shifted its weight as if coming to alertness. The guard looked around, his eyes passing sightlessly over the invisible crowd, then tugged impatiently at the dog's leash. It strained against the pull for a moment, then, with a movement that in a human would have been a shrug, followed its master. Evon looked at Mistress Gavranter, who gave him a nod of approval. Evon felt like a fool for not remembering the dogs before. Pray the Twins this was the only mistake he'd make tonight.

They slowly approached the front doors, the shielding magicians reshaping their spells to cover the groups from the sides as well as the front. Piercy's observations had paid off; they had timed their approach to coincide with the moment both guards were at opposite ends of the building, around the corners. Piercy slipped out from behind the shield and pressed his ear to the door, nodded, then quietly pushed it open and went inside. Moments later he reappeared and beckoned to them. Evon and Mistress Gavranter dismissed *desini cleperi*, and leading a file of magicians and agents, Evon followed Piercy through the door.

The entrance hall rose two stories into the air and seemed to extend all the way to the back of the house. Red and black tile made a geometric pattern on the floor, a *trompe l'oeil* that made the floor seem creased instead of flat. Creamy pillars marched around the room, supporting a gallery on the second floor from which someone could look down on the entrance or, if they had a very long pole, could tap the vast crystal chandelier hanging from the center of the ceiling. Dark halls led off the room on all sides, and two staircases ascended to the second floor on opposite sides of the hall. The walls were adorned with portraits of dark-bearded men and overweight women, all of whom glared at Evon's intrusion into their territory. The hall was otherwise empty. Evon checked his watch. It was nearly ten o'clock. Twenty-four hours since they'd taken her. He tried not to think about the many delays. Surely she would know he'd come after her. Did she think he'd abandoned her? His stomach was in knots. He realized he couldn't remember the last time he'd eaten—something along the route? He slowed his breathing and tried to concentrate. Time enough for self-recrimination later.

Mrs. Petelter's agents spread out through the room, disappearing down the halls, and Mrs. Petelter waved something that gleamed in Evon's direction before following. A mirror. *Contact me when you've secured the weapon,* she'd said, *and we'll pull out.* He didn't actually believe her. She needed to capture Rayner Valantis to keep from looking like an incompetent, and she wasn't likely to give up on that just because he told her they could leave. But he was willing to go along with the pretense so long as Kerensa was safe.

Mistress Gavranter signaled to Evon to lead the way up the left-hand stairs. No one had argued with her when she'd said Evon would go first; some of them, no doubt, hadn't wanted to be the one to draw enemy fire, and others were convinced by her argument that Kerensa would be more responsive to someone she knew than to strangers grabbing her. He had memorized the route and now took them along the second floor gallery toward the stairs at the back of the building, servants' stairs that bypassed the third floor and took them to the servants' quarters at the top of the manor. He cringed at every noise the magicians made, their heavy breathing and wheezing and one terrifying cough that ought to alert every person in the manor. But no one appeared.

Evon had just turned to Piercy to ask him to look down the next cross-corridor when a door opened and a rectangle of light appeared on the dark red carpet ahead of them. A woman stepped out and saw them. Her mouth opened. *"Desini cucurri!"* Evon said in an urgent whisper, but two other people shouted the same words and the woman fell over in the face of a triple paralysis spell. Inside the room, people began exclaiming in surprise, and someone looked quickly around the doorway and shouted, *"Frigo!"* A woman cried out behind Evon, and he heard the sound of a body hitting the ground.

"That's it," Mistress Gavranter said. "To the stairs, everyone, and be prepared for lethal force." She didn't say whether she meant to expect lethal force to be directed against them, or for them to use lethal force, but Evon had already made up his mind on that point. He raced toward the far stairs, Piercy dogging his heels and half a dozen magicians following. The same Speculatus magician shouted, *"Frigo!"* again, but someone behind Evon said, *"Retexo,"* and he heard the high-pitched whine of a spell aborting.

Halfway up the stairs, he heard footsteps running along the hall above toward them. He came bursting out of the stairwell at them at full speed, shouting *desini cucurri*, and wove through the falling bodies of nearly a dozen men and women before stopping to wait for the rest of the magicians to catch up. They were so *slow* it was driving him mad, but he had enough sense left to wait for them. Two were panting hard as they came off the stairs, and Evon told them, "Stay here and keep the stairs clear. We'll be leaving in a hurry." They nodded, and while they tried to look fierce, all they managed was gratitude.

He'd gotten a little turned around in his attack, and as he took a moment to look around for the right path, he heard a woman shout, *"Desini cucurri!"* The balding man shouted, *"Retex--"* and Evon felt *desini cucurri* brush past him as he whipped around, making the left side of his face tingle and his heart beat faster at the near-hit. Odelia stood only a few yards away, smiling. "Evon Lorantis," she said.

"The more fool me, for not guessing you were part of this. You found the girl, didn't you?"

"Twice now," he said. "I imagine it's killing you, not knowing how I did it. How many traps did you lay along our path?"

She began walking toward him, her black tiered dress swinging like a bell. "It doesn't matter," she said. "I've almost got the secret. How long have you had her? A week? And you haven't figured it out, or you wouldn't need her."

Evon wondered why the other magicians weren't attacking. She was distracted, she was taunting him, and they couldn't get off a simple paralysis? He flexed his fingers and said, "I'm not as ruthless as you are, I suppose."

"Quite the character flaw, I've always thought. *Desini cucurri!*"

Evon countered it with a flick of his left hand. "I'm not leaving without her."

"You're not leaving here at all. *Frigo!*" she shouted, and threw herself to one side as Evon shouted "*Recivia!*" and sent the spell flying back in her direction. She ducked, far too agilely for someone wearing that layer cake of a dress, and Evon took the opportunity to look behind him. His heart sank. Her *desini cucurri* hadn't gone astray; it had been aimed at the four magicians behind him, who now lay in varying frozen positions he would have found comical if he weren't fighting for his life. They were so *slow* and now he was on his own, which was what he'd always thought would happen, because the Gods were not on his side. He ran for a door and got it open to dive inside just as Odelia unleashed another *frigo* at him. She was good enough that any breaking spell she hit him with would splinter his bones. Across the hall, Piercy stood in the shelter of another doorway, glancing out occasionally. "I'll distract her, and you go," Evon called out, and Piercy nodded. Evon left his doorway long enough to direct four different spells at Odelia, and Piercy made his run as Odelia had to concentrate on defending herself. She half-turned in Piercy's direction as he passed her, and Evon cast his own *frigo* to keep her from pursuing him.

"Your shadow won't do you any good. There are plenty of guards on that room," Odelia called out. "Though I would like to know how you located her. I have enough obstructions on this building to block anyone, especially you."

"Oh, Odelia, you know I'm better than you are," Evon said. "Gold medalist. Top of the class. And your spellbuilding never did compare with mine. You had to cheat to even come close to matching me."

"I am not a cheat!" Odelia screamed, and the door behind Evon shattered, showering him with wood splinters. "You always had everyone believing you were the golden boy, they gave you all the chances and I had to claw my way to the top! I should have arranged an accident for you years ago, but I'll just have to settle for killing you now. *Forva!"*

The doorway burst into flame, and Evon rolled away from it and scrambled to the doorway Piercy had occupied. *"Recivia!"* he shouted, and the next *forva* rebounded on Odelia. He heard her scream and looked out just in time to see her extinguish the fire burning her tiered skirt. *"Forva!"* he shouted, snapping his fingers, and a circle of fire surrounded her. He sank back into the shelter of the room and tried to catch his breath. He was tiring, and losing his focus. At some point, his reflexes would slow enough that he couldn't cancel whatever she threw at him, and then he'd be dead.

Soft footsteps approached along the carpeted corridor, and he flattened himself against the wall next to the doorway. The footsteps slowed, and then —

"Frigo!" Odelia shouted, and the wall collapsed on him, knocking him to the ground and filling his lungs with plaster dust. He rose to his hands and knees and then cried out, hacking and spitting plaster, as she kicked him hard with her pointed boot. "Do you know how many ways I could kill you, Lorantis?" she said in a conversational tone. "I figured out your little shielding trick. I'd say it was brilliant, but it was really pathetically simple. *Presadi."* The shield sprang up around him, clinging to his nose and mouth, and with his last breath he gestured to cancel the spell. He sucked in air and threw himself away from Odelia, wincing at the pain in his side. *"Forva,"* she said, and again Evon rolled to avoid the fire that sprang up where he'd been lying. He wouldn't be able to last much longer.

"You see, Lorantis? I *am* better than you," Odelia said.

"Better at torturing people, possibly," Evon wheezed.

"Better at being ruthless," she taunted him. "Really, a trait you ought to learn." She stood over him where he lay on his back, feeling as paralyzed as if in the grip of *desini cucurri*. He had perhaps one spell left in him. The right spell.

He returned her gaze and saw mad obsession in her eyes. She would never stop trying to kill him and Kerensa both. And he knew what that one spell had to be. "All right," he said. *"Frigo."*

Odelia's neck snapped back so hard the crack was audible. Her shocked eyes met his once more before the life drained out of them and she collapsed to the floor.

Evon lay, breathing heavily, unable to move for a moment. He closed his eyes. He'd never killed anyone before. It had been far too easy. Then the horror of what he'd done struck him, and he rolled over and vomited up whatever it was he couldn't remember eating. It smelled of bile and the lemony tang of *frigo*. He crouched there on hands and knees, breathing heavily. He couldn't even swear he'd never do it again, if it meant protecting Kerensa, and he felt sick again to know he was capable of such a thing. *Time enough to hate yourself when she's safe.* He pushed himself to his feet and went wearily to the door.

Someone rushed at him, and he was too tired, he couldn't react before the person attacked him with his bare hands. No, it was Piercy, grabbing at his coat. "Evon, you have to come now," he said. "She won't let me take her. Keeps saying something about the spell. She'll listen to you. Come *now.*"

Fresh strength poured through him. *She's why I'm here.* He ran with Piercy down the corridor to the servants' stairs and down the narrow hall to the room he'd seen in *spexa*, passing the limp bodies of four men Evon didn't recognize, blood pooling beneath them. Piercy could be deadly when he wanted. They burst through the door and skidded to a halt. The red-bearded man, Valantis, stood in the center of the room with Kerensa bundled over his shoulder. She was struggling, but weakly, her legs hanging limply down her captor's chest, and Valantis seemed not to notice her exertions. "Out of my way," he said. His voice was deep and raspy, the voice of a man with a long tobacco-smoking habit.

"Put her down," Evon said.

Kerensa struggled harder and cried out, "Evon—"

"The weapon is mine," Valantis said. He reached up with his free hand and casually struck Kerensa on the back of her head, hard, and she fell silent. Evon shouted, *"Frigo!"* but he was too exhausted for it to do anything more powerful than make the big man sway where he stood.

"Not much of a magician, are you? Now get out of my way and I won't kill you where you stand."

Evon began circling to the man's right, limbering his fingers. Piercy went to the left, flexing his wrist and letting a knife fall into his open hand. Valantis shifted his weight trying to follow them both. "Clever," the big man said. He dropped Kerensa, making her cry out in pain, and whipped out a long knife and put it to her throat. "I'll kill her, and then neither of us will have the weapon. But I judge you care more about her welfare than you do about the spell."

Evon looked at Kerensa, whose face was set and white. She looked exhausted. He felt as if Valantis's knife had gone through his chest. "All right," he said, raising his hands in submission, his mind working frantically. "Don't hurt *desini cucurri!*"

He had never tried targeting only part of a person before, and it didn't work as well as he had hoped—Valantis could still move at the waist, but his arms and neck were frozen, and that was all that mattered. Evon carefully pulled Kerensa away from the knife before Valantis realized he was still conscious and that his legs were free. He wrenched the knife out of the man's frozen hands and gave it to Piercy. "Take him to Mrs. Petelter," he said. "I'll bring Kerensa."

"No," she said in a voice raw from screaming that made Evon wish he had the power to kill Odelia again. "You have to get everyone out of here. I can't hold it off much longer."

He knelt next to her. "You—the spell. You're keeping it from activating?"

She nodded. "I don't know how long. You have to get everyone out. I can feel it building."

Evon exchanged glances with Piercy. "Forget him," Evon said, nodding at Valantis. "Use the mirror to get everyone out of the manor. If he wants to live, he can find his own way. Do you understand?" he said to Valantis, who looked very confused. "You're about to see that weapon you were so interested in demonstrate its power. If you don't want to be part of the display, I suggest you start running."

Valantis gave him one more stunned look, then stumbled out of the room, his neck and arms unnaturally still, unbalancing him so he bounced off the doorframe on his way out. "Evon—" Piercy began.

"Get out. I'll help Kerensa. *Move!*" Piercy ran out the door. Evon turned to Kerensa. "This isn't a safe place for you when you're reborn," he said. "You won't be able to get out of the wreckage. Can you stand?"

She shook her head. "She broke my legs," she said. "You have to go."

"I told you I'd stay with you, didn't I?" He scooped her up in his arms, staggered a little under her weight, then headed toward the servants' stairs. "We'll go out the back. It might still destroy the house, but we won't be under it."

"I can't control it much longer," she cried. "You'll be killed."

"Just tell me when you're going to let go." He went down the stairs as fast as he dared with his burden. Kerensa tucked her head into his shoulder and clasped him tightly around the neck. Her skin was hot to the touch and reddening as he ran. She must have extraordinary willpower, to prevent a spell of that magnitude from activating for even a short time. He could hear her whimper every time he went down another flight of stairs, jogging her broken legs, and cold fury filled him to the point that he could barely see.

They reached the entrance hall and Evon turned toward the back of the house. He hadn't paid much attention to this part of the building, since it had nothing to do with the route to the fourth floor, and he was casting about for a door that might lead to the outside when Kerensa said faintly, "It's happening." Evon quickly set her down. Her skin was bright red and faint irregular lines of yellow began to form underneath it. He realized, too late, that his reserves were low and he had no idea if he could cast a spell strong enough to withstand this blast. Nothing to be done. He rolled into a ball and said, "*Presadi,*" just in time to see Kerensa convulse on the floor, and then he squeezed his eyes tight shut as the blast hit his shield.

The light was so bright it burned his eyes through his eyelids and the forearms he put up to shield his face. He felt himself buffeted by a wind that rolled him in his shield across the floor, bumping as if the smooth floor were made of jagged rocks instead. The airtight shield blocked sound as well, blocked it so completely that he felt as if the blast had knocked him deaf as well as blind. He kept his arms up, afraid to look, afraid he'd already been blinded, and waited for the shield to stop rolling. *No heat, isn't that lucky? I guess it works.* He was beginning to feel lightheaded. Was the event over? How long did it last? He wished he'd thought to ask Kerensa, then realized she was probably too preoccupied with dying to notice things like the passage of time. Kerensa. He dared open his eyes a crack and saw a red haze and the afterimages of the white, searing light. He needed air. He dismissed *presadi* and felt panic clutch at his heart; he couldn't see anything, not fire, not walls or masonry. He blinked, hard, and saw red and orange in the distance, and felt cold air that smelled of char and old stone on his face. Heat seared his palms, and he rolled onto his back and panted, drawing in deep breaths of the frigid air. Then he let out a cry and leaped to his feet, swatting at the back of his head and Kerensa's bag, still strapped to his back, where they had begun to burn. The searingly hot ground gave off waves of heat he could see in the moonlight and began to burn through the soles of his boots. "*Presadi,*" he said with a gesture, acting by instinct, and a flattened bubble appeared on the ground before him; he stepped onto it, wobbled, and found his balance. He really ought to learn to cast that shield as a wall rather than a sphere.

Things began to swim into focus, and far above he saw specks of light. Some of them danced and sparkled with rainbow light, and they were probably imaginary, but others remained stationary and he was fairly certain they were stars. The manor was nothing more than heaps of ash and still-flowing stone, rising at intervals around him that mirrored the walls and pillars. Steam rose from the cracked, blackened tiles beneath his feet. About twenty feet away, a dark shape huddled on the ground, weeping. Evon wobbled his way toward her by kicking *presadi* until it rolled, awkwardly, knocking him off balance with every rut and bump it went over. He removed his coat and draped it around her as he'd done once before, though what he wanted to do was take her in his arms and kiss her until her tears stopped.

"You're not dead," she said. Her voice was dull and emotionless. "I thought you would be dead."

"You have such little faith in me? I won't say it wasn't hard, but I do have some small skill as a magician. And—" He pulled her bag off his back and rummaged in it. "I brought you a dress."

She looked up at him, holding out the blue gown with a flourish, and began to laugh, somewhat hysterically, but it was a laugh nonetheless. He laughed with her. She would be all right, he thought, and turned his back so she could dress. "Your legs," he said suddenly.

"Reborn, remember? She—" Kerensa's voice cut off abruptly. "She mostly just tried to take the spell off, and that terrified me, but otherwise she didn't hurt me much."

"I know Odelia. I think you're lying to me."

"Well, I know you, and I think you're trying to make all of this your fault, so you can just stop that right now. I don't even feel any pain. You can turn around now." She was looking through her bag for her shoes. "The worst part was feeling like...like a thing. Like all they cared about was the weapon."

Evon felt sick again. "The magicians are here," he said. "They helped rescue you. I'm afraid some of them will see you only as a weapon too."

Kerensa put on her cloak and shivered. "Isn't there anything we can do?"

"I'm going to be lucky if Mistress Gavranter—that's their head magician—can arrange for me to stay here rather than be shipped off to Matra. I think I impressed her, and I did just manage to survive the weapon at its most powerful. But...it's likely they won't let me work on the spell anymore. I might be allowed to consult."

"That's so unfair."

"It will give me time to work on the other spell. The one that proves the Despot is the spell's target."

Kerensa came close enough to him that he could see her smooth face in the moonlight. "You really think that's true?"

"I try to trust my instincts. But not so much that I won't try to prove it before acting on it."

Kerensa took his hand and squeezed it, sending a thrill through his body. "Thanks for coming after me."

His vision was still a little blurry, but he could see her eyes, and his heart ached. He'd thought—he'd hoped, by the way she had clung to him as he carried her, that possibly...but no. The look she gave him had nothing but friendly affection in it. He managed a smile. "How could I do otherwise, and still call myself your friend?" *Though a friend wouldn't be feeling this way about you right now. Oh, Kerensa.*

The devastation extended far beyond the ruined manor, farther than Evon's blurry vision could see in the moonlight. The smoking ground was rough, and *presadi* was awkward, so it took them some time to cross the hundred yards or more to where the frost-burned grass began again. They saw no sign of life anywhere, all across the fields. They neared the forest, and Evon worried that the others might not have gotten out in time, that Piercy—

"There you are! You had me worried, dear fellow. I was about to come looking for you." Piercy detached himself from the trees and embraced him, pounding him hard on the back. "Kerensa, you look well."

"I feel well," she said. "The urge has passed. I thought you came with a lot of people."

"We're all here, Miss Haylter, and are astonished at that display," Mistress Gavranter said. "Belitha Gavranter, and I hope we will be able to discover the secret of that spell and free you from it."

"I hope so too, Mistress Gavranter," Kerensa said. "Was...was anyone killed?"

"Five of Mrs. Petelter's agents did not return, and two of our magicians were caught in the weapon's fury," she said. "Please don't look that way, young lady. It's not under your control, and they knew what the risks were."

Evon almost told her about Kerensa's holding off the blast for several minutes. He decided to wait until they were alone. If those magicians knew Kerensa could do something like that, they might draw the wrong conclusions. Better not to confuse them now.

"It's hard for me not to feel guilty," Kerensa was saying. "Even though I know it's the spell doing it."

"Well, I think we can rid you of it soon, with Mr. Lorantis's help," Mistress Gavranter said. "I suggest we go on to Ostradon and find shelter there. In the morning, if you don't mind, Miss Haylter, we'll begin our studies."

Evon kept his mouth shut. If Mistress Gavranter was going to ignore his summons back to Matra, he wasn't going to make an issue of it. He mounted, and took Kerensa up behind him, wishing her hands on his waist meant more than just her need to stay on the horse. His terror for her safety had dissolved into misery at his own situation. If he—if they—succeeded at freeing her, the magicians would take the spell to Matra, or to the Despot, and Kerensa would go home and back to her old life, and he would never see her again. She thought of him as the brother he'd claimed to be, would probably remember him fondly or with gratitude, and he would carry the memory of her face with him for the rest of his life. He clenched his hands on the reins. At least she'd remember him. It would have to be enough.

15

*P*iercy threw open a window, choking and gagging. "Evon Lorantis," he said, waving the thick orange smoke out the window, "you are my best friend, and I would do anything for you, but I am nearly to the point of tossing you out this window along with your noxious fumes."

Evon was coughing too hard to answer at first. Finally, his eyes streaming, he said, "You could get another room. You probably *should* get another room. I can't promise that won't happen again."

"If I acquired my own room, there would be nothing constraining you from staying up all hours and forgetting to eat. You and I will simply have to come to an accommodation. And I will find something to occupy me during the daylight hours, when you are busily engaged in finding new and unpleasant ways to fumigate a room."

"There was the one that ended with a flash of light and purple fire."

"All right, fumigate or illuminate a room, though I am not certain purple is anyone's color." Piercy stepped away from the window, ostentatiously holding his nose. "It is dinnertime," he said. "I will take myself off to the dining room, and you should away to speak to Mistress Gavranter. She kept Kerensa far too long yesterday."

"Kerensa looks exhausted still. I'd hoped it was just the effect of the weapon's activation, but I think the magicians are pushing her too hard."

"You are the one with the power to stop that, dear fellow. I cannot credit how those magicians' attitudes toward you changed when you walked out of that desolation unscathed."

"Not totally unscathed. My coat is never going to be the same, and the hair on the back of my head is still a little singed."

Piercy walked around Evon and tugged at the indicated hair. "You saw what remained of the deceased when they were retrieved yesterday. Everyone is shocked, amazed and awestruck that you did not resemble them. With good reason." Serious now, he added, "Evon, that was extremely dangerous. You had no idea your spell would even work against a fire of that magnitude."

"I promised I wouldn't leave her," Evon said. He went to shut the window, which was letting in a frigid breeze.

"She wouldn't thank you for killing yourself to keep that promise," Piercy said. "And I hope you don't think that risking your life will change her feelings for you."

Evon shook his head. He looked out over the rooftops of Ostradon, watching smoke rise from the chimneys of the tall, narrow brick houses. "I couldn't leave her."

Piercy sighed. "I know." He went to the door. "Eat something. Don't force me to bring you something vile from the kitchens. Hunger may be the best sauce, but it's murder on the intellectual faculties."

Evon heard the door close behind Piercy, then turned and moved things off the small round-topped table he'd appropriated from the downstairs hall of the inn. It was covered with a layer of orange dust, under which was a layer of brown crumbly things. He used a handkerchief to wipe the top of the table, sending dust and crumbly things to the floor. If he took a positive view, that was one more thing he knew *didn't* work. From a more negative perspective, it was one thing that didn't work out of what might be a million other non-viable possibilities. He sat heavily in his chair and stared at the bare table. He felt as though he was on the right path, but he couldn't work out which of the many things he'd tried were part of that right path. Piercy was right; he needed to eat something. No, first he had to extract Kerensa from the magicians' clutches. They'd all been awed by their first sight of the spell, but now that it was a commonplace, they had a tendency to forget there was a woman attached to it.

He went down the hall and up a flight of stairs to the third floor, which the magicians had appropriated for their use as sleeping and working quarters. He knocked on the door at the far end of the hall, then entered. Kerensa sat quietly in a chair, her caramel-golden hair bundled at the base of her neck, spell-ribbons frozen in place around her. Several of the magicians hovered over her, making notes or copying runes. It infuriated Evon that the magicians insisted on repeating his work, claiming that his perfectly clear notes were unintelligible. Such a waste of time. The slow pace of their work further infuriated him. They seemed to believe that the activation of the spell meant they had plenty of time before the urge struck Kerensa again. Evon kept having to remind himself that he was there solely because Mistress Gavranter had overridden Mrs. Petelter's demand that Evon obey the Home Defense command for him to return home. Mrs. Petelter, who'd failed utterly to capture Valantis, was in disgrace not only for that failure but because of the debacle that had gotten Kerensa kidnapped in the first place. She'd intended to send Evon home immediately, to avoid looking disobedient as well as incompetent, but Mistress Gavranter had taken her aside and had a few quiet words with her, then the two women had gone into Mrs. Petelter's room for a mirror conversation with Home Defense, and ultimately they'd emerged, Mrs. Petelter looking relieved, Mistress Gavranter looking smugly pleased. Now Mrs. Petelter avoided him, and Evon avoided her, just in case she changed her mind.

"Mistress Gavranter," Evon said. The magician was seated near the window, frowning over a page of notes. She looked up inquiringly. "Mistress Gavranter, I believe it's dinnertime, and I think everyone would do better with a little refreshment."

Mistress Gavranter's eyes went to Kerensa, then back to Evon. "Thank you, Mr. Lorantis, I think that is an excellent idea."

"It can wait another five minutes," Mistress Quendester said, not bothering to look at Evon, who had to stop himself making an angry reply. "Five minutes" was Mistress Quendester's habitual response to any suggestion by Evon that it was time to stop.

"I really need to stop, Mistress Quendester," Kerensa said. "Don't worry, I'll come back."

Mistress Quendester glared at Kerensa. "I'd think you would want us to work as fast as possible," she snapped.

"I wish you would," Kerensa said sweetly.

"Oh, let the girl go, Caris," Master Waldratis, the balding magician, said, stepping back and mopping at his forehead with his handkerchief. "I could use a rest myself."

"*Desini,*" Evon said with a sharper flick of his fingers than was necessary to dismiss *epiria,* taking advantage of Mistress Quendester's irritation and the distraction of the other magicians. They murmured crossly, casting dire glances Evon's way, but no one challenged him. It was good to have a reputation.

Evon offered Kerensa his arm, and the two of them went down the stairs to the dining room. "I'm glad you came in when you did," Kerensa said. "I was starting to get restless. Have you made any progress?"

Evon grimaced. "If you call several more explosive failures 'progress,' then yes."

"At least you know what doesn't work."

"That's what I told myself, but I knew I was lying."

She laughed and squeezed his arm. "Isn't there anything I can do to help?"

He looked at her cheerful face and thought of a million things he wanted to say to her. "Continue to cooperate with the magicians," he said. "Maybe they'll find a way to separate the spell from you, and then it won't matter whom it's targeting."

"I think some of them couldn't find a way to their own backsides without a map and a guide dog, but I'll try to be helpful."

"I'm sorry."

"Don't be. They're a lot more careful of my comfort than I expected. I think some of them believe I really do have control over the spell and are terrified I might repeat my performance at the Speculatus manor if they anger me. I haven't done anything to correct that impression."

"It seems I'm not the only one with a reputation for fearsomeness."

"They do walk softly around you. You must have been something to watch, back at the manor."

Evon thought of Odelia collapsed on the floor with her head hanging at an unnatural angle. "I did what the situation called for."

They entered the dining room and joined Piercy at his table. A waiter brought them somewhat dry roast chicken with boiled onions and potatoes. Evon picked at his food and went over his last failure in his head. Phosphorus wasn't working as a source of light, symbolic of guidance. Plus, it was dangerous and volatile. Wood and candle hadn't burned hot enough, and oil gave off too much smoke. What was left? Alcohol might work...in fact, a nice clear alcohol would be more symbolic than white phosphorus, clarity of liquor, clarity of purpose.

"Excuse me," he called out to the waiter, across the room. "Could you bring me a large bottle of grain alcohol? Or gin, if you don't have that."

The waiter gave him a skeptical look, but shrugged and left the room. Evon went back to his food and found Piercy and Kerensa staring at him. "Dare I ask why you want to make yourself very, very drunk at twelve-thirty in the afternoon?" Piercy asked.

"It's for the experiment," Evon said. He took a bite of chicken. It really was dry and unpleasant.

"That's a relief," Kerensa said. "I thought you'd gone mad with frustration."

"I have, but not enough to destroy my brain with a 190-proof beverage." Evon washed down the last of the chicken with water. "Kerensa, will you come to my room before you go back to the magicians? I need to copy something out from the spell."

"Evon, I think you need to have a rest," Kerensa said. "You have the strangest expression."

"Have I?" He'd thought he was behaving normally.

"You do, dear fellow. Your eyes are a little glassy and you look paler than usual."

"I feel fine." Now that he thought about it, he did not feel fine. He felt a little stiff from standing over the table all morning, and the room seemed too cold.

"I think you might be coming down with something," Kerensa said. She laid the back of her hand on his forehead and he flinched at how cold it was. "You have a fever."

"It can't be very serious, because I don't feel unwell," he lied. "But I promise I'll rest once I've copied out the spell. I have the runes, but I want to see them in order."

"All right," Kerensa said, and her look of concern forced him to turn away before he did or said something stupid.

The waiter returned with a large bottle of clear liquid and a small glass. "Thank you," Evon said, pressing a few coins into the man's hand, and pushed back his chair, taking the bottle and the glass with him.

"That man thinks you are going to your room to drink yourself to death," Piercy said. "I can see it in his eyes."

"He can think anything he likes now that I've got this," Evon said. "Kerensa, if you don't mind?"

She followed him up the stairs and into the room, where Evon soon had the spell-ribbons visible and stationary. "What are you trying?" she asked.

"I'm creating a spell to prove the existence of the entity," he said, squatting to look at a curve of spell-ribbon near her feet. "This is the hardest part because there's no real evidence that it *ever* existed, let alone that it exists now. But I've worked out the material components, I hope, and now I'm going to use the part of this spell that draws you toward the next target as an identifier."

"I don't know what that means."

Evon scratched out a rune and drew a different one. "The spell...might as well say it 'knows' what it's looking for. It knows the identity of its ultimate target. I'm treating 'fathlon' as the name of that target, which I think is accurate, and using the spell—" He coughed briefly. "Excuse me. I'm using the spell to tie that name to

185

the identity of the target. Then the glass there represents the concept of 'no soul,' emptiness. And all of those things together will say whether or not a creature with all those characteristics exists."

"Why does it matter? What if it's just the Despot that it's targeting, a plain old ordinary person?"

Evon coughed again. "The spell was made far too long ago for its makers to know about the Despot rising up in this time. It's targeting something more abstract, not just a person. Maybe its target is just some quality the Despot has in common with Murakot and all the other victims. But if your story is correct, and it's a creature separate from the Despot, then there's no reason it might not leave him for some other host. And if...if the spell is sent after the Despot when it's the entity it wants, it won't find the right target, and this cycle will just keep going on." He'd remembered, as he spoke, what would happen when Kerensa reached that final target. He felt guilty, now, about keeping it from her. She ought to know the truth. He coughed again. He'd tell her about it tonight, after the magicians were through with her for the day.

"You *are* sick," Kerensa said. "You should go to bed."

"I will as soon as I finish copying these out."

"...You're not going to bed, are you."

"No. But I thought I sounded very believable."

"You did. I just know you well enough to ignore anything you say when you sound that believable."

Evon stood, stretching against the aches in his knees and shoulders. "Thank you. That should be enough."

"Please promise me you'll rest," Kerensa said, and the look in her eyes made his heart thump harder. *If only you would see me the way I see you.*

"We can compromise," he said. "I'm going to try one more experiment and then I'll take myself off to bed. Will that satisfy you?"

"I suppose," she said dubiously. "Don't forget you promised me."

"I won't. Go on. I'm sorry you have to put up with the magicians all afternoon."

"It would be easier if I thought they'd be at all effective. I know they're good, but you're better."

Evon's face warmed. "Thank you. I hope your faith in me isn't unfounded."

"It isn't," she said, smiling, "because you didn't burn." He watched her leave the room, his body aching from more than just illness. He could just say it. He could say *Kerensa, you are the most beautiful woman I've ever seen, and I love you, my heart lifts every time you enter the room, and I want to make you happy.* And she could look at him with pity, and then everything would be awkward between them, and he would feel like even more of a fool than he already was.

He opened the bottle of alcohol and poured a splash into the bottom of the glass, thought about drinking it, then set it on the floor. With his coppery chalk, he began to copy the runes onto the table top exactly as they'd appeared on the spell-ribbons, scattered rather than in a straight line or a circle. He set the glass in the center of the table, snapped his fingers and said, "*Forva*," and the alcohol burned with a pure white-blue fire. Quickly, before the alcohol was consumed, he spread his left hand palm-down above the fire, feeling its heat on his hand, and said, "*Solto epiria.*"

Nothing happened. The fire burned a little longer and went out. Evon stepped back and surveyed the tableau. He'd gotten something right, but he wasn't sure what. The fire and the glass, that felt right to him, and besides, if he'd gotten that part wrong, the glass would probably have shattered as the magic tried to force its way through the wrong vessel. He cleared away the glass, juggling it a little because it was hot, and looked at the runes. This was the spell, he was certain, he knew exactly what it did, so why wasn't it working?

He looked again at his paper copy, then went for his notes. The magician who'd created this spell was sloppy. There were redundancies, not in places where they might have been actual safeguards, but in places where they looked as though they'd just been copied over twice. Evon got some paper and made a fresh copy of the spell he'd just read off Kerensa—if he was wrong, he didn't want to have to go in there to recopy it and take her away from the magicians, who would make a fuss he didn't want to deal with. Then he started crossing pieces off. Here, a rune that didn't do anything; there, a complicated sentence that could be written so much more simply.

After a while, he had a slimmed-down version of the spell that he was sure would still work. Too bad for those long-dead magicians that he hadn't been around back then. Of course, if he had been, he wouldn't have known any better than they did, so it was just as well. He coughed again, harder this time, then scrubbed off the table and wrote out his new version of the spell.

He set the glass in the center of the table, poured in more alcohol and lit it, then again said, *"Solto epiria."*

Something grabbed him by his sternum—he could feel the cold fingers wrapping around it, digging into his flesh, and he cried out in pain. He was somewhere dark and cold, suspended in air by the hand that gripped him. No, it was more like talons than a hand, sharp talons that felt as if they might rip his breastbone out of his body with no more effort than tearing a piece of paper. Evon cried out again, and suddenly black became red and he found himself inside something that pulsed unpleasantly and dripped fluids onto a floor made of glistening, puffy pillows of flesh. He continued to dangle, feeling paralyzed by shock rather than *desini cucurri*.

Something was there with him, something other than whatever had him by the chest. It didn't seem aware of his presence; its attention was elsewhere. Evon could hear distant whisperings he couldn't quite make out, however he strained. The...thing...radiated cold the way a fire radiated heat, in waves that varied in intensity and burned his face and hands. If he looked at it from the corner of his eye, he could almost see it, or pieces of it, the flash of an eye, the twitch of a limb. It looked and felt wrong, unnatural, like something that didn't belong in the world.

Whatever had hold of his chest wrenched at it again, and Evon screamed in pain. Instantly the thing moved, its awareness focused on him. He felt himself at the center of a scrutiny so intense it bore down on him like a boulder, pinning him to the wall, or the floor, he'd lost track of where he was, and he tried to scream again but there was no air in his lungs—

—and he was lying on the floor in his room, Kerensa pounding on his chest and shouting at him, and people crowding in at the door. He breathed in deeply and said, "That hurts."

"I should hope it hurts, what with you scaring me like that!" she shouted. "I came back here to make sure you had gone to bed, because I knew you wouldn't, and I heard you fall and you were lying on the floor, and your lips were blue and you weren't breathing. What in *hell* did you do to yourself?"

He sat up, supporting himself with his hands. He was freezing and his head hurt. "I found it," he said. "It exists. I didn't know the spell would do that."

Kerensa stood and glared at the people in the doorway. "He's fine," she said. "He's just stupid. Go on back to whatever you were doing. Go." She shut the door and turned her glare on Evon. "Into bed," she told him. "Right now."

"I have to do the location spell while the thing's identity is still fresh in my mind," he said. He wearily got to his feet, every joint in his body aching, and took a large roll of paper from beside the wardrobe. "Would you move that table?"

"I don't want anything to do with your mad desire to drive yourself into an early grave."

"If I have to move it, I might overexert myself and get sicker. You wouldn't want that."

Kerensa threw up her hands and dragged the table under the window, rattling the glass still resting at its center. "Piercy was right. You use guilt like a weapon."

"Only because Piercy doesn't respond to other forms of persuasion." He stood at one side of the room and unrolled the paper, revealing a map of the continent with country borders and cities marked out. "Stand on that end so it doesn't roll back up." He lifted Piercy's bed a few painful inches and slid it to rest atop one corner of the map, then did the same with his bed on the other side. He needed ink. There was an inkwell in the drawer of the dressing table; he had to walk around Kerensa to reach it, and she folded her arms across her chest and continued to glare at him. He smiled pleasantly at her, then coughed long and hard and had to wave away her concern. "I'm fine," he said, "just had something caught in my throat."

"Of course you did," Kerensa said sarcastically.

The door opened. "I heard you were dead, Lore," Piercy said. "I knew it was impossible, because you are too stubborn to allow death to take you in the middle of an experiment."

"He found the entity and it nearly killed him," said Kerensa, "and now he refuses to admit he's sick and he won't listen to me."

"Well, he won't listen to me either, if you were hoping for some sort of support. Sympathy, I have in large buckets."

"Both of you be still and watch this," Evon said. "It's fascinating. Unless it doesn't work, in which case it's just messy." He stood on the map over a dot marked OSTRADON with the inkwell in hand. He swung his left hand across the map, rubbing his fingers together as if sprinkling salt over it, and said *"Epiria separa."* Nothing happened.

"I'm so glad you risked your health for that outstanding display," Kerensa said.

"You have such a negative attitude sometimes, do you realize that?" Evon paused to cough, wiped his mouth, and added, "The interesting part comes next." He crouched above the map and tipped the inkwell so a thin stream of ink spilled out of it to fall on Ostradon. Just as the ink touched the page, Evon said, *"Reperto Fathlon."*

Instead of soaking into the paper, the ink gathered into a large bead about half an inch across and quivered like quicksilver atop the map. Its quivering sent out tiny tendrils in all directions like tentative fingers. After about thirty seconds of this, it appeared to come to a decision and began rolling across the map, slowly, leaving no trail.

"It's going south," Piercy said. Evon nodded. The ink continued rolling until it reached a point south of the Dalanine border, where it stopped moving and began quivering again. Suddenly, as if it were a bubble someone had just stuck with a pin, the bead of ink collapsed and soaked into the map, making not an irregular blotch but an intricate design of curves and circles centered on a single point.

"Where is that?" Kerensa asked.

"The back end of nowhere," Piercy said. "There isn't even a city there."

Evon pulled a silver coin out of his pocket and knelt near the ink design. "The Despot is there," he said, and held the coin so its edge just touched the ink. *"Reperto* Fathlon," he repeated, and a thin stream of ink ran up the coin and pooled in the groove around its milled edge and along the contours of some long-dead queen of Dalanine. Evon blew on it, and the ink disappeared, but when he tilted the coin to catch the light, it iridesced as if coated with a thin layer of oil. He tossed it at Piercy. "Hold it in your hand and do a slow turn."

Piercy raised his eyebrows at Evon, but slowly rotated in place. When he was about three-quarters of the way through his turn, he exclaimed, "It's hot!"

"It works like the children's game," Evon explained. "As you near the correct direction, it warms up. Cold, and you're facing the wrong way."

"Wouldn't it be cold anyway, since it's winter? Or hot from being kept in your pocket?" Kerensa said.

"That's part of the magic. Its temperature is always dependent on the spell."

Piercy handed the coin to Kerensa, who repeated his movements. She handed the coin to Evon and said, "Are you certain it's the Despot?"

"It's only instinct, and your story," Evon said, "but what I *am* certain of is that this coin will lead us to the spell's actual target. Even if it isn't the Despot. Which I think it is."

"You're starting to babble," Piercy pointed out.

"I feel a little light-headed after that." Evon sat down on his bed. "Tomorrow I'll have to convince the magicians to let me work with them on separating the spell from you, Kerensa. Once we figure that out, we can work out a way to take the spell to the Despot and release it without killing anyone but him."

"Or I could walk up to him and let the spell do its work," Kerensa said.

Evon and Piercy looked at each other. "That would not be wise," Piercy said. "The spell...once it fulfils its purpose, it no longer needs its carrier. You would die in destroying the Despot, and you wouldn't be reborn."

"Oh," said Kerensa. She blinked a few times, and again said, "Oh."

"So we have to find a way to release it from you before that happens," Evon said.

"I see," said Kerensa. She took a few steps and the map rolled up behind her. "How long have you known this?"

"A few days," Evon said. "We didn't think you needed to know, since there was nothing any of us could do about it, and—"

"I understand," Kerensa said. "You were trying to protect me. I don't really need that kind of protection." She didn't sound angry, she sounded tired.

"I'm sorry," Evon said.

"It doesn't matter." She raised her head and glared at him. "Now," she said in a more normal tone, "you've done the locator spell and you are getting into bed and staying there."

"I agree," said Piercy. He pulled the map free of its weights and rolled it up. "I'm going to take this to Mrs. Petelter. If it represents the Despot's current position, she should know about it, if only to communicate it to her superiors. She may even thank me. Evon, get into bed like a good boy and I'll be back to check on you later."

Evon sat down on his bed and began to take his boots off. "No, let me do that," Kerensa said. "You really did frighten me. Did you know the spell would be that dangerous?"

"No, of course not," he said, crawling under the blankets fully dressed. Now that he was lying down, he realized how terrible he felt. The bed was warm and soft and he felt himself beginning to drowse off immediately. "I don't know what happened. I was in its presence...I think it noticed me. I hope it doesn't know how to follow me here."

Kerensa sat on the bed. "Could it do that?"

"Possibly. I don't know. It doesn't have a physical presence...oh, no, I think I was inside its host's head. It was truly disgusting." Evon took her hand, as much to give himself comfort as to reassure her. "I think...it sounded as though it had to direct the host to do things because it didn't have the physicality to do them itself. So I'm safe."

Kerensa squeezed his hand. "Good. I was terrified that your illness was far worse than it seemed." She stood and walked across the room to Piercy's bed, sat down, and crossed her legs. "Now go to sleep. I'm not leaving until you do."

"I can't sleep if you're watching me." Evon yawned until his jaw popped.

"I think you can. I also think you're stubborn enough that if I leave this room, you'll get up and go back to work on whatever the next step is."

"You know me too well." It occurred to Evon, even in his sleep-fuddled state, that her knowing him that well should make her inclined to fall in love with him. Then he thought about all the qualities she knew about him, his stubbornness, his failures, his obsession with work, and had a moment's self-pity that he was, from that perspective, fairly unlovable. He rolled onto his side, facing away from her, and after a minute or two essayed a faint snore. "Don't even bother," she said, and he grinned. After a few more moments, he drifted off to sleep for real.

16

*E*von slept restlessly, woke after dark, slept again. He hurt
everywhere with a dull, throbbing ache he couldn't escape
from no matter what position he slept in. Piercy was there when he
woke, with water and a cold damp rag to lay on his forehead. He
shivered under the blankets. Shivering hurt. He couldn't stop coughing, though when he woke the second time to full daylight it had
subsided to a mild, dry cough that barely hurt at all. Piercy gave him
more blankets and he huddled underneath the mound they made and
wondered if he would ever feel well again. He had feverish dreams
about riding his horse across a bare, charred landscape that he knew
was the result of the weapon being activated to kill the Despot, only
its destructive force had taken everything with it. Kerensa was dead,
and he cried for her and for himself. Then his dreams turned darker,
and he was trapped in that fleshy red nightmare with the entity
searching for him, to crush him with its baleful attention, and he ran
through the pillowy pink flesh that kept sticking to his feet. The
Despot rose up in front of him, fifteen feet tall, but Alvor with his
mace stepped between them and swung at the Despot's head. The
stump of his missing finger shone bright gold, though Evon couldn't
see why. Shadowy figures joined Alvor, who shouted "Run!" at him,

and he stumbled away into another nightmare about the Witch of Marhalindor, though he knew nothing about her except that she was insane, and now he was looking for Kerensa to tell him a story about the Witch, and he remembered she was dead, and he wept again.

He woke, clear-headed, after full light, and wondered what day it was. His hair was matted with sweat and he felt uncomfortably warm beneath his many blankets. Piercy slept on his own bed across the room, his mouth open as usual. Evon stretched and found that he didn't hurt nearly as much as he had, and that his head didn't ache and his vision was clear. He felt sticky and sweaty all over, and he needed to relieve himself, but when he stood, he realized he was too weak to make it to the water closet down the hall, so he used the chamber pot under the bed and felt much better.

"I am grateful to see you mobile again, dear fellow, but I hope you do not expect me to empty that thing for you," Piercy said with a yawn.

"I didn't mean to wake you. You looked exhausted."

"And well should I be, what with caring for you for the last two days. No, no thanks needed, you would undoubtedly have done the same for me." Piercy sat up and stretched. "Fever gone? No more aches? You really do have the worst nightmares. Fortunate Kerensa was not here or you would both have been very embarrassed."

Evon flushed red. "Did she stay away? I wouldn't want her to catch this."

"No, she stayed well away," Piercy said, too casually.

"What is that supposed to mean?"

Piercy sighed. "Things became, shall we say, rather intense while you were on your sick bed. She..." He reached into his coat, which was hanging up at the head of his bed, and pulled out a folded piece of paper which he handed to Evon. Evon opened it and read:

Don't follow me, Evon. I mean it. Time's run out and this is the best option. You and Piercy won't be safe where I'm going and I couldn't bear it if you were hurt or killed. Thank you for everything you've done. You've been the best friend I could hope for.

Evon tossed the paper on the bed. "You let her leave?" he exclaimed.

"There was no 'letting' about it, dear fellow. She made a clean escape that I would admire if I weren't so worried. She told the magicians she was going out for the morning to do some shopping and she told me she would be with the magicians all day. Then she took her bag and left."

"But why did she think she had to go? I'm so close—I know I'll figure it out soon! She didn't have to do this!"

"As I said, dear fellow, things became rather intense while you were ill. You know I took the map to show Mrs. Petelter? She became very agitated over it and there were many communications to headquarters and much running about in the manner of poultry wondering where their heads have got to. Ultimately we learned that the Despot is pushing north at an alarming rate rather than waiting for spring as any sensible mad dictator would do, leaving nothing in his wake but destruction and brutality. When confronted with this terrible reality, one of the magicians whom I will not name because I am certain you can guess her identity rather vocally protested that there was no way they could figure out the secret in time. Kerensa apparently took her seriously, which, since none of the other magicians contradicted Mistress Quendester, is not nearly so foolish a thing as you might otherwise think. Kerensa disappeared yesterday morning."

Evon swayed to his feet and sat back down hard on the bed. "She doesn't have the coin, though. She's just going to get herself killed."

Piercy cleared his throat. "Actually, she does have the coin," he said. "It was the first thing I looked for after we learned she was missing. She must have taken it when she came to see how you fared, night before last. And I must say I'm relieved that she does. I hate to think of her wandering out there with no direction."

"I hate to think of her out there at all. That skin of hers might prevent her from being harmed by weapons, possibly, but there are a great many ways to hurt someone that don't leave a mark." Evon attempted to rise again and this time was successful. He began to remove his clothes. "Did you say she left yesterday morning? So she only has a day's head start on me."

"Evon, think," Piercy said, pushing him gently back onto the bed.

"You are in no condition to ride. Once you get to the border you'll be easy prey for any bandit or thug that comes along."

"I recover quickly," Evon said. "Get out of my way."

"The magicians are working on locating her. Let them track her down. You can't help her if you relapse."

"Did she leave anything behind?"

"No."

"Then the only way they can track her is by her name, and for that to work you have to know the subject well. They're never going to succeed at that. I'm the only one who can find her." He stood for a third time, brushed off Piercy's hand, and continued to unbutton his wrinkled, sweaty waistcoat.

"Evon, this is madness."

"No, Piercy, this is me riding off after the woman I love so she won't die pointlessly. I don't care if she never sees me as anything but a friend. If she dies because I didn't do anything to stop her, even if she saves Dalanine or the whole damn world, I will carry that guilt with me to my grave. Please try to understand that."

Piercy looked grim, but he nodded. "I'll start packing. You should bathe, you'll feel better for it. I'll find us clothing that is more suited to riding —"

"You're staying here," Evon said.

"I am certainly not staying here. You need my help."

"Piercy, if the worst happens and I can't get her free of the spell before we reach the Despot, I won't be able to protect all three of us from the blast. And I need someone here I can communicate with that I can trust."

"You can trust Mistress Gavranter."

"It's not the same. Piercy, you are perfectly capable of taking care of yourself on the road, you and I both know that, but this is going to come down to magic, and you can't follow me there."

"What happens when you have to sneak into the Despot's camp?"

"I'll wish you were there with me, and I'll muddle through. But you know this is the only sane course of action."

Piercy turned away. "I wish you didn't make so much sense

sometimes. All right. But I expect to hear from you every day, even if it's to say you've made no progress."

"Agreed. Will you still find those clothes for me?"

"If you promise to bathe. You are rather ripe, dear fellow."

Clean and dressed in a shirt and trousers that made him look like a well-heeled farmer, Evon ate quickly, ignoring the stares from the others in the dining room, packed what few things he thought he would need, and went to the stable yard. He was surprised to find Mistress Gavranter there, wearing a heavily lined purple cloak that she clutched around her against the cold. It made her look like a queen preparing to hold court. "Mr. Lorantis," she said, "I understand from Mr. Faranter that you intend to take a ride."

"Yes, Mistress Gavranter," Evon said. "I hope you approve."

"And if I did not, would it make a difference? I thought not. Good hunting, Mr. Lorantis." From the depths of her cloak she pulled out a folded piece of paper. "You may need this, or you may not, but I believe in preparing for all contingencies."

Evon opened it. It was a map of southern Dalanine and its borders, with shaded areas scattered across it and a silver dot near Ostradon. "Areas of magical concentration," Mistress Gavranter said. "The silver mark is attuned to you, which should keep you out of trouble unless you desire to wander into it. Whether you use it to find those areas or to steer clear of them is up to you, but you should remember that sometimes help is available from the least likely places."

"Thank you, Mistress Gavranter," Evon said, a little overwhelmed. He put the map away in his bag and mounted his horse. "I don't suppose you know if Miss Haylter took a horse with her?"

"I don't believe she did," Mistress Gavranter said, "which tells me that there is a part of that young woman that wants to be found."

Evon nodded to her, wheeled the horse around and trotted out of the stable yard. He retraced the route they'd taken the day they'd ridden to rescue Kerensa, and when he passed the side road that had led to Valantis's manor, Evon shivered a little. With Odelia dead, Valantis might give up on Kerensa...but it was foolish to think Speculatus had no other powerful magicians, and Evon still didn't know how they'd tracked her in the first place. Kerensa headed south into the hands of the Despot, with Speculatus following behind...Evon gripped the reins more tightly and pushed the thoughts away. There was nothing he could do about any of that. The only thing he had power over was finding Kerensa. He inhaled deeply and caught her scent making a clear trail along the coastal highway. How far could she have gotten on foot in one day? Perhaps he would catch up to her in Belicath. It might be just that simple.

Snow began falling around mid-afternoon, tiny cold specks that caught on his lashes and made him blink constantly. He pulled his wide-brimmed hat of felted wool further down over his eyes. These clothes were unexpectedly comfortable, though he felt a little exposed without his frock coat hugging his body. Piercy had compensated for that missing garment by providing Evon with a cloak as well as an overcoat. Evon thought he probably looked a little stupid, but he wasn't going to let that get in the way of comfort.

By the time he reached the outskirts of Belicath, at sunset, the snow was coming down more heavily and the lights in the houses he passed were little more than dim halos to either side of the road. Evon was following Kerensa purely by scent at this point, barely aware of the wide street and the pedestrian bridges arcing above the busiest intersections, and the appearance of the southern gate looming up before him startled him. He stopped his idiot horse beneath the last streetlight and looked off into the distance. The snow was falling so heavily now that he could barely see more than twenty feet ahead before everything simply went gray. He cursed vehemently. If he went on that night, he'd likely just get lost and freeze to death. He wasn't going to catch up to her tonight, anyway. Sleep, and an early start, and with luck the snow would have stopped falling.

He left Belicath early the next morning, the horse trudging through drifts four or five inches deep in places. The snow continued to fall, but in tiny specks once again, and despite the knot of anxiety Evon carried with him he was still able to appreciate what a beautiful day it was. He took out his map. The next town south of Belicath was Annaplen, probably a day's journey for the idiot horse and his first real chance at catching up to her. He tried not to think about the possibility that she'd found a ride with someone. As long as she was still on foot, he'd overtake her soon.

Dark fell before he reached Annaplen with no houses or villages in sight, but it was a clear night with a bright moon and it was easy to push on to reach the city, which, when he arrived, appeared to be host to a city-wide party. Men and women strolled together, even after dark, and shouted greetings to others across the street or to passing traffic. Evon was startled to be accosted in this way by several different women, all calling out invitations for him to join them and commenting approvingly on his appearance. They didn't seem to be prostitutes, but they were far more aggressive than the women of Evon's acquaintance in the capital, and he felt uncomfortably exposed by their attention.

He crossed most of the city this way and had begun to worry that Kerensa had come and gone when her scent took a sharp turn to the left. Gratefully, Evon followed it to a less crowded and less noisy neighborhood that was still heavily trafficked even at that hour, past a number of frame houses and businesses with their names painted in the windows and up to the yard of a small but pleasant-looking inn with a picture of a dancing pig hanging over the front door. Here, it seemed, was where all the noise had gone. Brightly lit windows revealed a taproom full of people drinking, laughing, eating, and in some cases dancing, though Evon couldn't hear any music. Kerensa's scent led straight through its front door.

The taproom smelled of warm beer and warmer bodies. Men and women sat or stood wherever they could find room, some of them even sitting on tables. Barmaids squeezed between customers, but cheerfully, not seeming to care if a careless drunk waved a little too broadly and clipped the edge of someone else's mug. A roar went up in one corner of the room, and a woman stepped onto a table, assisted by several friendly hands, and began belting out a song Evon had never heard before. Everyone in the taproom turned to watch her, and most of them joined in the raucous chorus when it came around. Evon shoved through the crowd, scanning the room as he did so. Drinkers kept stepping into his path, most of them without meaning to, though some clapped him on the shoulder and invited him to join the party. He declined with as good a nature as he could muster after a long day on the road and his irritation and frustration at being so close to Kerensa without seeing her. Perhaps she'd taken a room and had gone there to get away from the noise.

Then he saw her. She was seated at the bar, her back to him, a mug of pale beer next to her hand. She sat a little slumped over, though whether she was sad or simply tired he couldn't tell. He shoved harder and managed to make a free space next to her. "What are you drinking, miss?" he said.

"I already—" She looked up at him and her mouth fell open, then closed sharply. Her eyes narrowed. "I told you not to follow me."

"Yes, I know. Do you think someday you'll find a way to say it that will persuade me to listen?"

"Evon—"

"Let me see. It's dangerous, I'll be killed by enemy forces, you have to do this alone, you want to sacrifice your life for the greater good, it's dangerous, and I can't think of any other objections you might have."

"You said 'dangerous' twice."

"Well, I thought it might be extra dangerous, what with the war and all."

She covered her mouth to hide a smile. "Why won't you leave me alone?"

"Is this man bothering you?" A dark-bearded young man, very broad in the shoulders, loomed up behind Kerensa.

"Yes," Kerensa said, irritably.

The man looked Evon up and down and seemed to like his chances. "Let's see what we can do about that," he said. Evon felt someone else step up behind him. This might not end well.

"I'm her *brother*," he said, equally irritable. "I came to take her home. Our parents are worried about her."

"He's not my brother," Kerensa said. Evon felt hands grip his upper arms.

"Livian, why do you keep playing this game?" he said, trying to sound exasperated and sad at the same time. "You know Ma worries when you don't come home. I'm just glad you fell in with people who want to defend you, even if it's against your own brother. Really, fellows, it's good to know there are decent men left in this world who are willing to defend a lone woman's honor."

The hands relaxed, though they didn't let go entirely. "Is this true, miss?" rumbled a deep voice from behind Evon.

"No!" Kerensa exclaimed. She looked a little stunned. "He's making all of this up! I don't want to go with him!"

Evon projected as much sorrow into his voice as he could. "Livian, you know how it hurts me when you say that. Your own brother who's looked out for you your whole life, who only wants what's best for you. I'm sorry you had to hear that, fellows. I hope your own sisters treat you better than mine does. Please, Livian, let's just go home."

The hands released him. "I think you should go with your brother, sweetheart," the bearded man said. "Come back and have a drink with us another time."

"No—" Kerensa began, but Evon grabbed her hand and squeezed it hard. "Come along, *sister*," he said, and pulled her through the crowd and out of the taproom.

She yanked her hand free when they were in the yard. "How dare you do that?"

"I'm just pointing out how easily an unscrupulous man could take advantage of you."

"Someone as unscrupulous as you, you mean?"

"Kerensa, you're not safe alone on the road. An unescorted woman is a target for every evil-minded man out there. What were you thinking?"

"Evon, there's no more *time*. You and I both know those magicians are never going to find a solution before the Despot invades."

"What about me? You don't think I can do it?"

"How much progress have *you* made?"

It felt like a punch to the stomach. Kerensa looked at him for a moment, her eyes wide, then said, "I'm sorry. I didn't mean that."

"Didn't you?" He leaned up against the porch rail. "I can see where you might have lost faith in me."

"No. Never that. But I'm tired of waiting and being poked at and analyzed. I want to *act* and I want to stop feeling like a victim."

"Kerensa, we're talking about your life. If you manage to get into the Despot's presence, which is improbable, you won't come back from that. That's unacceptable to me. It ought to be unacceptable to you."

"Evon, every day the Despot moves a little farther north. He's destroying everything and everyone that gets in his way. What I'm carrying is the only way to stop him. I don't want to die, but how can I rate myself any higher than the thousands of people who will otherwise die at his hands?"

"That doesn't mean you have to throw your life away when there's another solution."

She sighed. "Then tell me what I should do. Tell me *your* solution. And it had better not involve those magicians, because I am not going back to them."

"No. Some of them, most of them, are decent people, but Mistress Quendester was right in saying they wouldn't find the secret before the Despot comes. But they're looking at it the wrong way. They still think they can extract the fire from you and use it as a weapon. They don't understand that the spell *is* the weapon, that breaking it down like that will only destroy it. If we're going to stop the Despot from tearing Dalanine apart, from tearing any other country apart, it will be through this spell. I just have to find a way to keep it from killing you."

"Can you do that?"

"I know I can. I refuse to believe otherwise."

"I'm going to keep traveling south. The sooner I reach the Despot, the less damage he'll do."

"Then I'll just have to figure this out while we're on the road."

Kerensa turned her too-smooth face so he was looking at her in profile. "Then what do we do?"

That "we" cheered Evon immensely. "Sleep," he said. "I've been on the road all day chasing after someone who thinks she can get rid of me with an uninformative note. I don't want to think about this before morning."

Kerensa smiled. "I knew it wouldn't work. But I thought, maybe for once he'll see reason. Is Piercy with the horses?"

"I made him stay behind. He's more logical than I am and an appeal to reason worked."

"I didn't think you went anywhere without him."

"Neither did I." Right then he wished Piercy were there with them. He was good with strategy, and if anyone could find a way through enemy territory into the heart of the Despot's army, Piercy could. He'd have to ask Piercy about it when he communicated with him that night.

"Well, we can't go back in there, and I left all my things in the room I rented," Kerensa said irritably. "Couldn't you have been a little more discreet?"

"You were the one who told the man I was bothering you. Did you want me to get beaten up by two half-drunken farmers?"

She ducked her head. "I was just being honest. I didn't think about how they'd react."

"And you think you're safe out here on your own. We can go in the back way and I'll find someone to rent me a room."

He took her around through the stable yard and in at the kitchen door, where the cook directed him to the innkeeper's wife, a stout woman who took his money and gave him what was probably the smallest room in the place, little bigger than the bedframe that filled it. Kerensa showed him where she was sleeping, just in case, and stopped him before he left. "I wanted you to follow me," she said, laying her hand on his arm. "I'm glad you did."

"That's good, because you won't be rid of me easily," he replied. Her eyes shone in the lamplight, and his mind replayed *I wanted you to follow me* and tried hard to turn it into *I want you*, with no success. "Good night, sister Kerensa."

"Good night, Evon, and don't worry, I'll still be here in the morning." She shut the door on the sound of her laughter. He stood still in the hall outside her door for a moment, then went back to his room to talk to Piercy. Between the two of them, they ought to be able to come up with a plan.

17

They had two days of beautifully clear weather as they traveled south, sunny and warm enough that even high in the mountains the roads cleared somewhat and they made excellent time. The first night, they stopped at a farmhouse where the farmer's grown sons appreciated Kerensa far more than made Evon happy. He wished he could have pretended to be her jealous husband, and had to settle for being her overprotective brother instead. Kerensa seemed oblivious to the glances and jostling for positions at the table next to her, which mollified Evon a little, but he still watched her carefully until Mrs. Tefinter, the farmer's wife, showed her to a room she would share with the woman's young daughters. Evon bunked down with the sons and tried to fall asleep to their chorus of whistling breaths and honking snores. Even Piercy never made that much noise.

He was impatient, the next day, to reach Holdplain; it had been impossible for him to make any more attempts at removing the spell from Kerensa that night, and he began to feel the pressure of moving south without any progress. According to his map, Holdplain was an easy day's ride from the farm, so after a hearty breakfast he took Kerensa up behind him and trotted away down the highway, which had begun to turn inland away from the coast. He'd offered to buy her a horse of her own, though he winced at the resulting leanness of his purse, but Kerensa admitted she didn't know how to ride, and he had to endure the guilty pleasure of having her body pressed against his back as they rode. He didn't remember her holding him this closely before, and cursed himself for being so sensitive to her presence.

"If the weather stays this clear, we should reach the border in just a few days, right?" she said. She leaned closer to him, her breath warm on his neck, as a wagon passed them headed north; it had given them only a few inches' clearance.

"I wouldn't count on it," Evon said. "Mrs. Tefinter said they're expecting another big storm in a day or two."

"That's too bad. I hate the delay."

"I don't. If a storm hits while we are safely tucked away in a little inn somewhere, that's more time for me to work. And even the Despot can't move his armies in a blizzard."

Another wagon approached, this one wider, and Evon went off the verge into ankle-deep drifts to avoid it. "Does it seem to you," he said, "that there are more wagons going north than before?"

"I counted yesterday," Kerensa said. "Seventeen, and some of them were families instead of cargo. The Despot is already driving people ahead of him."

"If they have time to flee, it's not yet dire," Evon said.

"Or too many people think they have more time than they do. Look, there's another one."

Evon once again went off the road. "Don't blame yourself."

"I'm not, but it does make me anxious."

"Holdplain tonight. Will you be ready for a few more experiments?"

"The way you say that makes me think you have something more in mind than simple study."

"I want to try a few more command words with *vertiri* to see if it responds to one of them. It will...you may feel fear again."

"I can endure that." She didn't sound as certain as her words suggested. Evon cringed to think of causing her pain, even if it was only emotional pain. He reminded himself that it was better for her to feel a little pain now than to undergo the ultimate agony of the spell's final activation. He had to find a way. There was no acceptable alternative.

But in Holdplain they ran into trouble of a different sort. "You only have one room?" Evon exclaimed.

"Sorry. We're a tavern and we only got so many rooms. You can bunk down in the stables if you've a mind." The tavern owner was a brusque, thin, bald man who stood behind the bar polishing the same glass repeatedly with a none-too-clean rag.

"But she's my *sister*," Evon said. "There's no impropriety in our sharing a room."

"Wouldn't be right, sister or no. This is a decent, Gods-fearing establishment. Stable or nothing."

Evon hesitated, then leaned close to the tavern owner. "Sir, I really hate to have to tell anyone this. You can see my sister looks like a beautiful, normal girl, yes? The sad truth is that she has fits sometimes. Froths at the mouth and everything. I try to take a room next door to her, so I can hear it if she falls down, because it's my duty to care for her in her trouble."

The bald man paused briefly in his polishing, his eyes widening just a bit. He glanced at Kerensa, who was seated at one of the tables, picking at something stuck to the table top. "Not that pretty little thing?"

"It's too true, sir. Now, I can understand your position. It doesn't look good for a man and a woman, not married to each other, to share a room. And I'll understand if you want me to take myself off to the stables. It's just that somebody needs to care for her, and if I'm not there, well, I'd need to know that you were ready to step up to help her." Evon wished now that he'd known about the room situation; he could have claimed they were married. Too late now. "She sometimes loses control of her bodily functions," he improvised, seeing the man's expression wavering.

The man looked at Kerensa again, reluctance and disgust at war on his face. "I suppose I can make an exception, given your situation, but just the one night, understand?"

"That's all we need." Evon took the glass and shook the man's hand vigorously. "Thank you for your compassion. I'm sure the Gods look favorably on a good man such as yourself." He quickly turned away and beckoned to Kerensa to follow him, just in case the good man changed his mind.

"You're sure there wasn't another room?" Kerensa said.

"Of course I'm sure. And yes, I could have slept in the stables, but I'm not willing to lose another night's study just because you don't want me snoring on your floor all night." The tiny room had one bed with a couple of thin blankets and no other furnishings. "I didn't realize Holdplain was so small."

"It's all right, I don't mind. I just feel sorry for you not having a bed."

"Don't worry about me. Look, why don't you sit down, and we'll try a couple of things. I planned everything out while we rode today, so it shouldn't take long. Then you can get some sleep and I'll dig into my notes a little further."

Kerensa sat on the bed. "How certain are you that this will hurt? Or be frightening?"

Evon hesitated. "Fairly certain."

"Then I need a minute to prepare." She closed her eyes and breathed out, slowly, then inhaled. Evon cast *epiria* while she relaxed her body. He watched her, mesmerized again by her beauty, even in her travel-worn state with her hair disheveled. He looked at the single bed, just wide enough for two people to sleep close together. What would she do if he suggested it? If he bent down right now and just kissed her? He turned away and did a little deep breathing of his own. She deserved better than to be assaulted, especially by someone who loved her, in a situation she had no way of escaping, and if he couldn't summon the courage to be honest with her, he needed to stop thinking about her that way.

"I'm ready," she said quietly, and Evon turned to see that she had gripped the edges of the bed loosely and sat upright, her eyes closed, waiting for him.

"I'm going to try *vertiri* again. I still don't understand why the spell reacted to it the way it did," Evon explained, and cast the spell.

Once again the spell-ribbons came to a halt, quivering, waiting for something to happen. "Now there are a few command words I want to try. I hope they won't hurt or frighten it, but this is when you should be prepared." Kerensa nodded. Her grip on the edge of the bed tightened. "*Cucurri,*" he said, and once again the spell-ribbons stretched like kneaded dough, and Kerensa made a whimpering sound through her clenched teeth. "*Desini,*" Evon said quickly, and gripped her wrist as she panted, her lips pulled back to bare her teeth.

"We can stop," Evon said, but she shook her head vehemently and said, "Try again."

Evon released her and stepped back. "Once again," he said. "*Vertiri. Sepera.*"

Kerensa's eyes snapped open and she arched her back, a hiss of pain emerging from her throat. Evon dismissed the spell and wrapped his arms around her, murmuring to her as she clung to him and sobbed silently. "I can't do this to you," he said. "Let's just leave it at that for tonight."

She shook her head, pressed against his chest. "How many more?" she whispered.

"Just one. One more."

"Then do it." She released him and wiped tears from her eyes. "I can handle one more."

"I don't know if *I* can."

"You can endure it if I can. One more."

Evon stepped back and waited for her to regain her composure, then raised his right hand. He was almost out of words that enacted movement and change. "*Vertiri. Trattuci.*"

The spell-ribbons went from being alert and still to raging about Kerensa, flying so fast they turned into a blue halo surrounding her. "Are you all right?" Evon said.

"I don't feel anything but dizzy," Kerensa said. "What did you do?"

One of the spell-ribbons rose above its fellows and began flowing away from Kerensa. Others began to follow. "I think I did it," Evon breathed, afraid to hope. "They're moving!"

Behind her blue halo, Kerensa gasped. "Moving? Moving away?"

The one spell-ribbon had become a stream of them. "Yes!"

Kerensa clasped her hands in front of her. "I can't believe it!"

The stream of spell-ribbons flowed up the wall and across the ceiling. It seemed to be looking for an outlet. "It's trying to get out," Evon said.

"So catch it! We still need the spell, right?"

The spell flowed down the wall and over the floor, swerving back and forth like a headless blue snake. It came to Evon's feet and flowed over them, then stopped. It came back and began twining up Evon's ankles, moving more quickly now. Evon felt a warm, unpleasant tingle flow through his legs wherever the spell touched. "Oh no," he said. *"Desini!"*

The spell flowed backward as quickly as it had come, returning to circle Kerensa's body as if it had never gone anywhere. "But—" Kerensa said in a small voice. "You said it was working."

"It was," Evon said, "but what it was doing was looking for a new host. Damn it, I should have let it take me. That would have solved our problem."

"By creating a new one," Kerensa said. "And suppose you weren't able to work magic on it because it was attached to you?"

"But you would have been free."

"It wouldn't be worth it at that cost. But Evon, you figured out the solution! We just need to find the right person to attach the spell to."

"How could you want to condemn anyone to what you've had to endure?"

Kerensa's face fell. "I couldn't. Not even someone evil. Well, maybe someone evil. But it would be hard to find the right person."

Evon sat on the bed next to her. "You're right, though. We found the right spell. Now we just need to know how to use it."

She leaned against him. "So it's a victory."

"Absolutely." He had to get out before he did something stupid. He stood and said, "I'm going down to the stables for a bit, so you can get undressed in private."

She looked as if she were going to say something, then changed her mind. "All right. And—thank you again, for not giving up."

He smiled at her. "You're stronger than I am; maybe I should thank *you* for not giving up."

He went out to the stables and brushed the horse, which had already been well cared for, and tried not to think about sleeping in the same room as Kerensa, only feet away from her. *Think about something else. Vertiri* and *trattuci. Vertiri* for change, *trattuci* for...the best translation might be "transfer." So the spell's reaction made sense, but why would its creators have made it respond to those commands? Suppose one host became unsuitable; they apparently wanted to be able to move it to another host without killing the first. So these magicians cared at least a little for human life; why would they build a spell that required someone's death to activate? And why set it up so it would find so many false targets?

He put the currycomb away and went back to the room. Kerensa was sitting on the edge of the bed in her nightdress, golden hair braided neatly and feet tucked under the hem of her gown. "Are you going to do some reading?"

"Yes, unless it will disturb you."

"No. I'm not very sleepy."

Evon sat on the floor and took his notes out of his bag. He found the runes comprising the spell to find the next target and compared it to the slimmed-down version he'd created to prove the existence of the entity. It really did look as if they hadn't known any better, as if the awkward, false-target-finding version was the best they could do. If the creators of the spell had used his version, Kerensa would have been drawn directly to the Despot and...he shouldn't be pleased that so many people had died because of the spell, but he would never have met her otherwise. Suppose all the spells could be adjusted the same way? Not that there was a purpose to doing that, unless he could alter the spell itself. He picked up a few more pages and set them aside. What was he looking for? Something that might tell him why the spell's builders had attached the spell to a person, since *vertiri* and *trattuci* proved it could move independently. If he knew that, he could figure out how to keep it free of a person. Probably.

"Can I ask you a question?" Kerensa asked. He looked up and saw her propped on her elbow in the bed. "Go ahead," he said.

"What will you do when this is all over?"

Evon blinked. "What makes you ask that?"

"What happened tonight...the whole time I've known you, it's been in the middle of this horror. I don't really know what you do when you aren't following me around."

He grinned. "I do very much as I've been doing this whole time. I invent and refine spells for whatever client Miss Elltis has brought in. We had a government contract when Piercy brought me the problem of the Fearsome Firemage."

"Who is—oh, no, Evon, did you really call me that?"

"Only at first. Anyway, I suppose I'll go back to doing that. Though Miss Elltis won't have me back. Mistress Gavranter says she may have work for me. So I don't know exactly what it will be, but likely it will look much the same as what I was doing before." The thought made him unexpectedly unhappy, and not because it meant never seeing Kerensa again. The prospect of spending the rest of his life in small, cold rooms researching spells depressed him.

"For the longest time I didn't think I had a future," Kerensa said, rolling onto her back to stare at the low ceiling. "Now I don't know what I want to do with it."

"I thought you were interested in university."

"It seems so impractical, though. Elkenhound isn't much bigger than Holdplain; what use would an Alvorian scholar be there?"

"There are other things to study. You might decide you're interested in something else as well. And...there's no reason you have to stay in Elkenhound, is there? Matra is a beautiful city, and there's so much to do, so many people to meet." *Could* she live in Matra? What might happen if they saw each other regularly, without the burden of this spell between them? On the other hand, could he bear to watch her fall in love with someone else?

"I'd miss my family," she said, but there was a question in her voice. "I don't know. I'm still a little afraid to make plans until...whatever happens. I'm sorry. I'm keeping you from your work."

"I don't mind. Tell me about your family."

"I live with my aunt and uncle. They took me in the year of the influenza, when my parents died. They're wonderful people, but I think my aunt—she gets this look in her eye sometimes, like she doesn't know what to do with me. Most girls my age are married by now or have permanent work somewhere. She doesn't understand why I'd work in the tavern when I could take a job in a shop, or marry Turley."

"Who's Turley?" Jealousy gripped him like a fist around his stomach.

"He courted me for a while, when we were both younger. I liked him well enough, but then he asked me to marry him and I knew I didn't like him as much as that. He follows me around back home with this lovesick look in his eye. I wish he'd find someone else to moon over. I've been gone long enough, maybe he has. At least he never followed me as far as you have." She laughed. "But you're much harder to send away."

"Nearly impossible."

"Only nearly?"

"I suppose you could have me stuffed in a grain sack and put on a wagon headed north, but that would only slow me down."

She laughed again. "I can't tell you what a comfort it is to have you here."

So he was a comfort. Like a blanket, or a stuffed toy. "I'm glad to hear it. I don't think you should be alone for this."

She fell silent, and he went back to his notes. After a few minutes, he heard her breathing change. She'd fallen asleep facing him, her head cradled on one hand. He watched her for a little while, until she made a sort of gentle grunting sound and rolled onto her back. He looked back at his notes. He wasn't going to get any more work done tonight. He gathered them up and put them away, turned out the light, then rolled up his overcoat for a pillow and wrapped himself in his voluminous cloak and tried to get comfortable. He had trouble not thinking about how close she was. He could think about runes instead. He was sick of thinking about runes. Kerensa began to snore, not very loudly but with a kind of intermittent irregularity that was impossible to predict. Not a very romantic trait, but Evon found it endearing and then mocked himself for being so smitten as to love even her erratic, annoying snore. He rolled onto his side, facing away from her, and began going over spells in his head, simple gesture and word combinations, more complicated spells which could be cast swiftly if you knew how to draw the runes in the simplest form that was still intelligible. *Spexa. Cleperi vertiri*, bitter and soapy to the taste. *Solto epiria.* The soothing monotony calmed his mind and eventually, despite Kerensa's snoring, he fell asleep.

"*T*he tavern keeper says another big storm is coming," Evon said, entering the stable after settling the tab. "I think it might be wise to stay here another day, wait it out."

"I don't want to wait." Kerensa drew her cloak more closely around her. Even in the shelter of the stable, a chill wind blew around them, bringing with it the aroma of baking bread and, below that, the icy smell of snow.

"Suppose we get lost in the storm?"

"You have that map. We can't get very lost with that. And there are little farming villages all up and down the road. We can find shelter somewhere, and be that much closer."

Evon looked out at the sky, which still looked clear. It was impossible to believe a storm was coming. "All right. But let's hurry."

They left Holdplain and went south under the clear blue sky, the sun turning the untrodden fields into carpets of sparkling white. Around noon the great highway ended, becoming a much smaller, unpaved road that was frozen hard into ruts where the wagons had passed. A wagon approached at that moment, forcing them off the road. Evon felt sorry for the passengers, who were jounced and jolted in the bed of the poorly sprung wagon as it passed over the ruts. "It makes the horse seem much more comfortable," he said over his shoulder.

"More refugees," she said. "Did you see how they had all those possessions loaded up? How far is it to the border?"

"Another seventy miles or so."

"Do you think the Despot has crossed yet?"

"Piercy says not, but he's close." He and Piercy still hadn't worked out how they might get near enough to the Despot for the weapon to work. Evon didn't think he and Kerensa were stealthy enough to work their way through the enemy camp and sneak into the Despot's tent without anyone noticing, and their wildest plan—to pretend Kerensa was a gift for the Despot—had so many disadvantages it had only been arrived at late one evening, when Piercy had had a little too much to drink and Evon was mentally exhausted and ready to embrace any mad idea.

Clouds began gathering soon after, high, thin clouds that obscured the sun but clearly didn't hold any snow. Evon looked at his map and located a village some ten miles further on. They ought to be able to reach it before dark. He put it away and glanced at the road ahead. No more wagons had passed since the first one. Far in the distance, a copse of trees stood on a rise, and beyond that, heavy clouds massed on the horizon. Evon cursed, then flicked the reins and urged the horse into a faster gait. "What's wrong?" Kerensa said.

"The storm is coming," Evon said. "I'm going to try to reach that village before it arrives."

"Aren't we running toward the storm?"

"We could turn around and go back to Holdplain."

Kerensa thought for a moment. "Do you think we can reach the village in time?"

"If we run."

But the road was too rough for a full-out run, and Evon's stomach clenched as they trotted into the oncoming storm with no shelter in sight. They should have returned to Holdplain. His stupidity was going to get them both killed. The sky was now fully overcast and the oncoming clouds blanketed the fields so completely that Evon could see the edge of the storm as it pressed on toward them. He pulled the horse up and took out the map; they were still a mile or two from the village. They would run into the storm long before they reached it. But there was nothing to do but move on.

The wind had picked up and blew tiny flecks of snow at them that bit into Evon's face. He pulled his hat low over his eyes and ducked his shoulders to keep his vision as clear as possible, which wasn't very clear. Kerensa huddled behind him, clinging tight; he glanced back and saw that she had pulled her hood well over her head. He turned around, and the wind swelled and the storm was upon them. Evon was blinded by the white, whipping snow that battered them both. It came in gusts, the wind occasionally dropping to a mere growl instead of a roar, glimpses of the road sometimes visible between blasts of snow and wind. The horse stood still, as placid as if this were a summer shower. Evon spoke to it and it moved forward, Evon leaning over to stare hard at the ground, looking for evidence that they were still on the road.

He lost track of time as they plodded slowly along, his eyes burning with effort and the blowing snowflakes. Once he felt the horse go off the frozen track and pulled it back; another time he saw the edge of the road just before the horse stepped off it. He had no idea how Kerensa fared, but her grip on his waist never varied and she made no sounds of distress. Then the wind picked up yet again, and Evon couldn't see anything at all. He stopped the horse and they stood still for a few minutes. "What's wrong?" Kerensa shouted.

"I can't see anything. It's not safe to move on if it's possible we could leave the road." Evon ducked under the warm, heavy folds of his cloak and made a space where he could safely pull out the map, then conjured a tiny light. His heart sank. They had made hardly any progress. It would be hours before they reached the village, and Kerensa, who already shivered now and then, would be frozen before that. He wouldn't be in very good shape himself.

"I think that's a light," Kerensa shouted, tapping Evon's shoulder. He put the map away, dismissed the light and looked around. He saw nothing. "There, that way, it looks like lamplight," she said.

"It's probably the snow blinding you," Evon said.

"No, I'm certain of it. Isn't there some way you can look ahead, or look closely?"

"I don't think I'd see anything but snowflakes, even if there were something there."

"I think we should take the chance."

"Kerensa, if we leave the road, we could wander until we freeze to death."

"We're already doing that. Please, Evon, I know what I saw."

Evon chewed on his lip. "All right," he shouted. "Point me the right way."

She stuck out her arm and pointed. Evon turned the horse and once again began their slow progress.

There was nothing but snow. Evon wondered if it would be possible to make their way back to the road using the map. There were so many obstacles the horse could trip over, and break a leg, and then they really would be doomed. He wondered if Kerensa could be killed by something like this. Would the spell's creators have built some sort of safeguard into it, to protect the host from dying in some pointless fashion? He blinked hard to clear his lashes of snow. There was a light—no, it was gone. Evon strained to see anything in the encompassing whiteness. There it was again. A lamp in a window, and someone passing in front of it, blocking it out occasionally. Evon urged the horse onward, feeling his despair begin to drop away.

"Did you see it?" Kerensa asked.

"Yes, and thank you for not saying 'I told you so.'"

"I wasn't even thinking it." Kerensa shivered again, a hard, convulsive movement. "I'm just glad I was right."

"So am I."

The rectangle of light grew larger and stronger until the outline of a house loomed up out of the whiteness. Evon had an impression of rough framing and two stories and then he saw the door. "Don't get down," he told Kerensa, and slid off the horse to go and bang at the door. Nothing happened. Whoever had been moving around behind the window stopped. He banged on the door again and shouted, "Can you help us?"

The door opened a crack. A suspicious-looking eye that might have belonged to someone of either sex squinted up at him. "What do you want?" The voice was old and pitched low for a woman or high for a man.

"My wife and I need shelter from the storm," Evon said, deciding at the last minute not to risk another Holdplain incident. "Can you help us?"

"No shelter here. Get along."

"We'll die if we don't find a place out of the storm. Isn't there anywhere we can stay? A spare room? We can pay, or—I'm a magician, I know many useful spells—"

"Don't need none of that. Get along, I said."

"*Please,*" Evon said. "My wife isn't well. We'll take anything. I swear we don't mean you any harm."

"I ain't seen a wife. Ain't seen nobody but you. You could be a murderer, kill an old woman in her sleep."

"Wait." Evon went back and helped Kerensa dismount. Her shivering was coming more rapidly now. Evon led her to the front door, then conjured a light so the old woman could see them both clearly. The suspicious eye flicked from one of them to the other. Kerensa smiled. Evon tried to smile, but felt his face was frozen.

"You can sleep in the barn around back," the woman said finally. "No fires. And don't think of tryin' to get in here once I'm abed. I got a little magic of my own."

"Thank you, ma'am, we truly appreciate it," Evon said. They went back to the horse and, clutching its harness, made their slow way around the farmhouse, then struck out toward the dim shape of the barn. Snow was packed against the base of the doors, and it took some shoving for Evon to pull one of them open wide enough for them and the horse to fit through. It was less cold than in the heart of the blizzard, but still freezing inside, and empty except for a sway-backed mule, though stalls and rusted pails showed that this had once been a dairy farm. The floor was swept clean, but a ladder led up to a hayloft which appeared to be full of messily stowed hay.

"I'll take care of the horse. Why don't you see if you can turn that into bedding of some kind?" Evon said. Kerensa nodded and gingerly climbed the ladder, careful of her footing in the near dark. Evon found a scrap of old blanket and rubbed the horse down, then led it into one of the empty stalls far away from the mule, which looked at him with a vicious eye. He could hear Kerensa up above, and the rustling of hay being shifted. "Would you push some of that over the edge for the horse?" he called up to her, and moments later large clumps rained down. He put the hay into a convenient trough, then scooped up several armfuls of snow into another trough and cast a furtive *forva* to melt the snow and warm the resulting water. He repeated the action, awkwardly, to fill the canteen hanging off the horse's harness. They didn't have any food, so water would have to do until the storm blew itself out. He tried not to think about what he would do if the storm lasted more than a day or so. He might become desperate enough to invade that woman's home and raid her larder.

He clambered up the ladder, hauling their bags with him, to find that Kerensa had piled some of the hay into two large heaps and was sitting on one of them, her cloak wrapped around herself. She was shivering hard now and looked miserable. Evon swiftly removed her cloak, spread it on the haystack, and sat on it, then pulled her down to sit with her back against his chest and wrapped his own cloak around them both. He held her tightly as she shook and only then realized what he'd done. *It made sense,* he told himself, *she wouldn't have gotten warm on her own, and I promised I wouldn't light a fire. I should have started a fire anyway. This is madness, holding her like this.* Her shivering body felt good against his, and he had to quell the impulse to kiss her hair, to turn her so he could cradle her against him and be filled with her wonderful smoky scent. As she gradually became still and warm, he desperately tried to think of reasons not to let her go. Shared warmth against the frigid barn? They could still freeze to death, on their own. He couldn't come up with anything that wouldn't make his true motives obvious. He ought to let her go, call up a light so they could see more clearly to settle into their separate hay piles, and try to sleep the storm, and his desires, out.

"More comfortable?" he said, hoping he sounded casual.

She sat silent for a moment, then turned sideways, put her arms around his neck and leaned against his chest, her head on his shoulder and her fingers brushing the hair at the nape of his neck. "I am now," she said.

At first he didn't understand. Kerensa's dark dress made her nearly invisible in the dim light; he could see only her hair and the lighter oval of her face, which she now turned up toward his. She seemed to be waiting for something, and suddenly he registered the feel of her body pressed against his, how her arms tightly circled his neck, and he thought he might have wandered into a dream, because what was happening was impossible. He laid his hand along her cheek and felt her lean into his touch, shifting so his fingers trailed across the smooth skin of her face. A million questions rose up in his mind, but then his lips found hers, and he forgot every one of them.

Her lips were still cold, but warmed with his kiss, parting a little in response. She drew him closer despite her awkward position, half in his lap and half on the floor, so he put an arm low around her waist and hitched her up to a more secure position, and felt her smile against his mouth. This was nothing like the chaste kisses he'd exchanged with certain young women of his acquaintance, proper and socially acceptable; nothing in his experience had prepared him for holding the woman he loved and feeling her heart beat faster with desire for him. She was beautiful and he was kissing her and, even better, she was kissing him with a wonderful eagerness, and that told him this was not a dream because it was something he had never dared dream of. He put his free hand to the back of her head and began pulling pins out of her hair until it fell in one glorious sweep to her waist, and he ran his fingers through it and shivered with joy. "Kerensa," he murmured, and she kissed him so fiercely that it burned all the way down his spine.

When they finally separated, Kerensa laid her head on his shoulder and sighed with such pleasure that another white-hot wave went through him, and he held her close and felt again the rapid beating of her heart. He ran his hand down her silky hair again, but paused when a horrible thought occurred to him. Surely she wouldn't...? He was trying to frame the words *Did you only do that because I was available?* as a more delicate question when she said,

"Did you only kiss me because I was forward, or did it mean something more?"

He felt the fist around his heart relax. "Shouldn't I be asking *you* that question, since you were the forward one?"

"I was so afraid of making a fool of myself, but I couldn't bear it any longer, not showing you how I feel. I figured if it was dark, at least I wouldn't have to see you when you rejected me."

Evon laughed and stroked her hair. "I would never have had the courage to do what you did. I intended to take my love for you to my grave."

She drew in an astonished breath. "You say that as though...Evon, how long have you felt this way?"

"According to Piercy, practically from the moment I first saw you. I was just too dense to realize the truth until you were kidnapped."

"That's still a long time for you to carry those feelings around. You couldn't have told me?"

"Not while you might think you should return those feelings out of gratitude."

"Oh. I suppose that makes sense." She shifted. "You were good at hiding your feelings. I thought you cared for me only as a sister."

"I thought you cared for me only as a brother."

"I'm glad you're not my brother."

"So am I, because this would be illegal."

"Immoral, certainly." She intertwined her fingers with his. "You came into the bar and started telling that story to those men that made me sound either crazy or whorish, I wasn't sure which, and I thought, He really is going to follow me anywhere, and I knew I never wanted to be without you again. And I hoped it meant you might feel something more for me than friendship."

"I had no idea how you felt. I nearly went mad when Speculatus had you. I've wanted to kiss you ever since then, and run my fingers through your hair, and hold your hand—" Evon lifted their joined hands and kissed the back of hers. She laughed, and the sound made his heart beat faster, so he bent and kissed her again, over and over until, laughing, she pretended to push him away and said, "Now I wish I'd said something sooner."

"I intend to make up for that lost time, so don't feel too much regret."

"I could think of it as being even gladder that I didn't wait longer."

"I agree." He kissed her once more, just because he could and because she loved him. In the darkness, with the snow howling around the barn outside, it was hard to believe it was real. He conjured a light and Kerensa winced against the sudden brightness. "What did you do that for?" she asked.

"Proving to myself that you are really here. It seems so unlikely, someone like you deciding to fall in love with me."

"What's that supposed to mean?" She leaned away to look at him more fully.

"Well, because I'm stubborn, and difficult, and I say stupid things because I become absorbed in my work —"

"And you're kind, and smart, and you've never let me down, and you are so handsome I can't stop looking at you."

"I am?"

"Of course. You're much better looking than Piercy, for one. You have those blue eyes, and that square jaw —"

"And yet Piercy is the one all the girls follow around."

"That's because Piercy is satisfied with flirtations, and you have been waiting for the right girl, and I imagine all of them knew that girl was me, so they didn't bother trying to attract you." Kerensa snuggled close again. "Evon?" She sounded unexpectedly shy.

"Mmm?"

"Do you think...would it be wrong for you to hold me while I sleep tonight? Because I would really like that."

"Wrong as in, we're not married, or wrong as in, we might do something only married people are supposed to do?"

"Either one." She ducked her head lower against his chest. "Evon, I have been alone for so long, and I trust that you will find a way to keep me alive, but I am still so afraid. I would just like to have that comfort for one night. And it is really cold in here. But I understand if you think it would be a bad idea."

He tightened his arms around her. "Kerensa," he said, "you would have far more trouble convincing me to let you go."

They shoved the two piles of hay together and made a bed from their cloaks, then nestled together, Kerensa falling asleep almost immediately. Evon lay wakeful for a while, surprised that he was untroubled by the impulses that had tormented him ever since he discovered he loved the woman in his arms. Perhaps the over-whelming surprise and relief at learning she felt the same way had satisfied him—for the moment, anyway. He kissed her beautiful hair, then turned his face so he didn't have to breathe through it. She loved him. It was like a miracle. *Now,* he thought as he drifted off to sleep, *I just have to perform a miracle for her.*

19

*E*von woke the next morning to find the storm had not abated, that the barn in the daytime was only slightly less dark than it had been the night before, and that he was starving. Kerensa lay peacefully asleep beside him, her hair tangled and a line across her poreless cheek where she had slept on a crease of the cloak. He gently shook her awake and saw her expression go from momentary confusion to awareness of where she was and then, wonderfully, such happiness when she saw him that it was impossible for him not to kiss her. She made a pleased sound when he did, and when he drew back, said, "I didn't say it last night, but I love you, Evon Lorantis, and I hope you'll always kiss me the way you did just now."

That, and the look in her shining eyes, made more kissing essential, until Evon had to release her because the desire that had been banked the night before was rising up in him again, and it seemed to him that Kerensa felt the same way. He was determined not to press his attentions on her, however willing she was, on a makeshift bed in a hayloft in the middle of a blizzard. So he kissed her one last time and retreated to arm's length while she sat and picked hay out of her tangled hair. "I never understood why you braided it at night," Evon said.

"This is why. Though usually there's less hay. Would you hand me my brush? By the Gods, but I'm hungry."

"The storm hasn't let up. I was thinking of approaching our unwilling landlady. I don't want to starve to death in this barn."

They bundled up and went over to the house and knocked on the door. When the suspicious eye appeared, Evon said, "Thank you so much for the shelter, ma'am, you've saved our lives. We were wondering if we could buy some food from you. We were planning to eat at the next village we came to, but you know we never made it that far. My wife would certainly appreciate it."

Kerensa jerked a little when he came to "wife," but said, "We really are very hungry. Don't you have anything you can spare?"

The eye examined her. "Show me your coin first," the woman said.

Evon pulled a handful of coins from his trousers pocket. The door opened a little more, a plump wrinkled hand reached out and scooped up all the coins from Evon's palm, then the door closed with a loud thump. Evon and Kerensa looked at each other. "She's worried about *us* robbing *her*?" Kerensa said in a low voice.

"I can break this door down. It would be easy."

"I'm beginning to think you might have to."

The door opened again. "Ain't got more to spare," the woman said, handing them a sack, then a keg the size of Kerensa's head. "And no fires. Don't need that barn burnin' down."

"Thank you, ma'am," Evon said, not daring to waste time opening the sack for fear she might change her mind. They retreated to the barn and discovered their reluctant benefactor had given them two round loaves of barely stale bread, a chunk of cheese as big as Evon's doubled fists, half a dozen slightly wizened apples, and a jar of preserves. The keg turned out to contain fresh cider, only a little hard. Evon found his pen knife and hacked off chunks of bread, which they smeared with the preserves and ate until Evon felt he could never eat again. Kerensa's appetite was better than his, and she finished off her meal with half the cheese, two of the apples, and a long draught of cider. "I've never known anyone to eat quite so much," he said, teasing.

She wiped her mouth with the back of her hand and said, "I've never been so hungry in my whole life. I'm going to give one of these apples to the horse. Poor thing."

"I'm going to study, if you don't mind," Evon said, pouring a little of the cold water from the canteen over his sticky fingers and rubbing them dry on his trousers.

"I wish I had something to do other than watch you study and groom the horse," Kerensa complained. "Not that I don't enjoy watching you do things. You get this furrow to your brow when you're studying that makes you look fierce, like a warrior out of Alvorian myth."

Evon grinned. "No one's ever mentioned that before."

"Probably no one's ever watched you as closely as I do before." She leaned over and kissed him. "I like that I can do that whenever I want."

"You are welcome to do that whenever you want. I positively encourage it." He shouldn't encourage it; as far as society was concerned her honor had already been compromised just by spending the night with him. But he could still feel the warmth of her body curled close against his, could still remember that look in her eyes when she'd woken next to him, and knew he didn't give a damn what society thought.

She kissed him again, then took her apple and descended the ladder. Evon stared after her for a while, then shook his head and tried to focus on his notes. He knew them so well by now that he probably could have written them out again by memory. Knew them well, and yet couldn't find the answer. He thought of the look on Kerensa's face when she woke, and picked up his notes with renewed determination. He just had to look at it in a new way.

His eyes passed over a rune, something that triggered a memory. It had been in Haderon's spell, the resurrection spell, and in the finding spell too. He did a little digging and found variations on it in every section of the spell. He spread the notes out on the hayloft floor so he could see them all at once, then found his lexicon and started reading the runes as if they were words, one slow rune at a time. So many were still missing, but it was easier, now, to identify those unknown runes by context, though he also had to translate the resulting "sentences" into modern language. The one he'd been looking at was "bind," or sometimes "bound." He took out a pencil and circled the rune wherever he found it, then stood up and took a few paces back. If he linked each spell by overlaying the "bind" rune....

Suddenly, a new pattern emerged. *bind the fire to destroy the one who has no soul,* he read. It wasn't a sentence fragment; he'd started in the wrong place. He ran his finger backwards through the runes and tried again. *To the destruction of the Enemy of life and the host that binds it.*

It was the spell. The whole spell, not just its pieces. The secret of the fire.

Fingers trembling, he read on, making guesses at the runes he didn't know.

From the heart of Nystrantor we make our instrument, blood and bone, host to the fire that she may defeat the Enemy. In her we bind the fire to destroy the one who has no soul. In her we bind the call. In her we bind our wills.

I, Minta, bind her that she may endure all but the fire.

I, Leandrie, bind her that she be drawn, host to host, to the one who has no soul.

I, Wadley, command that the fires be bound within her and released by the one who has no soul.

I, Haderon, bind her to return again if the one who has no soul escapes our instrument.

I, Danior, bind our commands as one and command that binding to seek out the enemy of life. May the Gods look with favor on our instrument, who chooses death that life may return.

Evon's heart sank. It wasn't a spell; it was an old-fashioned binding magicians used to use to connect spells. It didn't tell him anything new, since he'd already worked out how the five spells interacted. He read through it again. So where was the fire spell? This referred to it as if it were something separate, some other spell they had access to. And what was Nystrantor? The word had been spelled out, not written as a proper name, but it couldn't be anything else. He knew he'd heard it, or read it, before. If the magicians had created the fire spell separately, it was going to take a great deal more effort for him to unravel it.

"That horse is lonely," Kerensa said from below, and her head rose above the ladder. "It was far more affectionate than I was comfortable with. I almost wish we'd gotten that other horse to keep it company."

"Have you ever heard the word Nystrantor?" Evon asked absently. And what did it mean, "instrument"? They couldn't have known Kerensa would come along, a thousand years later, so there must have been some other woman bound to the spell back then. Was that important, that it was a woman?

"Of course. It's one of the places of power, the ones saturated with magic. The Witch of Marhalindor made it and it drove her insane. Why?"

Now he remembered. He'd learned of it in a geography class, in a series of lessons about those dangerous places and how to avoid them. "It says the magicians created the spell from the heart of Nystrantor. No, that's wrong, it says they made their instrument in the heart of Nystrantor."

"That sounds dangerous. Anything might have happened."

"They were probably very desperate." Something nudged his memory. Something about being changed. "What did you say happened to Carall?"

"Um...he became undead?"

"No, the pragmatic explanation."

"Oh. I said he probably wandered into one of those places and was changed by it into something not quite human."

Evon began pacing. Something felt wrong about all this. "And there's no fire spell," he said. "I'm certain of it. Five control spells and nothing to control." Unless the fire came from something else. *From the heart of Nystrantor we make our instrument host to the fire.* They *made* the woman an instrument. She was —

"Sit down," he told Kerensa, who was watching him pace with curiosity. He took her arm and guided her to the pile of hay where they'd slept.

"Evon, what's wrong?"

"I hope nothing. Just sit." He cast *epiria*, then, in quick succession, *vertiri* and *trattuci*. The spell-ribbons went wild and once again started to flow away from Kerensa's body.

"You found a solution!"

"I don't know. Just...don't say anything for a moment, all right? I'm sorry. I didn't mean to be impatient. I just need to think."

The blue snake of the spell once again cast about until it found Evon's legs and began spiraling up them. The warm, unpleasant tingle grew into a mild burning itch. He resisted the urge to scratch and held his arms well away from his body, in case he was wrong.

"Evon, what are you doing?"

"Just tell me if you feel strange." He felt very strange himself, with the spell-ribbons weaving around his body, past his waist and creeping up to his chest. Kerensa was nearly free of them now. "I feel wonderful," she said, her face glowing. Evon took a closer look. She really was glowing, her skin pinker than usual.

"You don't feel too warm?" he asked.

"No. I feel comfortable for the first time since we left Holdplain." She took off her cloak. "Do you suppose the storm is letting up?"

Her skin was rosy now, almost red. He reached out to touch her face and felt heat radiating off it. "*Desini!*" he screamed, and the spell-ribbons reversed their course, but her face grew redder and beads of sweat appeared at her hairline. She looked at him, uncomprehending, but frightened at his terror. He grabbed the canteen and emptied its contents over her face; the water steamed, and Kerensa cried out in pain. "What's happening?" she said, then saw the red skin of her hands and screamed. Evon grabbed her and held her close to him, hoping this would speed up the process of restoring the spell to her. She was hot to the touch and the smell of smoke was stronger than it had ever been. He closed his eyes and prayed he hadn't been so much the fool that they were both about to die and take this barn with them in the conflagration.

Nothing happened. They were both surrounded by flying ribbons of blue, which made it impossible to tell which of them the spell was attached to, but at some point he realized Kerensa's skin was cooler and, when he drew back to look at her, no longer red. She looked at him, confused and terrified, and he released her and turned away. It was a guess that had turned out to be horribly right.

"What did you do?" she whispered. She looked at the backs of her hands again, shivered, and went to retrieve her cloak.

"I...tested a theory." How could he explain it to her when he barely understood it himself? All he really had were a few ancient lines and his well-honed instincts. "I've been looking for a spell," he said, beginning to pace again, "something like the ones that urge you toward a target, that releases the fire when the spell activates. I haven't found anything because there isn't anything to find." He couldn't bear to look at her. "A thousand years ago there were five magicians who were looking for a way to stop Murakot, or the entity riding him, however you want to look at it. They found a woman who volunteered to...she knew it was suicide, but she agreed to be their instrument to kill the entity. They took her to Nystrantor and used the loose magics there to make the changes, probably. Then they built these spells to control what she'd become."

He paused, hoping she would understand and he wouldn't have to say the words, but she sat silently on the hay. He could feel her attention on him, and it broke his heart. "The fire wasn't a spell," he said. "It was a part of her. The magic changed her, and she became host to the fire. I don't know what happened to you," he went on quickly, as he heard her draw breath to speak. "Maybe you're descended from that woman; Alvor killed Murakot, and the fire was never needed, so she probably lived to have children and go on with her life. Maybe it was the entity's re-emerging into the world that woke up whatever lay dormant inside you. All I know is that the fire is a part of you, and there's nothing I know that will remove it from you. If I transfer the spell to someone else—well, you saw it. It's all that's keeping the fire from consuming you. I'm sorry, Kerensa, I'm so sorry, I don't know how to save you and I know I promised but there's nothing I can do—"

"But you said," Kerensa said quietly, "you said you would find a way."

"There isn't any way." He finally summoned the courage to look at her and saw that her eyes were empty, her face expressionless, and he moved to embrace her, but she stepped away, her eyes never leaving his.

"It can't be right. You said you would find a way," she said. Her voice was emotionless, that same terrible empty voice he'd heard the first time she'd ever spoken to him.

"I'm sorry. I'm sorry," he said.

Her face crumpled into tears. "I don't want to die," she said, and finally she let him hold her while she wept, tears running down his own face. "It's not true. You promised. It's not true."

Every word struck his heart like a spear tipped with ice. "I know. I'm sorry. I love you, and I don't know what else to do. I don't."

She wrenched herself free of his grasp. "Then *think*," she said, furious even though she was still crying. "You know more about magic than anyone else alive, you know it's true, and you know this spell better than anyone alive. They had to use magic to make the fire, they couldn't have...couldn't have just *wished* it to happen! They did this to me and you love me and you *will* figure this out."

"But—Kerensa, it's not a spell, I don't even know what it was they used to make it happen! For all I know, they didn't do anything but let Nystrantor work its will on her!"

"So? The magic is inside me. Find it and take it apart."

"I—"

"If you tell me you can't, I'll walk into that blizzard and keep walking until I meet the Despot or die."

Her eyes were wild, her voice shaking, and Evon had no doubt she meant what she said. He looked at her, so beautiful and so convinced of his abilities that he began, against reason, to feel hope rise up within him. "I won't let you die," he said. "I worked out the first spell. I'll learn to defeat this one too."

"Good," said Kerensa. "Then let's get started."

20

"Where in the hell have you been?" Piercy demanded. "I realize you have many demands on your time, dear fellow, what with riding into what is fast becoming a war zone, but you may recall that you promised to speak with me every evening. I have been arguing with myself about whether the advantages of contacting you outweighed the possibility of my dulcet voice alerting enemies to your presence. As I am an expert arguer, you can imagine how that conversation is going."

"We were caught in a snowstorm, and I was...preoccupied," Evon said, reddening. It wasn't as if he couldn't share the news of his changed relationship with Kerensa with his best friend, but he felt a little shy about simply bursting out *She loves me*, she *loves* me, *I spent the night with her and it was wonderful* like a burbling fool. And there were more important things to discuss.

"I made a discovery that changes everything," he went on, and began to explain the true nature of Kerensa's magic. The small circle of Piercy's face grew increasingly confused as Evon spoke, until he shook his head and said, "Stop. You are making very little sense. The spell isn't a spell, but it *is* a spell, just not the same one?"

"No. Look, we're dealing with two things. The *magic* is the fire.

The *spell* is what controls it. I can remove the spell, but the fire is part of her. So we're going to find a way to remove the fire and still use it to kill the entity."

"I see. 'Magic' and 'spell' are different. Can you do it?"

"I'll do my best. But that's what I have to tell you. We're turning aside and going east, to Nystrantor."

"By the Gods, Evon, why would you want to go to that desolate place? Is fire suddenly calling to fire?"

"In a sense. Nystrantor is where the magicians changed the first volunteer. I'm hoping to learn how they did it."

"You know the Despot is moving closer every day. If you go east, you will end up walking into the middle of our army. It's unlikely they will simply let you pass."

"I know, but I don't see that we have any other options if we want to use the weapon and not kill Kerensa doing it. It shouldn't take more than four days' journey, allowing for climbing the mountain. The storm's starting to abate, and we'll ride out as soon as we can. We're both tired of this freezing barn."

"You're sleeping in a barn? Evon, I had no idea your situation was so primitive. Do you huddle together for warmth?"

Evon grinned. "We do at that. But we would do that anyway, since it turns out she loves me."

Piercy's jaw went slack. "Evon...that's incredible. I'm thrilled for you both, though she's clearly deranged to think of you as a viable romantic prospect. I trust you are treating her with the respect she deserves?"

"I won't say it isn't hard, but we've both managed to keep our baser desires in check, thank you for asking."

"Now I'm glad I didn't come with you. Romance is very well, but watching other people moon about after one another, even if it is my best friend and my almost-sister, is positively exhausting. Though I assume her affections have spurred you to even greater effort?"

"You assume correctly. I won't let her die, Piercy. I just need to understand this thing better. The magicians changed their volunteer; maybe I can work out how to reverse that change."

"I don't understand how Kerensa could have ended up with the magic. No one took her to Nystrantor, correct?"

"I think she's a descendant of the volunteer, and that change was something that gets passed on to children, like height or eye color. Isn't it sad, that that woman's name didn't get recorded anywhere? She was incredibly brave."

"I know I would have trouble walking into one of those places of power voluntarily. Are you certain it's safe, dear fellow? There are tales of people wandering into one and wandering out fifty years later. Your solution might be too late to stop the Despot."

"Kerensa says Nystrantor is fairly well known. No time alteration, just the burning lands. Not that it isn't dangerous. I'd say I'll be careful, but at this point I'm desperate enough to risk anything."

"I'll tell you to be careful anyway, Evon. Stay in contact. The magicians are still trying to track you, and Mistress Quendester is furious with me that I won't provide them with your location. I am, naturally, devastated that I cannot help the war effort, but since you won't tell me where you are, I have no way of using the mirror to discover that." He winked. "Mistress Gavranter has lectured me quite sternly on my recalcitrance. She speaks repeatedly of your stubbornness and her hope that it hasn't gotten you into trouble on your journey, which I interpret to mean that she wishes you luck."

"Thank you for convincing Mistress Gavranter to let you be my contact. She means well, but she would want updates more frequently than I have information."

"I am still endeavoring to discover a way to get you and Kerensa close to the Despot without being killed. Our information on his forces increases, sadly because said forces draw ever nearer, as I believe I've mentioned."

"Well, you now have more time to figure it out. I'll speak to you again tomorrow night, all right?"

"Yes, and I will attempt to learn more about the location of Dalanine's forces as well. Don't let your mooning about cause you to forget our appointment. Perhaps I should task Kerensa to remind you. She is probably less likely to be distracted from the essentials despite her affection for you."

"I don't know. She thinks I look like a warrior out of Alvorian myth."

"By the Gods, is it as bad as all that? You two deserve each other, and I mean that in all seriousness." Piercy smiled. "Good luck."

"Thank you." Evon glanced over his shoulder. "Were you listening to all that?"

"I was, until you told Piercy that I love you," Kerensa said, "and I got distracted thinking about that. We do moon about a little, don't we?"

"I spent a great deal of time wishing you felt for me what I did for you, so I deserve to do a little mooning."

"The storm's let up to the point that I think we can leave," Kerensa said, coming to sit beside Evon. "Is there a road to Nystrantor?"

"Most of the way." Evon took out the map. "We go a little farther south to here, to this village, and buy supplies. Then we take that road there that leads east into the mountains. From there we have to find our own way to the burning lands, assuming we can also evade the army. If we move quickly enough, we can pass through before they come far enough south."

"I'm worried about your safety," Kerensa said. "I should be immune to the fire, but you won't be."

"Unless you're *not* immune because your fire came from the same place."

"I hadn't thought of that. I guess now I have to worry about both our safety."

"Time enough for that when we get there." Evon stood and offered her his hand. "If you've packed everything, I suppose we should say goodbye to our oh-so-gracious host."

No part of the old woman made an appearance when they knocked on her door, and Evon forbore to leave her any more money. He hoped he had enough left to supply them for the rest of the now extended journey. They rode back across the fields under a light sprinkling of snow and watched the southern sky clear as they rode in its direction. The winds had prevented much snow from building up, though Evon only recognized the road because it was a long, mostly straight stretch of snow through which no stalks of yellow dead grass protruded. Kerensa took charge of the map, though they didn't need it as long as the road remained clearly marked. She held on to Evon's waist and leaned against his back, and he marveled at how different it was now to have her riding behind him, occasionally laying her cheek against his shoulder and hugging him tighter. It was hard to remember that they were riding into danger and possible death.

They reached the village by midafternoon and Evon, reluctantly, took two rooms at the town's lone inn. The memory of waking up next to Kerensa that morning made him long to represent her as his wife so he could share her bed again, but the way his body responded to the idea made it unlikely that he would be able to restrain himself, and by the look in her eye Kerensa was thinking the same thing. So he called her his sister, and offered her his arm instead of his hand, and hoped his eyes didn't give them both away. They bought staples, long-lasting foods like cheese and apples, and stowed their purchases in Evon's room for safekeeping, then ate supper and went to their separate beds. It took Evon a long time to fall asleep, and when he finally did he was plagued by dreams of Kerensa bursting into flame and taking him with her, over and over again.

More snow was falling when they left the next morning. Evon hated the snow. He couldn't remember a time when the world wasn't made of snow. His hands were freezing inside his gloves, which was stupid because gloves were supposed to keep your hands from freezing. He pulled his ugly hat down over his ears and glowered out at the world over the horse's head. He knew that horses were reasonably intelligent, but whoever had sold him this one must have laughed himself sick at unloading it on Evon, because it was surely one of the stupidest creatures ever given breath by the Gods. If he didn't goad it, it would stand in the snow until it froze to death. He should have sold it and bought a better one.

"Evon," Kerensa said. "Look at me."

He turned his head and was utterly surprised when she pressed her lips against his. The cold tip of her nose rubbed across his cheek.

He automatically put out a hand to keep her from overbalancing and falling off the idiot horse, and felt his bad mood melt away. By the Gods, but he'd needed that.

"You had the most unpleasant expression on your face," Kerensa said, "and I thought you shouldn't be allowed to go on thinking whatever horrible thing you were thinking." She sat back, and Evon made a noise of protest. "We don't have time to stand around kissing, Evon."

"We have a *little* time." He took the horse off the road and dismounted, then lifted Kerensa down and circled her waist with his arms. "And I like this way better." He pushed her hood back from her face and proceeded to kiss her all across her face and exposed neck while she laughed and pretended to struggle to free herself. Eventually he found his way to her lips and they kissed, slowly and intently, until Kerensa lifted her head and said, a little breathlessly, "Feel better now?"

"Much." Evon rested his forehead against hers.

"That's good, because someone's coming and I don't want us to be a spectacle for everyone's amusement."

Evon turned to see riders approaching from the direction of the village. There were four or five of them, coming along slowly, but as Evon watched they broke into a run. He boosted Kerensa back onto the horse and mounted, moving further off the road. If they were in such a hurry, better to let them pass now.

"I wonder why they started running suddenly," Kerensa said. Her words made Evon feel uneasy. He fumbled around until he found his quizzing glass, gestured and said, *"Solto spexa."* The lens glowed with a greenish light like the belly of a firefly, and Evon held it to his eye. It felt as if he'd leaped forward to stand near the riders, and he swallowed against the lurch in his stomach. Five riders, their faces hooded against the cold...and one rider with a red beard that spilled over his collar. Valantis.

"It's Speculatus," he said, shoving his lens into his pocket and kicking the horse out of its mindless stupor. "Hold on tight."

Stupid the horse might be, but it had a turn of speed that had Evon hoping Kerensa wouldn't be flung off. They galloped down the road, the horse's footing unexpectedly sure on the frozen ground beneath the snow. "How are they faring?" Evon called out.

"I think they're drawing closer," Kerensa replied. "Where are we going?"

"Away," Evon said. "Get out the map and let's see what's ahead."

He felt her moving around, one hand clutching his waist, the other spreading the map across his back. "Evon, there aren't any villages for miles," she said. "What are we going to do?"

He cursed. "They'll kill me and take you back. We should choose our ground, see if I can't eliminate a few of them." He didn't say that Valantis was likely to have brought magicians, or that they'd be prepared for him to attack. He was desperately running through spells in his head, trying to find ones they wouldn't know to defend against. *Presadi*, but that was one target at a time, and the others would be on him in seconds. If he knew how to use *solto olficio* or *solto spexa* against another person, those would be disorienting...but "if" was pointless now.

Kerensa still held the map against his back. She shifted to look behind, then said, "I have an idea, but it's dangerous."

"More dangerous than those five men?"

"It's possible danger versus certain death."

Evon felt the horse stumble a little and drew in on the reins slightly. "What is it?"

"There's a place of power only a quarter mile from here."

"That could kill us all by itself!"

"Maybe. But they certainly will. There's no name, so I don't know anything about it, but I think it's worth the risk."

Evon pressed his lips close together. "How close are they?"

"It will be a race to get there ahead of them. And there's no guarantee they won't follow us."

Evon nodded, then flicked the reins to urge the horse back into a full-out run. "Let's just focus on getting there."

Now he crouched low on the horse's neck and felt Kerensa grip him as if she were afraid of falling off, which was probably true. The rough road and the horse's speed made Evon a little afraid of falling himself. He imagined he could hear their pursuers' horses drawing nearer, though he knew that was impossible because if they were that near, they were near enough to cast spells. He risked a glance over his shoulder and saw that they were about a hundred yards away, and they were gaining. One of them raised a hand, and Evon shouted, *"Retexo!"* just in case, nearly falling off the horse with gesturing over Kerensa's head, but either the magician's aim was bad, or he was just too far away, because nothing happened.

"Turn off the road now!" Kerensa shouted. "Right, right! Turn right!" and he yanked on the reins and the horse veered right, stumbled a little over the verge, and took off running across the field. If it broke a leg now, they were finished. But though its gait went erratic, it didn't step in any holes or trip over fallen branches, not that there would be any branches in the middle of this treeless, horribly exposed stretch of land. In the distance, a copse of trees, their branches bare and spiky, stood huddled like travelers crouched around a campfire. "How far?" he called back to Kerensa.

"We're nearly there. The silver dot is starting to vibrate. I don't know what that means."

"It might be reacting to the presence of free magic. Not something we can do anything about. Keep your head down!"

Flames burst up on their left, melting snow and producing a huge cloud of steam. *Forva.* He twisted around quickly to look at their pursuers, only about a hundred yards away now, faced forward long enough to make certain the horse was still pointed in the right direction, swung around and tossed the same spell back at them. One of the riders, unfortunately not Valantis, screamed and fell off his horse, beating at himself and rolling in the snow to put out the fire that engulfed him. Evon grinned, though he knew he couldn't count on that kind of luck again.

Then the horse screamed, and lurched, and Evon shoved Kerensa away as the horse fell hard on its side and began thrashing. He barely missed being crushed under its massive body, but had the wind knocked out of him and lost precious seconds trying to recover. Kerensa came to crouch next to him, casting terrified glances back at Valantis and his riders. "Evon," she said, "now what?"

"Get the bags and get clear of the horse. Keep running until I tell you to stop." Evon backed away from their pursuers as quickly as he could, passing the helpless horse and silently apologizing to it for their desertion. He hoped it had just stumbled and hadn't broken a leg. He kept his hands raised, and was heartened to see the men slow as they neared and then match his pace, keeping about fifty feet of space between them. It was good that they knew his reputation. That might keep him alive.

Valantis, at the front of his little band, pulled his horse up and dismounted, holding his hands well away from his sides to show that he was unarmed—or at least that whatever weapons he had on him weren't in his hands at the moment. He continued to approach Evon on foot while his men pulled back a little, each also displaying empty hands, though if they were all magicians, that was more a threat than a reassurance. "Kerensa, stop!" Evon shouted without looking behind him. He continued to back up; Valantis continued to follow.

"You saved my life," Valantis said. "Though you probably didn't mean to."

"That's correct. I should have killed you for what you did to Kerensa."

"That was Cattertis. She liked pain far too much for my comfort, but she did her work well. You have your revenge, though. She died in the fire."

"I had my revenge before that when I snapped her neck," Evon said, raising his voice to make sure all the riders heard him. Two of the men glanced at each other uneasily. If he had time, he could take advantage of that. He probably didn't have time.

He became aware of Kerensa's presence just before she put her hand on his elbow to steady him. "How close are we to the place?" he asked in a low voice.

"I'm not sure. I don't dare pull out the map right now. We might be right on top of it."

"In any case, I owe you a life," Valantis continued. "I'll spare you if you give us the woman."

"Mr. Valantis, has anyone in the history of the world ever accepted that offer?"

"You'd be surprised at what people will do to save their own necks." Valantis pushed back his hood so Evon could see his face and held up a palm-sized glass sphere. It was pulsing with a cool violet light. "I'll just keep coming after her if you don't."

Evon ground his teeth. They'd been using a simple tracking spell, far less complex than the one on the coin, the kind of thing any ten-year-old who could say *reperto* could perform. If he'd been thinking at all, he could have countered it. "I can render that useless," he said.

Valantis shrugged. "We have other methods. Come, Lorantis, be reasonable. I swear I won't hurt her. You can even have her back when I've gotten what I want out of her."

Evon was watching Valantis's men as he said this, so he saw the look that passed over one rider's face that said more than one person intended to get what he wanted out of Kerensa, and fury swept over him. *"Forva!"* he shouted, and immediately after, *"Presadi!"*

The man went up in a column of white fire, making his horse squeal and fling him off before dropping to the snow itself to soothe its burns. Valantis's remaining two magicians raised their hands. And a six-foot-tall iridescent bubble of *presadi* sprang up around Evon and Kerensa. Whatever spells the magicians cast struck the impermeable shield and bounced or trickled off harmlessly. Valantis gestured wildly at his men, then pulled out a highly illegal dueling pistol and aimed a shot at Evon's head. It ricocheted off the shield and Valantis ducked just in time to have the bullet zing past his ear. He began gesticulating and presumably shouting at Evon, who innocently tapped his ear and shook his head.

"I can't begin to tell you how impressed I am right now," Kerensa said. "But aren't we trapped here?"

"Not exactly. We'll probably look stupid, but there isn't anyone here whose opinion I care about." Evon walked to the far side of the bubble and put his hands against it. "If we walk and push at the same time, we can make this roll all the way to the dubious safety of that unknown magical place."

Kerensa put her hands against the bubble and followed his movements. "I thought the shield spell was small."

"So did I. I took a chance that I could make it bigger. If it failed...I used most of my reserves to cast this, and we would have been defenseless. So I'm glad it worked."

"*I'm* glad you didn't mention that before." The bags tumbled against Evon's ankles, rolling with *presadi*. The copse of trees grew nearer.

The shield shivered a little. Evon glanced over his shoulder and saw Valantis hacking away at the bubble, his lips spewing soundless invective. "I wonder if I could combine this with *recivia*, make a shield that returns blows with equal force on the attacker," he mused.

"Evon Lorantis, you really are always thinking up new spells in the back of your head."

He reddened. "I try not to let it interfere with other things, but sometimes I become moderately obsessed. Something you should no doubt know about me."

She smiled and laid her hand atop his. "Your obsession is going to save my life. I can hardly complain about it. But when all this is over, you can expect me to give you gentle nudges when your obsession interferes with your life."

"I welcome it. I look —"

With a soundless burst, blinding red light flared up around them on every side.

*B*linking back tears of pain, Evon squinted to see what had attacked them. They were surrounded by a ball of sparkling crimson light, sometimes flaring like a flame given new fuel, sometimes spitting like water dropped into hot oil. Valantis was gone. Evon couldn't see anything past the red light, which, it occurred to him, was exactly the same size as *presadi* and formed a wall in front of them, exactly where they'd been pushing the shield along. Evon reached out and put his palm flat against it, and it gave a little, just like *presadi*. He looked down and saw that the crimson light ran under his feet as well. He walked back to what had been the rear of the bubble and tried to see out, but the light was opaque as well as coruscating. It was starting to become a little stuffy where they were. *"Desini,"* he said, and a thin mist of black dispelled the shield and made the flickering red light vanish.

They stood about a hundred feet from the copse of trees. Previously bare, the trees now clung to the last of their autumn leaves, which covered their roots in inches-deep color. There was no snow on the ground, which felt soft, not yet frozen. Valantis and his men were nowhere in sight. Evon turned to say something to Kerensa and took a step back. "You're glowing," he said. She was surrounded by flying spell-ribbons, dark blue and dormant, but also by a flickering golden light that limned her silhouette and the lines of her body. It looked as if someone had used a burning taper to outline her with fire.

She looked down at her hands and gasped. "I don't feel anything," she said.

"I think there's something about this place that makes magic visible," Evon said. "As if it had a kind of permanent *epiria* cast over it. There's the spell, and...that must be the fire magic."

"But *epiria* never showed this before."

"*Epiria* is for revealing spells, organized magic, not raw magic. This place must be incredibly powerful to do something like that."

She turned her head to look over her shoulder. "It's *everywhere.*"

"It's beautiful," Evon said. "You look extraordinary." He reached out and took her hand. "It's not actually fire. I can still touch you."

"Thank the Gods," Kerensa said, and flung herself on him. She was shaking. "I'm sorry," she said, "it was just facing Valantis, and now this...."

Evon held her close. "Be glad," he said. "I might be able to figure the fire out here, without our having to go all the way to Nystrantor."

She nodded. "This place seems sort of peaceful, flamboyant visual displays aside. I wonder when we are." They began walking toward the copse, which lay still in the face of the slight breeze that brushed their faces. Even the dying leaves were motionless.

"It looks as though we've gone back in time a few months," Evon said, scanning the ground ahead.

"Or forward by nearly a year. Or several years. Or a millennium."

"You're right. I just hope we don't stay offset in time when we leave. If we return to find a landscape decimated by the Despot's armies, I don't know what we'll do."

They reached the copse, where Evon had to duck a little to avoid the low-hanging branches. Leaves brushed softly against his hair and face, dry but soft, like old parchment. "Let me get that," Kerensa said, and removed a rust-colored oak leaf from his hair. "How long do you think we should stay in here?"

"I don't know. I was thinking we should circle around and come out at a different place." Evon looked at the map again, then folded it and put it away. "Though if this doesn't restore itself, we could end up very lost."

"Better than very dead." Kerensa found a fallen tree to sit on and dragged the bag of food into her lap. "Do you want something to eat? Mortal terror seems to make me hungry."

He sat next to her and accepted a hunk of wax-coated cheese. Something stirred in the bushes behind them, and he whipped around to see—nothing. "I'm still edgy," he laughed. The rustling started again, louder and more persistent. "I'm suddenly thinking about the kinds of fauna places like this might produce."

"So am I. But isn't it just as likely that the creatures are friendly plant-eaters?" Then she leaned away and said, "What is *that*?"

Evon turned to look behind him and saw what looked like a shimmering square, radiant with blue and green and yellow, ripple through the air several feet above his head. "Ambient magic," he guessed. "With magic being visible here, if the place's magic were part of the landscape, everything would glow. It must pool together, or something similar."

"Or weave together. That looked like cloth," Kerensa agreed. "There's another one, way up there."

Now that he knew what to look for, Evon saw the magic every-where. It didn't seem to be self-aware the way Kerensa's spell was, but it had enough instinct to avoid obstacles, such as trees or his head. They sat on the tree and watched the magic for a time, mesmerized by its beauty.

The rustling started again. Something kicked up the leaves fallen at the base of one of the trees. "I didn't see anything," Kerensa said, alarmed. "And I just realized we haven't seen a single bird."

Evon pulled out the glass and cast *epiria*, which sent out white tendrils like hair-thin vines to tangle around the lens; he tried wiping them away, but his fingers passed through them without feeling anything. Shrugging, he held the glass out in front of him and scanned the ground where the leaves had been disturbed. "I don't see anything," he began, and then he did. "It's a chipmunk," he said, handing the glass to Kerensa. "A normal chipmunk, except that it's invisible."

"Why doesn't the *epiria* of this place reveal the creatures?"

"I have no idea. It makes no sense. I wonder what else is invisible."

Kerensa swung the lens up to look at the sky and exclaimed, "I saw a raven!"

Evon looked where she pointed and saw nothing except a blue and red cloth of magic undulating across the sky. Suddenly it rippled as if shuddering, then for a brief moment he saw a flying bird outlined against the cloth, then the cloth wrapped itself around something that struggled and cried out weakly. The cloth constricted, twisting as if it were a rag being wrung out by invisible hands, until it was twisted nearly in half. Then it spun open and continued undulating through the air. Seconds later something hit the ground nearby with a soft *thump*. Evon and Kerensa looked at each other, aghast.

"And now we know why the animals are all invisible," Kerensa said.

"I wonder that we haven't been attacked," Evon said.

"Maybe we're too big to be enveloped?"

"Or perhaps they just aren't that hungry yet."

"I like my explanation better."

Evon took Kerensa's hand and squeezed it gently. "I want to see whether I can work out how the fire is attached to you," he said. "It won't hurt, I promise."

"If you find a solution, I don't care if it hurts," she said, but her voice was a little wobbly. "What do you want me to do?"

"Just sit there." He stood and surveyed her body, trying to look at the golden fire objectively and not think about how perfect her figure was and how it felt to have it pressed against him. He pinched the bridge of his nose to clear his thoughts and tried again. The spell-ribbons were a manifestation of the binding spell. They were attached to that spell. Therefore, it followed that the golden fire he saw must be attached to the fire magic deep within Kerensa. Suppose it was visible all the way down? If he could see inside her body....

"This may take a while. I've only ever read about it and I don't remember it very well because I wasn't planning to go into medicine." A spell that let doctors look inside the body, something about *spexa* and some other command word, something unlikely...why couldn't he remember? Another cloth of magic drifted past, this one hovering only a few feet above Kerensa's head; he waved it away and the draft he caused made it flutter a little before continuing on its path.

"All right," he said finally. He held his hand out, palm upward and fingers spread wide, and said, *"Spexa torpia."*

Nothing happened aside from a spicy-sweet taste filling his mouth. There was a silvery-green thickening of the air as an oculus tried to form, but failed to open. "Hmm," Evon said. No, of course, *torpia* was too obvious. He paced around the clearing, feeling Kerensa's eyes on him. Another iridescent cloth passed near him, brushing his shoulder, and he flicked it away. "Let's try this," he said, coming to stand in front of Kerensa and repeating the gesture. *"Spexa madi."*

An oculus with a rim made of silvery-green light opened in front of Kerensa's chest, and Evon winced. It was like a round window on her innards, heart pulsing, lungs pumping, blood flowing through her veins. "What?" Kerensa asked, alarmed. She craned her neck to try and see through the oculus. "No, don't," Evon said. "It's really better that you don't look."

She gave him a narrow-eyed look, but said nothing more. Evon turned his attention to *spexa madi*. Golden fire outlined each organ, each rib; it was, again, beautiful, if also a little grotesque. The fire didn't seem to be connected to any of the things it touched. "Um...*torpia auctata*, I suppose." The rim flashed pale blue briefly, and the image quivered. He repeated the spell with the same results.

"What are you trying to do?" Kerensa asked.

"See deeper into your body. But it's beyond my reserves." His lower back ached. The spellcasting against Valantis's people, and performing the unfamiliar *presadi* spell, had wearied him. A cloth woven of pink and green brushed his hair, and he ducked away from it.

"What does that mean?"

"I told you that spells give focus to the incomprehensibility of magic, right? Well, when a magician uses command words, he's using his body to shape that focus, but the spells shape him too, drawing power through him. Or her. The amount of magic a magician can wield is called his reserves, and they deplete and replenish the way...well, it's a little like how you start feeling tired when you're hungry and you're alert again when you've eaten. That *presadi* took a lot of my reserves to cast." He sat beside Kerensa and saw that the oculus, from this side, was opaque black and rippled from the center as if a steady stream of water were dripping into it. He looked up and watched one of the cloths undulate past. "I wonder," he said, and flicked his hands up and out. *"Desini cucurri."*

Red ropes surrounded the cloth, tangling it in an irregular web like the work of a drunken spider. The magic convulsed and went entirely stiff, then drifted to the ground. Evon went and picked it up. It tingled in his fingers, a pleasant sensation like the purr of a cat. It looked like a heavily starched napkin, if napkins were made of loosely-woven blue and white threads that sparkled.

"This is essentially pure magic," he told Kerensa, who came over to touch it. She smiled and stroked its surface. "I think I can use it to boost my own power, but...you should step back, probably." He turned to face away from her, clasped his hands together while awkwardly clutching a corner of the cloth, and said, *"Presadi."*

The shield came into being explosively, knocking Evon down and blazing with red light that pulsed and flared with a sound like a roaring bonfire. Kerensa came to his side and gripped his shoulder. "Are you all right?"

"Yes," Evon said, dazedly. He looked at the magic in his hand. The threads had come a little loose and one or two had pulled free of the weaving and waved free in the air. He dismissed the shield and got to his feet. "That is a *lot* of magical energy."

"Is it safe for you to use?"

"I think so." Now that he knew what to expect, he thought he could draw on a portion of its power instead of using the whole thing. "Stand still." He bent the cloth a few times until it was a little more pliable, then wrapped it around his left forearm. It gripped him when he overlapped its edges, which worried him, but otherwise simply continued to purr. He cast *spexa madi* again; it took almost no effort. It was a pity these things probably couldn't exist outside of this place. "*Torpia auctata*," he said, and the rim went from green through blue all the way to dark violet, and the view shifted to display a nebulous, pinkish substance that quivered with energy. It was as deep as it was possible to see, and he felt barely any strain. He also saw no golden fire anywhere. "*Torpia adenuo*," he said, and the lens's rim flashed backward through the rainbow until it was dark red, and the view reverted to the semi-revolting sight of Kerensa's organs outlined in fire.

"Well?" Kerensa said.

"I don't—actually, would you cross your arm over your stomach?" The binding spell had said something about blood and bone, and maybe that was literal instead of metaphorical. Kerensa's arm came into view, the edges of the bones fiery. He leaned in close. "*Torpia auctata*," he said. Kerensa's forearm filled the oculus. Evon's eyes widened. "Your bones are *covered* in patterns," he said. "It's as if someone took an awl and scratched designs into them. It's...actually it's beautiful. All these curves and spirals."

"Forgive me if I don't share your enthusiasm," Kerensa said. Her voice was a little shaky.

"I'm sorry," Evon said. "I forgot again. I told you I was prone to say stupid things."

"And I love you anyway," Kerensa said. "Is that what you needed to learn?"

"It's part of it. *Torpia auctata*." Soon the image showed a close-up view of one of the lines, a long gray highway across a white field of bone. "I don't see anything. I expected to see the fire connected to this in some way, but...oh, by the Gods, look at that." Tiny spheres of gold drifted past, following the line in the bone as if they were travelers on that highway. Where they collided with each other, they merged with a little flicker of flame.

"Look at *what*?" Kerensa shrieked. "Evon, don't say things like that!"

He looked in her direction. "I'm sorry, that came out all wrong. There's nothing to worry about, Kerensa, it's just not at all what I assumed."

Her gaze flicked over his shoulder, and she said, "Evon, that thing is coming awfully close."

He turned to see a flying cloth, orange and purple and somewhat larger than the others, descend toward his head. He lifted his arm to fend it off and shouted as it wrapped itself around his right hand and arm to the shoulder and began to squeeze. Kerensa screamed and started beating at it with her fists, while Evon tugged at its edges with his left hand trying to pull it off. It felt as if his arm was being pumped full of air, swelling painfully until he thought it might pop. His left forearm, still wrapped in the paralyzed cloth, brushed against it, sending up sparks of orange fire. The attacker shuddered, but didn't release him. Evon slammed his left arm against the thing over and over again, creating showers of sparks every time and accidentally striking Kerensa once or twice. All at once the thing loosed its grip and drifted to the ground, convulsing as it fell. Kerensa shrieked and stomped on it until it was half-sunk into the earth. Evon examined his hand closely. It didn't look puffy; it was crisscrossed with the imprint of coarse threads and hurt a little when he put pressure on it.

"Are you all right?" Kerensa said, breathlessly.

"I think so, if my heart will just slow down. That was stupid. I should have paralyzed it, but I panicked."

"I thought you needed both hands for *desini cucurri*."

"Oh. True. I must *really* have panicked."

"They just look so harmless, it was like having a baby rabbit turn on us."

They both looked at the cloth wrapped around Evon's forearm. "I think we should get that off," he said.

They tugged at it, Kerensa trying to pull it off like a glove, Evon picking with his fingernails at the seam where it overlapped. Between the two of them, they had it removed just as it started twitching free of the paralysis. Evon carried it far away from them and did his best to crush it into the ground. "It probably wouldn't try to attack, it's so small, but I'd rather not have another incident like that," he said.

"But now you won't be able to finish what you were working on," Kerensa said.

Evon smiled. "I already did. I was just distracted by being almost eaten by a tablecloth." He dismissed the oculus and picked her up by the waist and swung her around, unable to contain his relief. "The fire is drawn to those grooves on your bones, or they confine it, or something like that. Those grooves are the alteration, not the fire. The fire isn't part of you! I'm certain the alteration was to make the original...I suppose she was a host, too, like the Despot is to the entity—anyway, it was to make her able to hold the fire, to make her a, a *hospitable* environment for it. The fire can be removed. I don't know how, but it *can* be removed and I swear to you, Kerensa, I swear I'll find out how."

"I know you will," she said, smiling up at him. Then her eyes shifted to look past him, and her face went white. "Evon, *look*," she whispered.

He turned to follow her gaze and saw a great dark blot a few hundred feet away, dozens, hundreds of flying cloths, all coming directly at them. Coming *for* them.

"Get your bag," he said, shouldering his own bag and the backpack full of food. Individual cloths were now visible, drifting downward and toward them in a casual way that felt more menacing than if they'd swarmed them directly.

"If we get under the trees, they won't all be able to follow like that," Kerensa said.

"Good idea. Let's keep moving."

They struck out in a random direction; Evon had lost track of the way they'd entered, and now all he wanted was to get them away from the aggressive magic. They left the copse and crossed a piece of bare ground before entering another, slightly larger grove of trees. They stumbled on in the late autumn light, Evon wondering where the sun was and if it ever set, or if the light even came from the sun at all. He looked behind them, occasionally, and saw nothing following them, but they passed smaller magics now and then and Evon was afraid to assume they were safe. Eventually, though, he saw that Kerensa was breathing heavily and had her hand pressed to her side, and he realized his chest and legs ached and that he wasn't breathing easily himself. "Stop," he gasped, and Kerensa immediately sank to the ground and tried to calm her breathing.

They were in another small clearing just like the first, except that there was no fallen tree, so at least Evon knew they hadn't been running in circles. Running had been stupid. They should have found the way they'd entered and taken their chances with Valantis. Now they were lost, with no functional map, in a place of power that might well have taken them out of their own time a millennium or more forward or back. Evon staggered to sit next to Kerensa and put his arm around her shoulders. She leaned into him and said, "We're lost now, aren't we?"

Evon nodded. "I'm sorry. I panicked again. Those things really unnerve me."

"I panicked too, so it's on both of us if we never get out of here."

He laughed, a little breathlessly. "We'll find a way out. I can cast—"

"I think it was casting spells that drew their attention."

He stopped. "I...think you are correct. Well."

Kerensa dug in her pocket and pulled out something that shimmered. "But I think this still works, even in here."

The coin with the finding spell. "You are brilliant."

"I like hearing that."

Evon's heart was still pounding from the near catastrophe. Pounding too hard, really. Then he realized the thrumming sound was coming from outside them both, hoof beats on the hard ground, and they were coming closer. Kerensa looked at him. "Could Valantis—?"

"Get behind me," he said, backing them both into a sheltered corner between the thick trunks of two trees. Too late he realized they had left their bags in the open, but the rider was too close now for them to do anything about it. He thought about casting *presadi* until he remembered that the bright red light would draw any attacker right to them, and limbered up his hands for *desini cucurri*. He'd have to risk drawing in more of the flying cloths if it meant protecting them both. Was it Valantis? He'd gotten turned around, couldn't remember which direction they'd entered by to tell if the rider was coming from the same place. Kerensa gripped his shoulder, then released him as if she'd remembered he would need his hands and arms free for spellcasting. The sound of hoof beats turned from one horse into several, and Evon's heart sank. Even with the help he'd taken from the magics, he was still tired from all the spellcasting, and if there were too many of them, or if they were magicians, he and Kerensa would be hard pressed to defend themselves.

The first rider trotted into the clearing. He was bearded, like Valantis, but his beard was black rather than red and there were streaks of gray in it. He wore old-fashioned chain mail over a loose-sleeved white shirt, stained at the cuffs, and dirty leather trousers with boots scuffed and scratched from heavy use. His right hand rested on something laid across his lap. His eyes scanned the clearing and lighted on Kerensa, and he said something in a strange language and pointed with his left hand at her.

Kerensa let out a strange sound halfway between a gasp and a squeak. She slipped past Evon and approached the rider. "I can't believe this," she said. Evon reached out to grab her arm and she shrugged him off. "Evon, *look at his hand*," she said in the same breathless tone. The man raised his hand and pointed at Kerensa again. The middle finger of that hand was missing and the stump shone golden in the autumn sunlight.

"It's *Alvor*," Kerensa said, and turned her face up to address him.

The man lifted an enormous spiked mace from his lap and swung it at Kerensa's head.

22

*K*erensa screamed and flung herself to the ground. *"Desini cucurri!"* Evon shouted, gesturing sharply. The man's arm froze in mid swing, tangled in red cords, and he was nearly jerked out of his saddle by the motion. He roared something in that unfamiliar language and sawed at his horse's reins one-handed, yanking its head around to face Kerensa in preparation for trampling her. She scrambled backwards on all fours and Evon ran forward to pull her up, out of the horse's reach. His muscles ached. His reserves were running low.

Two other riders emerged from the woods, calling out words inflected like questions. The big man ignored them and urged his horse onward. *"Desini cucurri!"* Evon shouted again, and the horse froze mid-step and went over hard, taking its rider with it. The man let out a cry of surprise that turned into one of pain as he hit the ground. One of the riders, a woman, raised both hands in such a familiar gesture that Evon called out, *"Recivia!"* almost before the woman cast her own *desini cucurri.* A flashing mirror spun out of nowhere between them, turning the spell back on the woman, who only barely dodged it; Evon saw red cords wrap her right arm tightly. The other rider spurred his horse forward, drawing a short blade. Evon felt his breath coming too rapidly. He didn't have enough in him to block this man's attack.

The woman shouted *"Forva!"* and Evon threw himself to the left just in time to avoid taking a blast of liquid fire—*liquid?*—to the chest, then rolled again to get out of the path of the rider with the sword. The rider jigged around to face him, and Evon backed slowly toward Kerensa, risking a glance over his shoulder to see if she was unhurt. "Kerensa, *no!*" he shouted, and ran toward where she crouched near the fallen man, trying to help pull his leg from beneath the horse. Alvor, if it really was Alvor, grabbed her arm and dragged her off her feet and into a chokehold.

The man with the sword took another swing, which Evon barely ducked under. He dove at Kerensa and tried to pull Alvor's arm away from her neck. She clawed at Alvor's hand, her face red and her eyes bulging. Alvor snarled something at Evon and kicked at his knee with his one free leg. Evon stumbled, then cried out as the sword struck him across the back, the blow turned aside by the folds of Evon's thick cloak. The man with the sword spoke to Alvor in the same unintelligible language, and Evon took advantage of his brief distraction to rise and kick Alvor in the face as hard as he could. The big man roared and released Kerensa to cover his nose, which began pouring blood. Evon took Kerensa's arm and dragged her into the shelter of several close-growing aspen trees. She was coughing and gagging and her eyes watered, and Evon put her behind him and turned to face their attackers. "You *bastards*," he shouted, not caring that they probably couldn't understand him any better than he understood them. "Leave her alone! What kind of people attack a defenseless woman?"

The man with the sword dismounted; the woman did as well, one-handed and awkward, then, to Evon's amazement, touched her frozen arm and said, *"Sepera,"* and a glittering fall of crystal nearly obscured his view of her flexing her arm as if it had never been paralyzed. The two approached Alvor and began trying to pull him free from the horse. They spoke among themselves in low voices, occasionally glancing in Evon and Kerensa's direction, their eyes flickering over the trees as if scanning for danger. "Are you all right?" Evon asked.

Kerensa nodded. "Can't speak," she mouthed.

"My reserves are low. I don't know how many more spells I can cast. I don't know how good that woman is—"

Kerensa mouthed something, then made a face at Evon's incomprehension and drew the word DANIA in the dirt at her feet. "You really think so?" Evon asked. Kerensa nodded vehemently. "I thought Alvor fought in defense of others. That man tried to kill you. Twice. It's got to be an illusion or some sort of trick this place is playing on us."

The woman said something more loudly. Evon looked up to see her watching them warily. Her dark hair, cut short to brush her chin, was mussed on one side as if she'd just risen from her bed. Slowly, she raised her hand and gestured, then spoke a single word. Evon's brow furrowed. *"Cleperi,"* he said, then repeated the word accompanied by the gesture the woman had used and did the same thing for Kerensa.

A tone rang in his ear, a low-pitched hum like the sound of a thousand bees hovering just behind his head, and the air around them quivered, distorting everything around them for the space of two breaths. As the tone faded, he heard the woman begin speaking: *"Ia tromos e tradsem* for *ke sapeke ke iem.* You *cerrat bel jeset* of the *fathlon* in you—"

"Fathlon," Kerensa whispered, pounding Evon on the shoulder in her excitement. He gestured her to silence. The woman continued to speak, though she occasionally paused to cast *cleperi* on her companions.

"—and we have *yav letica* it in *beli* forest, which we *ecklat* leave. We cannot *epiros* why you *presadi beli* woman if she has *fathlon* in her. *Aste* she *presados* Alvor—" she gestured at the man on the ground, who was finally free of the horse and having his ankle palpated by the other rider. "So she cannot be *meron* enemy."

"Why isn't it translating all of her words?" Kerensa whispered. She was regaining her voice, though she still coughed occasionally. Evon was afraid to hand her their canteen, afraid to take his eyes off this woman who he was increasingly certain was the real Dania, looking quite lively for a woman a thousand years dead.

"The translation spell has to have a base to work from. The more she talks, the more it can translate. That's why she's talking so much." In a louder voice, Evon said, "I think what you're saying is that Kerensa—" he pointed at her—"has the Enemy inside her. What she's carrying is a spell with the Enemy's name on it that is intended to kill him. It. However you're tracking the Enemy, it must have identified Kerensa falsely. Her spell has the same problem. Do you understand me yet?"

"For the most," Dania said. "Say again what it is that the Enemy has done in her?"

Evon explained again. Dania said, "Such a spell is impossible."

"You can see it for yourself," Evon said, pointing at Kerensa wreathed in blue ribbons and outlined in fire.

"It resembles the shadow of Murakot," Dania said, "but the fire is unfamiliar."

Evon gave her a summary of what he'd learned. Dania circled Kerensa and seemed taken aback at how Kerensa beamed at her. When Evon finished speaking, Dania turned to look at her companions. "I believe him," she said.

"It's an improbable story. He might be lying to protect the woman," said the second rider. He was tall and thin and his skin had a waxy, unhealthy sheen to it. His eyes, when he looked at Evon, were as empty as Kerensa's had been the day he met her. "The Enemy twists minds to believe what it wants."

"If that were so, he would not have cast *desini cucurri*, he would have attempted to kill me." Dania took a few steps toward Alvor, still sitting on the ground next to the paralyzed horse. "Are you well?"

Alvor's face and beard were gory with blood, and he glared at Evon. "As well as could be expected after receiving a boot in the face," he growled.

"Then you shouldn't have tried to kill me," Kerensa said. "It was dishonorable."

Alvor barked a laugh. "No honor to be won in fighting the Enemy fairly," he said. "Do you not agree, my friend?"

Evon thought he was talking to him, but before he could answer, something detached itself from the trees next to him and placed the edge of a blade across his jugular. "Agreed," someone said in his ear in a rasping voice, the person's breath hot and stinking of raw meat. Evon froze. A moment later, the blade was withdrawn and the person slid past him to crouch next to Alvor. He, or possibly it, wore a dark green cloak with the hood pulled well down over his face. He rested his hands on his knees, and Evon saw, not a blade, but ivory claws just retracting into his hands. There was something wrong with his legs, as if the knees had been attached backwards, and the shadow of the face inside the hood wasn't entirely human.

Kerensa clutched Evon's arm. "They came here," she whispered. "When they vanished, this is where they came. Why didn't they return? Evon, what if this place won't let us go either?"

"Let's make certain they don't still plan to kill you before we start worrying about that." Evon surveyed the sky for more of the flying cloths. Two flew high above, specks against the featureless sky. If they were drawn to spellcasting, they weren't yet aware of the battle.

Kerensa nodded, then stepped around Evon and walked over to Alvor before Evon could do more than catch at her sleeve. "Can we start over?" she said. "My name is Kerensa and this is Evon."

Alvor glared at her. "Your man tried to kill me."

"You tried to kill me first. Would you not defend the people you love from death?"

Alvor glanced at Dania, then at the other rider, who had to be Carall. "Alvor," he said, saluting her by inclining his head and pressing three fingers of his left hand to his forehead. "Carall, Dania, Wystylth. If you seek the destruction of the Enemy, then we have common cause."

Evon could tell Kerensa could barely keep from vibrating with excitement. "How did you find us—I mean, find what you believed was the Enemy?" he asked, before she could start asking irrelevant questions about Alvorian myth.

Dania pointed at her horse, which bore a plate-sized version of Evon's quizzing glass. "Two hours ago the Glass became active. It has been dormant for over three years."

Two hours ago. They hadn't even entered the place of power then. Evon's heart sank. It was increasingly likely that time here was askew, variable, and that they could very well come out far too late to have any chance of stopping the Despot.

"We killed the Enemy," Alvor said, hitching himself along until he could use a tree to hoist himself to his feet. "I am certain of it. And yet it appears again. Perhaps this spell is merely a remnant of the Enemy's presence in this world, that the Enemy itself remains dead?" Alvor sounded as if he were looking for reassurance, which to Evon's mind was ludicrous, given the size and ferocity of the man.

"There is no smell of the Enemy on her," Wystylth said in that rasping voice. "Only the smell of smoke."

"We know where the entity—the Enemy—is, and we know who its host is," Evon said. "We were on our way there when we were attacked and forced into this place of power." Now that the confusion of battle was over, questions began arising in his mind. Did Alvor and the others know what had happened to them? What *had* happened to them, for that matter? If he told them that a thousand years had passed since they disappeared from the world, how would they react?

"Lead us there, and we will destroy it again," Alvor said. "Dania, if you wouldn't mind?"

Dania went to the horse's head and laid her free hand on it. "*Sepera*," she said, and the cords shriveled away and the horse fell into a heap, all flailing limbs and tossing head, crying out its panic. Alvor stood to one side and waited for it to sort itself out, then helped it stand. Evon breathed in sharply. "Teach me that," he demanded, then realized how abrupt he'd sounded and his face went red.

"Do you not know? I am surprised." Dania examined the horse, apparently to check the efficacy of her spell. "You seem a most formidable magician despite your age."

"Probably a lot of knowledge got lost between your time and ours," Kerensa said.

Dania stopped halfway to restoring Alvor's right arm. "What time is that?" she asked, narrowing her eyes.

Kerensa and Evon exchanged glances. If they didn't know how long they'd been wandering.... "It has been almost a thousand years since the four of you disappeared," Evon said.

"It has been no more than three weeks that we have wandered in this place," Carall said. There was a gap between his two front teeth and air whistled through it when he spoke. "This is another trick of the Enemy."

"No, sir, it is a trick of this place," Evon said. "Its natural properties have been overridden by the free magic. If—when we find the way out, we might emerge an hour, or a dozen years, or two millennia from the time we entered." The words "two millennia" made him feel ill.

"How could such a place draw us so far forward in time?" Carall asked Dania.

"I do not know why you look to me for the answer. I am as mystified as you," she said.

"Some places fold in on each other," Kerensa said. "You might have walked the same path a thousand times. A thousand thousand times, even. And it would have felt like a single time."

"Then prove this to us," Carall said, approaching Evon, his bony head thrust forward, menacing. "Prove that we have traveled outside our time. Prove that you are not liars sent by the Enemy."

"Carall—" Dania began.

"There's no sky here," Kerensa began, "no sun I mean, and probably no stars, but when we step outside this place, Wystylth will recognize that the stars aren't in the right places—they've moved in the last thousand years. And Dania, you likely realized that we speak your language, only a much altered version of it. I'd ask Evon to dismiss the translation spell and prove it," she added with a grin, "but I don't want any confusion that might end up with people being dead."

Carall looked at Alvor, who said, "We have tried to find a way out of this forest without success. How do you propose otherwise, Kerensa who is strangely well informed about our abilities?"

Kerensa glanced at Evon. "To be honest, I'm not sure we'll be able to leave, either," she said. "But we have a spell to find the

Despot—that's the Enemy's host in our time—and I hope it will lead us to somewhere we can exit this place. And if it's capable of tracking the Despot from in here, that might mean we'll come out close to our own time. So if you want to throw in your lot with ours...."

"Then let us be going," Alvor said. He mounted his horse in a swift, fluid gesture completely at odds with his bulky appearance. "I look forward to doing battle with our Enemy again."

"You can't," Evon said without thinking.

Alvor looked down on him. He'd washed most of the blood off his face, but enough clung to his beard and the creases of his skin that he looked savage. "You do not tell me what I cannot do," he said.

"The spell Kerensa is carrying will destroy the Enemy forever, not just for a thousand years," Evon said. "You must allow us to complete our task."

"We saved this country—no, belike we saved the world," Alvor said, raising his voice. "Dare you tell me that our work was in vain?"

"Alvor, your work gave the world a thousand years of peace," Kerensa said, laying her hand on Alvor's calf and making Evon want to grab her and drag her out of his reach. "But this spell was made by magicians in your time who were willing to sacrifice anything to see the Enemy destroyed forever. Don't let their work be wasted. Help us use it against the Enemy."

Alvor sat back in his saddle. His eyes looked out over the clearing, rapt in memory. "Free us from this place," he said finally, "and we will speak more of this."

Kerensa nodded and took a step back. Carall and Dania mounted, and the three of them looked at Kerensa for directions. Wystylth, on the other hand, kept his eye on Evon, and Evon thought he saw the shadowy face smile. He looked away, trying to seem unconcerned, but wondering what interest the man, or whatever he was, might have in him.

Kerensa took out the coin and closed her fingers over it, then turned in a slow circle until she was facing the direction Alvor had arrived from. "This way," she said, and shouldered her bag and began walking. Evon quickly picked up the other bags and followed her, trailed by four people out of history and myth. He walked close beside her and said, in a low voice, "This is not good."

"What are you talking about? This is *amazing*. I just spoke to Alvor! You traded spells with Dania and Wystylth nearly cut your throat! I have so many things I want to ask them all. Some of the myth *has* to be wrong, you know. Passing down stories from generation to generation, they must have gotten some of it wrong."

"Kerensa, this is not the time for planning an attack on the Alvorian canon. If they decide to head off after the entity, I can't stop them."

"Maybe we should let them do it."

"What?"

Kerensa wouldn't meet his eyes. "We still don't know how to remove the fire and keep it a weapon. Wouldn't it be easier to just let the heroes take care of the entity?"

"Kerensa, if they kill the Despot, you're doomed to carry that fire for the rest of your life. You'll go on burning to death and being resurrected and that cycle will never be broken."

"If you figure out how to take this fire out of me —"

"*When* I figure it out."

"All right, when you figure out how to take this fire out of me, couldn't you transfer it to someone else? Someone evil?"

"I'm not comfortable judging the comparative evilness of other people. And you ought to know better than anyone that good people die because of this weapon too."

Kerensa ducked her head lower. "I don't need a reminder."

"I'm sorry. But you know it's true. Besides, even if we let Alvor kill the Despot, we've already seen that his solution isn't permanent. In a thousand years the entity will return and someone else will have to endure what you have. It might even be your descendant. Can you really condemn someone else to that fate?"

Kerensa sighed. "You're right. But it was nice, for a few minutes, to pretend it was all over." She stopped and turned around. "We should probably join hands, or something," she said. "I've heard that sometimes people cross the borders of these places and end up separated. Sometimes separated in time as well as location. So we shouldn't take any chances."

Alvor nodded. Kerensa stood between Alvor and Dania and hooked her elbows around their ankles so she could hold the coin as she walked between their horses. Evon wrapped his fingers around Carall's ankle and then, hesitantly, held out his hand to take Wystylth's. This close, he could see that Wystylth was definitely smiling. His mouth was slung forward a little, like the muzzle of a cat, though he didn't have the fangs Evon half expected to see. Wystylth's palm was rough like sandpaper, but the back of his hand was smooth, almost silky. The ivory claws were fully retracted, giving his fingertips a bare, unsettling look. "I don't bite," Wystylth said in a low voice, and bared his teeth. They were perfectly normal human teeth.

"I didn't expect you to," Evon said, embarrassed that his voice had a little quiver in it. He remembered the sharp claw pressed against his throat and was extremely conscious that both his hands were occupied. Would he dare use magic against a legendary hero? Absolutely.

They began walking forward again, somewhat less gracefully now. Wystylth's walk was a sort of bob, as if he weren't used to walking on two legs. "Your woman is beautiful," Wystylth said into the silence, his smile growing broader.

Fear for Kerensa made Evon forget fear for himself. "Stay away from her," he hissed. "I can make you wish you'd never been born, or however it was you came into this world."

Wystylth looked at him for a long moment. "I left my lady wife behind the day we rode off into this place," he said. "The Gods only know what she thinks happened to me. I meant no disrespect."

Evon wanted the earth to swallow him whole. "I apologize," he said. "That was...by the Gods, I am so sorry. I thought...."

"I know what you thought," Wystylth said. "It is what everyone thinks. And I did threaten to slit your throat." He smiled again, and Evon realized, looking more closely into the shadowy hood, that his eyes were merry. "You have the look of a man newly in love and not entirely certain what he did to deserve it. She is an unusual young woman. One who tries to help a man who attempted to kill her."

"She is extraordinary," Evon said, wishing he had Kerensa's hand in his right now instead of Carall's too-thin ankle and a hand that wasn't quite a paw. "And I am lucky."

"I had a feeling, all these weeks, that I would not return home to Merenna," Wystylth said. "But it is not the same as learning she has been dead for a thousand years. Still, we were ten years together, and that is better than no years at all."

"I'm sorry."

"Thank you. I think you understand a little of what I feel. You will have to tell me, ten years from now, whether you understand better." Again that flash of a smile. Evon felt as if his world were being rearranged so quickly that if he let go with either hand, he would tumble to the ground.

"I think —" he began, and the world jerked, and his foot came down not on bare, cold earth, but snow that crunched beneath it.

---

*E*von stumbled a little bit, and Wystylth grasped his hand more firmly and kept him from falling. It was a clear, starry night, the still air several degrees colder than it had been just a moment before. Evon dropped Wystylth's hand a little faster than was polite and saw the man grin at him; he returned the grin sheepishly. He let go of Carall's ankle and suppressed the desire to wipe his palms on his trousers.

"Wystylth?" Alvor said.

Wystylth took a few bobbing steps forward, scanning the sky. "We are not in our own time," he said. "But the sky is not so much changed that I cannot see we are still in southern Dalanine."

"I don't see Valantis, or his men," Kerensa said. "Evon…."

Evon looked around. It was dark enough that he couldn't tell if they were anywhere close to where they'd entered the place of power, and he had no way of knowing whether they had emerged the same day, or weeks later, or even years. Inspiration struck him, and he took out his mirror. "*Eloqua* Piercy Faranter," he said, and the mirror frosted over. He waited; no response. Alvor and his companions moved forward, talking quietly among themselves. Evon followed them, his attention absorbed by the mirror. If they were so many years in the future that Piercy was dead...or if the Despot had destroyed all of Dalanine....

"There are signs of other horses passing this way," Wystylth said. He was crouched low now and examining the ground. Evon saw nothing but drifts of snow, but Wystylth leaned down until his nose was less than an inch from the drifts and said, "Three horses. Their tracks end here, as if they too passed into the place of power."

"Look there," Kerensa said, and ran forward, her steps slowed by the snow-covered ground. Evon looked up to see her pointing at a dark hump on the ground. "It's our horse. Poor thing, they killed it." At that moment, the mirror cleared, and Piercy's familiar face filled its small circle.

"Good evening, dear fellow, and how goes the hunt?" he said.

"Did I speak to you yesterday evening?" Evon demanded.

Piercy's eyebrows went up. "Have you forgotten already? I was not aware that love could so disorder your faculties."

"Did I?"

"Yes, Evon, why are you so agitated? Do you have news?"

Evon glanced over at where Alvor and Carall were having a low-voiced but intense argument. "I...no news yet. We may not be going to Nystrantor after all. I'll tell you as soon as I know what our plans are. Do you know where the army is? Our army, I mean?"

"North and east of your position, based on where you were last evening. I'm told they will engage the Despot's army in two or three days. You ought to be able to circle north of them, but I have to say, Evon, my confidence in your plan is waning."

"It...might not matter. Things have changed."

"Evon, you sound shifty. Are you keeping something from me? Because you know that never ends well for either of us."

"I'll tell you everything, Piercy, as soon as I understand it myself."

Piercy made an exasperated noise. "You had better do," he said, and vanished.

Evon put the mirror away and looked around again. If Valantis and his men had followed them into the magic place, it was impossible to know where, or if, they would emerge. They needed to move on immediately, though even as he thought that he had a brief image of Valantis face-to-face with Alvor, and it made him smile despite his anxiety. He went to join Alvor and Carall, who had finished their argument but were still, as Evon saw when he approached, angry about something. "We thank you for bringing us out of that place," Alvor said.

"Though Dania's Glass would no doubt have done the same, had we waited a little longer," Carall muttered.

"They deserve no less thanks for all that," Alvor said sharply. "Now I would have you explain why we should not pursue the Enemy as we have done before."

The abruptness of the question startled Evon. "Ah," he stammered, "I mean no offense to you, but if you kill the Enemy as you did before, it will only come back again centuries from now." He explained what he had learned about the spell and the inferences he'd made about the nature of the entity. Alvor listened, his face a dispassionate mask. Carall kept putting his skeletal hand to the pommel of his short sword, his eyes watching Alvor instead of Evon. Dania's eyes were closed in thought, her head bowed. And Wystylth watched Evon closely, all traces of the smile gone. The more Evon spoke, the more dispassionate Alvor's face became, and Evon began stammering under the weight of his scrutiny.

"So is the young woman to die in order to destroy the Enemy utterly?" Alvor asked, after Evon's explanation trailed off.

"I won't let that happen," Evon said.

"And yet you do not know how to prevent it."

"Not yet."

"Possibly not ever."

"As I said, I won't let that happen."

"So you will wander until you discover a solution, while your Despot continues to ravage the land? And you consider *my* solution an impermanent one?"

"Your solution condemns Kerensa to a life of suffering and some future generation to the depredations of the Enemy." Evon felt his voice shake.

"We should not stand here arguing with the boy," Carall said.

"He's not a boy," said Dania. "Alvor, his argument has merit."

"It has uncertainty," Alvor said. "We are expected to simply stand by...every feeling revolts against it. I am sorry," he told Evon, "but we have seen the destruction wreaked by the Enemy and we cannot afford to wait on you. We will carry you to the nearest settlement as repayment for your aid, but then we must bid you farewell."

"No!" Evon exclaimed.

"Alvor, please don't do this!" Kerensa cried out. "You were always a man of action, and I know this goes against your nature, but this *is* the right solution."

"You are a brave woman, Kerensa," Alvor said, and offered her his hand. "Ride with me and tell me what the people of your time remember of us."

"You're making a mistake," Evon said, his teeth clenched.

"Alvor's decision is the right one," Dania said. She leaned over and pulled Evon up on the horse behind her. "I would know more of this spell that binds the fire." She added, in a lower voice, "Perhaps with my assistance you will find the answer you seek, and then, who knows?"

Evon said nothing. Four legendary heroes would pursue the Despot and kill the entity, and Kerensa would be doomed. *You didn't have a solution anyway,* a cruel voice inside his head whispered. *You were willing to see the world devastated by the Despot to prevent the death of the woman you love. Not quite the heroic type, are you?* He looked ahead to where Kerensa was in vehement conversation with Alvor. Maybe she could argue him around to her way of thinking. But Alvor had an amused, condescending look on his face, the kind of indulgent look parents give their children when they perform a clever new trick. Evon responded to Dania's next question absently. At least she was willing to help. But unless that help produced results before they reached the next village, however far that was, Evon's journey was over.

Dania deserved every bit of the reputation history and myth had given her. She grasped the implications of Evon's research immediately and from that was able to independently come to the same conclusions he had. "Nystrantor may have the solution you seek," she said, "and one that will not require you to use the magic on the Enemy." This close, Evon could see that her dark hair had gray in it and the corners of her eyes and mouth were lined. They were all four of them much older than he had imagined.

"You know Alvor is wrong," Evon said desperately. "Why don't you tell him so?"

"Alvor is my *Kiere*, which by your expression is a word your language no longer has," Dania said. "It means...not a lord in the sense that he is my superior, but someone to whom I owe respect and loyalty and therefore give my obedience. I follow where he leads, even into death. I will not cross him."

"But don't you give him advice?"

"Advice, yes. Orders, no. Evon, you should realize that Alvor is not a man made for patience. It grates on him to be told he must sit quietly in a corner while someone else is a hero."

"I don't want to be a hero."

"Neither did Alvor, once on a time."

"Kerensa says he was just a man who became great because the times demanded it."

"That is very accurate." She sighed. "It seems so long ago that we were all just ordinary folk wondering at the rumors of war we heard coming out of the northlands. Well, not Carall. He was a prince of... how strange that I cannot now remember it."

"Is he...undead?"

Dania glanced over her shoulder at him. "Undead? That is a rumor I had not yet heard. No, he was touched by a malignancy that now eats at him, bone and blood. I have some skill as a healer and yet I cannot restore him. It makes him angry, to be so weakened. He was not always so hostile to strangers."

"I understand," Evon said, not understanding at all. "Dania, isn't there anything I can do to change Alvor's mind?"

"It is not a mind that changes easily," she said. "Prove to him that you can do what you intend to do. Enlist his aid. He is not proud, but he dislikes feeling useless."

Evon lapsed into silence again. He still couldn't prove that the fire could be removed from Kerensa. He was willing to beg Alvor for help—he wasn't that proud—but he didn't think there was much point. His mind fell back into the pattern of going over and over everything he'd learned, looking for an answer. He ought to be asking Dania about magic in her time; the Gods only knew what lost spells she might know. But the idea depressed him. She didn't know the one spell that mattered most to him and to Kerensa, if it even existed. He looked ahead to where Kerensa rode with Alvor; they appeared to still be arguing. This was the opportunity of a lifetime for her, the chance to trade stories with her hero, comparing fact with legend. Instead she was still valiantly trying to argue him around to their point of view. That depressed him further.

Dawn came while they were still on the road, illuminating a town on the distant horizon. Evon felt himself begin to droop and struggled not to fall asleep on Dania's shoulder. The woman had to be twice his age and she was still alert and fresh as if she'd slept all night instead of riding. He peered at the road ahead. It seemed to be moving. He blinked and rubbed grit from his eyes and looked again. Dozens of wagons came ponderously toward them along the road, preceded by horsemen moving more swiftly. Alvor pulled up and the others followed suit. "What is this?" Alvor said.

"They must be fleeing the Despot's armies," Evon said. "Piercy said his forces were advancing swiftly."

"The better for us, that we do not have far to go to hunt him down," Alvor said. "Dania, does your Glass recognize the Enemy's presence?"

"It does, though the sign is not clear. I cannot tell how distant the Enemy may be."

"Then let us proceed." Alvor motioned them forward.

It was less than half an hour before they encountered the first riders. One of them stopped nearby, controlling his unquiet mount with difficulty. "You oughtn't go that way," he said.

"We have no fear of the tyrant," Alvor said.

The man looked confused. "What's that then?"

"He says we have important business in the town," Evon said. Without the *cleperi* spell, Alvor's language was only gibberish to the rider.

"You ought to rethink that. The Despot's armies are on their way and it's only a matter of hours before the town is overrun." The man eyed Wystylth dubiously; Wystylth grinned at him.

"We don't expect to stay long," Evon said.

The rider shrugged. "Oughtn't take the ladies into the battle," he added. "Despot's armies aren't kind to women."

"Thank you for the advice," Evon said. The man shrugged and rode on.

"It sounds like the Despot is close," Kerensa said.

"All the better for us." Alvor rode on, followed by the rest. Evon looked down and saw Wystylth looking back at him. Throughout the journey Wystylth had loped along beside the horses, sometimes disappearing for a stretch but always returning again, usually to speak to Alvor. His face was in shadow again, but Evon thought he saw sympathy in his smile.

They now rode among the wagons, piled high with people and boxes and in some cases furniture; Evon saw a wizened old man perched on an enormous rocking chair, teetering high atop a mound of crates. None of the wagoners, or their passengers, met anyone's eyes, except for several small children who hadn't grasped the somberness of the situation. They laughed and waved, and Evon waved back, but their enthusiasm depressed him still more. He caught Kerensa's eye as she happened to glance behind her, and smiled weakly. She didn't smile back. If he was feeling despondent, she must be miserable. She wasn't arguing anymore; she was listening to something Alvor was saying, all her attention on him. Maybe he was telling her a story after all.

It seemed every inhabitant of the town was in the streets, loading wagons or horses and shouting at everyone else. Alvor led his procession through the streets at a slow walk, giving anyone who tried to interfere with him a level gaze that promised violence if that became necessary. They ended up in the stable yard of a small coaching inn, all the coaches of which had been pressed into emergency evacuation service. Only two horses waited in the stalls, and as they dismounted, a woman came out of the inn to saddle one of them. She ignored their little party despite the extremely old-fashioned dress of four of its members.

Alvor dismounted and helped Kerensa down. Evon got down with no assistance and went to Alvor's side. "Please," he said, "help us reach Nystrantor. We'll never make it on our own. I'll separate the weapon from Kerensa and we can destroy the Enemy forever."

Alvor looked at him curiously. "You are that convinced that your weapon will wreak such damage?"

"I've seen it. Nothing survives. Alvor, I'm positive this is the right way to do this."

"Is his assessment of the weapon's power correct, Dania?" The woman nodded. "Then you know how to save this young woman and still destroy the Enemy?" he said to Evon.

Evon hesitated. Alvor looked at Kerensa. "Will you still argue against my point?" he asked her.

"I can't," Kerensa said. "You're right. About everything."

The woman saddling her horse mounted and rode out of the stable yard. Evon glanced at her as she left, then looked back to see that Kerensa had begun to cry. "What—" he began, and someone shoved him hard from behind, knocking him to the half-frozen ground, and knelt on the small of his back. Rough-palmed hands grabbed his and immobilized them. "No," he shouted, and struggled hard against Wystylth's grip to no effect. "Don't do this!"

"Thank me for saving your life," Alvor said. He sounded regretful. "She is going where you should not follow."

"Leave her alone! Go on, kill the Despot your way, just leave her alone!"

"He's not forcing me, Evon," Kerensa said, her voice choked with crying. "There's no more time. I can't let any more people die when I can stop it happening."

"Kerensa, I can find a way! Please—" He bucked and kicked as rope went around his wrists and bound them tight. "*Please*," he begged.

From where his face was pressed into the mud, he saw her kneel beside him, felt her lay her hand on his cheek. "I love you," she said.

"And not just because you've done more for me than anyone else. You have to let me do this. There's been too much suffering already."

"Alvor made you think this way," Evon said, "he made you think it was hopeless but it's *not*, Kerensa, I swear it's not. Just give me time."

"There's no more time." She kissed his cheek, her tears falling onto his face. He struggled more, but Wystylth shoved him harder into the ground and he grunted in pain. "Don't hurt him," Kerensa said, her words barely intelligible through her tears.

Evon shouted incoherently, desperately, as more rope went around his ankles and Wystylth heaved him off the ground with no more effort than if he'd been a child. "Don't fight me," the man said in his rasping voice, and cuffed Evon so hard across the head that he bit his tongue and his vision went blurry for a moment. When he could see clearly again, he was in one of the empty stalls and Wystylth was tying the long end of the rope binding his ankles around the brace supporting the feeding trough. "I am sorry about this," Wystylth said, and shoved a piece of cloth into Evon's mouth. "But we cannot have you rescued too soon." He came around and tugged on the rope around Evon's wrists, testing the knots. Then he was gone. Evon heard the sound of horses riding out of the stable yard, and then there was nothing but the horse in the other stall snuffling at the food in its trough. He was alone.

24

$\mathcal{E}$von strained against the ropes binding his hands, twisting and stretching until his wrists felt raw. It was too much to hope that Wystylth didn't know how to tie a knot. Eventually he sagged, breathing heavily through his nose. Beyond the stable, he heard the sounds of shouting and the occasional scream, all of it too far away. No one was going to find him and free him in time. It was over. He closed his eyes and saw again Kerensa's face, what little of it had been visible with his own face ground into the mud, remembered the touch of her lips on his cheek, and despair overwhelmed him. Of course this was how it had to end, because the Gods were not done playing with him yet. *You've barely known her three weeks*, a cruel voice inside his head taunted him, *in a year you'll find someone else and she'll be a sad memory*. Had it really only been three days since she'd put her arms around him in that dark, freezing barn? He remembered waking next to her, the look on her face when she'd seen him there, and his heart broke into splinters inside his chest. She'd trusted him, and he'd failed her.

In his memory, Kerensa raised her face to his, her hazel eyes shining, and said, *I know you'll find a way*. It was like an electric jolt to the chest. No. He was *not* giving up yet. Evon dashed away tears he didn't remember shedding and strained at the ropes for a few seconds before remembering how stupid that was. He needed a different approach. If he could speak, he could cast spells — awkwardly, probably, but if he was the best magician of his generation he had damn well better be able to manage it with his hands tied behind his back.

The cloth Wystylth had stuffed into his mouth had a trailing end; he could feel it brushing his cheek. He began scooting along the muddy ground, folding himself so his nose nearly touched his knees, then began scissoring his legs, trying to catch the loose end of the gag between his knees. He twisted his head, lifting the cloth, trying to flip it over one of his knees, and finally he was able to pincer it and unfold his body, pulling the cloth slowly out of his mouth as he did. He spat out the last of it, coughed, and spat again, trying to moisten his mouth enough to speak. *"Fri—"* he began, then couldn't stop coughing. *"Frigo,"* he said, and gestured at the ropes binding his hands. He hoped.

Nothing happened. He strained at the ropes again, but they gave only a little. He groaned. The ropes weren't brittle enough for *frigo* to affect them. *"Frigo,"* he said again anyway, and again nothing happened. He needed to make them dry enough to snap, and maybe if he'd had a few days he could have invented a spell for that, but as it was he knew nothing that would turn damp rope dry and breakable.

But that wasn't entirely true, was it? There was a spell that would do just what he needed. Evon's palms went damp with sweat. Quickly, before he could talk himself out of it, he snapped his fingers and said, *"Forva."*

Excruciating pain circled his wrists and sent tongues of fire up the backs of his hands. Evon gritted his teeth, counted a slow three, then ground out, *"Desini."* The fire went out — at least, he hoped it had, because while the heat was gone, his wrists still felt as if they were on fire. He shook tears, these of pain, out of his eyes, and said, *"Frigo."*

With a crack, the fibers of the rope separated, and Evon's hands flew apart. Shaking, he brought them around to examine them. If he'd permanently damaged his hands—there were burns like black-red bracelets around his wrists just where the ropes had been, and streaks of red ran up the backs of his hands, but he could flex his fingers, and that was all that mattered. He started prying at the knots binding his feet, feeling sweat prickle his armpits and bead up on his forehead despite the chill. It wasn't too late. He could still catch them, and—and do what, exactly? Snatch Kerensa off Alvor's horse and ride very fast with her in the opposite direction? And then four legendary heroes would probably kill him, leave his body behind and take Kerensa off to her doom. He needed a better plan than that.

The knots loosened, then came apart. Evon sat rubbing his ankles and panted from his exertions. The first thing was to catch up to them. He would figure out the rest when the time came. *You're out of time*, the cruel voice said. He grabbed at the edge of the feeding trough and hauled himself upright. In the next stall, the horse regarded Evon with a kind of offhanded curiosity. Evon reached out and stroked its nose while he waited for his legs and feet to stop tingling. The sensation reminded him of *vertiri* and *trattuci*, of the blue spell-ribbons flowing away from Kerensa and twining themselves around his body. If only he could have made the fire leave her so readily. *Something* had to make it leave her, if it had passed from host to host over the generations—

That electric jolt struck him again, leaving him breathless. Of course. It was so damned obvious he felt like an idiot for not having seen it before. But—*could* he save her, was it even possible? Evon headed for the stall door. It might be possible. It would take perfect timing, and he would need every ounce of magical power he possessed, and it still might not work. But it was more of a chance than he'd had before. And he was certain he could convince Alvor to let him try.

The stall door seemed very far away—too far. Evon looked back and saw he'd moved only a foot from where he'd started. He took another step toward the door. It was no closer than before. Evon took a few more long strides, then began running. It felt as if he and the door were both moving, the door always three steps beyond his reach. *Dania.* He stopped to catch his breath. It was almost a compliment, that they'd assumed they would need more than one deterrent to keep him from following them. Now that he knew what to look for, he could see the heat shimmer where the trap was triggered by Evon stepping into it. Evon moved backward—at least Dania's spell allowed him to do that—and pulled out his quizzing glass, wincing as his burned wrist brushed the edge of his coat. "*Epiria*," he said, passing his hand over the lens.

Tiny violet bursts of light shone out on both sides of the stall door, clustering along the hinges and the latch. Evon raised his left hand, began to speak, then shut his mouth hard. He shouldn't have cast *epiria*. He could not afford to use any more of his reserves; if they didn't replenish in time, it could mean he wouldn't have enough for the sequence of spells his subconscious mind was working out. There had to be another way.

He turned the lens to examine the rest of the stall. The violet lights diminished the farther he went from the door, leaving the back third of the stall free from the spell's effect. Evon dismissed *epiria* and backed up until he was pressed against the feeding trough. He looked at the horse again. It was a brown mare with a white blaze on her forehead. She nodded at him as if in encouragement. She seemed a good deal more intelligent than his last horse, though that couldn't have been a very high bar to meet. "If Piercy had set this trap, he would have extended it to cover the stalls on either side of me," he told her. "Let's hope Dania isn't as cunning as Piercy." He clambered up to balance on the feeding trough, which creaked a little under his weight, got one leg over the side of the stall, then swung his other leg around and dropped heavily to the ground next to the horse. Slowly, feeling a little superstitious that Dania's spell might notice him and figure out what he was doing, he approached the stall door and let out a deep, relieved breath when it opened easily. Evon turned and eyed the horse again. "Let's you and I save a life, shall we?" he said.

He saddled the horse quickly and furtively, not sure what he would do if the mare's owner emerged from the inn. Beat him senseless, probably, with how keyed up he was feeling at the moment. The mare stood patiently as Evon mounted and obediently moved forward when he urged her into the street beyond.

The crowds had gone from frightened to panicked in the time Evon had taken to free himself. Wagons stood crosswise in the center of the street, their owners shouting at other wagoners trying to go the other way. Nervous animals made the air fragrant with the stench of their bowels. Children clutched at their parents and screamed or sobbed. In one place, the traffic jam was caused by a fully loaded wagon that had been abandoned in the center of the road whose owners had decided that fleeing was harder when they had all their possessions with them. The wagon's shafts rested empty on the ground, and three large men were trying to shift the heavy load without the help of horses. It felt to Evon as if the crowd were trying to sweep him away backwards out of the town, as if the refugees were stepping into his path on purpose, just to slow him further. A few of the men and women who approached him looked as if they were considering separating him from the horse, but the occasional forceful application of his boot saw him clear of the town and out on the open road heading south and east.

Here, on the great plains below the mountains, snow had not fallen so heavily and the road was clear, if still frozen. Hard as it must be on the horse's hooves, at least it wasn't mud churned to soup by the passage of thousands of refugees. Evon held on to the reins and prodded the horse into a gallop. He had no way of knowing how close the Despot was, couldn't even tell how far Kerensa had gotten, had nothing but the scent of smoke in his nostrils and a terrible burning anxiety in his chest. She only had to come close to the Despot and the weapon would do the rest. Having met Alvor, Evon had no doubt the man would be able to get Kerensa as close as she needed. Then it would be over.

A few miles down the road, the way forked, but Evon discovered that Alvor and Kerensa had struck out across country, into the hills. He guided his mount the same way. It was both intelligent and docile, not a combination he expected to find in a horse, and he felt a momentary guilt at having robbed someone of what must be a rather valuable animal. Call it assisting in the war effort.

Fifteen minutes after leaving the road behind, he felt as if he must be the only man left alive in the world, the plains were that empty.

He looked north, wondering if Dalanine's army was close enough to see, but a long, low arm of the mountains hemming in the plains northward obscured his vision. He ought to be hoping for Alvor's success today; it would spare thousands of lives. Thousands of lives saved at the cost of the only life that mattered to Evon. He definitely wasn't a hero. He gritted his teeth and urged the mare to run faster, following Kerensa's trail as if it were penciled across the landscape.

Low gray clouds massed overhead, and more billowed thickly across the horizon. Evon looked again and realized those clouds were smoke. His heart pounded faster for a few beats before he remembered that the weapon would likely not make that much smoke, or any smoke at all, and that he was not too late, he couldn't be too late now that he'd figured it out. He could feel the horse straining beneath him; she was already running as fast as she could, and forcing her to greater effort would only kill her and leave him stranded in the middle of these wide plains. He glanced up. Would it be rain, or snow, that fell from those clouds? Either would be the kind of delay he could not afford.

Thunder cracked, high and sharp, nearby, and something passed his ear with a whining hum. He turned around and saw another mounted figure coming up fast behind him. The rider's hood was pulled well forward over his face against the cold, but his red beard was easily visible even in the dim light. *Valantis*. Where in the hell had he come from? He waved something that gleamed in the dim light at Evon—a gun?—and kicked his horse's sides. Now Evon could hear him shouting, and although the words were unintelligible, there was no mistaking the fury in the man's voice. Evon leaned forward over the horse's neck and wished he knew a spell that would make it move faster. He wouldn't have dared use it even if he did. He glanced over his shoulder. Valantis was gaining on him. He could smell Kerensa's trail preparing to turn left to avoid—nothing, there was nothing there, no reason for the path to change, but he didn't have time to wonder about it. There was nowhere to hide on this barren plain, nothing to save him, but all Evon could think was *I'm not going to make it in time*. He had no way to fight Valantis, neither weapon nor spell, and his horse was tiring, and—Evon felt despair rising in him again and kicked it back into the dark corner of his mind it had come from. It wasn't over until...he refused to finish that thought.

"Stop or I'll shoot you dead, Lorantis," Valantis shouted over the noise of both their horses' hooves. He was only yards away. Evon pulled up and turned to face Valantis, whose hood was still pulled low over his face.

"It's too late," he said. "Kerensa is near the Despot's army now. If you ride after her, you'll only be killed."

"It's not the girl I want," Valantis said. He pushed his hood back, and Evon's shock at the man's appearance transmitted itself to the horse, who took a few sidelong steps until Evon calmed her. Valantis's red hair and beard were streaked with white, and wrinkles were carved into his face like wind-worn channels. He looked nearer sixty than the forty Evon had guessed his age to be. "I wandered for *years* in that Godsforsaken place thanks to you." His voice was still raspy, but weaker than it had been.

"It can't have been years," Evon said without thinking, "or your clothes would have fallen apart."

Fury swept across the big man's face, and he leveled his gun at Evon's heart. "Taunt me, will you?" he shouted.

"I'm sorry," Evon said, not meaning it. He looked furtively around for something that would get him out of this. Kerensa's scent was strong now; he had to be close to her, and maybe there was still time.

"You're going to fix it," Valantis said. "Right now."

"I don't know how," Evon said.

"Figure it out." Valantis's hand was trembling with either age or fury, not that it mattered, since either would be enough to make him squeeze the trigger by accident.

"Ah...." Evon looked around again and was startled to see an unexpected shimmer only a few feet away, directly athwart Kerensa's trail where it made that inexplicable turn. If Valantis hadn't attacked him, he'd have run right into it. Perhaps Dania had a little of Piercy's cunning, after all. He certainly hadn't thought to be looking for more traps. He edged the horse in that direction, then stopped when Valantis waved the gun at him.

"Don't move," he said, "and don't think about running. I'm not so desperate to have this reversed that I won't enjoy watching your blood water this earth. Do it. Now."

"Put the gun down first. You don't want to shoot me before I've restored you," Evon said. The horse moved a few more steps. If he could put the trap between himself and Valantis….

"I said *don't move!*" Valantis shouted, and fired the pistol just as Evon kicked his horse in the direction of the trap. The shot went wide, and Valantis swore and yanked on his horse's reins to bring it around. Evon swerved to avoid the trap, swerved back to put it between himself and Valantis, and prayed to whichever of the Twins was listening that Valantis's bigger and faster horse was also less agile than Evon's stolen mount. At that moment he heard something large hit the ground, and turned around in time to see Valantis, caught by *desini cucurri* in mid-shout, catapult from his fallen horse's back and land face-down in the frozen turf. The horse had dropped in mid-stride and looked like a toppled statue; Valantis, with his knees bent and his rump in the air, just looked ridiculous. *He's going to come after me again,* Evon thought, but that was the only thought he had time for. He shouted at his horse, who plunged into a gallop, and they were off again on Kerensa's trail. He was beginning to feel as if all he had ever done in his life was follow Kerensa across Dalanine. Well, if he could reach her in time, that would stop. *It will stop if you don't reach her,* the cruel voice said. He wished he could make it shut up.

Clouds of smoke continued to gather along the horizon as if the land itself were burning. The Despot must have tens of thousands of soldiers at his command. Tens of thousands of soldiers, and who knew how many of those tens stood between Evon and the Despot. The idea that Alvor, legendary hero or not, might be able to fight his way past them seemed suddenly ridiculous. The Gods only knew how much harder it would be for Evon Lorantis. The horse slowed a little going up a short incline, and when they reached its crest, Evon pulled it up sharply and stared, disbelieving, at the bowl-shaped valley below.

He was too far away to make out individual features; instead, the valley teemed with soldiers the way an ant hill might overflow with tiny, scrambling bodies. They marched in sloppy order, squares and columns distorted into rhombi and curves, but there were so many of them their lack of martial discipline hardly mattered. Blood-red standards bearing the image of a black raven and topped with some object too small for Evon to make out dotted the field, but his eye was drawn to one twice the size of the others. It bore two ravens, each clawing and gouging at the other, neither appearing to have the upper hand, and it was borne by a soldier wearing silvery armor that winked with light even in the gloom. Several horsemen stood near it, but at this distance Evon could not see any distinctions between them that might mark the Despot. He heard no shouts of battle, saw no frenzied movement that would indicate combat, but he also couldn't see Alvor and the others anywhere. He kicked his horse into a gallop again and plunged down the side of the incline. They had to be here somewhere. He knew he hadn't gotten ahead of them; Kerensa's scent led straight—no, it was turning to the right, away from the army—

More smoke shrouded the hillside ahead as if one of the storm clouds had descended to roll along the plains. This one, however, was white, and something inside it flashed briefly, reflecting light that did not come from the sun. It reminded him of something, one of the only things he'd known about Alvorian myth before meeting Kerensa, something one of the heroes had said...Dania's Glass. One of the Four Talismans. Alvor's Mace, Dania's Glass, Wystylth's Claws. Carall's Breath. A concealing mist that protected the four as they surrounded Murakot just before killing him.

Evon began shouting and waving one arm as he urged the horse directly into the center of the cloudbank, which was moving rapidly toward the army. It was so thick he could barely see the horse's head less than two feet from his, and he slowed the horse to a walk, afraid of getting turned around. "Wait!" he shouted. "Alvor, wait! I know how to save Kerensa! Please!"

The only thing he heard were his own words reflected back at him by the thick fog. *"Please,"* he said. *Please,* came the echo. He could see nothing except his hands on the reins and the blackened burn stripes circling his wrists. His pulse sang in his ears, high and fast. The horse nickered at nothing and shook her mane as if shooing flies.

Then, *"Solto spexa,"* Dania said, and it was as if the fog bank was nothing more than a light gauze through which Evon could clearly see three horses and a shorter, crouching figure about ten yards from where he stood. "I underestimated you," Dania said.

"I was lucky," Evon said. "And I know how the magic works. I can free Kerensa and still use it to kill the Despot."

25

*A*lvor looked at him, his eyes narrowed. "Desperation drives men to many things," he said, "but I think you would not dare to lie to me."

Evon shook his head. "I swear to you, sir, the Enemy will die today. I just need the four of you to defend me while I cast my spells. Hold them off for five minutes. Dania, will you paralyze the Despot when we see him? I intend to cast some very complicated spells and I will need all of my reserves to do it."

"If you tell me what you intend, perhaps I can assist you," Dania said.

Evon shook his head again. "The truth is, I'm still working out everything in my head, and I think if I tell you what I have in mind, you will all simply be distracted. Please. Five minutes. Ten at the most."

"Evon," Kerensa said, "please don't do this. I don't think I can bear it if you give me false hope."

"It's not false hope, I swear it." Evon dismounted and went to her side, looked up at her where she sat behind Alvor. She had been crying, though she was dry-eyed now, and when he reached out to her she slid awkwardly down and threw herself into his arms.

"Just...when we near the Despot, just hold the weapon in check for as long as you can, and I'll do the rest." He put his fingers under her chin and tilted her head so she had to look at him. "Please. If it doesn't work...."

Kerensa drew a deep, shuddering breath, then nodded. "If it doesn't work...Evon, promise me you'll shield yourself before the end. I don't want you to die."

"I promise. But it won't be necessary." He looked at Alvor. "Ten minutes. If it doesn't work, then Kerensa will...." He couldn't bring himself to finish that sentence any more than he could the previous one.

The heroes looked at one another. Wystylth said, "I believe I can occupy the Enemy's guards for at least that long. I have seen them as closely as I dare, and I do not believe they are entirely human. Something upon which I am something of an expert," he added with a grin.

"It will be like the battle at Riskin Falls," Dania said.

Carall scowled. "I should hope not. I was knocked unconscious at Riskin Falls and woke to find the battle over. I would see my blade run red with blood today."

Alvor gazed steadily at Evon. "I think you are desperate to save the woman you love," he said.

"I am, sir, but I also know what I'm doing." *I hope I know what I'm doing. This could mean my own death, and theirs.*

Alvor took a deep breath and let it out slowly. "Then we will try this your way," he said, "and I hope you are not mistaken."

"So do I, sir."

"We should be moving," Carall said. His horse jigged nervously as if picking up on Carall's restless movements. "The Breath cannot be stopped once it is set in motion, and it will leave us behind soon."

Evon led Kerensa to his horse and helped her mount, daring Alvor to make an issue of it. Alvor said nothing, merely wheeled his horse and set off toward the army. The others gathered behind him, Evon at the rear with Kerensa holding tight to his waist. There was so much he wanted to say to her, but none of it seemed very important right now. Time enough for that when this was all over. He reviewed the spells in his mind; the sequence was important, and so was the timing, and there were so many things he was leaving to chance, but he had to believe it was possible. Kerensa shifted a little behind him, but said nothing. What was she thinking? Her voice had had that same dead tone he remembered from Inveros. He prayed she hadn't given up again. This would only work if she could keep the weapon from activating immediately.

They came over the top of another small rise and saw the army spread out before them. The edge of the Breath had only just begun to reach the first soldiers, none of whom seemed to notice anything amiss. "Ride out, Dania," Alvor said.

Dania cracked her horse's reins and set off down the hill at a gallop, the others following her, Evon trailing a little behind because the command had taken him off guard. They rode without speaking or shouting, the only sound the thrumming of their horses' hooves on the snowy frozen ground. Evon wasn't sure exactly when the soldiers heard the sound of hooves, but they hadn't done more than stop and begin to turn when Dania raised both her hands, snapped her fingers and shouted, *"Forva!"*

White fire exploded through the ranks, so hot Evon could feel his skin tighten. The Breath vanished, vaporized. Five rows of soldiers sagged and fell, and the air was filled with the smell of smoked meat and the sound of screaming. Part of Evon gaped in astonishment at Dania's unparalleled abilities, another part made a mental note to have her teach him that when this was all over, but most of him was occupied with not falling off his horse, which might be an excellent animal but clearly didn't have the experience the heroes' mounts did with *forva* that could crisp your eyeballs.

Dania gestured again and the fire divided, burning hotly on both sides of a cool corridor that led deeper into the heart of the army. Alvor hefted his mace, Carall drew his sword, and to his left Evon saw Wystylth's claws fully extended and his hood tossed back to reveal a head of blond hair much like Evon's own. He didn't have time to notice more than this, because then they reached the first rank of soldiers and battle was joined.

Evon wished he were watching this from the outside, not only because it was less dangerous but because the four heroes fighting together must be what legends were made of. Alvor laid about him with the mace that no ordinary man could have lifted, let alone broken heads and backs with. Carall was more subtle but equally deadly, his blade flicking from soldier to soldier and leaving piles of bodies in its wake. Dania cast spell after spell Evon couldn't even recognize, sending enemy fighters to the ground with their bodies contorted or their faces blue with asphyxiation or, in a few cases, turned completely to ash. And Wystylth was everywhere at once, snarling defiance, his hands and claws bloody from tearing out the throats of anyone stupid enough to come within arm's reach of him. Evon could only keep his horse under control and pray that no one got close enough to him or Kerensa that he would have to fight back. In the back of his mind he again ran through the sequence of spells he needed, testing their order—he would have one chance to do this, and it had to be perfect and perfectly timed.

They were somehow pressing forward through the masses. Dania found a clear spot and cast *forva* again, though it was not as big as the first one because they were all too close to the enemy soldiers, and cleared out a few more ranks so they could advance more quickly. Alvor swung at another head, crushing the skull, and raised his voice to say, "I think we are near our Enemy."

"We are," Kerensa shouted, and Evon craned his neck to see that she'd gone pale and was sweating. "I can feel the urge pulling at me. It's strong."

"Then ware guards," Alvor said, ducking a sword thrust and booting the soldier in the face so hard his neck snapped.

They fought for a few more seconds before Carall shouted, "I see them!" and spurred forward a bit to exchange blows with something whose head and neck weren't quite right. Its forehead bulged high above tiny eyes, and the tips of fangs protruded from its lips. Its neck was as thick around as Evon's thigh and corded with sinew so tight you could have plucked it like a harp string and seen it vibrate. It roared in Carall's face just before Carall's blade took it in the throat, then shook itself so hard Carall nearly lost his seat and his sword. Carall withdrew and stabbed at its stomach, striking below the heavy hide armor it wore to cover its chest. It shrieked and collapsed. "They die as any man does!" he shouted.

"Then we shall have to assist them in that endeavor," Alvor called out, and began laying about him with his mace. Evon had thought they were fighting well before, but now the blows came furiously on all sides and Evon could see their forward progress had stopped. He clenched his fists. So close. Should he help? He couldn't afford to. But if they failed to reach the Despot....

A gap opened up near Evon, and Kerensa groaned and her entire body went rigid with concentration, her fingers digging into his side. Evon looked around just in time to see the two-raven banner hovering nearby, framing a man in a shining steel cuirass on a massive horse armored for war. Standing, he would have been a full head taller than the inhuman creatures battling around him. His long hair hung lank and greasy around his face, and Evon could smell the sour odor of unwashed body wafting toward him on the cold breeze. The Despot kicked one of his own guards out of the way, and Evon heard a crack as the thing's leg broke, but the man's face showed no anger or cruelty, only a chilling impassivity more frightening than either of those. Evon jigged the horse away from the Despot, but he ignored Evon and Kerensa and made straight for Alvor, whose mace was gory with blood too red to be human. He was fighting two of the inhuman guards at once and had no idea that death was coming at him from behind.

Evon shouted a warning that was lost in the furor of battle, then spurred his horse toward the Despot, though he had no idea what he would do—beat him over the head with his fists, maybe? He could not afford to waste any of his reserves on offensive spells. Kerensa groaned again as they neared the Despot, shoving through the melee, and Evon realized he was screaming incoherently and waving his arms. He pushed his way in front of the Despot's horse, between him and Alvor, and the Despot looked at him with that impassive expression, then brought his sword around to strike at Evon, and Evon raised his hands because there was nothing else he could do—

"*Desini cucurri!*" Dania shouted, and the Despot froze in midswing, then fell face down and hit the frozen ground, his right arm still outstretched with the enormous sword clutched in it. The horse reared up and screamed, then came down on the Despot's shoulder, crushing it. Terrified, Evon kicked at it to make it flee. Everything hinged on the Despot being alive for this. "Whatever your spell is, you should cast it now!" Dania yelled at him, and turned her attention to one of the deformed things that was trying to disembowel her.

Evon leaped down from the horse and helped Kerensa dismount, then smacked its rump hard, hoping it might find a way out of the melee. Kerensa's face was fixed in concentration, tears leaking from her closed eyes. "I can't hold this for much longer," she said. Her skin was already a little too pink. Evon took a few deep breaths. He wasn't allowed to give in to panic.

"Take his left hand with yours," he said, "and press your first three fingers against his pulse." He pushed up Kerensa's sleeve and drew runes along the inside of her forearm with his coppery chalk, then turned his attention to the Despot only to realize the man was wearing hardened leather vambraces with rusty, tight-fitting buckles. He tugged at the straps with his fingertips to no avail, then pulled out his penknife and began hacking at the leather where it attached to the buckles. It was hopelessly inadequate to the task.

Movement caught his eye, and he looked up from his work toward the Despot's head. The shadow under the man's cheek seemed to shift in the dim light. Then Evon realized that nothing else, under the pall of smoke and the higher clouds, was casting a shadow. "*Wystylth!*" he shouted, acting on instinct. "*Help!*"

Then Wystylth was by his side, looking where Evon pointed, and without a word threw himself atop the Despot's frozen body and sank his claws deep into the man's temples. The shadow quivered, lay still, quivered harder, strained to get away, and finally fell still. Wystylth grinned. "I have seen the Enemy before," he said, "and it evaded my Claws. This time it is not so lucky, I think. And I am curious as to what you intend." His grin tightened as the shadow made another break for freedom. "Knife, on my belt," he added, jerking his chin, and Evon snatched the knife from its sheath, nearly cutting himself on the sharp blade, and sliced through the leather straps of the vambrace as if they were wet paper.

He yanked the vambrace away, then shoved the sleeve of the Despot's shirt away from his arm and chalked other runes there. He put his hand over the two joined ones, traced a rune on the air, and said, "*Vertiri. Torpia misca ademi.*" His mouth burned as if he'd swallowed a live coal, and a throbbing pain went through the small of his back as he cast the powerful, complicated spell. It felt as if someone had tied a knot in his spine and was pulling it tighter. Evon gritted his teeth and ignored it. He would have enough reserves for this. The alternative was unacceptable.

Kerensa gasped, and her skin went a shade pinker. "That feels strange," she said.

"Stay focused. It's just making the Despot a suitable host for the fire," Evon said. It wasn't as straightforward as he made it sound. This was the part he was least certain of, and if there had been more time...but there wasn't more time, and Evon had had to guess. *Ademi* was doing something, he was certain, because he could see the Despot's muscles twitch as part of his body began to change. Evon just hoped it was the right part.

He ducked low as a saber struck at his head, heard the cry of its wielder cut short as Alvor hit him so hard with the mace that the man flew back into two of his fellows. The twitches came more slowly now. Wystylth grunted as the entity tried to break away again. Kerensa closed her eyes and moaned a little behind her clenched teeth. The twitches stopped. "It's almost time," Evon said. "Just one last thing." He released Kerensa and the Despot's joined hands and began unbuttoning her dress. Kerensa's eyes flew open and she reached up with her free hand to stop him.

He met her eyes, so beautiful and so full of pain. "Do you trust me?" he said. He removed her hand and continued to unbutton her bodice.

She nodded. "But I don't understand."

"I know," he said. "I'll explain everything later." He laid his palm flat against the hot skin of her chest, between her breasts, and chalked an awkward left-handed rune on the back of his hand. "I love you. *Vertiri. Desini madi.*"

Kerensa's eyes went wide as all the air rushed out of her lungs.

Evon felt her heart give one final beat and stop. She blinked once, her hand reaching to her throat, then the life left her eyes and her hand went limp and fell to her side.

Evon caught her before she could hit the ground, though she was now beyond caring. Dry-eyed, he twitched the edges of her bodice closed; he couldn't spare the time to button it. Modesty was another thing that no longer mattered to her. Her skin had already begun to cool, returning to its normal hue. He laid her down next to the Despot, took out Wystylth's knife and hurriedly began carving runes into the frozen ground, making an uneven oval around Kerensa and the Despot. Now was where he learned whether he was right.

Wystylth was looking at him as if wondering if Evon had gone insane. Evon wasn't sure about that himself. "It makes sense," he shouted over the noise of the battle raging around them. "There's only one control spell. If the —" The knife caught on a clump of dead grass, and Evon hacked at it until it gave, feeling panic rise up in him at even that small delay. "If the original volunteer's children inherited the fire," he went on, letting this recitation of logic calm him, "it would burn them when they were born — maybe burn them in the womb, even. It was the...modifications...that were being passed on. And yet the fire and the spell survived for a thousand years, so they were being passed on too, just not at birth. In death. One host dies and it finds another one, and the spell goes along with it." He made a final cut and then stabbed the knife into the ground, where it quivered for a moment from the force of the thrust. His reserves were almost gone. Flashes of light darted before him, and he scrubbed his eyes to dispel them. *No distractions.*

Wystylth's shoulders tensed, and he snarled as the entity made another break for freedom. "But suppose the Despot is not a descendant?"

"That was the first thing I did. I made the Despot's body mimic Kerensa's, part of it anyway, so he would be the nearest available host. At least I hope I did." Evon gestured at Kerensa's lifeless body. "And now we see. *Solto epiria.*" It felt like a knife driven deep into his back, and he closed his eyes briefly as the battlefield swayed around him. *No falling unconscious, Lorantis. Stay focused. She's counting on you.*

The familiar blue ribbons came into view, along with a shimmering golden haze that surrounded Kerensa's body. Evon breathed out in relief. He also hadn't been certain the improved *epiria* rune circle would show free magic. There had been a lot about this situation that he hadn't been certain of. He checked his watch. Maybe four minutes left before it was too late for Kerensa. He wanted to wave his hands at the golden haze to make it move faster. He clenched his fists instead.

Then it moved, pouring like melted honey across the gap between their bodies and settling around the Despot. The spell-ribbons flowed after it. Evon flexed his hands; this was where timing was essential. The golden haze settled into the Despot's body. The spell-ribbons' glow began to increase. Evon raised both hands and shouted, *"Desini cucurri!"*

The spell-ribbons stopped in place, but they shivered, straining against the paralysis. It would take no more than a minute for them to overcome it. "You should go now," Evon said. "When the spell breaks free, it will complete its cycle and release the fire, and I am only able to shield myself and Kerensa from that." He hoped. He was nearly at the limit of what he could manage.

"If I go, the Enemy will go free," Wystylth pointed out. "And I find I am eager to meet Merenna beyond the gates of the Underworld."

"But—" Evon began, then met the man's eyes. "I understand," he said.

"Do you?" Alvor said. He stood beside Evon, his mace hanging heavy in his hand. One of his arms was bloody and he held it at an awkward angle. The fighting was less fierce, though Dania and Carall were still heavily engaged with holding off the enemy forces. "We none of us came into this expecting to survive. Think you that we are such craven weaklings as to allow this young woman to face her death alone? We were prepared to die when last we fought the Enemy. This is simply fate delayed."

"But—" Evon said again.

"I hope for your sake you can revive her," Alvor said. "Now, Evon, finish this." He turned away and raised his mace to take another soldier in the chest. Evon stared after him in wonder. *Kerensa will never forgive me if I do not remember,* he thought, and spared a few precious seconds to look at them all, at Alvor roaring defiance at the horde, hurling soldiers away from him with his mace, at Carall's undead eyes so intent on his bloody sword slashing and impaling his enemies, at Dania sweeping her arm and sending fifteen soldiers to the ground with their heads hanging limp from broken necks—did they know what was coming? As if she could hear his thoughts, Dania turned briefly to look at him, and smiled, a rueful, resigned smile that told him everything he needed to know. Evon exchanged one last glance with Wystylth, who nodded at him in salute and grinned that now-familiar grin. Evon took Kerensa's body in his arms, curled them both into as tight a ball as he could manage, and said, *"Presadi."*

An iridescent bubble sprang up around them, just large enough to encompass their bodies. He hoped there would be enough air to get him through this. Two and a half minutes left. He closed his eyes and buried his face in Kerensa's hair.

Light blazed so brightly it burned pink through his eyelids, even as well guarded as they were. He felt a silent blow ring through *presadi* that rattled his bones and made him bite his tongue, a blow hard enough to send them flying as if they'd been kicked by a giant's foot. For a moment Evon felt weightless, and clutched Kerensa's body in an irrational fear that she might be left behind. He clenched his eyes shut tighter and prayed to both Belia and Cath for survival; he hadn't considered what the spell's explosion would do to *presadi,* and he was aware that even if *presadi* protected against external attacks, it would do nothing to prevent his ribs being cracked or his neck being snapped from being tossed off a cliff. Then they hit the ground, hard, and Evon cried out in pain just before *presadi* bounced, then bounced again, and after what seemed like hours came to a rolling halt. For a moment, Evon just lay there, curled up around Kerensa, then shook himself, dismissed the spell and laid Kerensa on her back on the stony ground. He wiped the back of his hand on his shirt to remove the chalk, laid his palm against her skin once more, and said, *"Vertiri. Madi sepera."*

Nothing happened except the taste of cinnamon passing across his tongue. Her skin no longer looked poreless and felt smooth and too cool beneath his hand. He repeated the spell, pressing harder into her chest. One minute left. His reserves were drained. *No. I did everything right. I can't fail now. Dear Gods, I just need one more miracle.* He pounded at her chest, shouting the words over and over again, drawing the runes between her breasts and striking her again in desperation. Nothing. He forced himself to become calm and thought again, trying not to picture the seconds ticking away. Carefully, he scrawled runes across her forehead, pushing her hair out of the way, pulled her eyelids open and said *"Vertiri. Torpia cucurri."*

She blinked, dragging her eyelids away from his fingers, then took a deep breath and pressed her hands to her chest. Confusion deepened. "You *undressed* me," she said. "And—where are we? Where's the Despot?"

"He's gone," Evon said, tension draining out of him. "He's gone. It's over."

She blinked at him again, her fingers pulling her bodice closed across her chest. "It's over?"

Evon nodded. Kerensa's eyes went wide, her mouth opened and closed soundlessly a few times, then she began to cry so hard her whole body shook. He gathered her into his arms and held her tightly. "I'll tell you all about it," he said, "but I would like to sit here with you, just for a moment, because you were dead and I am so, so grateful that we're both alive now."

She nodded vigorously, drawing in a deep breath as she tried to control her tears. "It doesn't seem real yet," she said. Then she sat up quickly, breaking his grasp. "Evon, what is *that*?" she exclaimed.

They were on a low hill, sitting in about an inch of snow, completely alone, but far in the distance lay blackened ground three hundred feet across around which tiny figures lay collapsed like broken ants. Further away from that center, more tiny figures milled in confusion. Smoke, warm and wispy, drifted toward them, smelling not of burned flesh or grass but sweet, like honey. In the center of the blackened area rose a column of shifting, translucent fire, probably thirty feet tall, that put out short tongues of flame all along its length. At the top, the fire fountained up and out, letting off sparks that faded before they touched the ground. Not a fountain, but a flower with a million petals that it shed and then grew again. It swayed a little in the wind.

"I think that's what the fire was trying to be, all this time," Evon said. "It's beautiful. It's a fitting memorial."

"For the Despot?" Kerensa wiped her eyes and made a face. She began buttoning up her dress. "And you *wrote* on me, too."

"It was to save your life," Evon said. "But now I think I should tell you one last Alvor story."

EPILOGUE

The stiflingly hot, high-ceilinged room in Mistress Gavranter's cooperative wasn't much of an improvement over Evon's old room at Elltis and Company, whose windows couldn't be opened more than a crack, winter or summer. He couldn't remember Matra ever being this hot in early autumn before. Knowing that the room was closed off by his own choice didn't make matters any better. He stood with his back to the maple-paneled wall and regarded the shielded table at the other end of the room. Putting it off was simply cowardly, but he was tired of being thrown all over the room.

He sighed and picked up an old-fashioned military saber and approached *presadi*. It had an opalescent, mostly opaque look to it; he probably ought to correct for that, knowing from experience how unsettling it was to be inside a shield you couldn't see out of. That could wait until later. He took a deep breath, tensed in anticipation, and swung the saber at the shield as hard as he could.

The backlash took him off his feet and sent him skidding on his rump over the smooth tiled floor. When he finally came to a stop, he checked the marks chalked along the floorboards. Eleven feet. Enough to dissuade an attacker without the magician using up all of his or her reserves on the shield. He'd finally done it. The government would have its spell, and Evon would have one more defense against Valantis, if he ever appeared again. Piercy assured him that the government had enough evidence of Valantis's crimes that he didn't dare return to Dalanine, especially since Speculatus had disavowed any awareness of said crimes to protect itself from prosecution, but Evon didn't intend to take his safety, or Kerensa's, for granted. He got to his feet and winced at the pain in his backside. That was probably another bruise to add to his impressive collection. Kerensa was either going to make sympathetic noises or laugh at him, and he would bet on the latter. He loved hearing her laugh.

"By the Gods, Lore, this room smells of sweat and...what *is* that?" Piercy said, putting a cautious head round the door. He'd been present for Evon's earlier, ill-advised experiment with firearms.

"An herbal concoction that's the key to this new spell. Its components are a state secret."

"I cannot believe anyone might want to know anything about anything that smells that bad except, perhaps, how to stay far away from it."

"It won't smell that bad out in the open. And I'm certain the government will find many uses for this spell. I hope to earn a good deal of money from it."

"Enough to pay for a wedding, dear fellow?"

Evon put his hand on his trouser pocket. "If she agrees."

"Evon, only you could possibly believe your suit might be rejected."

"It was important that we learn to know one another under more normal circumstances. Suppose we discovered we didn't actually like each other? I haven't even met her family yet, Piercy—what if they won't give their blessing? And now she knows how impossible I am to be around, and how obsessed I can be about my work, and there are all those men at university who share her interests—"

Piercy crossed his arms over his chest. "You are my best friend, and I have seen you at both your best and your worst, so you must know that when I tell you that you are out of your very talented mind I do so out of love."

Evon took a deep breath and let it out slowly. "I know you're right and I'm being stupid. I'm just nervous about this evening. It's not as if I've proposed marriage to anyone before." He mopped his forehead with his sleeve. "I feel as if I've sweated enough for two men."

"You should open a window. Or, and this is simply speculation on my part, but isn't there some spell to cool a room?"

"I had to keep the windows shut when I was doing the projectile tests. I didn't want bullets flying out into the streets. And there isn't any such spell. Yet."

"I heard that," Kerensa said, pushing the door open wider and smiling at Piercy as she passed. "That was the sound of Evon Lorantis adding yet another project to the roster. Don't you ever get tired of being brilliant?" She was dressed in a lightweight gown patterned in blue and wore a modish hat rather than a bonnet and looked, to Evon's eyes, more beautiful than ever. She kissed him lightly on the cheek, wrinkled her nose and added, "What is that *smell*?"

"Herbs and Evon," Piercy said. "He says it will make him rich, though in my opinion such an aroma will not sell well to the ladies."

"The smell is a side effect," Evon said. He took a few steps away from Kerensa, conscious of his state of undress, his neckcloth and frock coat discarded on the deep window casement behind him, and of the awful smell he was sure came off him in waves. "The new shield works, more or less. It should be done by this afternoon."

She followed him. "Not too late, I hope, because you've promised to dine with me tonight and I'll be embarrassed for you if you come to the table dressed like that."

Evon had to stop himself putting his hand on his pocket again. "I haven't forgotten," he said. "And I promise I clean up nicely."

"I know," Kerensa said, with a mischievous smile on her lips and a look in her eyes that dispelled all his uncertainty.

"Will you join us for dinner now?" Piercy asked. "Though since Evon will need to clean himself up it could be a rather late dinner."

"Can't," Kerensa said. "I have a lecture in an hour. But thanks for the invitation."

"Getting, or giving?" Evon said, picking up his neckcloth.

"Very funny. I'm sure Master Killiter would have kittens if one of his first year students took his lectern. But I've been invited to speak on the meaning of Alvor's descent into the Underworld to one of the university literary organizations next week."

"Prodigious work from our prodigy," Piercy said. "Evon, I'll meet you at my club in...shall we say one hour? I'd rather not loiter in your front hall where your odious cousin might find me. She is an unholy terror and quite makes me believe in compulsory year-round schooling. Kerensa, my dear, always a pleasure." He bowed and shut the door behind him.

Kerensa looked around for a seat and failed to find one. "Did you really have to remove all the chairs?"

"After I was flung into one the third time, I learned how stupid it was to keep unnecessary furniture in here. But it's wonderful about the speaking invitation! What do people think, about your radical interpretation of the stories?"

"That they're radical. It's been so difficult to find historical support for what little I learned from Alvor, since I can't say that my knowledge came from the source." The smile vanished. "And yet I wish we'd had even more time."

"I wish we could tell anyone that you were responsible for defeating the Despot." Evon shrugged into his waistcoat and began buttoning it up. "Or that Alvor really did return. I suppose I could tell the *Weekly Gazette*, but it seems like sullying his good name to let that rag have more fuel for their ridiculous theories."

"Isn't it better that people don't think we're mad? The idea that the military had an experimental weapon is slightly more believable, if you don't look at it too closely."

"Piercy and Mistress Gavranter know the truth, and so do the ministers responsible for spreading the cover story. All those magicians and Mrs. Petelter's Home Defense agents who saw the weapon activate at the Speculatus manor must have guessed what happened. And the government hasn't been able to explain the thirty-foot pillar of fire at the center of a new place of power," Evon said. He put on his frock coat and hat and wished summer dress for men weren't so much like winter dress for men. "But the idea of Alvor's return is so fanciful, no one would believe it no matter how much evidence we had. It just seems a shame that there's no way for the truth to be told."

"We know the truth. That satisfies me." Kerensa held out her arm to Evon. He looked at it. "Kerensa," he began.

"I want you to escort me back to campus. It's on your way home."

"I'm sweaty and unkempt —"

"And still the most handsome man of my acquaintance." She hooked her arm through his and drew him close to her. "Whenever you meet me on campus, all the women have the most jealous expressions."

"And all the men wish I were dead."

She laughed and put her free hand around the back of his neck. "Don't be silly," she whispered, "they all know I'd never look at anyone but you, even if you were dead," and kissed him. He slid his arm around her waist and pulled her close. She smelled of strawberries and fresh air and her lips tasted of sunshine.

"Even if I were dead?" he murmured in her ear. "Waxy and cold like Carall?"

"I'd rescue you before that happened."

"I'm happy to know you'd come after me, because I'd do the same for you."

"I know," Kerensa said. "You already have."

COMMAND WORDS AND SPELLS

ademi—"same," duplication spell.

cleperi—"hear," in combination with other command words alters hearing or sound.

cucurri—"move," limited telekinesis; with *vertiri*, used in healing spells.

desini—"stop," turns off a working spell, among other things.

desini cleperi—"stop hear," silence spell.

desini cucurri—"stop move," paralysis spell.

desini spexa—"stop see," limited invisibility; with *vertiri*, causes blindness.

eloqua—"speak," long-distance communication spell; requires both parties to have a mirror, but can be performed by even the least experienced magicians

epiria—"reveal," make a spell visible. Usually requires a lens of some kind, but can be done with a rune circle for larger areas.

epiria sepera—"reveal go," preparation for mapping spell.

forva—"burn"

frigo—"break," make things shatter. Only works on relatively dry things, like wood or bone.

madi—"center," specifically the human heart or other vital organs when used with *vertiri.*

misca—"mix," complicated spell in which two objects interchange certain physical traits.

olficio—"smell," in combination with other command words, alters smells or the sense of smell itself.

presadi—"guard," shield spells. Type of shield depends on the gesture used.

recivia—"reverse," returns a spell to affect its caster.

reperto—"find," locator spell. Requires item belonging to or identified with whatever you're seeking, or thorough knowledge of subject.

resarva + sense—"close" sense, decrease the sensory enhancement.

retexo—"annul," cancels a spell before it can take effect.

sepera—"go," used mostly as a trigger to make very complicated spells with multiple command words operate at the right times. Also the command word for a lost ancient spell that dismisses *desini cucurri.*

solto—"open" in the sense of making something greater. Magnifies the effect of certain command words.

solto epiria—"open reveal," more powerful and complex version of *epiria.*

solto spexa—"open see," cast on lenses for distance viewing. Can be cast on eyes, but this is not recommended.

spexa—"see," alters vision. Basis for clairvoyance spell. Can be cast on walls or doors to see through, and on air to see at a distance when you know the subject or location well.

spexa madi—"see center," x-ray spell.

torpia—"body," used in healing spells to link other command words to specified parts of the body.

torpia auctata and *torpia adenuo*—"body grow" and "body shrink," commands for manipulating a *spexa madi* oculus.

vertiri—"change," used in biokinetic/healing spells. A kind of preparatory word to attune the spell to something living.

vertiri + *trattuci*—"change + transfer," move something from one place to another. Used in healing spells to increase blood flow and align bone, among others.

ABOUT THE AUTHOR

Melissa McShane is the author of many fantasy novels, including the Crown of Tremontane series, beginning with SERVANT OF THE CROWN; The Extraordinaries series, beginning with BURNING BRIGHT; the Company of Strangers series; and THE BOOK OF SECRETS, first in the Last Oracle series.

After a childhood spent roaming the United States, she settled in Utah with her husband, four children and a niece, four very needy cats, and a library that has finally overflowed its shelves. She wrote reviews and critical essays for many years before turning to fiction, which is much more fun than anyone ought to be allowed to have.

You can visit her at her website www.melissamcshanewrites.com for more information on other books.

For information on new releases, fun extras, and more, sign up for Melissa's newsletter: http://eepurl.com/brannP